continued . . .

OCEANS OF FIRE

"Christine Feehan boldly goes where no writer has ever gone . . . Erotic, exotic, suspenseful." —*Fallen Angel Reviews*

"Brimming with exhilarating action sequences and sultry love scenes." —*Publishers Weekly*

"[A] magical series about the sisters with something extra . . . *Oceans of Fire* is a rousing romantic thriller and a true classic!" —*Romantic Times*

"Fascinating and mysterious . . . enjoy a little bit of magic, a dash of intrigue and all the romance to be found in *Oceans of Fire*." —*Romance Reviews Today*

"Christine Feehan has brought paranormal romance to a new high with *Oceans of Fire* . . . Plenty of spine-tingling action . . . and simmering passion." —*A Romance Review*

"The Drake series is a complex blend of fantasy and suspense." —*Booklist*

"Combining a touch of whimsical magic with a tense thriller . . . tremendous romantic suspense." —*Midwest Book Review*

Further praise for the novels of
"THE REIGNING QUEEN OF PARANORMAL ROMANCE"*

MIND GAME

"Swift-moving and sexually-charged . . . electrifying." —**Publishers Weekly*

"[A] compelling and spectacular series. The amazingly prolific author's ability to create captivating and adrenaline-raising worlds is unsurpassed." —*Romantic Times*

"Explosive . . . An exciting, thrilling read . . . A phenomenal plot. Ms. Feehan has really outdone herself . . . The sexual chemistry is literally a scorcher . . . *Mind Game* is a definite page-turner." —*Fallen Angel Reviews*

SHADOW GAME

"[A] swift, sensational offering . . . the sultry, spine-tingling kind of read that [Feehan's] fans will adore."

—Publishers Weekly

"Intense, sensual and mesmerizing . . . Feehan is a rising star in paranormal romance."   *—Library Journal*

"Never slows down until the final confrontation. The story line is fast-paced and loaded with action."   *—Midwest Book Review*

"Sizzling sex scenes both physical and telepathic pave the road to true love . . . Action, suspense and smart characters make this erotically charged romance an entertaining read."

—Booklist

"Feehan packs such a punch with this story it will leave one gasping for breath . . . Guaranteed not to disappoint, and will leave one begging for more. A must-read book, only cementing Ms. Feehan's position as a genre favorite for yet another round."   *—The Best Reviews*

WILD RAIN

"Readers . . . will be seduced by this erotic adventure."

—Publishers Weekly

"Ms. Feehan is unsurpassed in romantic fantasy; her imagination knows no bounds in creating unique and fresh tales that abound in steamy sensuality, fantastical imagery and lyrical prose."   *—Rendezvous*

"A powerful tale that pumps up the adrenaline . . . A fabulous jungle love story."   *—Midwest Book Review*

"Beautiful imagery, edge-of-your-seat suspense and passionate romance . . . The sex is spicy enough to singe your eyebrows."   *—Romance Reviews Today*

"[A] terrific new series . . . Fascinating."   *—Romantic Times*

Turbulent Sea

CHRISTINE FEEHAN

JOVE BOOKS, NEW YORK

THE BERKLEY PUBLISHING GROUP
Published by the Penguin Group
Penguin Group (USA) Inc.
375 Hudson Street, New York, New York 10014, USA
Penguin Group (Canada), 90 Eglinton Avenue East, Suite 700, Toronto, Ontario M4P 2Y3, Canada
(a division of Pearson Penguin Canada Inc.)
Penguin Books Ltd., 80 Strand, London WC2R 0RL, England
Penguin Group Ireland, 25 St. Stephen's Green, Dublin 2, Ireland (a division of Penguin Books Ltd.)
Penguin Group (Australia), 250 Camberwell Road, Camberwell, Victoria 3124, Australia
(a division of Pearson Australia Group Pty. Ltd.)
Penguin Books India Pvt. Ltd., 11 Community Centre, Panchsheel Park, New Delhi—110 017, India
Penguin Group (NZ), 67 Apollo Drive, Rosedale, North Shore 0632, New Zealand
(a division of Pearson New Zealand Ltd.)
Penguin Books (South Africa) (Pty.) Ltd., 24 Sturdee Avenue, Rosebank, Johannesburg 2196,
South Africa

Penguin Books Ltd., Registered Offices: 80 Strand, London WC2R 0RL, England

This is a work of fiction. Names, characters, places, and incidents either are the product of the author's imagination or are used fictitiously, and any resemblance to actual persons, living or dead, business establishments, events, or locales is entirely coincidental. The publisher does not have any control over and does not assume any responsibility for author or third-party websites or their content.

TURBULENT SEA

A Jove Book / published by arrangement with the author

ISBN: 978-0-7394-9836-1

JOVE®
Jove Books are published by The Berkley Publishing Group,
a division of Penguin Group (USA) Inc.,
375 Hudson Street, New York, New York 10014.
JOVE® is a registered trademark of Penguin Group (USA) Inc.
The "J" design is a trademark belonging to Penguin Group (USA) Inc.

PRINTED IN THE UNITED STATES OF AMERICA

For my parents,
Mark and Nancy King,
who taught all of us how to love

ACKNOWLEDGMENTS

As with any book, I have many people to thank: Domini Stottsberry, who did so much research and worked hard to pull this book together; Cheryl Wilson, an amazing friend and writer even under stressful circumstances. I owe a lot to Rich Campbell, bass guitarist for the band *America*, who graciously took time out of his busy schedule and gave me so much help, attempting to teach me about touring and life on the road. If I have made any mistakes, they're mine alone, as he was out touring and I couldn't double-check everything. Last, but not least, Jeri Stahl, retired Aurora, Colorado, police detective, now doing consulting work for Denver, who answered all my questions patiently and worked through my scenes with astonishing clarity.

"Turbulent Sea"

Darkness lives inside me
A secret that I hide
The light that comes from all the rest
Is lost upon the tide

A touch of lightning—magic
Has left me marked and cold
I want . . . I need . . . I crave for me
A love that sells my soul

Like a turbulent sea
Pulling at me
I'm drowning in passion and fear
With all that I am—or ever will be
I must fight for what I hold dear

And I fight
For what is right
But shadows follow . . .
Me into the night

I sing and I cry and I scream at the night
To change an unchangeable fate

The wave crashes
In my heart
Darkness follows
Light departs

Like a turbulent sea
Pulling at me
I'm drowning

—Sheila Clover English

1

JOLEY Drake stared in a kind of sick dread at the mob of people crowding the gates and fence. She had forgotten what after parties were like, or maybe she'd just blocked them out. Women pushed against the car windows, lifting their tops and mashing their bare breasts against the tinted panes. Some waved thong underwear in various colors. They shoved at the car, pulling on door handles and screaming. She doubted any of those women knew who was in the vehicle, but they were clearly willing to sell themselves to get an invite inside.

"My God, Steve," Joley muttered to her driver, "sex, drugs and rock and roll are such a cliché, but it's so true." Even to herself she sounded jaded.

Steve Brinkley's gaze met hers in the rearview mirror. "You stopped coming to these things years ago; what made you change your mind tonight? I was shocked when I got your call."

That was a question she didn't want to answer, not even to herself—especially to herself. She pushed her forehead into her palm. "I haven't been to one of these in so long, I let everything but the music just fade away. I didn't want to think about what goes on, but now that I'm here, I might just throw up." She meant to sound light, joking, but the pounding on the hood and the hands trying to yank open doors were impossible to ignore.

She felt like an animal trapped in a cage. It was surprising how often she felt that way. And if the mob knew who was inside, they would have begun dismantling the car to get at her.

She hadn't wanted to remember this part of her life. Those first heady months as a megastar, when everything she wanted, or needed, or even thought of was handed to her and the band—that had been so long ago, a dream come true that had quickly turned to a nightmare she tried to forget.

She had been born with a legacy of gifts, but even she had been overtaken by the magnitude of what was offered to her in that first flush of success, being treated like a star, godlike, given anything, wanted everywhere. Like so many stars before her, she'd fallen into the trap of selfish egotism, believing she deserved to be treated differently.

Being a Drake with special gifts prevented her from using anything poisonous to her body, but her band hadn't been so lucky. She'd seen the results, and more than once had walked into a hotel room to find naked bodies writhing everywhere and drugs and alcohol flowing freely. Her boys, as she called them, were more than just friends—almost family—and the excesses of alcohol, drugs and women crawling over one another for a chance to be with a member of a band, to do anything for him, had nearly destroyed their minds and their lives.

Most of the band members lost families to that lifestyle. It hadn't taken Joley long to become disgusted with the way they were all living. She'd walked out, turning her back on music—on the band—on fame. They knew it was her voice that had taken them to the top and without her the band would topple quickly. In the end, her manager and the band members had convinced her they would set rules and abide by them.

Joley knew she couldn't dictate to the band, but she could establish guidelines she could live with. She didn't ever pretend not to have a wild streak, but that didn't include illegal substances or sexual orgies. And it certainly didn't include underage boys or girls performing sexual favors and getting totally wasted with her band. The terms had been agreed to, and Joley rarely went to parties other than with the band immediately afterward. And she never went where someone might be providing all the things she'd most objected to—until now—until tonight.

"Why do you suppose these women feel the need to service bands? What do they really get out of it, Steve?" she asked her driver. "Because I don't understand. They line up to give the band and even the roadies blow jobs. Actually stand in line in the halls, hoping to get the chance. They don't really care if anyone knows their name."

"I don't know, Joley. I don't really understand half of what people do or why they do it."

The guards pushed the crowds back to make room so the car could approach the high, wrought iron gates. All of the guards were carrying guns—and not just polite police-issue handguns beneath smooth jackets either. Those were semiautomatic weapons cradled in their beefy arms, right out in the open like in some gangster film. Joley's stomach lurched as she observed the guards through the tinted glass. These weren't rented security—these men were the real deal—professionals every last one of them. They didn't wear boredom on their faces; they wore masks, and their eyes were flat and cold. She knew if she were to reach out and touch one of them, even lightly, she'd feel the chill of death.

Her cell phone went off, interrupting her train of thought. Flipping it open with a little grimace, she answered. "Gloria, I told you I'd take care of it. I'm getting Logan now. You dragged me out of bed and I said I'd do it, so give me some time and I'll have him there." She knew she sounded bitchy, but really. Gloria Brady, the mother of Lucy Brady, psycho-stalker from hell, every band's worst nightmare come true, was once again demanding to speak with her sax player, Logan Voight. He'd had a brief encounter with Gloria's daughter, making the mistake of seeing her more than once, and now Lucy and her demented ways would haunt him forever.

Joley snapped the phone closed and shoved it into her pocket. She'd been pacing her hotel room when the first frantic call from Gloria came in. Joley had latched on to the excuse, dragging her driver out in the middle of the night, lying to herself that she was coming to the party to deliver the message to Logan and see to it personally that he took care of the problem. Now that she was here, she realized how utterly stupid she'd been. Others might look at the guards and think they were cool; she looked at them and wondered how many people they'd killed.

A guard tapped her window, making her jump, motioning for her to let him see her. Her driver objected, but she rolled down the window and peered at the guard so he could visually identify her. She saw the instant flash of recognition. Joley

Drake, legendary singer known simply as *Joley*. For one brief moment she thought he might ask for her autograph, but he recovered and waved her through the gates.

Sergei Nikitin had been inviting her to his parties for months, but she always made excuses not to go. Sergei was a wealthy man who ran in the in circles. He knew politicians and celebrities of every kind. He maintained the public image of a charming businessman who liked the good life and surrounded himself with household names—movie stars, race car drivers, sports figures, models, public figures and of course the most famous bands.

Very few people knew he was reputed to be a Russian mobster with a violent, bloody past and a penchant for making his enemies disappear. Most of those who had heard the rumors thought they only added to his mystique. It seemed inconceivable that the suave, charming businessman might actually order vicious, sadistic deaths to further his already abundant wealth—to everybody but those in law enforcement—and Joley—thanks to her brother-in-law, who was a sheriff.

"Just stop here," she instructed and waited until Steve had pulled to the side of the drive, still a distance from the house, before opening the door. She remained in the seat, hesitating.

The party was in full swing. Music blasted from the house, filling the air around it. Joley could almost feel the building expanding and contracting with every boom of the bass. Even the windows vibrated. She sat in the car with the door open and studied the house. Nikitin would know she'd come. His security people would have radioed the house immediately so Nikitin could be ready to greet her. It would be a victory of sorts for him. Finally. Joley Drake. He'd been pursuing her for months. Another celebrity he could be photographed with.

"Are you getting out, Joley?" Steve asked.

She met the driver's eyes in the rearview mirror and made a face. "I don't know. Maybe. Do you mind just waiting, Steve? I feel bad for dragging you out tonight."

"That's what you pay me for," he reassured her. "If you want to sit here for a while, it's fine by me. I was surprised you wanted to come," he added, a note of worry in his voice.

It had surprised her, too, but she'd lain awake staring at the ceiling until she'd wanted to scream in frustration. She rarely slept, was a total insomniac, and she couldn't do anything but pace back and forth in her hotel room. The frantic call from Gloria begging her to find Logan had been all the excuse she'd needed. Gloria's daughter was in the hospital having Logan's baby and had already called the media and was making a scene, threatening to kill herself if Logan didn't show up.

Joley told herself she'd come to the party to make certain Logan knew what he was doing, to send lawyers and security as well as her manager, but she could have done it all with a phone call or two. Lucy had already agreed to turn over the baby to him, and the papers had been drawn up, but everyone knew Lucy wouldn't go away that easily. There would be one scene after another.

Joley shook her head as she turned her attention to Nikitin's grounds. There were people everywhere. They milled around the rolling grass, some making certain to be seen by the mob at the fence. A few hopeful starlets and male models even signed autographs through the gate. Cries and pleas and drunken laughter were every bit as loud as the booming music.

She spotted Denny Simmons, her drummer, walking in the distance with a blonde, not his current girlfriend. She bit her lip hard. She didn't want to know any of them cheated. "Men are dogs, Steve. That's why I don't date anymore. Hound dogs."

He sighed, watching Simmons. "They have too much, Joley. You know they drink too much or do a few drugs and they don't have a clue what they're doing."

"Denny's been divorced once already and he acts as if his girlfriend is his world, but look at him now." She narrowed her eyes as Denny stopped to kiss the girl, skimming his hands over her ample breasts. The woman jerked his shirt out of his pants and her hand went to his zipper. "Damn him for this. I really like his girlfriend, and she has a child. I'm never going to be able to look her in the eye again."

Men were dogs—*all* of them. Not a one could be trusted. Well, maybe her sisters's men, but not the ones Joley fell for. She liked them hard-edged and dangerous and that added up to . . . "No, not dogs, Steve. I like dogs and they're loyal. *Snakes* is a better word for what men are."

"Maybe you shouldn't be here."

She detested the compassion in his voice. Her rapid rise to fame had created this situation, and now their lives were little more than tabloid fodder. She tried to steer the other band members away from the life of excess, but it had been impossible when everything came so easy. And men like Sergei Nikitin knew how to use fame and popularity to get what he wanted. He'd supply the drugs and women and even the pictures for the tabloids if it furthered his own cause. And once he got his claws into a person . . .

"Men can be weak," Steve said.

So could women, Joley surmised. Or she wouldn't be here, chancing ruining her life. And for what? "That's just a cop-out, Steve. Everyone has choices. And everyone ought to know what the people in their life are worth. And men should have more self-respect—and honor—than to abuse the people who love them."

His gaze narrowed and Joley looked away from the mirror. She couldn't bear to see the knowledge in his eyes—or in her own—that she was really talking about herself. How hypocritical was it to condemn Denny for making wrong choices when she'd probably come here for that very thing. She couldn't even bring herself to admit the truth, hedging in her mind, pretending it was to help Logan save his child when the real reason was purely selfish.

Her body was on fire. Hot. Needy. Ultrasensitive. Her nipples brushed her lacy bra and sent streaks of white lightning zigzagging through her straight to her groin. Her body pulsed with life, with need, with want . . . Oh man did she want. She brushed a hand over her face to hide her expression from Steve.

A crush of what looked like teenage girls dressed in too-tight clothing, too much makeup and heels to make them look older came rushing around the walkway toward the front door. They were giggling loudly and pulling at their clothes, trying to look as if they belonged. Joley swore under her breath as memories flooded back. Young girls servicing band members and roadies. Groupies, looking to do anything with someone famous. Drugs and alcohol to deaden their inhibitions.

In the early days she had tried to stop it. Now she knew she couldn't. What others did and what they could live with was on them. The only stipulation she'd adamantly enforced was that any groupie had to be old enough. The girls didn't look it, but she was getting older and everyone seemed to look about thirteen to her these days. Maybe she was just jaded. Her manager and certainly the band would never break that one taboo, and risk losing everything.

The rush of excitement the show had produced drained away, even the fire racing through her veins, leaving her feeling tired. As if reading her thoughts, Steve cleared his throat and leaned out the window to get a better look at the girls.

"I swear, Miss Drake, looking at those girls, I'm feeling ancient. They look like they should be home playing with dolls."

"I must be ancient, too," she conceded, watching as one of them broke away and dashed around the corner to hide in some bushes. The girl pulled out a cell phone and quickly made a call.

Her eyes were bright and she couldn't stop smiling, her excitement at the opportunity of mixing with the band members and all the celebrities at the party nearly palpable. She was pretty. Young. Even with the makeup she looked no more than fourteen. Innocent looking. Definitely in need of protection. The poor girl had no idea what she was getting into. Joley pushed the door open even wider and swung her feet out of the car.

"We're not supposed to tell anyone they're letting us in," one of the other girls called out. "You'll get us kicked out. They told us not to tell anyone."

Joley glanced at Steve. "That doesn't sound good. If someone told them not to tell, they have to be underage."

The girl with the cell phone hastily snapped it closed and shoved it into her purse out of sight. "I left a message for my mother that I'd be late," she said and ran to join the group.

Joley got out of the car, frowning. She wouldn't have her band members or even the road crew picking up young teenagers. That was the one hard-and-fast rule the band had sworn never to break, and if any of them had been a party to the invitation for the teens, they were gone. Just like that. She'd quit before she'd have this kind of thing going on, and they knew it. She'd done it once and she'd walk away again. She could only hope her own crew had no idea who had been invited to this party. In any case, the teens had to leave immediately.

She took a couple of steps toward the group just as a limousine with tinted windows pulled up between her and the girls. Even as Joley started around the large vehicle, the door to the house swung open and several men came out. Joley recognized two of her roadies as they intercepted the girls. Relief flooded her until one of them laughingly put his arm around the girl who had made the cell phone call. Fury swept through her. The girl couldn't be more than fourteen. He had to see that.

"Dean!" She shouted his name. He was so fired. If she had any clout in the industry, he would never work for anyone in the business.

Dean spun around, the smile slipping from his face. The other roadie half turned and then said something, throwing up the hood of his sweatshirt so she couldn't get a clear look at him. The girls instantly stopped laughing and ran around the corner of the house, both roadies and two other men following after them, urging them to hurry.

Brian Rigger, her best friend and lead guitarist, stepped out of the house, a frown on his face. He looked around as if a little bored and then over at her. A smile broke out in greeting. "Joley! When did you get here?"

"Just now, Brian. I saw Dean and some friend of his with some teenage girls." She had to shout to be heard above the noise of the music and party pouring out the open door. "They took off that way." She pointed, even as she tried to walk around the absurdly big car that had pulled up at an angle to her. "And I need to find Logan."

"He's not here. Gloria called Jerry shrieking at him to get Logan to the hospital. It's a big mess, apparently. Logan took off with Jerry."

Joley sighed. Of course Gloria would call the band's manager, Jerry St. Ives. And being nearly as psycho as her daughter, she wouldn't stop there. Logan had given her Joley's cell number to use in an emergency. Joley was *so* having the number changed immediately. "Well, I hope he has an attorney with him." She hadn't really needed to come at all. Now she didn't even have an excuse to be there. "Go find the girls, Brian, and get rid of them."

"It's done," Brian assured her and took off briskly in the direction she indicated. Joley took a step to follow, but the door of the limousine swung open, blocking her path. She sent one panicked glance toward her driver before she composed herself and turned a look of sheer, utter contempt on the man who emerged from the backseat.

"Well, well, well. If it isn't Nikitin's new playmate. RJ the Reverend. Or should I say the predator? I thought you'd be in jail by now."

Her heart was pounding too hard, so hard she was afraid she might have a heart attack. She didn't want to step back, or show fear, but as his bodyguards surrounded him, she moved to position her feet for better defense. Up on the balls of her feet slightly, shoulder width apart and one back, relaxed, one arm across her waist in a casual pose while the other hand was tucked under her chin where she could use it to block any incoming punches. The tallest one was the most aggressive. He'd struck her once before, weeks earlier, and she kept a wary eye on him.

RJ glared at her. She noted that he had to assure himself he was surrounded by his men. His fingers curled into fists, and maniacal hatred shimmered in the air between them. She had exposed the Reverend on national television when she'd gotten him on live tape claiming he could end Joley's wild ways by tying her down, flogging her and having sex with her to drive out her demons. The media had played the clip endlessly for weeks after, and clearly RJ hadn't forgotten that any more than she had.

"Joley Drake. Whore of the devil. I've wanted to talk to you for a long while."

She raised an eyebrow. "Talk? I doubt talking is on your mind. Unless it's to hear the sound of your own voice. You're cruising for women, you and your little pack of wolves, so don't even try to give me your idiotic spiel about saving souls. Save it for someone who doesn't know what a sick pervert you are."

The taller bodyguard stepped close enough that she could smell his cologne. It seemed absurd that he was wearing something spicy and nice smelling. "You bitch."

Joley rolled her eyes. "Can't you come up with something a little more original?"

"Now, Paul," RJ said in a soothing voice. "I do want to talk with Ms. Drake. She needs our sympathy and compassion. You're right, Joley, I am a human male. And my body often betrays me, but I try to overcome the weaknesses of the flesh." He spread his arms to take in the house. "Wickedness and debauchery are taking place in this establishment and I mean to aid those who will listen."

"Do people actually believe you? You're here for the sex and drugs, nothing else. At least the rest of them don't lie about it."

"Is that why you're here?"

The question caught her by surprise and she inwardly winced, keeping her famous smile plastered on her face. She might pretend to the rest of the world that she'd come to do a great deed, but she knew better and his question had hit a little too close to home.

"I'm not doing this with you." She glanced over her shoulder to try to see the young girls, but they were out of sight along with the roadies and Brian. Logan was already gone and she wasn't siccing the Reverend on him. If he knew Logan's unwed girlfriend was giving birth, he'd race to the hospital and try to grab headlines at Logan's expense.

"I overheard you say there were teens here. If that's true, perhaps I can be of some assistance." RJ moved closer, crowding her personal space.

She should have shifted, stepped to the side to give herself more room, but the taller bodyguard, Paul, blocked her path. She found herself surrounded, in a tight circle.

"Get in the car, Joley," RJ said. "We can discuss this without all the noise. If the young people need to be saved, I can do it. You have to believe in me. One slip only makes me human. Let my record speak for me."

His voice had dropped a bit, and she recognized the famous charismatic note he could produce. She nearly laughed. She was a Drake, and her legacy was spell-singing, the most powerful gift of sound in the world. If the Reverend wanted to engage in a battle of sound, he had chosen the wrong opponent.

"I suppose everyone is human, RJ," she conceded, dropping her voice into a low, sexy drawl, one designed to slide over a man's senses. She saw the Reverend's shiver of awareness, felt the rising heat in the circle of men and realized she was playing with fire. Paul crowded her even closer so that she could feel the brush of his thigh against her hip.

That was stupid, Joley! Are you trying to get yourself raped or worse?

The voice slid into her head. Male. Humming with a kind of sexual fury. Her heart jumped and her stomach did a small, crazy flip. She didn't dare take her eyes off of the men surrounding her, but in spite of herself, she felt relief along with absolute exhilaration.

She tried to retreat, to get out of the circle, realizing the back door of the limo was still open and she was only a step from it. She glanced up at Paul as his arm came sweeping around her waist. Determination to toss her onto the backseat was on his face.

She spun away from his body, shooting her elbows out as weapons, trying to gain inches so she could use her feet. With her body weight behind a kick to the knee, she could easily bring him down.

Without warning, another man moved into the circle. He glided in total silence. Complete and utter confidence surrounded him. Everyone froze, including Joley.

And just like that, Joley couldn't deny the real reason she had come in person rather than make a few phone calls. *This* was what she'd come for. Ilya Prakenskii. Russian bodyguard to Sergei Nikitin. A dangerous man with a murky past, death in his eyes and a dangerous, volatile appeal that sang to every one of her senses.

That look on his face. Ilya Prakenskii was always in control, always cool and expressionless. His eyes ice-cold, and never, *never* could she just read him like she could others— unless he wanted her to, unless he opened his mind to hers deliberately and let her catch small glimpses of the real man. She had never really seen him angry other than at her. She had power over him whether he wanted to admit it or not—and maybe that was what made him angry. He wanted her. It was in the heat of his gaze, the set of his mouth, the hot lust when he looked at her, but most of all, in his mind-to-mind touch— possession and promise and a dark need that bordered on obsession.

He was why she couldn't sleep. He was why her body felt

hot and tight. She wanted to claw at everything and everybody. She swallowed fear and stood still, afraid that if she moved, if he touched her, she would wrap herself around him and be lost forever.

"Paul." Ilya said the bodyguard's name in a low voice, but one that carried the razor edge of a knife. "I suggest you keep your hands to yourself."

"I see you've come to save your boss's little pet," Paul said.

Despite his bravado, Joley found it significant that not only did Paul move away from her, but all of the other men did as well, including RJ.

"He sent me out to save you," Ilya corrected. "Getting your ass kicked by a girl would be embarrassing, especially with so many people watching." He caught Joley's wrist and tugged until she came to his side. Instead of placing her beneath his shoulder, he brought her just one step behind him so he could shield her body should he have to. "Sergei is waiting for you, RJ."

"He's the Reverend," Paul corrected. "Everyone calls him Reverend."

Ilya merely stared at the man until he shepherded RJ and the others up the walkway to the house.

In the ensuing silence, Joley feared Ilya might be able to hear her heart beating. She tried not to notice the width of shoulders, or the heavy muscles on his chest. He wasn't obvious about his strength until you got up close, but more than his physique, more than his perfect masculine body and his tough, heart-stopping face, she was drawn to his mental strength and intellect.

Everyone gave in to Joley. Everyone wanted to please her. She was strong, smart, famous, wealthy, and she had the gift of sound. With all that, she was beautiful, with satin skin, bedroom eyes and a sexy, curvaceous body. She was also stubborn and liked her way. She could read people—except for Ilya. He was every bit as smart, every bit as strong, and he had every single psychic gift her family had, each well developed. Aside from that, he was the sexiest thing alive and she was mesmerized by him.

"Trouble?" His gaze followed the men before he turned his full attention on her. Those ice-blue eyes drifted possessively over her face and down her body, touching her breasts, sliding over the curve of her hips and down her legs with a long, slow perusal that should have struck her as rude but instead sent her pulse skyrocketing.

Her entire body reacted with scorching heat. She felt herself go damp. Even her breath came in a little rush, lifting her breasts and unsettling her even more. Her face flushed. He knew what he did to her.

He turned her hand over, the hand he had zapped with some sort of spell months ago, the hand imprinted with his touch, his scent, the hand that marked her as belonging to him. It had happened so fast—in a little place on her home turf. She'd been dancing and he'd come in with his boss. Even then she could barely breathe when she saw him. And now, thanks to the little psychic mark he'd branded her with, she could always sense where he was, and how much her body craved his. Her palm—his mark—itched. And nothing seemed to alleviate the itch but Ilya being close.

Pride demanded she pull away from him, but the pad of his thumb moved in a delicious pattern over her palm. She felt each stroke humming through her bloodstream. Her womb clenched, and she felt the flood of liquid heat begging to welcome him deep inside her where he already seemed to live.

"It's got to be said, Joley, your driver-slash-bodyguard seems a bit useless to me." He flashed Steve, still in the car, a look of contempt and tugged on her hand until she followed him, moving out of the glare of the floodlights, into the deeper shadows where reporters might not notice that Joley Drake had come to Nikitin's party.

"You've got to stay away from the Reverend and his moronic group of badasses, Joley," he added. "They're capable of doing you great harm."

"I know." She did know. And she wanted her hand back, because if he kept it up, she was going to strip and fling herself into his arms and she'd never forgive herself.

"I'd have to kill them. You know I would. Just stay away from them."

"No one ever *has* to kill anyone." She wanted to cry—or scream in pure frustration. He was so matter-of-fact about it, as if killing could solve the world's problems instead of *being* the world's problem.

"You're naïve to think that, Joley," he said softly and

brought her hand to his mouth. His lips were firm and cool. His mouth was hot and moist. He nibbled on the tips of her fingers.

He knew what he was doing to her. He had to know. And he had to know she'd come there to see him. Joley tugged half-heartedly at her hand, but he merely tightened his grip and she let it go. There was no saving her self-respect.

"Why can't you let me have some peace?"

"You know why. You belong to me and I'm not willing to give you up because you're afraid."

She felt the first flush of smoldering anger. "I'm not afraid of you. I don't like what you are or who you work for. There's a difference."

"Is there?" He smiled as he scraped the pads of her fingers with his teeth, sending streaks of fire racing through her bloodstream and sizzling along every nerve ending.

She jerked her hand away and wiped it on her thigh. "You know there is. I'm not going to deny I'm physically attracted, but I have a certain weakness for jerks. Don't ask me why, but I have 'losers apply here' stamped on my forehead. You're just the kind of man I want to avoid."

His palm curled around her throat, a gentle touch, yet it seemed a flame burned against her bare skin. A faint grin touched his mouth, turned his eyes to a deep blue. "Am I really?" The smile was gone, leaving him looking more lethal than ever.

She swallowed the sudden lump of fear before she choked on it. His thumb slid along her neck in the smallest of caresses, sending shivers of awareness down her spine. Sexually, she was very susceptible to him. She suspected him of spell casting, but when she touched him, she couldn't find evidence of it. He often whispered to her at night, urging her to come to him. And she wanted him day and night. Even her songs were beginning to reflect her need of him.

She had come here intending to sleep with him—just getting it over with—but now that she was with him, she knew it would be a terrible mistake. He would own her, she'd never be free of him. Her only hope was to hold out and hope her obsession with him passed.

"You're a hit man. It isn't glamorous or cool. It's disgusting. You kill people for a living."

"Do I?"

He never raised his voice or seemed to take offense, even when she was being deliberately rude.

"Don't you?" She was desperate. *Desperate.* Someone had to save her from herself, because this man had her so tied up in knots she couldn't think straight. She wanted to claw at his face, rake his body with her fingernails, fight for freedom, and yet at the same time, she craved him, needed him, wanted to wrap her body around his and feel him deep inside her, possessing her, claiming her. She nearly groaned in despair.

"Kiss me, Joley."

Her stomach somersaulted. Her gaze jumped to his mouth. He had great lips. Very defined, very masculine. Kissing would get her into more trouble and she was already in way too deep. Ilya Prakenskii seemed so cool on the outside, ice water in his veins, but inside he smoldered like a living volcano, all molten heat and roiling lava.

He leaned close, his lips inches from hers. His warm breath was against her face and he smelled of spice and mint. "Kiss me." The command was low, his voice soft, almost tender. Her toes were beginning to curl.

She didn't know if she moved to cover that scant inch or if he did. She only knew that his hand shifted to shape the nape of her neck and that her body went soft and pliant, molding against his incredibly hard frame. And that his mouth was on hers. His lips were firm and cool. His teeth scraped and tugged at her lower lip and then it wasn't cool anymore. Fire ignited.

He took control before she could think or breathe, the flames sweeping up and through her, consuming her, taking her over completely. She gave herself to him, wrapping her arms around him, sliding one leg around his to bring her body some relief from the terrible tension that built and built along with the firestorm his mouth created.

His hand caught her hair and held her with a tight, ruthless grip, the bite of pain only increasing her need to be closer, to wrap herself up in him. Her hips moved, sliding her body intimately against his thigh. She needed—*needed*—release, a respite from the continual sexual pressure that never seemed to let up. Night and day her body was on fire for this man.

The heat from his mouth spread like flames licking over her skin. She heard herself moan, and he deepened the kiss, exploring her mouth, taking everything she offered and demanding more.

The world spun away for Joley until there was only his strength and his hard body and the racing fire storming out of control. Her breasts ached, felt swollen and tender, the tips sensitive as they rubbed against his chest. The junction between her legs was hot and damp, demanding release. She slid along his thigh, applying pressure, seeking the relief only his body could provide.

"No." Ilya lifted his mouth from hers, his fingers reluctantly releasing her. "Not like this. When you give yourself to me, it's all the way and forever. This is too easy."

Joley flung her head back, glaring at him. "You're saying no to me?"

"We're not doing this, not like this. You want to get off, you can come home with me and get into my bed where you belong."

She studied his implacable expression, wanting to belong to him, knowing he would take her over, knowing she couldn't live with what and who he was. She would end up loathing herself more than she already did.

He was rejecting her. She'd flung herself at him after months of enduring his constant assault on her senses, she'd given in, driven by an obsession, a craving he'd planted, and *he was rejecting her.* Humiliation fed fury. She took a deep breath and flung back her head, chin up. "Fine. I don't need you. I can walk into that house and go home with any man I want."

Ilya heard the complete confidence in her voice and knew she was stating the absolute truth. She looked passionate, untamed, so sexy his heart nearly stopped. Her eyes were fairly shooting sparks. Her hair was wild and disheveled, as if he had already made love to her. She looked wild and unpredictable and so beautiful he ached.

Ilya caught her wrist again, turned over her palm. "Do you see this, Joley?" His hand slid over her upturned palm, sending shivers along already sensitized nerve endings. "I don't care what happened before I put my mark on you, but make no mistake, Joley, ever since I put this on you, you belong to me. I don't share well with others. Do whatever you feel you have to do, but be willing to live with the consequences. Just know you're going to make things unnecessarily hard on yourself."

"Why are you doing this to me?" Her palm, the one marked by his brand, itched to slap the tough angles and planes of his face. He led her on and then rejected her. "You can't tell me no and then say I can't be with anyone else. Damn you to hell for this."

"You need a man, and I don't mean some spineless wimp who is going to give in to your every whim. You need someone who can rein you in and control your tendency to act before you think."

"That's so sexist. As if I can't take care of myself." She gave a little sniff of disdain, furious with him. "I'm a famous, highly successful woman who's been all over the world, Prakenskii, and I do a darned good job of taking care of myself."

He shook his head. "You don't and you know you don't. Everyone thinks you're tough, Joley, because that's what you want them to believe, but you're not. And you're way too impetuous. You rush in to act without thinking. The Reverend and his pathetic excuse for bodyguards are a perfect example. What did you think would happen when you exposed him for his sleazy crimes on national television? He intends to pay you back. A man like that doesn't forgive and forget. He gets even."

"And you think I need a man to protect me?"

"Yes. Call me sexist all you want, but in the end, it won't change the truth. You're running because you know you need me and you don't want to need anyone."

"Joley!" Brian called her name and she spun around. Denny, her drummer, was walking with him toward her, looking guilty.

Joley loathed herself in that moment. She wasn't any better than Denny. She'd come here for sex with a man she was certain was the worst kind of criminal. And he had rejected her advances, humiliated her, threatened her, and she still was on fire for him. What did that say about her? She pushed away from Ilya and ran to meet Brian and Denny, choosing to escape before she did something she couldn't take back.

2

"I'VE done something so stupid, Hannah." Joley paced back and forth, skirting the furniture in her hotel room as she held the phone to her ear. "Really, really stupid."

"I'm not going to mention that it's three in the morning and you're scaring the hell out of me," Hannah said amid a great deal of covers rustling and her husband Jonas whispering in the background. Hannah shushed him. "I know you're not hurt because all of us would know."

"I *am* hurt." Joley kicked at the bed. She'd already thrown the pillows and every other thing she could find in the room that couldn't be destroyed. "I can't sleep. I can't eat. All I do is think about *him.*"

Hannah might be completely across the country, but she didn't have to ask who *him* was. "What happened?" She tried to send her sister waves of reassurance, but the distance separating them was too great.

"I couldn't sleep. I ached, Hannah, inside and out. I swear I feel like I'm in heat or something. Nothing satisfies me. I don't know what to do anymore. When I do sleep, which is rare, I dream about him. And they're not just any dreams, either. Total erotica. I loathe him. I despise him. How can I want him like this? What's wrong with me? I desperately want to be normal, Hannah. Make me normal."

"You sound scared. Tell me what happened." Hannah used her most calming voice and breathed slowly, in and out, in the hopes that her sister would follow suit.

"He's like a drug addiction," Joley said, "I can't get over him no matter how hard I try. I need to come home. I need to be with you. I'm drowning here."

"Do you think your obsession for him will be better if you come home?" Hannah asked, her voice cautious. Joley was volatile when it came to Ilya Prakenskii. The connection between the two of them was strong, and seemed to be growing stronger.

Joley put her hand over her face, shaking her head, even though Hannah couldn't see her. "No. No, it won't. I went to a party tonight. I told myself I went because I couldn't sleep and I was bored, but I really went to see him."

"Did you go home with him?"

"No! I didn't, but I would have had sex with him." Joley squeezed her eyes shut tight. "He said no. He *rejected* me, Hannah, and that made me want him even more. He knows he has power over me. I feel like I'm caught in his trap and I can't get away."

"Is it possible he used a spell on you?"

"All of you examined me. You didn't find one. There's nothing but the zap on my palm and his voice in my head. He talks to me. His voice is so sexy, it turns me inside out. Except now he isn't talking and that feels so much worse. I'm really in trouble, Hannah." Joley knew she was talking too fast, but she couldn't stop herself. "I have to hear his voice, or I go crazy in my head. But if I reach out to him, he's won." She sank onto the bed. "Hannah. Tell me what to do."

"I'll come out."

Joley shook her head, forcing herself to do the right thing. Hannah had been brutally attacked and nearly died just a few short months earlier. The last thing she needed to do was to fly anywhere in public when she was still trying to heal. "No, no, we're leaving for Chicago in the morning. I can do this. I can get him out of my head."

She rubbed her palm frantically up and down her thigh. Ilya Prakenskii was already deep inside her and he wasn't going to let go of her without a fight. "Why do I go after men who bring out the absolute worst in me? I don't understand why I'm so different from all of you. Look at Libby. She wouldn't be attracted to a man like Ilya. Only me. Just me."

Joley sounded so filled with despair, Hannah was alarmed. "Look, hon, I'm catching the next plane. Hang on and I'll be there. I'll meet you in Chicago."

Joley wanted her sister to come. She felt safer when Hannah was around, when any of her sisters were with her, but she was an adult and this was her problem. She had to learn to manage her cravings for the Russian bodyguard because she knew the need wasn't going to just disappear. Hannah would ease the symptoms, but she couldn't stay forever and then the desire would be back at full strength and Joley would be right back where she started. She took a breath in an effort to calm down.

"I don't want you to come, Hannah. I just needed to hear your voice. Tomorrow I'll be onstage and the energy carries me a long way. I'll be all right. I just need to find a good, decent man. Maybe if I'm with someone who respects me and sees the good side of me, I'll get over my weakness for really bad men."

She'd tried being alone, refusing to date anyone, because she was attracted to the wrong sort of men, but once Ilya had come into her life, she couldn't think about anyone else, let alone the idea of someone else touching her. But she would get over that. People could change—*she* could change.

"Are you sure, Joley, because I don't mind?"

"I do. I don't want you to have to fly across the country to hold my hand." Besides, she was already losing her mind and knew she was already lost. Joley glanced around at the amazing mess she'd made of the hotel room, throwing a fit because Ilya Prakenskii wouldn't have sex with her. He'd made her feel cheap—no—she'd made herself feel that way, throwing herself at him because she *needed* sex—not just any sex—sex with him. And he was responsible for that, talking to her day and night in that incredibly seductive black velvet voice and zapping her palm so she itched and burned. Damn him.

She lifted her chin and took another calming breath. "I'm going to be fine."

"Joley, you're really upset. Don't pretend you aren't," Hannah cautioned. "That's when you always get into trouble. Think before you do anything."

"Why do people always say that to me?" Joley said. "*He* said I don't think. He said I needed a man to tell me what to do because I couldn't take care of myself. As if. He's stuck in the Stone Age."

Hannah knew she'd struck a nerve and tried to recover. "He is very dominating. I noticed that whenever he's around you and he doesn't like you to cross him."

"Well, he can go to hell. I don't know what game he's playing, but I'm not playing it with him. I'll be glad to get out of this city." Joley flung herself on the bed, trying not to notice that her body ached and she felt hollow and empty.

"Europe was good?" Hannah asked.

"Very good. We sold out every concert and we actually scheduled a few extra because the sales were so high and we hated turning away fans. I'm exhausted, but it was great."

"You had fantastic write-ups in the newspapers, and even the tabloids treated you fairly well. There were only a couple of scandals."

Joley laughed, and for the first time it was genuine. "I told the reporters to go easy on me because my parents believe all the lies they tell."

Hannah laughed with her. "I read that quote and knew you'd really said it. Mom's going to have a few things to say to you."

"That's not unusual," Joley said. "Go back to sleep, Hannah. And tell my brother-in-law I love him, even though he's semi-friends with Prakenskii when he should be arresting him."

"I've got news."

There was a small silence while Joley sat up, the note in Hannah's voice tipping her off. "What?"

"Abbey is getting married next month, as soon as you get home. They're having the ceremony on the Drake beach and the reception here at our house. They only want immediate family at the ceremony. You know how Abbey is. And I'm pregnant."

"Oh my God! Oh my God! For real? You're going to have a baby for real?" Joley stopped, the smile fading from her face. "Wait a minute, Hannah. What does the doctor say? Are you sure you'll be all right? You're still not completely healed."

"Libby doesn't know if I'll be able to nurse. There's a lot of scar tissue, but we'll see. I'm so happy, Joley, and I can't wait for you to come home to share this with us."

"Libby's the best doctor in the world," Joley said of her sister. Libby had special healing gifts, and thanks to her, Hannah's scars were barely visible. "Jonas must be walking around with a big balloon head. What have you gone and done, Hannah? He's going to be impossible to live with."

"I heard that," Jonas called.

"Well, it's made him bossier," Hannah said, laughing.

Joley could hear the joy in her sister's voice, and deep inside, where no one could see, she wept for her own loneliness. She wanted someone to share life with, to laugh and cry and hold at night. Her life was spent moving from city to city in an endless tour of shows, living out of hotels and buses. She loved it, but she wanted someone with her. She was so happy for her beloved sister, Hannah, but Hannah's happiness only intensified her own lonely existence.

"Wasn't Abbey going to call me?" Joley asked, somewhat hurt that her sister hadn't given her the news of her impending marriage.

"Don't be silly," Hannah said. "You were in Europe and they just decided. They're waiting on the actual date to speak to you. You're going to stand up for her, remember? And Kate and Sarah and Libby will be married at Christmas."

"Finally. I thought they'd never actually do it, just talk about it."

"If you get married, Joley," Hannah asked, "how will you want your wedding?"

"Since it's never going to happen, I don't think about it. I'm going to be the favorite aunt," Joley pronounced. "The fun one who always lets the kids get in trouble."

"You'll find someone, Joley," Hannah reassured her. "You just have to be more open and let it happen. You've always been so fiercely independent."

"It's more than that and you know it. I despise men weaker than me and hate men stronger than me. That pretty much leaves me with nowhere to go."

"I thought I wouldn't be able to live with Jonas, Joley, but when you love each other you find a way to compromise. Jonas does get bossy with me, but I've found that I have as much power in the relationship as he does."

"I know you're perfect for each other," Joley said. "I think I always knew it, but Jonas is different. He's a good man and he loves you more than anything else in the world because you're you. Hannah, you deserve to be loved that way."

"And you don't?"

Joley was silent.

"Joley." Hannah's voice was soft with love. "You're a great person. You sacrifice for everyone. Don't do that to yourself, don't sell yourself short."

"I don't." But Joley knew things about herself Hannah didn't know. Dark things she craved, maybe even needed, in a relationship. She loathed that part of herself, driven by sex and danger, suppressed most of the time, but so strong the need fought her continually. She wanted to be loved, but what decent man could ever love someone like her? Sometimes, like now, when she felt driven to the brink of madness, she wished she wasn't a Drake and she could drown herself in alcohol and drugs and not feel the pain.

"Tell everyone I love them, Hannah," Joley said. "I'll be home soon."

"I really will fly out," Hannah offered.

"No you won't. You'll stay right there and do whatever Libby tells you to do," Joley said. "And Jonas. Tell him I said bossing you around right now is a good thing."

Hannah laughed. "I'm *so* never telling him that!"

"Get some sleep. I'm much calmer now," Joley lied, forcing cheerfulness into her voice. "And wish me luck in Chicago."

"You don't need luck, Joley. Your talent sells tickets. Have fun, and call me if you need me. You know I'll come. Love you lots."

"Back at ya." Joley hit the end button and tossed her cell phone onto the bed before sinking down on it.

Hannah would come to her, but Joley would never ask her now, not when she was pregnant, especially after the vicious attack. Hannah was special, and Joley always turned to her when she felt in crisis. Hannah dealt with everything in her own sweet way, wanting to make the world better for her sisters. She had been a success as a supermodel, but Joley knew she'd be even more of a success as a mother.

Joley was closest to Hannah, loved her dearly, and it had been Ilya Prakenskii who had saved Hannah's life. He had stopped her attacker and kept her alive until the Drakes had gathered together to help heal her, and for that alone, Joley would always feel a connection with the man.

"You have Jonas," Joley murmured. Jonas was tough as nails when he had to be, and he loved Hannah. Everyone had known it but Hannah.

Joley ran her hands through her hair several times, before she flung herself backward to lie staring up at the ceiling. She'd killed an hour talking with Hannah, but she had a long way to go before the night was over. The hotel had an exercise room. She could go there. Alone . . . again. If only the tabloids really knew what her life was like.

Joley. Party girl. Lovers all over the world. *Not.* It was more like Joley up all night writing songs and going to the exercise room to keep from going into sexual meltdown.

"Damn you, Prakenskii. You're punishing me now, deliberately not speaking to me. Well, you know something, I don't need you. And I don't want you." She leapt up and grabbed her hotel key. Sexual frustration was really good for writing songs. Her best songs had come from detesting, no, loathing Ilya Prakenskii and wanting him with every breath in her body.

The workout room was deserted, and she grabbed a bottle of water and programmed the treadmill for a run up and down hills. In her head she could hear musical notes with each step she took. Fury at Prakenskii was the pounding beat of the drum. The saxophone was purely erotic, the guitar riff—the blood sizzling in her veins. The keyboard was the breath moving in and out of her body steadily, necessarily. She could hear the bass in each slap of her foot on the surface, deep notes that set her heart pumping.

There was euphoria in music, the only place she could escape who she was, what she was. She had six sisters and she admired every single one of them. She was fiercely protective of them, although she was second to the youngest and all of them had incredible gifts. They all knew she had a weakness for dangerous men, but they had no idea just how terrible her craving for Ilya Prakenskii really was. And he was the epitome of everything she stood against.

She believed in the order of the universe. She believed in good and evil, in the balance of nature. She believed in the right to defend oneself, of course, but she deeply and sincerely believed it was wrong to harm another. It was rumored that Ilya was a hit man, and she could never, under any circumstances, have a relationship with a man who was evil. The problem was, he didn't feel evil. He felt hot and sexy, with that terrible edge of danger she seemed to crave.

She had been in his mind many times. He could communicate with her telepathically, and that meant he had to open his mind to hers. She had caught glimpses of violence, terrible things that made her afraid, but she'd never seen a memory of him murdering in cold blood—and if he was as evil as a hit man would be—then why couldn't she feel it when she could tell so easily with others?

"Joley?"

She nearly jumped out of her skin, whipping her head around and gaping at her lead guitarist, Brian. "You scared me. What are you doing here this time of the morning?" She kept running, turning her head away from him, afraid the guilt would betray her.

"You seemed so upset when you left, Joley. You barely said a word. I saw the Reverend there and I know he and his entourage are confrontational with you, so I was worried."

"I'm fine." She glanced at him. "You should get some sleep. We have a show tomorrow in Chicago."

"Stop that thing and talk to me. This is Brian, not some schmo off the street. We've been friends for years." He held out the water bottle as an offering.

Joley let out her breath and allowed the treadmill to slow to a stop. She took the towel from Brian and wrapped it around her neck before taking the water bottle. "I thought you were allergic to exercise. What are you doing here?"

"You're always here when you're upset."

"I'm here to work out. And I sometimes come up with my best songs late at night."

"Tell me what happened. What were you doing at Nikitin's party?"

She shrugged and swallowed a long gulp of water. "I couldn't sleep and thought I'd check it out. Once I got there, I remembered why I hated those things." She dried off her face. "Did you manage to run down that little weasel Dean whatever his last name is and his friend? The ones hanging with the girls who couldn't have been older than fourteen."

Brian shook his head. "I never found them. Denny helped

me look for them, but we couldn't find them anywhere. We checked the pool, the gardens, the garages, everywhere, but they must have made the girls leave."

"If he shows up in Chicago, Brian, I'm having Jerry fire him." Jerry St. Ives was her manager, and she was just as angry with him as she was with Dean. He had promised to oversee the parties and make certain that no young kids were taken advantage of.

"Joley, you know very well anyone could have invited those girls. For all we know Nikitin did. At least talk to Dean before you give him the axe. He could have been escorting them off the property."

"He ran when I called him."

"Honey, come on. Joley Drake angry is a scary thing. I'll talk to him if you don't want to do it, but at least let's give him the benefit of the doubt. This is America. Innocent until proven guilty."

She rolled her eyes. "And what's with Denny and the blonde?"

"He was afraid you saw that."

"You think? She was blowing him right on the grounds in front of anyone and everyone."

"He was pretty screwed up."

"Is that supposed to be an excuse?" She shoved her hand through her hair in agitation. "I like his girlfriend. Lisa's a really good person and she deserves better than him." She knew she sounded disgusted and judgmental, but it was the truth. "I'm not going to be able to look at him."

Brian shook his head. "Joley, not everyone is perfect."

She burst out laughing. "Is that what you think I am, Brian?"

"We all do."

"I was there for the same reason as Denny. I just didn't go through with it." She pushed past him and threw the towel in the empty basket. Housekeeping had come and gone long ago.

"What the hell are you talking about?" Brian demanded.

"I was lonely. I went to the party with the idea of bringing someone home. I'm not perfect, but I'm also not committed to anyone. Denny is. He should be a man and tell Lisa he needs other women. That's only fair."

Brian rubbed the bridge of his nose, narrowing his eyes and frowning in disapproval. "I don't believe you."

She didn't pretend to misunderstand. "Well, it's true. The saint is really a sinner. Sheesh, Brian, you've known me for years."

"You don't sleep around."

"How do you know what I do or don't do while you're at the parties having a great time?"

"I don't believe any of this. You're just upset."

"You don't believe I can get lonely, Brian?"

"Hell, Joley, if you're lonely, I'm lonely, too. Maybe we should just make all the rumors true and hit the sack together." He wiggled his eyebrows at her.

She studied him over the bottle of water. For one, horrible moment, she even considered the idea. They were both alone. They liked each other, were best friends, maybe if they got to together . . . Prakenskii had turned her down and her pride was wounded. She'd always been able to wrap Brian around her little finger. And he was nice. A very nice guy, but she wasn't the least attracted to him, nor was he attracted to her. She sighed. "I like you too much," she said.

"What the hell does that mean?"

"It means I'm not going to sleep with you and ruin a perfectly good relationship. I like you, Brian. I don't like the men I want to sleep with."

"Okay, now I'm confused, but that isn't unusual around you, Joley." He rubbed the bridge of his nose. "Most of the time we're all confused."

"Me, too." She grinned at him. "At least we can agree on that."

He smiled back at her. "We've got to catch a plane first thing in the morning and catch up with our bus. Are you going to sleep tonight?"

"You go ahead. I was in the middle of composing."

"You were in the middle of trying to run yourself into the ground. Did seeing Denny really upset you that much, Joley?"

"That and a lot of other things. I'm tired of this life, Brian. I want a home and a family."

"You love performing."

She shrugged. "Maybe I do. I love music. I lose myself in it. But in the end, no matter how good things are, I don't have anyone to share my life with me. Maybe that's why I get so upset with Denny. He's had wonderful people to share happiness with, women who love him for who he is, not what he does, and he throws it away for a few minutes of pleasure. How many chances should he have before none of it's real anymore? Until every woman who goes near him wants him just because he's in a band and not because she loves him? And then we stop playing and he grows old and he's all alone. I guess he can look back and say he counted a few thousand blow jobs and that will comfort him in his old age."

"You're just down tonight."

She drank more water and nodded, agreeing with him because it was what he wanted. "Yep, that's what it is."

He studied her face. "You really aren't thinking about quitting, are you? We're on top. Every song we release is a number one hit. No one does that. No one. Every concert is sold out. Our albums are double, triple platinum. Come on, Joley, tell me you're just having a bad night and you're not serious."

"Does it matter what I say?" She pushed past him toward the door.

He caught her shoulder and stopped her. "Of course it matters. You always matter. I hate that you're unhappy. I'll talk to Denny."

"He can't change who he is. But I'm not lying to Lisa for him. I'd never want you to lie to me if my boyfriend was screwing around on me, and I won't do it for or to any of you."

"That's fair enough," Brian said. "It was one party, Joley, one that got a little out of hand. Nikitin's parties are notorious for excess, but we don't usually stay long. We make an appearance, have a few drinks and leave."

"He supplies women." She made it a statement.

"He has women on the guest list; most hosts of parties do."

"You know what I'm saying. I know what he is, what his reputation is. He's seducing the band, don't you see that? Supply drugs and alcohol and women. Take a few blackmail pictures and hook the boys on the high and he's got you all under his thumb. That's how he operates."

"Nikitin throws some killer parties, Joley, which is why everyone goes when he invites us, but he's not offering anything we can't get anywhere else. Hell, Jerry can get us any drug we want, any woman we want. That's not why we like hanging out with Nikitin."

"You like him? Nikitin?"

He shrugged. "If he isn't already a billionaire, he's close, and yet he's cool, and I hardly think he needs to supply our band with anything to get us under his thumb. What would be the point? I don't know him very well, but yes, I like him. He's personable and intellectual. You know me. I don't hit the party scene hard, but I do like conversation and he's an interesting man. We've been talking quite a bit. He doesn't do drugs that I've seen, so we hang out, have a drink or two and talk world affairs. He's very knowledgeable in a lot of areas I'm interested in."

"Such as?" She wasn't touching him, but his aura had changed slightly, enough for her to know he was uncomfortable with the conversation.

"Well, the market for one, what are good stocks. What makes a good investment. He really knows his stuff. He has advisors, but he does a lot of his own research and makes solid choices."

She could hear the admiration in Brian's voice and it alarmed her. "What about his men?"

"His men?" Brian echoed, his frown deepening. Now his aura changed sharply, throwing out a mixture of colors—annoyance—disturbed—even anger. "What men?"

Her eyebrow shot up. "The ones with guns everywhere. Did you notice them? Those guns are real, my friend."

"Well the threats to him are real as well. You ought to know about that. You need bodyguards. Which reminds me, where were your bodyguards when you came to the party? Why was Steve just sitting in the car like an idiot? With the Reverend there, anything could have happened. Jerry warned you that the threats against you have been escalating. And you have that nutcase fan fixating on you and trying to tell you he loves you. His letters are very disturbing. Twice he's managed to get nearly onstage."

She sighed. "I might have a bodyguard or two, but I sure don't have men with automatic weapons guarding my gate. What's up with that?"

He shrugged. "It's probably a necessity."

"Why, Brian?" She persisted, wanting to shake him.

"Wouldn't a bodyguard or two be enough, or some rented security? Have you taken a look at those men? And what about Prakenskii?"

Brian's head went up sharply. "I saw you with him. Did he make a move on you? Scare you? Because I can talk to Nikitin about him."

She gave a short laugh. "You really have no clue what's going on there, do you? Nikitin would never fire Prakenskii. He's afraid of him, just like anyone else with a brain. And those guards you think he needs, they're all trained soldiers."

Brian gave a growl of total frustration. "You have no idea what his life was like in Russia. He had a lot of enemies. That's why he has a man like Prakenskii working for him."

"A man like Prakenskii?" she echoed. "What has he said about his bodyguard?"

"Just that he's very dangerous and not to cross him. He advised me to stay out of his way." Brian lowered his voice as if the walls had ears. "I think he's killed a lot of people."

"Is that what Nikitin told you?"

Brian shook his head. "He implied it. And the other bodyguards defer to Prakenskii over everything. I've never actually heard the man talk. He looks at people and they just jump into action without him saying a word. Frankly, he scares me and I wish Nikitin would get rid of him. I know he doesn't altogether trust him."

Joley went on alert, radar suddenly going on with a loud warning shriek. She was instantly protective, everything in her rising up to defend Ilya—which was silly—and stupid—but she couldn't stop herself. "What does that mean? Why would you have a bodyguard you don't trust working for you? He's the man who takes the bullet for you."

Brian narrowed his eyes, suspicion creeping into his expression at her sudden change of attitude. "I don't know, but a couple of times I've seen one of Nikitin's other guards, a man by the name of Pavel Demidov, come in and whisper to Nikitin. They both always look around to see where Prakenskii is. If Prakenskii is watching or is close by, Nikitin waves Demidov off. Within a couple of minutes he makes excuses to me and tells Prakenskii to watch things while he disappears for a while. Nikitin almost always goes to a phone and has a heated conversation in Russian. He definitely doesn't want Prakenskii to hear or see him. There's no question he trusts Demidov and not Prakenskii. What's Prakenskii to you?"

"I'm just curious." Joley widened her eyes in innocence. "What does Nikitin say?" Nikitin felt evil, unlike Prakenskii, who felt—well—sexy. She nearly groaned aloud. She was so far gone she wasn't even hiding it from Brian.

"They talk in Russian, how the hell would I know? And I can only pretend to look for a bathroom so many times before Nikitin or Demidov gets suspicious that I'm trying to eavesdrop."

"So you *were* trying to find out what was going on." Joley pounced on that.

Brian shrugged. "I find those parties boring. I'm not going home with a woman; I'm not into public blow jobs or orgies. I have to watch my drinks, so what the hell is there to do other than observe people? If Nikitin isn't available to talk to, there's not much going on for me."

"I thought you were seeing someone."

"Yeah, well, that didn't last." He made a face at her. "I'm too nice."

Joley laughed and poked him, using the towel to keep from making skin-to-skin contact. "That you are, my friend. Very nice. One of my favorite people in fact, next to my sisters and Jonas. You got dumped? Cuz I'll go hunt her down and kick her ass for you if you want me to."

"Naw, but thanks for the offer," Brian said, laughing with her. "But I bet you could do it. You still taking lessons from your karate man?"

"I have several trainers." It was another way to get through the long days and even longer nights. She liked physical exercise; it was a great way to sublimate.

"You're so crazy, Joley, why do you take that stuff? You have security and a personal bodyguard, who," he looked around him, "never seems to be on the job."

She grinned at him. "The poor man has to sleep sometime."

"His job is to guard your butt, not sleep. And he wasn't sleeping. His lazy ass was sitting behind the wheel of the car."

"I like being alone when I'm working out. He's off the clock and he's actually a good guy, Brian. I wouldn't have him, but Jonas convinced my family I need a personal protector, so

Steve pulled the short straw and ended up guarding me as well as driving."

"I'll bet Jonas doesn't know you don't use Steve half the time."

"I do too."

"He wasn't guarding you at Nikitin's party."

"He was too; he drove me there, but I didn't want him following me around at the party and told him I might need a fast getaway so to stay with the car."

Brian rolled his eyes. "Good plan, Joley. Good use of a bodyguard. And what did happen between you and Prakenskii?"

She shrugged. "He pulled me out of a situation with RJ and his little gang of thugs, so I think he felt entitled to lecture me." Her palm burned. She rubbed it up and down her thigh and hoped her face didn't flame with her blatant lies.

"Nikitin is sure strange about that man." Brian shook his head. "He seems to rely heavily on him yet he keeps him out of the loop part of the time. I find it fascinating."

"Why?"

Brian held open the door for her and Joley followed him out. "Human nature fascinates me. I like people. I like to know what makes them tick."

"Sex," Joley blurted.

Brian laughed. "Don't be so nasty about poor Denny. He's going to be slinking around avoiding you as it is. If you give him one of your superior, you're-a-bug-under-my-shoe looks, he'll be squashed."

"It doesn't stop him from being such a hound dog. Seriously, Brian, what about the others? Was everyone there getting wasted and screwing around?"

"Do you really want to know?"

She considered. "I don't want Nikitin to have any surprises for me. Have any of them done anything illegal he could get them on? Or done anything he could blackmail them with?"

Brian whistled. "You really don't trust the man. Seriously, hon, do you think a man like Nikitin cares what any of our band members do?"

"I think I wouldn't want to find out. He isn't all he seems, Brian. I have a lot of information because I have so many family members and friends in law enforcement. He's not a nice guy."

"He told me he grew up in the Russian mob. He said a lot of his men were caught up in that life, but he's broken away, gotten legit and tried to give men like him a chance to have a decent life."

"And you believed him? Looking at the men who work for him, the guns they carry, you believed him?"

"If he did manage to break away from the mob, Joley, especially the Russian mob, with their history of retaliation and violence, I can see why he would feel he would need guns and men who knew what they were doing."

"And how many mobsters actually get out of that world, Brian?" She gave a harsh laugh. "Do you also believe in Santa Claus?"

"You really ought to take some time to get to know him before you judge him," Brian said. "I think you'd like him."

"You've forgotten one teeny-tiny but very important fact, my friend." Joley keyed her room and stood in the open doorway, turning back so he could see her expression. "I'm a Drake. We're not normal. I read people through touch, which is why I'm so careful to rarely touch any of you. I don't even have to touch Nikitin to feel the violence and evil in him. Don't be dumb, Brian, stay away from him, and keep our boys away from him, too. He'll chew you up and spit you out and not even think twice about it. And you can take that to the bank." She closed the door on his shocked expression.

3

HER palm itched. Really itched. Joley rubbed her hand up and down her denim-clad thigh, clenching her teeth together, all the while trying not to reach out with her mind to find—*him*—Ilya Prakenskii. Looking out the open door of her dressing room backstage, she could feel the energy in the arena, swelling and rolling like waves on the sea. Ten thousand restless people, excited, waiting, anticipating her performance, yet she knew—absolutely knew—that Prakenskii was somewhere in that vast crowd.

Adrenaline raced through her system, adding to the excitement and the building waves of sheer energy the crowd produced. Heat rushed through her body at the thought of the Russian bodyguard. She couldn't get near him without sizzling chemistry arcing between them. Sometimes, like now, she swore she could still taste him in her mouth. She touched her fingers to her lips, pressing hard, trying to erase the memory of his kiss. He ran in her veins like a drug, a bad habit she couldn't kick, no matter how hard she tried.

"Joley? You up for this? It's crazy out there." Brian shot her a grin. His eyes were shining and he looked as sexy as hell, just the way the females in the crowd liked him. Tight-fitting jeans, shirt open to his flat stomach, chest showing and black hair tousled. The women would go wild when he took the stage.

She stepped into the hall and matched his grin. The rush of the crowd was exhilarating, but it was the music that always moved her. She thought in music—actually could see in music.

Sometimes she could smell and taste it. Notes and melodies floated through her mind when she was talking casually to others. She heard music in the rhythm of the world around her, and sometimes, in silence, she found the most perfect songs. But now, when the energy was so powerful, she saw musical notes dancing in front of her, in colors, like tiny fireflies flashing in the air around her.

One of seven daughters of a seventh daughter and endowed with special gifts that could be both blessing and curse, when she opened her mind, she could feel the hopes and dreams and disappointments in the lives of her audience. She rarely sought out and touched a single mind, rarely invaded privacy. But sometimes she interspersed melodies and slower ballads between the foot-stomping, get-up-and-dance rhythms of the rock and roll she was so famous for, in order to bring peace and contentment to any troubled people she sensed in her audience.

"Good choice for a warm-up band," Brian said. "They have a way of getting the crowd going."

"Yeah," Joley agreed, "I really like them. And they're not bad to travel with."

"Chicago is great," Rick Henderson, the bass guitar player, announced. He came up behind Joley to air hug her.

Although he hadn't even brushed against her, she moved forward, an automatic response from childhood. She rarely touched anyone other than her sisters. It was a good way to ruin friendships. Fortunately her band had been with her a long time and they respected her personal space.

She spun around and smooched the air at Rick. "Chicago is awesome. I love it here." To be honest, she was just a little nervous. After the Nikitin party in New York she was somewhat depressed. She had a few enemies and the threatening letters had been more plentiful than usual lately. The Reverend and his followers were protesting her concerts and she knew they would be trying to cause a scene here as well.

"Chicago always has a good crowd," Brian agreed, high-fiving Rick. He flashed another smile at Joley. "You aren't worried are you, hon? Seriously, we have extra security everywhere."

"That whack job Reverend RJ is here," Joley said, and bit down hard on her lower lip, wishing she hadn't mentioned him.

She'd done a stupid, stupid thing, challenging the perverted man in front of the television cameras, but worse, she'd used her voice on him. He had enough charisma to gain followers, but Joley's voice could make men obsessive. She'd been careless, and she knew it. What was worse, Ilya had seen the entire thing. That also had made her feel cheap and dirty. She certainly knew how to make a fool out of herself around him. She didn't want to appear as if anything bothered her. That was her trademark—happy-go-lucky Joley. Laughing at life and moving through the world like quicksilver. She hid scared well—always had. So well that her sisters, able to read others with ease, never guessed that she'd embarked on her world tour with trepidation. The recent attack on Hannah had terrified her. She knew the Drake family had bitter enemies, and the threats on her life had grown numerous.

"The Reverend shows up just to get the press," Brian said. "I caught his act the other day for a few minutes, how repentant he is for his lustful thoughts, and how he spent a week on his knees begging the lord's forgiveness for lusting after you. He says he wants to save you as well. He's forgiven you for tempting him, you daughter of the devil, and now he only wants to reach out and pull you from hell's claws. I think he's trying to get the world to believe you're a lesbian or at least bisexual, because then he could really crucify you."

For a moment Brian sounded bitter, but when she glanced up sharply, he shrugged. "He's a fucking weirdo, Joley. Don't let him rattle you."

"Well I wish he'd just disappear."

"He got a lot of press time for his little act with you," Rick added, threading his fingers through his long blond hair in typical Rick fashion. He had gorgeous hair and the women went wild for it. Knowing that, he used every opportunity to draw attention to the shimmering golden strands, which made the rest of the band laugh.

"Anyone near you can pretty much stay on the front pages. And now the Rev's hanging with Nikitin," Brian added, pointing his finger at her. "I told you it was a mistake to ignore Nikitin. If you were his friend, he'd never let the Reverend come near his parties."

"You ought to know. You've gone to them even when I asked you not to," Joley said and glared at Brian.

Brian looked uncomfortable. "I didn't know about him, Joley."

Rick shrugged, unrepentant. "He always has the best booze and women. What can I say? His parties rock."

She ignored him and turned her attention to the warm-up band as the rest of her band members crowded close. Denny stayed to the back looking sheepish and avoiding her gaze. Leo Meyer, on keyboard, looking good in jeans and an open vest, blew her a kiss, his eyes shining with excitement.

Logan forgot all about her personal space and picked her up, swinging her around. "I'm a father, Joley, can you believe that? She's the cutest baby I've ever seen."

Brian nudged him. "That's not hard, they're all kind of squishy and sort of undercooked."

Logan set Joley on her feet and hugged her hard. "Man, she's got the tiniest fingers and she looks at me and I melt." He glared at Brian, who grinned unrepentantly. "And she's not undercooked. She's just a little squishy."

Joley poked both of them. "She's new, not squishy. Is she still at the hospital?"

"Under guard." Logan nodded. "They're letting her go home with me tomorrow. Jerry's trying to find a nanny, but I have to be careful. I don't like the idea of hiring someone we don't know."

"What about Tish? She's a teacher and so good with kids. Have you considered her?" Joley was careful to extricate herself from Logan. His joy was overwhelming her, along with his fears of fatherhood. She couldn't afford to have those emotions inside her when she went out to perform. Her voice could affect the entire audience.

Logan rubbed at the deliberate five o'clock shadow on his chin and glanced around the tight circle surrounding him. They were all silent, watching him. "I think I burned that bridge pretty effectively."

When the band was first starting out, it was Logan's wife, Tish, who'd taken care of them all, sold their CDs at the bars and made their posters and even got them gigs. She was the one who had first connected with Joley, which had eventually brought their band to fame. Tish had come up the ranks with them and they all adored her. They'd known her since high school, and all of them missed her—especially Logan.

"You won't know until you try, bro," Leo said. "Tish isn't with anyone else and she never divorced your sorry ass. You told me that yourself the other day."

Joley's eyebrow shot up. "Have you been keeping tabs on her?"

Logan looked sheepish. He shrugged. "Maybe. A little. I ask some of our old friends how she's doing, that's all."

"Well, ask her then. She can only say no," Joley said to encourage him. "She knows the ropes, the way we work together. She's always fit in."

"You really think she's going to want to take care of someone else's baby?"

"*Your* baby," Joley pointed out. "If Tish thinks a baby— and you—need help, she's going to come, even if it means risking her heart." She pinned him with her dark, straight gaze. "If she comes, because she's generous like that, see that you don't abuse her trust. I mean it, Logan. Don't ask her, flirt around with her and then throw some groupie in her face." Her gaze strayed to Denny.

Denny ducked his head, looking miserable. With a small sigh, Joley went to stand in front of him. He offered a hesitant smile. "I know you're angry with me."

"Disappointed," she corrected, "but it's your life, Denny. You aren't married to Lisa. I just know how upset you get when you break up with someone you profess to love, and you're always the one sabotaging the relationship."

"I get high and the women are all over me and I can't seem to say no. She was trying to kiss on Nikitin and she looked so hot. He kind of pushed her away and she crawled under the table, right in front of everyone, like she was an animal in heat, couldn't get enough, you know. One minute I was drinking with Nikitin and laughing, the next, I was so burning hot for her I couldn't think straight." He rubbed his hand over his face as if he could wipe out the incident. "I wish I could tell you that I'll never forget it and she was awesome, but I can't remember most of it. I threw Lisa away for something I can't even remember." He shook his head.

He was miserable. Joley could feel desolation rolling off him in waves. His distress was genuine, not feigned to get back in her good graces. Denny had a weakness for women, but he'd made a commitment to Lisa and told the band members that he wanted to be faithful to her, because she mattered to him. Joley had believed him and now, feeling his unhappiness, she still did.

"Denny, had you been doing drugs?"

He shrugged. "Nothing much. Less than I normally do at a party. I have no idea what happened, but I told her. I called her last night when I got back to the room." For a moment tears swam in his eyes, and he blinked and looked away from her. "I wanted her to hear it from me, not read it in the tabloids, and I know they got my picture, the bastards. I spend my life hurting people I care about."

Joley frowned, not liking Denny's explanation of what happened. He might be a hound dog, but he always took responsibility. If he said he was sick and dizzy and the memory was foggy, she was suspicious that someone had slipped him a drug without his knowledge. But why? "You might have had a little help this time," Joley said before she could stop herself. Again she glanced at Brian, whose gaze slid away from hers. Was Nikitin up to something or was she simply overreacting because she didn't trust the man?

"Whatever happened, I think I've lost Lisa, and I can't blame her." The drummer's eyes swam with tears.

Joley's heart jumped. She'd never seen him cry over a woman. They were about to go out and perform for thousands of people and Denny was falling apart right before her eyes.

"It isn't over until it's over, Denny. You have a chance with Lisa. She's worth fighting for. We'll all help you. Is she here tonight? Did she come?"

Lisa had promised to be in Chicago for their concert, and Denny had been looking forward to seeing her. The band had been in Europe for weeks and Lisa hadn't been able to make New York, so Chicago was to have been their reunion.

"She flew in last night. I called her at the hotel, which only made it worse. I have no idea if she decided to come to the concert. If she did, she didn't pick up her backstage pass and she didn't check in with Jerry. I asked him to watch for her." Denny sounded more miserable than ever.

"I'll do what I can to help you, Denny," Joley promised rashly. "Jerry can find out if she picked up her ticket or not. If she's here, I'll do what I can to persuade her to give you another chance, but if you mean what you say about her, stay away from the parties. Leave when I do. Come back with me and we'll play Scrabble or something, anything at all to keep you out of trouble."

The other band members nodded. "We can play that Monopoly game, the one that never ends," Rick said. "We'll party with Joley."

Denny snorted his derision, but he looked much happier.

"Yeah, cuz Joley's such a partier," Brian said. Onstage the warm-up band broke into their final number. "That's the windup song, we're on in a few. Come on."

He put out his arm and they huddled together with Joley in the middle of their circle as they always did before each concert. It had become a tradition and they all were superstitious now. If they didn't come together like now, arms around one another with Joley in the center, Brian giving his standard pep talk, they all knew it was going to be a terrible show, everything that could go wrong would. Joley, like a lot of performers, did one standard sound check when possible, not wanting to chance ruining her voice. They ran through their songs, but tried not to have to repeat too much.

"Let's do it," Brian yelled and they took off running for the stage.

Joley hung back, listening to the screams and booming applause as her boys took the stage. She loved to hear the way the crowd went wild when her band picked up their instruments. They worked hard, contributed so much, each a genius in his own way, and she was proud of their music. The music swelled and she heard her name. *Joley*. Just Joley. And it was enough. She ran out into the glaring lights and it sounded like thunder.

For a moment she stood there, her body absorbing the rhythms and sounds, the currents of energy coming at her. She waved and sent the crowd her famous smile, and they went wild.

Immediately she launched into the first number, her voice low and sultry, slipping in and out of the swelling music as only she could do. The rhythm had the crowd on its feet; it was impossible for them to stay in their seats, clapping, swaying, some jumping up and down, others dancing, while her voice sank into them and turned them inside out with her music.

ILYA Prakenskii looked down at his hand. It was trembling. He had fought for survival since he was a toddler. He could withstand pain and torture. He'd been shot, knifed, hit with bats, and he had remained rock steady. He had sewn his own flesh. He had killed—numerous times. Nothing shook his calm. That place inside him, that cool detachment was what kept him alive.

He could even allow a woman to service his body, as he could hers, and still remain completely detached and in control. But he couldn't stop his hands from shaking or his body from reacting just looking at—or listening to—Joley Drake.

Emotions could get a man like him killed, so he'd been very careful never to feel. It had been so long since anything touched him, he was shaken, realizing that his deep need of that one small woman wasn't going anywhere anytime soon. She took his breath away. She stole all reason. He didn't get involved—*ever*—not emotionally—with anyone. People around him frequently ended up dead. Emotion was a weakness, something that could too easily be used against him. But Joley Drake . . .

Ilya hit the back of his head against the wall as if he could jolt her out of his mind. But she was already wrapped inside him and he was never going to be free of her. He knew that now, knew that no matter how disciplined he'd always been, his control went out the window whenever he laid eyes on Joley. And discipline wasn't going to save either of them this time.

He couldn't take his eyes off of her as she moved across the stage. Her voice swelled with power, vibrating through his body until he couldn't think with wanting her. He could have lived with that. The chemistry between them was so damn potent he ached every minute of every day, but there was so much more than sex. He belonged to Joley Drake. Body and soul. Men like him didn't ever belong to anyone—and no one belonged to them. Worse, she was slowly stealing his heart. He could take the craving for her body. He could even live without his soul, but if he allowed her access to his heart, he would be lost.

His eyes narrowed to slits. His gaze shifted to take in the crush of people, noting automatically every small detail and storing it so his mind could process all the information even as his body absorbed Joley—everything about her—the curves of her body, her far-too-erotic rhythm as she moved with the pounding music. Every step, every sway, every note screamed sin and sex. She couldn't help the way she was put together or the way her voice seduced and the way her body shouted, "fuck me." But it still pissed him off—and kept him awake at night.

He wished a good fuck was all he wanted, but that was the least of it. He wanted to make love to her. Hard and fast, slow and easy, memorizing every sweet curve and sinful valley. He wanted to know every intimate detail of her body and mind. He wanted to tie her to him any way he could. And he'd tried. First with his magic. Always with his magic. He used his voice shamelessly as a weapon because he knew that sound was the key to Joley. He understood, in ways she still barely perceived, that they were locked in a battle for life. And he wasn't about to lose.

The roar of the crowd swelled, building until the noise was deafening. Bright lights flashed, and Joley moved across the stage, in and out of the lights, almost as if she were making love to the shadows. Nothing in Ilya's barren existence, all the training given to him, all the hard-won experience—none of it—had prepared him for Joley.

Her voice had seduced him first. That perfect pitch that slid into his body, past every defense, and stroked and caressed until every nerve ending was on fire. Then he'd seen her, all soft inviting curves, full rounded breasts, small tucked-in waist and flared hips built to cradle a man. Her skin was flawless, looking so soft it was an invitation to touch. But her face, those classic lines, large dark eyes and full pouting mouth— he hadn't been able to drag his gaze from her the first time he'd seen her. His breath nearly strangled in his lungs and his body had turned harder than a rock. He'd been that way ever since.

More than all of that, her fierce spirit had drawn him like a moth to flame, all fire and passion, a woman in need of protection who thought she could take care of not only herself, but everyone around her. He saw how vulnerable she was. He saw inside of her, to that place she kept hidden, where she thought no one could love who she really was. If there was such a thing as love, if there was truly that emotion, then he loved her, damn it, with every breath in his body.

He'd never been in a relationship, let alone a family, and the Drake family was as alien to him as trust. Joley came from such a different background—hell, she'd managed to get under his skin, make him forget the discipline that was his life, and worse, she shook his control. He needed to be in control. *Needed* it. She had no idea of what a little stick of dynamite like her could do to a man, especially a man as dangerous and as lethal as he knew himself to be.

Ilya's body tensed as a man suddenly detached himself from the crowd and rushed the stage. Joley didn't miss a beat as security swarmed around the man, stopping him before he could climb up onstage. Ilya had already moved, a big man, fast on his feet, utterly silent, ready to protect her with his life. He took a breath and resumed his place against the wall where he could monitor the rows closest to the stage.

Joley had been raised in a loving environment. She had a large family with a lot of siblings, and parents who adored their children. Ilya had no idea what a family was like. If he had parents, he sure had no memory of them, and he only had vague memories of his older brothers. He was different and he would always be different. His training had shaped him. Trained to be a spy, an assassin, to work in the shadows and endure whatever hardship was needed in order to get the job done, he had been raised in a cruel, violent environment and had no idea how to live any other way. He'd never thought of living any other way, until he'd met Joley Drake.

Ilya spotted a man in the third row who had a look of rapture on his face as he stared up at Joley. Sweat beaded on the man's forehead and he was breathing fast. Ilya shook his head. She had half the men in the audience so tied up in knots it would be a wonder if there wasn't a riot. She was using her voice shamelessly, maybe unintentionally, but it had to stop.

He reached out to her. A slow, deliberate caress that slid like so much velvet down her arm to her palm, to the brand that marked her as his. He felt the first flutter of awareness, her mind touching his. The startling, stunning effect he always seemed to have on her. He loved that—the way she responded to him in spite of herself. She didn't want to open her mind to his, but she never could quite resist his touch.

She had power over him, had turned his life upside down, and he was working his way through his anger at that, but each time he touched her, he knew he had the same power and control over her.

And what was a relationship after all? Hell if he knew, just that melting inside, the fierce, urgent demands of his body and the terrible need to protect her, to be with her. And with him there was more—the need to dominate, to enforce his will on her, because in the end, he had to take control back.

When you're up on that stage and you're working the audience, all I can think about is slamming you against the wall and burying myself in you over and over, so deep they'll never get us apart. Deliberately he drawled each word, low and sexy, the smoldering heat slipping inside her until he saw the change on her face.

His breath strangled in his lungs as her expression turned even more sultry, the pouring out of her voice passionate, her lips a sinful invitation, her body moving with a natural sexiness that couldn't be hidden, and her eyes, heavy lidded, almost drowsy, bedroom eyes, promising paradise when a man sank his body into the soft silky heat of hers.

Stop it.

She hadn't even missed a beat, gliding across the stage, moving under the lights, which could only mean she wasn't nearly as far gone as he was. Damn her. He was crawling out of his skin. She shook him on such an elemental, *primitive* level that he knew he'd never get over her. There was no walking away. No being sated by her soft, sexy body. He would never be free of her. If any other man approached her with the same possessive obsession, he'd mark him as a stalker and end him as soon as it could be arranged, yet even with knowing that his need of her wasn't normal, he knew he was taking her for himself—because whatever he felt—she was feeling it, too.

He saw her gaze slide through the first few rows as if looking for someone—not him. Never him. Jealously was a black, empty emotion that threatened to choke the sense out of men. Who was she looking for? Her gaze touched on the man in the third row and moved on. Ilya understood she was looking for a specific person. A man?

She'd been angry enough at him last night, but he would have known if she'd turned to another man. He'd left her alone all night because he'd wanted so badly to reach out and touch her mind with his. And he'd be damned if he'd give in to that kind of obsession. He was going to be in control one way or the other. The problem was, he'd lain awake all night, his body so painful, tight and hard he knew he couldn't let things continue this way.

He slid his mind intimately into hers, once more allowing her to feel the depth of his sexual appetite for her. Her gaze jumped to his, her face flushed. He could see the rise and fall of her soft, full breasts beneath the tight shirt she wore.

Up onstage, Joley knew she sounded as desperate as she felt. Her entire body was on fire. She detested letting him know he was getting to her, but if he didn't stop the audience was going to witness spontaneous combustion.

I'm working.

Is that what you call it? Working? You're shaking your sexy little ass in front of that idiot, third seat from the middle, and he's nearly comatose. If you do it again, he'll do something stupid like run up onstage to grab you and then I'll have to kill the poor bastard and you'll be angry with me.

You can't talk to me now. I mean it. If he'd wanted to talk, he should have done it all through the long night when she couldn't sleep, when she'd lain awake on her bed waiting to hear his voice.

Her breasts ached and her nipples were hard pebbles rubbing against the lace of her bra with every movement of her body. She was on fire, throbbing and pulsing with hot desire. *He* did that to her with just his voice. A look from his eyes. A touch. He could reduce her to pure physical need. If he wasn't all the things whispered, rumored about him, he still was a dangerous man. She could lose herself in him. There was a part of her that craved his arrogance, his domination, his complete confidence and power.

Onstage she owned the world—she had the power, but with his voice in her head, he slowly took it from her.

Stop fighting me.

She closed her eyes, wanting him. Craving him. *I can't let*

you win. You know I can't, Ilya. You'd take everything from me.
Her pride. Her self-esteem, not that she had much left. Her
soul. He'd own her.
*I won't lose. You're running, but you're not getting away
from me. I'll give you everything and that's what scares you
the most. Don't worry,* milaya moya, *I have never run away
from a battle. I won't be going anywhere.* The tender note in
his voice scared her. Sex she could handle, but not the sheer
intimacy when he dropped that caressing note into his voice.

She forced herself to sing to the audience, to sing to Lisa,
concentrating, pouring her soul into the song about regrets
and mistakes and a true love so deep one needed to give it a
second chance. She thought of Tish and Logan, two people
who belonged together and were torn apart by stupidity, how
she didn't want that for Lisa and Denny.

Without warning, the drums stopped. Just stopped. The
band faltered and Joley swung her head around to look at
Denny. In trying to block out Ilya, she'd gone way too far, using her voice inadvertently and not sending directly to just
Lisa. She sent a look of total desperation to Brian.

The crowd realized immediately that drama was in the
works and quieted. Denny moved out around the drums and
walked across the stage to take the microphone from Joley's
hand.

"Dude, you've got your hands all over my woman and I'm
about to ask security to throw your ass out. I may have
screwed up, Lisa, but there's no one, *no one* in this world I
love more than you and your son. Marry me. Take me back.
Tell me what you want me to do. If you want me to leave the
band, I'm gone. Whatever it takes, but give me another chance
and I swear you'll never regret it."

Joley shaded her eyes to study Lisa's face. She was crying.
The man with her whispered something to her and moved a
little away, making Joley think he was a friend doing her a fa-
vor, rather than someone she'd picked up. Lisa looked utterly
miserable, her face covered by her hands.

Denny shoved the microphone at Joley, crouched at the
edge of the stage in front of her and held out his hand. "I'll
spend my life making it up to you, Lisa."

Joley moved next to him, placing one hand on the drummer's shoulder for support in the event Lisa rejected him.

Everything inside of Ilya coiled. Joley had just placed herself in a very vulnerable position. Security lined the rope in front of the first row, but they were looking at Denny and Lisa, not at the audience or Joley. He immediately glided into a better position, his gaze taking in the first few rows, but his mind settling on the man in the third row he'd noted earlier.

In a way this was his fault. He had distracted her, knowing she would never let down her audience. Joley had continued to sing under sexual duress and had been unable to control the notes in her voice, soft and sultry and purring like a huntress for a mate. The effect on the men was obvious, in particular on the face of the man in the third row.

Denny suddenly jumped from the stage. Joley gasped and stepped closer to the edge as if to follow him. Lisa stood up. Security rushed to protect Denny. The man Ilya was watching made his move, springing over the seats, nearly kicking a woman in the head as he leapt over her to get to the deserted aisle in front of Joley. Ilya took off running, shoving security out of the way as they surrounded Denny.

He burst out of the crowd just as the man launched himself onstage, reaching for Joley. *Move, damn it.*

In his hand, Joley warned him as she tried to back away.

Ilya caught the man from behind, taking him to the floor, locking his wrist behind him in a hold that threatened to break his arm. "Don't move," he hissed.

Joley laughed softly into the microphone. "He's just enthusiastic, no problem," she said. "Lisa, hon, come on up here and put Denny out of his misery so we can get these folks back on their feet."

The security team already had the man who had rushed the stage surrounded and were hauling him out. The band began to play, and Lisa, somewhat reluctantly, slipped her hand into Denny's and took the stage. Joley noted that she avoided his kiss, letting his lips only skim her cheek to the wild screams of the audience. Denny led Lisa back to the drums and took up his position. Lisa slid backstage, but sat where he could see her.

Joley let her heart regain its normal beat as she swung into a song, all the while looking for Ilya. He had disappeared in that way that he could. She had no idea if the man rushing her had had a weapon and if he'd managed to injure Ilya. Security had responded immediately and Ilya was gone as quickly as he'd arrived.

The rest of the concert went fairly smoothly, with only one equipment malfunction, which no one really seemed to notice. They took the stage twice more to yells, stomping and clapping before they called it quits.

Denny disappeared immediately with Lisa, and Logan hurried to call the hospital to check on his baby, so Joley visited with Brian, Leo and Rick while the crowd thinned. They were pumped up after the performance like always, stumbling over one another to talk. No one noticed that she said very little. She couldn't think of anything but Ilya, but pride wouldn't let her reach out to him. The longer he was silent, the angrier she became at him.

In the darkened van, she sat in the passenger-side front seat and rolled down the window as Steve took her out the back way. Die-hard fans that followed her from concert to concert knew she never traveled in the limousine or the decoy car, but stayed late and came out in the nondescript van. She always signed autographs for the ones who waited so long.

Steve knew the routine and he slowed the van as he turned onto the street. The rest of the band had come outside and stood behind the gates, watching as security milled with the crowd. These fans were polite, not rushing the car, but forming a loose line as they handed over programs and pictures for Joley to sign. She knew quite a few by name and greeted them with smiles, not for a moment letting how tired she was show.

A woman shuffled up to the car and handed her a picture. Joley didn't recognize her, but smiled and said hello. When she glanced down to sign, she saw that it wasn't her picture, but that of a young teenage girl.

"My daughter," the woman said. "She's missing."

Joley looked from the woman's grief-stricken face back to the picture. "I'm so sorry," she murmured.

"She was at your concert in New York, and afterward she was invited by your band to go to a party. She left me a message saying she was there and would be home late, but she didn't come home. I was working. I clean office buildings. She knew I wouldn't pick up the message until it was too late to stop her. Please. Have you seen her? She's only thirteen." Tears swam in the woman's eyes.

Joley took another look at the young girl. *I know that face.* For a moment she could barely breathe. "Steve? Does she look familiar to you?" She leaned close to him, whispering to keep the woman from hearing her. "Isn't she the girl who made the cell phone call and seemed to know Dean?"

Steve frowned, shrugged and shook his head, but said nothing.

"Please." The woman clutched at Joley's arm, digging her fingernails deep.

At once grief and fear overwhelmed Joley. Her stomach lurched.

Jerry St. Ives materialized from the crowd. "Is something wrong?"

The woman was hysterical now, trying to pull Joley out of the van, clutching her arm with one hand and yanking on the door handle with the other.

"You're bleeding. What did she do to you?" Jerry demanded.

The door began to swing open, and Jerry kicked it shut while calling for backup. Security swarmed around the woman and pulled her back, yelling at Steve to drive.

"No!" Joley protested, but Steve saw the blood on her arm and stomped on the gas, driving away from the crowd. She looked back and saw the woman struggling with the security detail. "Stop, Steve. It's not like she was trying to hurt me; don't let them turn her over to the police."

"Jerry says no, to keep driving. He'll fire me if I don't get you out of here. Your safety has to come first."

"You work for me."

"My job is to protect you."

"From a woman whose daughter is missing?" Joley turned around in her seat. "Get on the phone and tell Jerry we saw that girl with Dean. What if she's hiding out with him? Traveling with the band from concert to concert? We'd be liable. That should shake him up. She's *thirteen.*"

Steve shot her a quick glance.

"Do it!" Joley stared down at the picture, suddenly afraid. Had anyone in her band issued an invitation to the girl? It would be horrible if she'd run off with a crew member. Or worse, what if something had really happened to the girl? "And tell him I want him to find that roadie tonight and deal with this. Dean whatever. Brian knows him. I want Jerry to talk to him tonight."

"Okay, okay," Steve said soothingly. "I'll tell Jerry. He'll handle it, that's his job."

Joley breathed a sigh of relief. Jerry was very good at handling things, that's why he managed the band. She rested her head against the seat and closed her eyes.

4

JOLEY paced back and forth along the narrow aisle in her tour bus. "They should have Dean here by now, Brian," she snapped. "Where is he? It's been a week since that girl's been missing, Brian, and no one has talked to him about it. Jerry said he would take care of it and I trusted him to do it. We've had two shows since Chicago when we found out the girl was missing. This should have been done already."

"We don't even know for certain if it's the same girl, Joley. Steve said he couldn't positively say so, that she looked like her maybe, but the girls look so much alike it could be anyone."

"I said I was positive."

"Maybe the girl's gone back home by now."

Joley scowled at him. "Why do you think I'm upset all over again, Brian? I called the police in New York and she's still missing. Jerry had better take this seriously. I not only want Dean questioned, but everyone else. I had Jerry make copies of the photograph to distribute to the band and crew, and he hasn't even done that yet."

"It's not like Jerry doesn't have a million things to do, Joley. Be reasonable. The schedule's so tight the buses barely make it from one city to the next in time to set up. The crew breaks down the set and they have to roll. By the time Jerry gets things done, they're already gone."

"And you don't think a child's life is more important than a concert? What's wrong with you that you don't think we should look into this?"

"That's a job for the police. *If* she was at the same party, big deal, and that's a pretty big if. That doesn't mean we're responsible, Joley. You always take on way too much. She's a kid. She might have run away." Brian crossed his arms, a stubborn look on his face.

"Maybe, but she might have run away with Dean. And that makes it our problem whether you like it or not, because if a member of our crew touched her, or ran off with her, we're looking at a lawsuit that will never end, not to mention it's *wrong*."

"Joley, give me a break here. Dean probably saw the kid for a few minutes and forgot all about her. Do you think they remember all these girls they're with? They have sex, they get blow jobs, they do drugs with them. They aren't in love."

"That just proves my point. We can't waste any more time. I want her picture shown to everyone before they all lose their memories. And stop trying to handle me for Jerry. The coward. He knows I'm upset and he's hiding. If he doesn't get this done, he's gone right along with Dean. I mean it, Brian. I'm at the end with all of them."

Brian held up his hand to stop her rant. "Listen to yourself, Joley. When was the last time you slept? Or ate, for that matter? You're not taking care of yourself. And Jerry told you we should skip Red Rocks this year, it's too small, but you insisted and we have to drive all night now and set up for a back-to-back concert. Everyone's exhausted, you included. You're acting like no one but you cares about anything."

"Well Jerry and I just don't see eye to eye anymore about much of anything, do we?" Joley dropped into a chair and covered her face with her hands. Maybe she was acting like a diva. She couldn't tell anymore. And Brian was right, she was exhausted.

"Jerry wants whatever you want. He scheduled the stop in Red Rocks because you asked him to do it."

"Red Rocks is magical. When the sun is setting and the energy is right . . ." She trailed off. She couldn't explain it to Brian. You either felt it or you didn't. She was so tired she could barely think, but Red Rocks would recharge her, it always did, even when they had to do one concert right after the other to fit it in the schedule.

"We're going to have to get going in order to make the schedule, Joley. Try to get some sleep."

"Is Jerry checking on this girl right now?"

Brian shoved both hands through his hair in agitation. "You're like a bear with a sore tooth. We don't even know if it's the same girl, Joley. Calm down and think about this logically. She could have drank too much and gone to a girlfriend's house and is afraid to go home."

"And she's still not home after a week?"

"Okay, maybe she did shack up with Dean and they think they're in love," Brian said, exasperated. "Although I don't think the entire crew would be protecting him."

"But you're certain he worked the last two concerts?"

"He was there. Everyone saw him. According to a couple of his friends, he didn't realize any of the girls were underage until you yelled and they started giggling. He was stupid and ran, but he made them leave. He doesn't want to lose his job. The others said he went back to the hotel that night to catch a shower before leaving the city with the bus and he's been working hard ever since. That's as much as I know. And they certainly haven't seen the girl with him."

"Could she have stowed away in the bus? Did anyone check their bus?"

"They're checking it now. They were already on the road, but Jerry had the driver pull over and they're searching it before continuing. He'll call if they find her. And if we don't get moving, Joley, we're not going to make it in time for our next concert. Jerry's doing everything he can to find this girl, but we've got to get out of here now. There's nothing more we can do. She'll be found."

Joley pressed her fingertips to her eyes. The girl wasn't going to be found, not if that terrible feeling in the pit of her stomach was right—and it usually was. She couldn't exactly explain that feeling to Brian. "Fine. I'm sorry. I know I'm getting crazy here, but the mother said someone in our band invited this girl—this thirteen-year-old child—to an after-hours party. Who would do that?"

"Anyone could have issued the invitation, not necessarily a band member or one of our people. Come on, you know that. Nikitin or any of his crew could have or someone else coming to the party. We'll show the picture to everyone tomorrow, and if we're lucky, the police will tell us she turned up and is now home safe. I promise, tomorrow morning, as soon as we hit

Red Rocks, I'll talk to Dean personally and so will Jerry. I'll
make certain of it. In the meantime, try to get some sleep. I
know you didn't get any last night." He leaned closer to her. "I
mean it, Joley. We don't want to have to cancel due to your exhaustion, and it could happen. Go to sleep."

"You've all been talking again." She knew that when the
band was worried, they appointed Brian to be the spokesman.
"I'll go to bed." She would, but there would be no sleeping.
"Logan and the baby?"

"He's going to meet us in Red Rocks early in the morning.
He said he'll call Tish and see if she'll take the nanny job. I
think after your song, all of us believe in second chances."
Brian's gaze was steady. Maybe even a little accusing.

Joley felt the color rising in her cheeks. "Okay, I poured a
little too much into that song. It was for Lisa, but I was a little
distracted. I thought Denny was going to personally kick that
man with Lisa. I've never seen him like that, have you?" Brian
had known Denny since they were in kindergarten.

Brian grinned. "Denny's got it in him when you get him
riled, but no, never over a woman. I think Lisa's the real thing.
She slapped him though, right across the face, very hard. And
she was crying. I saw him go over to her after the performance, and she just hauled off and let him have it."

"Good for her. Then what did she do?"

"She was crying and he kept trying to put his arms around
her. She didn't run away, but she belted him a couple of more
times in the chest. Girlie punches though."

"So is he on the bus?" She didn't want to lose her drummer.

"He's driving with Lisa so they can talk. I think they rented
a car. He'll follow the bus."

"Joley! Brian!" Steve called out from the driver's seat.
"We've got to go now. Brian, if you're riding with us, I'm taking off."

Brian's eyebrow went up. "I'll stay if you want me to. We
can talk things out if you like, because, seriously, Joley,
you've got to lay it down."

Joley shook her head, suddenly weary. "I'll try to sleep."
She placed the picture of the missing girl on the small built-in
stand beside the couch. "I'll see you in Red Rocks."

Brian nodded and waved at Steve, before shutting the door

between the driver and the rest of the bus, which was Joley's home on the road. At once, the vehicle rumbled to life, and Steve pulled out of the parking lot onto the road.

Joley waved to Brian and watched him sprint for the second bus before she slid the privacy screen in place and heaved a sigh. It was going to be another long night. Was she really being ridiculous over the missing girl? It was entirely possible her band and crew had nothing at all to do with the underage teens being at the party. And Brian was right, she was exhausted and fixating on the missing girl.

Maybe she was crazy and it really wasn't the same girl— Steve didn't think so, but every time she looked at the photograph, she was more convinced than ever. She was angry with Jerry and Brian because six days had gone by and Dean hadn't been questioned—but truthfully, she was angry with herself. The Columbus concert, she'd flown in, done the sound check, and the roadies had broken everything down and were on the move before she remembered. She'd been upset because Ilya hadn't been there and he hadn't talked to her since the night in Chicago. She'd been thinking about him instead of the girl. She was used to handing everything over to Jerry to handle and she just let herself forget.

The Auburn Hills concert she'd remembered just before going onstage, but afterward, she didn't remember again until she was about to leave, so she hadn't asked Jerry if he'd spoken with Dean. The road crew was already gone. It was easier to blame Jerry and Brian, but ultimately, it was her responsibility to make the inquiry if she wanted it done, because she was really the only person who believed it was the same girl. She was so used to everyone doing things for her, and what did that make her after all? A diva. She really was messed up, mostly because she desperately needed to hear Ilya's voice again.

She considered calling one of her sisters, but they'd compare notes with Hannah, and one—or all—would come running. She didn't want to disrupt their lives, especially when they would see her glaring character flaws. It was fine to turn it all into a family joke—"Loser Apply Here" stamped to Joley's forehead—but it was altogether different for her sisters to witness it. And yet laughing with them, she could pretend it wasn't that bad, but when she was out on her own, alone in the bus, with no one to share either problems or laughter, she knew she could easily get into trouble.

Joley made her way to the back of the bus. Maybe if she rested, she'd manage to pull herself together. As she passed the small closet, a large hand snaked across her mouth and an arm slid like an iron bar around her waist. She was jerked back against a hard male body. Warm breath fanned her neck.

"Don't scream."

She knew who it was instantly. His scent. His aura of danger. His hard, masculine body, far stronger than he looked. She drew in a breath, struggled and tried to sink her teeth into his palm. He let her. She knew he let her bite him. He didn't utter a sound, or flinch, but his body crowded closer to hers, and she felt the press of his arousal, strong and full and unapologetic. She went still and waited for him to release her.

Instead Ilya Prakenskii trapped her between him and the closet door, his body pressed tight against hers. He rubbed his palm over her full lips, as if he expected her to kiss the bite better. And she was tempted. As it was, she couldn't keep her tongue from touching the small wound. He tasted masculine and sexy. The heat of his body crept into hers, a slow assault on her senses. She could feel the band of his arm sweeping up her rib cage to halt beneath her breasts. At once her skin felt too tight, her nipples hard and aching, and between her legs, already, the first flush of dampness signaled her response to him. It didn't help that the bus swayed as it rolled over the asphalt and his body brushed against hers intimately with every movement.

"How did you get on the bus?" Her voice sounded breathy. Her heart hammered and her stomach did a slow somersault. "How did I not see you?"

He bent to her neck, his teeth scraping over her skin, tugging at her earlobe before his mouth settled leisurely on the side of her neck. She closed her eyes, leaning into the heat of his body, feeling his thick shaft nestled tight against her. "That's what I do," he replied, in between bites along her neck. "It's my job not to be seen. Bodyguards are supposed to fade into the background."

"Really?" Self-preservation demanded she move. Self-respect demanded she feign shock. She did neither. His arms made her feel safe when she should have felt threatened. His mouth on her skin sent little flames darting through her blood-stream. Her brain said to move, but her body refused to acknowledge the command. "I think you're too much of a presence to fade into the background."

"You never notice I'm around unless I want you to notice," he pointed out. He turned her into his arms so that she was crushed against the broad expanse of his chest. "Look at me."

"If I do, you'll kiss me," she said, her voice muffled by his shirt.

He laughed softly, and she was instantly aware it was something he did rarely. "I've been craving the taste of you ever since I kissed you in New York. A week is a long time, and I don't think I can wait any longer."

She inserted a hand between them in an effort to get space, but his body was immovable and his arms had locked her tight against him. She lifted her face, and his lips were inches—*inches*—from hers. His breath was warm with the promise of temptation and sin. She wanted both.

His mouth settled on hers, teeth tugging at her lower lip in-sistently, until, without much resistance, she opened for him. Lost in his intoxicating, sensual taste, all male and sex and ur-gent demand, Joley went pliant, melting against him, hands sliding around his neck to press even closer.

His mouth didn't just promise sex and sin—it tasted of it, delivered it, sent fire streaking through her body like light-ning, and somewhere music played, vibrating through her en-tire body, singing in her veins. She melted into him, skin to skin, sharing breath until her toes curled. She gripped the front of his shirt for support as her knees turned to rubber and every nerve ending in her body caught fire.

Ilya didn't give her time to think or breathe. He simply took her body over, stealing her soul with scorching kisses, his hand sliding up to cover hers, to pry her fingers from his shirt, his thumb sliding in a caress over her palm.

Her entire body clenched in need. Her womb pulsed and throbbed. Joley gasped and tore herself out of his arms. How could he do that? One touch of the pad of his thumb across her palm and her body was scorched and trembling, so in need she could barely think.

Joley blinked back the tears glittering in her eyes. "You have to go, Ilya. I'm going to call Steve and tell him to let you off someplace you can call for a car." Even her voice trembled.

He shook his head and caught her chin, tilting her face up so she was forced to look at him. His hands were incredibly gentle, but his fingers were firm, keeping her from pulling away. "Not tonight. I'm staying with you. Just relax, *lyubimaya moya*, I'm not going to hurt you."

She took a breath and laid her palm against his chest, over his heart. "Yes, you will, Ilya, and I don't think I'll recover. So, no, you can't stay with me tonight or any other night."

"Why would you think I would hurt you?"

She blinked up at him—seeing him—seeing his aura—seeing inside of him. Each person, through individual experiences, created his or her own symphony, and she "saw" it when she looked at them. It was the reason she could pour compulsion toward a specific person into her song. She could pull out a short thread of his melody and match the exact pulsations. She could "feel" the vibrations of each musical note running in his brain, registering as various instruments and creating pieces both complex and simple, pieces filled with joy or sorrow, compassion or driving ambition—everything passionate, and especially the passions of good or evil.

She didn't see Ilya as evil—he didn't have that sick taint to his color—but neither was there light. There was power, far too much of it. Power corrupted, and he overflowed with control and authority. Strength and violence swirled around him, almost interchangeably. Where most people were a blend of light and dark and shades of all colors, Ilya was all shadow, and most of that was impenetrable and murky, so dark she couldn't see through the unrelenting blackness.

"Joley, answer me. Why would you think I would hurt you?"

His melody was wild and turbulent with the guitar riffs, fiery and passionate with the keyboard, so controlled with the percussion instruments, yet splashed with the violence of cymbals. There was smooth harmony accompanied by blasts of wind, streaks of lightning as guitars warred, and interludes of the tripping notes of a saxophone. He was fierce and controlled, dominant and mysterious, even in his music, the very essence of his being. She couldn't hope to understand his melody without examining each note, and she didn't dare get that close, not when her heart—her very soul—was at risk.

Joley let her breath out. "You know why. You have gifts."

"It's because of those gifts that I know we belong together."

She pulled away from him, not wanting him touching her. She couldn't read him, but it was possible he was reading her, and that wasn't safe. She was too mixed up in her feelings for him.

"Kiss me again. We don't do so well when we talk, but when we kiss, we're a perfect match."

She wasn't so certain of that. She'd like to think she matched him, but it was more like he took her over and she just melted into him until they shared the same skin. She shook her head. "I think it's pretty clear that you can never be in the same room alone with me. You can't ride all the way to Red Rocks with me." Joley wanted to weep with frustration. All she could think about was stripping and relieving the terrible ache, the emptiness that never went away, but she didn't dare take the chance, not after that kiss. She was too far gone when it came to Ilya.

He studied her for a moment then settled into the chair opposite her, more than satisfied with the flush on her face, her swollen, very kissed mouth, the rise and fall of her breasts. He'd gotten to her. And he'd marked her neck, putting another brand on her. "You're safe enough—for a while. Sit down, Joley, before you fall down."

"Why is it that everything you say sounds like an order? I was going to sit down . . ." Basically, she had to before her legs gave out. Just looking at Ilya made her weak, and kissing him was lethal. "But now, because you gave a royal command, I feel like I have to defy you just to keep myself."

"Well you don't."

She had no idea she was within his range, but sprawled out lazily, with his legs outstretched, he simply hooked her ankle and spilled her backward into the chair. "There. Decision made. No problem."

She threw a pillow at him, detesting his control when her heart was still racing and her body was on fire. Mostly she was upset with herself for not being able to handle him the way she handled everyone else. He was the only man who could shake her, and she didn't like feeling so exposed and vulnerable.

He snagged the pillow out of the air and placed it behind his head. "Thanks." He watched her with cool blue eyes. "Have you always had problems with authority figures?"

Joley regarded him with a kind of fury sweeping through her that gave way to sudden laughter. "You're impossible." How many times had she heard her father tell her she *obviously* had trouble with authority figures? She eyed him with suspicion. "You haven't been talking to my dad, have you?"

"I don't need to talk with your father to know this about you, Joley."

She shook her head. "You're not an authority figure, at least not to me."

"I don't believe you. Why do you think you fight me all the time?"

"Because you're reputed to be a hit man. I don't date men who kill for money."

"I'm a bodyguard."

"You're denying the rumors?"

He sighed. "Joley, you practically live in the tabloids. Is any of what they say true? Ever? Even with photographs as evidence, it seems they make things up about you. Why would you assume what you hear about me is the truth?"

He had a point, and she was a little ashamed that she believed *everything* she heard about him. He was so dangerous looking. He carried death in his eyes. And when she touched his mind, he *felt* deadly. He looked it, sounded it, and even inside, where she could see, darkness swirled, but . . . He was right; she was guilty of believing things about him without having facts to back up the rumors.

"I don't know. You're right. So I'm asking you, are you a hit man? Do you kill people for money?"

"Do you think a sniper is a hit man?"

She frowned at him. "It's a simple enough question, Ilya."

"Not really. It's a complex question. But you're smart. You'll figure it out. Why haven't you been sleeping?"

If she'd had another pillow handy, she would have thrown it at him. Ilya frustrated her no end. He never seemed to answer a direct question that mattered to her. She considered denying the truth, but what would be the point? "I don't sleep. I'm an insomniac. I have been since I was a kid."

"So have I. You had a good childhood, Joley?"

She heard the question, or maybe he was touching her mind and she felt his sudden stirring, as if something wasn't quite as right as it should have been, as if she'd better have had a good childhood or he would take it in his hands to do something about it. His expression hadn't changed, but something dark and disturbing moved in him and frightened her. "I did. My parents were very loving. I had my sisters and Jonas and life was great, one adventure after another. I was always in trouble."

"I can imagine."

But he liked the idea of her as a child doing naughty, defiant things and having loving parents who shook their heads and loved her all the more for it. She pulled that thought right out of his head and it made her feel warm inside. Even intimate. As if they already had a close, very personal relationship and he loved her childhood stories. The uneasiness inside her lessened.

She smiled at him. "My mother had all the psychic gifts so she thought she could keep up with me, you know, always know what I was going to do before I did it. By the time I was three, I was very aware she was watching me, so I set out to prove I could get away with things. I was the child always climbing on the roof and trying to fly, or walking by myself to the store because they said no, they couldn't take me. And homework was for everyone else. I've played the drums since I was four and never went anywhere without my sticks." She pointed to the drumsticks just inches from her hand. She'd removed them from her back pocket and tossed them on the chair when Brian came onto the bus. "If it made noise or music, I had to have it. My dad nailed my window closed because I kept escaping."

His eyes lit up, but he didn't smile. "I'll bet you were a hellion growing up. I've considered tying you to a bedpost upon occasion, and more than once I've wanted to turn you over my knee."

"I might have liked it," she said with a saucy grin. "But I'm so glad you restrained yourself just in case."

His eyebrow shot up. "In case you liked it? Knowing you, you probably would have. My punishment would have turned into a reward and then where would I be?" He reached out and snagged her hand, holding it up in the air between them. "Wrapped around your little finger like everyone else."

He let her go, slowly, reluctantly, the pads of his fingers stroking down her bare palm, where he had marked her, before his hand dropped away. His touch was electric. She felt that caress not only over her palm, but deep inside, between her legs, so that her womb clenched and liquid fire throbbed and burned.

Joley stared at him, horrified that he could touch her *inside*, that his mark was not just a brand, but a sexual stimulant, so strong even her nipples had peaked and her breasts felt heavy and swollen. Her entire body ached for his. Her tongue touched suddenly dry lips. Did he know what he was doing? She was in way more trouble even than she'd first thought.

"You're lethal. I don't think we can stay alone in this bus together. It isn't safe for you." But she didn't want him to leave. Just looking at him did something strange to her, filled her with a mixture of excitement and anticipation, but also peace, safety, as if she could lay everything down for a while and just let him take care of it.

This time he did smile. Her heart nearly stopped. There was a heady exhilaration in knowing he rarely smiled and she'd managed to get the genuine article.

Ilya pressed his palm over his heart. "You amaze me, Joley, all the time. One moment you lie your sexy little butt off, and the next, you're so honest you break my heart. I am sorry, you know. You took what happened last week entirely wrong."

Joley stiffened. "I don't know what you're talking about."

The smile lit his eyes—changed his entire face. He looked younger, more relaxed, still as tough as ever, but less intimidating. "There you go lying again. I did hurt you. I thought I might have, but I've never actually been in a relationship so I have no idea how to handle certain things. It would be best if you just told me the truth and made it easier for me. When we have children, we're going to be in trouble, you know that, don't you?"

Her breath stilled in her lungs. He had never had a relationship? *Ever?* The idea was both fascinating and terrifying.

"I'm not having children. Whatever put that idea in your head? I'm not ever getting married. I'm going to be the favorite aunt and make all my sisters crazy by letting my nieces and nephews do whatever they want."

Did she sound as scared as she felt? The idea that Ilya might want more than a quick, frantic session in bed scared her to death. He was the kind of man who controlled all things in a relationship, and Joley needed freedom like she needed air to breathe. And yet, like the proverbial moth, she raced to the flame.

"I really hate ruining your plans, but your idea of your future doesn't match what I have in mind for you."

"And that matters?"

He nodded. "Definitely." He not only looked completely confident and complacent, he sounded it as well.

She wasn't touching that one. Call her cowardly or smart, it didn't matter, whatever Ilya said, they were alone and she didn't trust herself with him if he started talking long-term. Men like Ilya didn't do long-term. They were one-nighters and they were gone. No commitment. No strings. He'd just admitted it. She took refuge in attack.

"How long was your longest relationship?"

His blue gaze held hers. "I just told you, I've never had a relationship."

"*Exactly.* Because you don't have relationships, Ilya, you have one-night stands. You have sex and you leave. Fast. You probably don't remember her name or face afterward."

"Like you planned to do last week?"

She had the grace to blush. "I'll admit it. I thought if we had sex, it would get you out of my system and I wouldn't have to lie awake thinking about you anymore, but you said no, and I'm good with that."

"Are you?"

His foot touched hers, the gentlest of taps, but her heart jumped in response.

"I don't think you're telling me the truth again. Are you afraid I'll forget you, Joley? Because frankly, *lyubimaya moya*, I don't think that's possible."

"Whatever." She bit her lip, not believing she'd said that. She'd just lost every bit of respect for her own ability to argue her way out of anything. It was just the way his voice turned husky and intimate when he spoke Russian. *Lyubimaya moya.* She translated it as "my sweetheart." The phrase was far more romantic in his language.

For a moment there was silence between them, filled only by the sound of traffic flowing around the bus. Ilya touched her shoe again with his. "I want you more than I've ever wanted anything in my life, but you were hoping to have sex and walk away without ever looking back. That's not what's between us. That's how you're looking at me—at us—and I'm not willing for that to be all there is."

He was throwing down the gauntlet with a vengeance. She looked around her bus, her home away from Sea Haven, and desperately wished herself safe within the protection of her sisters. The simple act of inhaling took him into her lungs. He seemed to dwarf everything in the bus, including her. And the last thing she wanted to talk about was how she had humiliated herself by going to a party she clearly didn't want to go to in order to throw herself at him only to be rejected. Not when he was so ready to cooperate with her now.

Abruptly she got up and yanked open the fridge, peering inside blindly. "You want anything?"

"I don't drink alcohol."

She turned back toward him, her eyebrow raised. "Why not?" Was she finally finding a chink in his armor? A weakness?

He shrugged. "In my line of business alcohol can get a man killed—and it doesn't really affect me the way it does others. As with you, I imagine, any type of drug or drink poisons my body and is rejected."

She knew the truth when she heard it. She didn't drink either, because being a Drake made it nearly impossible to be anything but violently ill if she indulged. "Bottled water or juice?"

"Orange juice then."

She took a deep, calming breath. She could do this. She could handle Ilya Prakenskii. She forced a smile as she handed him the bottle of orange juice. "Ice cold. Should be good."

She tried not to watch him drink, not to watch his throat as he swallowed. How in the world she found it sexy, she didn't know, but even the way he held the juice bottle by the neck, his eyes on her while he drank, made her womb clench. She sank back into the chair opposite him and touched her tongue to her lips. "What were you like as a child?"

Ilya's breath caught in his lungs, the question bringing up a time he kept hidden and refused to examine too often. *Afraid and hungry.*

His first thought was so strong he wasn't certain he had repressed it in time to hide it from her. Ilya searched his memories to give her a piece of himself that wasn't too bad. He didn't want pity. His life had been shaped by his childhood, and if he had to give up something to her, he wanted it to be something she might be able to relate to.

"I craved knowledge of every kind. Every book I could read on any subject. Every physical ability and way of fighting, and of course the use of psychic gifts—anything and everything, I soaked up like a sponge. I needed to learn all the time."

Because knowledge was power and it meant he would survive. It meant he would grow strong and invincible, that he could use his body as a weapon. That he could use his knives, guns, thin wire and anything else. That he could use his brain to stay alive. He needed to be stronger and faster and smarter than his enemies, and in the end he would see fear in their eyes instead of that little boy shivering in a corner, trying to make himself small so no one would notice him.

She caught glimpses of a small boy with dark curls huddled beneath a table. Terror consumed him, spread through her and left her close to tears. The memory was gone almost immediately.

To cover her reaction, Joley took a long drink of water, keeping her gaze above his head. What did she really know about him? Absolutely nothing. She had judged him mainly on rumors and his looks. She stole a quick glance.

His shoulders were wide, his chest thick and muscular. Dark hair made his blue eyes all the more startling. There was an innate toughness about him, and etched into his face were lines of hard experience. More than all that, danger clung to his aura, a dark, moody color and scent that felt violent and frightening, and where she might be able to ignore everything else, she couldn't ignore what her senses told her. He might be a bodyguard, but he was much, much more. That danger drew her like a magnet and yet repelled her at the same time.

"Do you have siblings?"

He shrugged his broad shoulders, a mere ripple of muscle, the movement casual, his gaze hot. "I have six brothers, but I didn't grow up with them. I've never been able to find them." And he had abundant resources all over the world—which meant they were dead—or they didn't want to be found.

"How sad for you—and for them. My family is everything to me. I can't imagine what it must be like to know you have someone but not be able to be with them."

"As I don't know them, it doesn't much matter."

She blinked. It made sense, but he wasn't telling the entire truth. He stayed close to her mind, sliding in and out at will and leaving behind impressions. He had wanted a family, and her family made the yearning all the more sharp. She didn't want to feel sympathy for him, or to picture him as a little boy with a mop of curls, scared and hungry. It made her all the more vulnerable to him.

"Why did you come here tonight?"

"You haven't been sleeping." He kept his gaze fixed on her.

She had thought his gaze cold, but the piercing blue had turned into something altogether different—glittering, hungry, almost like a very cunning animal waiting to leap and devour prey. She shivered and willed her blood not to surge so hotly in her veins. "You stopped talking to me."

"Is that why you can't sleep?"

"I wasn't sleeping when you were talking to me," she pointed out. "And I'm too exhausted to have a battle of the wits with you. What do you want?"

"I'm going to lie down with you and get you to sleep."

She nearly snorted water out her nose. "Are you crazy? I'm not getting in a bed with you. We wouldn't be sleeping."

"One of us has discipline."

"Really?" Her eyebrow shot up, and deliberately she slid her gaze over his body in a long, slow perusal. Her tongue touched her bottom lip while her fingers instinctively stroked the mark—his mark—on her hand.

He moved. It was a subtle shift, but there was no doubt in her mind he was easing the sudden tightness of his jeans. She could see the thick evidence in his lap that the stroke over the mark affected more than just her. Dark lust glittered in his eyes, and the hunger grew ravenous.

"You're playing with fire," he said softly. "I came here to help you sleep, not for anything else. Don't force the issue before you're ready."

She had learned a few things about Ilya from their brief encounters, and he rarely wasted words. He wouldn't warn her again. The perverse part of her wanted to see him out of control and reap the benefits of it, but the intelligent think-of-the-consequences part of her held her in check. She dropped her hand and rubbed her palm on her thigh in a reflex action, hoping to soothe the burning.

"I'm not ready," she admitted. "You scare me."

"I'm always going to scare you. That isn't the issue."

She shook her head. "I have more than one."

"I know. It won't be so bad, belonging to me. You'll always be safe."

"Will I?" She doubted it. "It's been my experience that extreme macho men are usually jealous, possessive, tend to hit women and cheat on them."

"I've discovered I can be jealous, and there's no doubt that what belongs to me stays with me, but men who hit women and cheat have no honor, no code. They aren't men, and you should know the difference."

The low, caressing note in his voice wrapped around her like a velvet blanket. He would take her apart, and when he put her back together, the most important pieces of who she was wouldn't be hers anymore. Ilya would own her.

"What about bossy?" He would rule her life. He was dominating, and there would be no denying that; she'd touched his mind. He would want to rule every aspect of her life, and Joley guarded her independence fiercely.

"You have to trust me with you, Joley. You don't trust anyone, you never have."

"That's not true. I trust my family."

He shook his head. "You don't trust them to see inside you and love you anyway. You guard yourself from them because you don't think they would understand your needs or what drives you."

Horror blossomed, and she pressed her hand to her suddenly churning stomach. He had been in her mind. She hadn't kept him out the way she thought she had, and Ilya was a ruthless man. He would be relentless in his pursuit of her, and now, having been in her mind, discovering her darkest secrets, he would use them against her. He had psychic gifts, and she could never forget, not for one moment, that he could use them against her.

She nearly groaned aloud. She could see his melody. She could see his aura. Could he see hers? The darkness in her? Not just shadows, but actual darkness?

"Joley." He said her name in a low caress. "There's no reason to be so afraid of me. I really did come here to help you get some sleep."

"How?" Because she couldn't imagine closing her eyes when he was in her bus. It was intimate—and it would make her far too vulnerable.

"There's always hypnotism."

She knew that utter distaste showed on her face. He laughed, and immediately her complete attention was riveted on him. The sound was husky, sexy, so low and brief it was more of an impression than reality, but all the more captivating because of that. He turned her inside out, and if he kept it up, she would melt into a puddle at his feet.

"Somehow I was fairly certain you wouldn't like that idea. We'll go back to the very simple way. You're going to lie down and close your eyes and I'm going to guard you, watch over you so you can rest."

"I'm afraid of you. And I don't trust anyone enough to sleep in front of them."

"I'm giving you my word nothing will happen, and my word is gold all over the world."

Joley took a breath. She was tired, but she couldn't imagine really falling asleep with Ilya in the close confines of her bus. "I don't know . . ."

He tapped the table beside him. "Just try for me, Joley. I'm not asking you to give yourself to me."

"In a way you are. You're asking me to trust you."

"Just to keep you safe. It is my job after all."

5

ILYA stood up, his gaze dropping to the small end table as he pushed himself up. He picked up the photograph. "Who is this?"

Joley braced herself against the sway of the bus as she stood up to view the photograph. Lights from oncoming cars flashed through the interior and illuminated Ilya's profile. His face could have been carved in stone. She tried not to fixate on his all-too-mesmerizing mouth by examining his eyes. He had long lashes. She'd never noticed that before, when she thought she'd noticed everything about him. She took the photo from his hand and studied the young face as if that could give her a clue to the girl's whereabouts.

"She's missing. She went missing at the New York concert. Not the concert, but the party—Nikitin's party. I saw her there."

Ilya shifted, drawing her immediate attention. It wasn't a movement so much as the rippling of his muscles, the sudden focus of a predatory animal watching her with cunning intelligence. His expression didn't change, he looked *exactly* the same, but he was entirely different. Joley had wanted color in his aura, but not like this. Never like this. Blood-red poured into the edges of the black, mixed and swirled, darkening the shadows and turning the color to violent death.

The musical notes representing him clashed and burned with passion and darkness, feeding on violence and swirling with the need to destroy. She wanted to press her fingertips to her eyes, to keep the images from her mind, but there was no escaping the sound and sight.

Breath strangled in her throat, and her heart slammed hard in her chest. Knots formed in her churning stomach. She was looking at the grim reaper. She'd had a brush or two with the death collector, but at that moment, watching the way the colors around him changed, she recognized with a sinking heart what she was seeing.

Ilya could smell her fear. Hell, he could see it on her face. She took two steps away from him, never taking her eyes off of him. Foolish Joley, thinking those meager steps would make her safe. She turned to run toward the front of the bus and what she clearly thought was the safe harbor of her driver's presence. Ilya caught her when the bus lurched, and she almost went down. Drawing her against him, he caged her between his much larger frame and the door of the closet. He could feel tremors running through her body.

He stood for a moment in silence, absorbing the satin heat of her skin, the silk of her hair and the soft feminine curves molded against him. He inhaled her, the scent feminine and clean, yet holding a hint of spice and more than enough sultriness for ten women. She kept her head down, holding herself still, like a cornered mouse, though he knew she was a tigress when riled.

"Why are you suddenly so afraid of me, Joley?" His hand cupped the nape of her neck, his fingers sliding in the thick wealth of her hair. "What do you see in me that frightens you?" His other hand held her wrist loosely, keeping the palm of her left hand—the one he had marked—pressed against his hip.

For a moment he thought she wouldn't answer, but Joley wasn't timid. Even afraid, she would face him. He felt her steel herself, that tremor that ran through her body, and she straightened, her back stiff, shoulders rigid. Respect and admiration rose in him. He tightened his fingers around her wrist and pressed her palm hard against his thigh. He felt his mark on her like a burning brand, right through the denim of his jeans.

"Your aura." Joley choked getting the words out. "Your face gives nothing away, but I see what's inside of you." A volcano, on the verge of erupting into a violent maelstrom that would blast anything and everyone out of his path. He would mow them down as if they were straw in the wind. The truth of what and who he was terrified her, because if there was one man totally capable of death and destruction, she was standing in front of him, with his mark on her—all over her.

"She's a child. What? Thirteen? Fourteen? Do you think I shouldn't be affected by her disappearance simply because she's a stranger?" His voice was gentle, low and caressing, reassuring. "She's a teenager at most, and she was in a place she shouldn't have been. I was there to keep an eye on things, to prevent anything like this from happening. Instead, my eyes—and my attention—were on you, and this child slipped past me."

It was the melody in him that soothed her now. Once again his song had changed, and the notes were comforting and calm, as if that violent rendition had never been. The steady beat of his heart was strong and precise, the beat that set the rhythm for his life. Calm. Exact. Absolute. The symphony rising around him sang to her, touched her where words might not have gotten through.

"That wasn't concern I saw in you just then." Her mouth was still dry, although her heart had calmed and the adrenaline rush was fading.

"You grew up very differently from me, Joley. In the world where I live, when young girls disappear, very unpleasant things happen to them."

Joley let her breath out and nodded. "Unfortunately, this time I have to agree with you. I'm afraid for her, Ilya. I have a bad feeling about this. She called her mother to tell her where she was even when she wasn't supposed to, and that speaks of someone who wasn't running away from home."

"I'll find her." Ilya spoke with that same absolute confidence his heart beat with. Rock-steady and deliberate.

She stared up at his face, mesmerized by the determination there. His expression was one of the same utter calm, but his eyes glowed like a fierce warrior of old. Whatever Ilya was or was not—he cared about that young missing girl. Joley didn't doubt for a moment that he was going to find her one way or another. He would never stop, never give up, until he had knowledge of what had happened to that child. He hadn't given up on Hannah when the odds of saving her had been impossible, and he wouldn't give up on the missing girl.

Joley yawned and hastily tried to cover it. She took a step

toward a chair as exhaustion settled back into her body. She stumbled and Ilya caught her waist.

"You're so tired you don't even know what you're doing." He tugged on her wrist and walked her to the back of the bus, where her bed was. "Lie down while we talk so I know you're at least resting."

"I've never done this." The confession felt silly. She had never closed her eyes with a man in her room. She didn't have that kind of trust. The simple act of lying on the bed made her feel vulnerable. "I don't sleep with others in the room."

"It's not going to hurt."

Joley sighed and complied, crawling to the far side of the bed and lying down, feeling small and vulnerable. She was too tired to argue, and it wouldn't take all that long for him to realize she really couldn't sleep.

Ilya bent down to remove her shoes. He tossed them aside and ran his hands over her feet in a rough caress that felt like he was taking her over. His hands made one pass only, but she trembled, the blood heating instantly in her veins.

He sank down onto the mattress, sitting with his back to the headboard, his legs stretched out. The heat from his body warmed her as she lay stiff and wary beside him. "Relax for me, Joley. We're just going to talk."

"I feel like I'm lying down with the big bad wolf."

He leaned over and brushed a kiss across her temple. "What big eyes you have, *devochka moya*. Close them now." He dimmed the light.

Joley moistened her lips, so aware of him there in the darkness. Every sway of the bus sent her body sliding against his. "How often have you gone to sleep with someone else in the room with you?"

"Never. But I'm in a line of work guaranteed to make enemies."

"That's a nice way of saying you have trust issues."

He tugged at her hair, so that she felt a small bite of pain before his fingers soothed with long, caressing strokes. "We fit."

She wasn't certain she wanted to hear that. She still feared he could see her aura the way she could see his, but she wasn't certain she could face him knowing, so she didn't ask. "We fight all the time."

"That's just you running. Why do you think I'm here, Joley? You haven't slept in days and you're not at the top of your
game. I want you back at your fighting weight when we do this
thing, so later you can't say I took unfair advantage."

She found herself smiling. "Liar. You don't want me at my
best; I'd kick your ass and you know it."

"We'll see." He leaned down and brushed a kiss across
each eyelid. "About this girl who's missing. Are you absolutely certain you saw her at the party? Maybe she just
looks familiar to you."

"Steve doesn't think it's her," Joley answered honestly,
"but in my heart, I'm absolutely certain. She was there with a
group of other young girls. I wasn't looking when they first
got there, so I don't know which car brought them, but they
had to come through the gate. Whoever was on guard duty
should remember them. Maybe five girls. All very young. One
of them, this one," Joley opened her eyes and tapped the photograph he was once again holding, "made a cell phone call. Another girl shouted at her that she wasn't supposed to tell
anyone that she was there. That confirmed it for me that they
shouldn't have been there."

"Joley." Ilya took her wrist again and brought her hand to
his chest. "Did you notice anyone around? Anyone who would
have observed you there at the time?"

"Sure. Dean, one of my crew, and another man who I
didn't get a good look at seemed to know the girls. They all
took off running together when I shouted at them." Joley
closed her eyes, replaying the scene in her head as she lay in
the dark. "Brian came out and went to find them. Denny and
some blonde were a distance away, and RJ and his bodyguards
had driven up. I know they saw the girls and heard me talking
to Brian. There were other people milling around as well. And
Steve saw the girl, too. We both thought all the girls with her
were too young to be there. Steve and I discussed it, but they
were a distance away and we didn't get the best look at them."

He stroked his fingers through her hair. "You take too
many chances."

Joley frowned. "What does that mean?"

"It means you should never have gone to that party and
gotten out of that car without your bodyguard right beside
you. And earlier, the moment trouble broke out in the arena,

you should have backed away, not gone to the edge of the stage where someone could reach you. I don't understand your security people. They know you've been threatened . . ."

"How do you know that?"

"It's common knowledge in your family, Joley. That man was with the Reverend's demented flock, and he had a can of spray paint in his hand to mark you as the devil's harlot. Your voice really affected him, which is why he was too slow to do any damage. I was lucky I got to him before he got to you."

She didn't think it was luck. Ilya didn't rely on luck. "Well, thank you for keeping me from being spray painted. It wouldn't have been pleasant."

"It could easily have been a knife."

"I know. I'm well aware, after Hannah, what can happen with knives and how easily they're concealed."

He brushed back her hair again, his touch this time comforting. "I didn't mean to bring up bad memories, *laskovaya moya*. Don't think about the attack on Hannah. Instead, tell me what you and Brian were arguing about. Your music was playing and I only caught a few sentences."

She sighed. "I shouldn't have yelled at him. I was really angry with myself for not inquiring about that missing girl and I took it out on him. Ever since that night, I've been wishing I'd done something. Maybe if I hadn't left it to Brian to run them down, that girl would be safe at home with her mother."

"When did you find out she was missing?"

"After the Chicago concert, a week ago. And yes, she's still missing; I called the police department to check. After a show I often sign a few autographs for the fans who follow all my shows. The girl's mother was there and she grabbed me." Without thinking she rubbed her arm.

Ilya pulled her sleeve back to examine the scratches in the dim light. The pads of his fingers soothed over the fading marks. "She did this to you? Where the hell was your bodyguard? And where was Jerry? He's supposed to be watching out for you." He brought her arm to his mouth, brushing his lips over the scratches.

Her stomach did a little somersault at the feel of his lips, soft and firm, pressing against her bare arm. She forced her mind to think when everything in her seemed to be turning to mush. "Don't worry, everyone acted crazy and pulled her off of me. I tried to tell them I wanted to talk to her, but no one listened to me. Steve drove off and wouldn't stop even when I told him he had to. The last I saw of her, they were dragging her away."

"Good. They at least did their jobs—after the fact. She should never have gotten close enough to do that kind of damage."

Joley opened her eyes again and glared at him. "I don't think you're a restful person—*at all*. The woman was scared and worried about her daughter. She wasn't trying to attack me."

Ilya stared down at her with a long, accusatory stare. For some reason his expression made her squirm. She rolled her eyes.

"Okay, she tried to pull me out of the van, but that was because she was so upset."

"One of these days, someone is going to get hurt, *laskovaya moya*, and life as you know it is going to be over."

She shoved at his immovable body. "That's exactly why we don't get along. I just go about living my life as normally as I can, and you throw out stupid statements like that. What does that mean? Is that some veiled threat?"

"I don't know how veiled it was." His tone was mild. "I think the threat was clear enough. Once we're permanently together, you're going to have a bodyguard who actually protects you."

She sniffed, showing disdain for his confidence, but her wayward body reacted. "I don't do permanent." She glared at him. "And neither do you."

"All that's about to change."

She was disgusted that she could be so physically attracted to a man who handed out orders as if born for it. A part of her felt she couldn't come to life unless this man was dominant, and yet she had to fight him until there was no hope of any relationship. She needed emergency therapy, but she was afraid it was already too late. Everything about Ilya both drew and repelled her. She needed him to take charge as much as she needed to fight him for trying to dictate to her.

He brushed back her hair. "Don't look so upset. You're going to be fine. You just need a little sleep and you'll be back in fighting form."

"I don't want to be attracted to you."

He didn't even wince. He simply nodded his head. "I know. But we fit. We belong. I'm not willing to walk away because you're afraid."

She closed her eyes against her own melting body—the clenching of the tight muscles in her feminine channel, the heated pulse and flip of her stomach. She betrayed herself—everything she was and believed in—for this man. It made no sense, but she was too tired to figure it out. "You're a dictator. Why in the world would you think for one moment—even one—that someone like me with a need for control would fit with a personality like yours? You take control, you insist on your way. I'd drive you even more nuts than you'd drive me. We'd end up hating one another."

"I don't dictate other than in matters of safety. And someone needs to do that for your protection."

She peeped out from under her lashes to see if he'd gone up in flames for that lie. "Even you, Mr. No Expression, can't keep a straight face. It's a wonder lightning didn't strike you dead. You're a dictator. You want every little thing your way."

"Only with you."

"I'll ask Nikitin sometime if that's the truth."

Something dangerous swirled in the depths of his eyes. "You stay far away from that man. I mean it, Joley."

She started to sit, anger sweeping through her, but his heavy arm simply dropped across her, holding her down. Joley suppressed the childish urge to bite him. "I'm not being soothed here. I thought you weren't going to make me crazy. I think *you* made my point for me."

"I don't particularly give a damn if you get mad, just for once in your life listen to someone who knows more than you do. Nikitin is dangerous, particularly to you, so stay far away from him. You don't like him, so there's no reason for your childish defiance."

Joley studied his face. Something wasn't quite right, but she couldn't put her finger on it. "Now you're deliberately provoking me. Why? I wonder." She reached up a hand and slid her fingers over his face, tracing the lines and shaping the bones.

He turned his face to press his mouth against her palm in a slow, burning kiss. Her entire body clenched, the demand urgent. Every nerve ending flared to life. Deliberately, his gaze holding hers, he lapped over his mark with his tongue, a long, slow lick that stole her breath as she felt it deep inside her, in her most feminine core. His tongue drew a lazy circle, and a moan escaped her throat. Her body was on fire, damp and needy, the pressure building as if his tongue was buried between her legs. She felt hot and dizzy, unable even to lift her head in protest. She couldn't think with the pleasure bursting through her.

He stroked again with his tongue, made the same circles until the throbbing between her legs built and built. *He isn't doing anything but touching his tongue to my palm.* The thought was terrifying. She was close to an orgasm, feeling his tongue on her clit rather than on her palm. How? She and her sisters had gifts, but to her knowledge, none of them had ever experienced anything like this. She didn't understand it, or how Ilya could possibly be the one to take over her body when she was always the one in control. When she was with him, her body melted, gave itself to him like a sacrifice, and there seemed little she could do to prevent it.

"There's no giving you up," he murmured against her palm. "This says you belong to me, and me to you."

Mutely she shook her head. Or maybe it wasn't mutely, maybe she was whimpering her denial. She had been so needy for so long, her body craving his to the point that she'd thrown herself at him in the hopes of ridding herself of the obsession. Now he was so close, larger than life, dominating her personal space, the scent and heat of him surrounding her. His melody suddenly took on dark erotic notes that tugged at her nipples until they were pebble-hard. Sensual notes throbbed and pulsed and moaned, licking over her skin and setting her on fire.

"You're mine," he insisted. Keeping his gaze locked with hers, he once more bent his head to the center of her palm.

The brush of his lips sent streaks of fire rippling through the wall of muscles until she nearly spasmed with an orgasm. She was that close—so close—and she wanted more. She pressed her palm against his mouth, a low moan escaping.

His aura suddenly expanded, the darker colors swirling around her like a cloak, enveloping her colors of purple and iridescent pink and vivid orange, the jeweled tones that represented her. His darker colors bled into hers, mixing and swirling until she could feel a thousand fingers brushing over her skin, tongues lapping at her nipples and between her legs.

And then he bit down right in the center of her palm. She heard herself scream as her body convulsed, as pleasure burst through her. Her orgasm was strong and long, rippling through her from head to toe, a bright blast of rockets that sent colors and musical notes scattering like gems around her head and bursting behind her eyes.

Ilya held her to him, closing her fingers around her palm to make a fist, holding it against his heart while she fought for breath and control. He had claimed her body for his own, showed her that he could own her—he did own her—and she couldn't go back. She looked up at him with a mixture of terror and awe.

"What did you do?"

He kissed her forehead. "Lie down and go to sleep now." She looked so confused, beautiful and a little desperate that he gathered her closer. "My gifts are a little different from yours and your siblings'."

She drew in her breath and tried to gather her scattered wits about her. If he could make her body explode just by kissing her palm, what the hell was going to happen to her if he ever decided he was going to make love to her? "Ilya, don't you think that's a little scary?"

"Only if you decide to retaliate."

"Could I?" She opened her fingers and looked at her palm.

He caught her hand. "Don't even think about it, because I swear, if you try anything, I'll strip you down to bare skin and you'll be under me all night. I came here to get you to sleep. Now go to sleep."

There was steel in his voice, but she caught the uneasiness in his eyes. He wasn't as nearly in control of the situation as he wanted her to believe and that gave her some satisfaction. She let her breath out and lay down again. "Soothe me. You said you could. And right now, I'm not feeling soothed." On fire maybe, her body still rippling with aftershocks, and the sexual tension slowly draining away, but she wasn't soothed by a long shot.

He stroked caresses over her hair. "Go to sleep, Joley. Just let yourself relax. You should learn meditation."

She scowled at him. "I know how to meditate. I've got things on my mind."

Things like a man giving her the orgasm to end all orgasms by teasing her palm. That just wasn't right. And could she really do the same thing back? She'd like to give it a try, but knew there was no handling the consequences. She wasn't sure of him yet—not yet.

Things like young girls disappearing with members of her band—well, not the band, but her crew. And the poor mother who had been dragged away from the van when she was only trying to get answers. She must have been desperate.

"You're sighing. I'm considering stronger measures than I've already taken."

She didn't want to think what those measures might be. In any case his hand continued to brush back her hair, and the feel of it was almost mesmerizing. His voice had dropped another octave and came out a husky whisper, the sound sliding into and through her body like the sound of a beautiful musical instrument. And this time, her body responded by relaxing. She didn't question it, she was too tired.

"I don't want you to worry about anything right now except going to sleep," he said.

"I can't help thinking about that poor woman and how upset she must be, not knowing where her daughter is," Joley admitted, turning on her side and curling up. She was exhausted, and for the first time in a long while, in spite of his presence—or because of it—tension began to drain from her body. "I need to talk to Dean, and then both of us should go to the police and at least tell them what we know. We may have been the last people to see her."

"Let me handle this, Joley. I'll question your crew and make a report to the police."

"I'm firing him if he dared invite that child to a party. Her poor mother."

His hand moved over the back of her head, stroking silky strands. "I'll find her. You stay out of it. It could be a very dangerous situation. Tell me about the man who was with her. Dean. What's his last name?"

"Walters. Dean Walters. And he had another member of the crew with him. Funny," she mused, "I used to know them all by name. I even knew their families. The same crew always stayed with us in the early days, but a couple of years ago some just up and quit. Now nothing is the same. Jerry had to tell me his last name was Walters."

There was a small silence broken by the sound of cars on the highway. "What happened a couple of years ago to break up your crew?"

"I don't know." She turned slightly to look over her shoulder. "I don't know. That's a good question. Everyone seemed happy enough, but then there were all the parties and Tish got fed up with Logan and walked out on us. Maybe she was the glue that held us all together. One by one, the old crew, the soundmen and the roadies who always traveled with us just up and quit. They didn't show up for work." She snuggled back into the coolness of her pillow. "Since then I don't bother so much with learning who they all are because we have a big turnover."

"Is that common?"

"It wasn't, but it seems to be now. Traveling is always hard on families. I didn't think our group would ever break up. We treated them like family and paid very well, but drugs and alcohol take their toll on everyone. And after Tish left, we all were depressed. It was hard to keep going."

"Tish was Logan's girlfriend?"

"Wife. They were married, and still are, although we don't talk about it. Logan and Tish went to school with Rick, Leo and Denny. Brian was in a private school, but he spent summers with them. When they formed a band, Tish did their website, got their bookings and sold their CDs. I heard them play at the Caspar Inn when I was just out of high school. I talked with Tish for a long time that night and ended up giving her a recording of my voice. She was the one who brought us all together. I loved their sound and they loved mine. The road crew were friends of theirs from school as well. We all learned the business together."

She yawned. Her eyelids were suddenly very heavy, and it was too difficult to keep her eyes open, so she curled deeper under the comforter he pulled up over her. His fingers eased the knots in the nape of her neck.

"Has Walters been traveling with your band the last two years?"

"Jerry would know. He handles everything on the road, but I've seen him often, at least enough that I recognize him and wave. He's never made an effort to talk to me, but then I haven't really talked to any of the crew other than the sound crew. And I don't know most of them very well anymore."

"You aren't having much fun performing, are you? Why do you keep doing it?"

"I love to perform. I love the energy of the audience, being with my band and the music we make together. I even love the pressure of putting together new material." She was lonely though. And she missed Sea Haven and her family. At least she could laugh with them and feel as if someone in the world cared about her for herself, not because she was a celebrity. "I'm just tired. We've been keeping a grueling schedule."

She could feel herself drifting under the influence of his massaging fingers. The motion of the swaying bus added to the dreamlike feeling pressing down on her. "I'm going to make a list. That's what Libby does and it always works for her."

"Libby is a brilliant woman," Ilya said of her sister. "And wise. What is this list for?"

"The pros and cons of being with you. I'm going to put them down on a piece of paper and then call my sisters to see if any of it makes sense."

Her voice was a thread of sound, low and muffled by the pillow and comforter. She sounded a mixture of sexy and drowsy, and he shifted to ease the nearly permanent ache in his body. "Are there cons to being with me?"

"You're so bossy. I hate that."

Honesty poured into her voice like warm honey. She really was drifting in a dream, or she would never have admitted she was contemplating making a list and discussing him with her siblings. He found her drowsiness incredibly sexy. He nearly groaned, holding on to discipline and control to keep from taking what was his.

"You're always telling me what to do and you just take me over. But when you kiss me, everything just goes to hell fast. I can't even think straight when you kiss me."

He found himself smiling. "I would think that should be put under pro."

"No, no. You don't understand. That's not a good thing."

He swept her hair away from her neck and bent until his lips could brush her ear. "Kissing me is on the pro side for certain. If you're going to make a list and talk about me with your sisters, at least be honest. Kissing has got to be a huge pro."

She gave a little sigh and her mouth curved. For one moment her eyelashes fluttered as she struggled to surface. "Maybe both sides."

"No way. That would cancel both entries out, and I have a feeling I'm going to need everything I can get on the pro side. What else are you putting on this list?"

She yawned and turned into him, fitting her face beneath his shoulder. "I'm trying to think of things I like about you."

"My charm."

There was amusement in his voice and it captivated her. "I wasn't aware you were charming. But you did save Abbey's Aleksandr when you could have been caught by the police."

"I wasn't worried about the police," he replied, "so I'm not certain we can count that."

"And you saved Hannah at a great cost to yourself." She wanted to open her eyes and look at him, but her lids were too heavy and she couldn't make herself lift her head. Besides, his fingers were pure magic, melting her body so that she was boneless. Her fingers slid along his thigh, up toward his rib cage, until he caught and held her hand over his heart. "I don't know if I really thanked you for that. Did I?"

"You can put that on the pro side," he said and brought her hand to his mouth to tease her fingertips with his teeth. "And yes, you thanked me."

"Hannah is special."

Ilya could barely hear her anymore. She was falling asleep, cuddling into him like a sleepy kitten. He kissed her knuckles and sat watching her face. She looked so young and innocent, angelic in her sleep, although her mouth promised paradise, a lush curve that kept his body hard with urgent demand.

The first time he'd ever heard of Joley Drake had been on the radio. Her voice had come on and his world had stopped. That voice. Pure and perfect, it had slid into his mind and lifted the shadows as if sunshine had suddenly burst through heavy layers of dark clouds. His world was violence and dirt, the dregs of society. Nothing shocked him anymore, and he had long since given up all illusions of finding good in a world of debauchery and excess indulgence. He had stopped believing in anything, and only his personal code kept him from destroying everyone around him.

He had spent two years investigating a child pornography ring that had taken him around the world, and the things he'd seen still haunted him—and he'd been hardened to the sins of man a long time ago. His orders had been to take the ring down, dispose of the guilty leaders and walk away without anyone ever knowing he'd been there. He followed leads from England to Brussels to Thailand. One by one he'd exterminated vermin until he'd found the man responsible for organizing the ring in the first place. The man had offered to share two little boys and a girl with him, but hurry, he was making a special video with these three.

By the time Ilya had worked his way through the maze, he found three dead children, killed in a snuff film of indescribable sickness and depravity. His control had slipped, always a dangerous thing. He had become a rabid animal, and he still couldn't examine too closely his behavior. For a short time his mind had shut down and the trained killer had taken over.

It was then, when he was at this darkest hour, that he heard a song on the radio. Joley's voice had given him peace for the first time in years. He hadn't believed anything could lighten his soul, but listening to her, it had been as if the sun had burst for the first time into his life and shone down on him. There was no redemption for him. He didn't expect or want it, but he craved the sun on his soul, those few moments of peace and contentment. She had saved his sanity. He would have left her alone, just collected her music, but their paths had crossed in the unlikeliest of chances. Now that he'd seen her, been in her presence and felt her warmth on his skin—on his soul—there was no going back. He needed her as a barrier between him and the unrelenting shadows of his life.

His fingers tangled in the silk of her hair. She'd been a shock to him, when he thought himself impossible to shock. She wasn't a perfect angel from heaven—one he couldn't relate to—she was human. Sexy as hell. Flirty. She'd drive a man mad in seconds. She was fiercely loyal. A tigress when it came to her family, and he'd begun brooding over that trait in her, drawn to it, drawn to her capacity to protect those she loved. She knew what it was like to need to do whatever it took to protect those weaker than she was. And he desperately needed someone to save him—to love him—to be as fierce for him as Joley Drake was in the protection of her sisters.

There had been a photo in a tabloid. The headline had read *Joley Caught In Her Love Nest.* He had been furious, not disillusioned; he knew she was no angel—that her lover hadn't protected her from that kind of exposure. Then he'd found out it hadn't been her at all, but that she'd dyed her hair and taken the blame to keep her sister from nasty gossip that might have harmed her sister's career. In that moment she'd ripped out his heart and took it into her keeping for all time.

There was no getting around wanting Joley. His body ached when he thought of her. And when she sang—or talked—or just stood there in silence—he found he was more aroused than he'd ever been in his life. She brought out things in him he hadn't known were there. Tenderness. Gentleness. Emotions that had never been in his life, not even as a child. She introduced him to laughter. She made him a better person, and she'd replaced despair with hope.

Ilya bent his head again and brushed a kiss along her cheekbone. "Life with you will never be dull." She also brought out the worst side of his nature, the need to dominate and control, his own protective instincts honed into fighting skills and determination. Ilya always won, no matter the cost, and he would win Joley. He had marked her because he couldn't stop himself from doing so, and that had scared the hell out of him. It was rare for him to lose control, and he knew putting his mark on her was not something he could take back. They were irrevocably bound together.

He shifted a little to slide down beside her, resting the back of his head on the pillow. She stirred, eyelashes fluttering before lifting. Her eyes, large and dark and glorious, smiled up at him. She nearly stopped his heart.

"Go to sleep, Ilya. I'll make sure nothing happens to you." She wrapped her arm around his waist and slid closer to lay her head on his chest.

His heart ached. An actual pain to rival the one in his groin. Even asleep, she'd felt his need, maybe it had registered in his voice. He was used to being alone. He didn't know any other way, had never considered anything else—he didn't know how to trust enough. But she made him want to learn—want to take a chance. She was the first person in his life who had offered to take care of him—ever. She had to be asleep and unaware.

"You talk in your sleep." He nuzzled the top of her head with his chin.

She smiled without opening her eyes. "I don't sleep."

"You're sleeping now—with me. For me."

Her smile widened and her arm tightened around him, before she relaxed completely into him again. "Because you're such a dick—tator."

He found himself smiling all over again.

6

ILYA was gone. Joley kept her eyes squeezed shut tight, trying not to feel alone and panic-stricken. She hated waking up to the sound of silence. Growing up in a large family, she loved being home and hearing the comforting sounds of the household stirring to life. As strange as the night had been, she had fallen asleep and actually rested.

She sighed, opened her eyes, rolled over and stared up at the ceiling of her bus. She knew they had to be in the Red Rocks parking lot or the bus would still be in motion and Ilya would still be inside with her. Holding her arm up, she opened her fingers and stared at her palm. There was no visible mark, but she felt the faint itch that was often present, reminding her that Ilya had zapped her with something she couldn't get rid of. She hadn't realized how powerful it was, or just how the mark had tied them together. She ran the pad of her finger lightly over her palm. Nothing happened. Nothing at all.

With a little frown, Joley sat up and shoved back her hair. She needed to make her list of pros and cons. And the pros needed to outweigh the cons when she discussed it with her sisters, because she was already lost. She paced across the room to the small kitchen to put on the kettle while she got ready for the sound check. They only had a few hours to get things pulled together for tonight's concert. It was difficult to do two shows in a row, but Red Rocks was worth it to her. She already wanted to go outside and just breathe in the air. She was definitely going to go running and do a little exploring, as Red Rocks had to be one of the coolest places on earth.

She could still feel Ilya's presence in her bus while she showered. Had Steve seen him when he left? She doubted it. Ilya wasn't the kind of man to be seen when he didn't want to be, and somehow she was fairly certain Ilya would try to protect her reputation. And that was going on the pro side of her list. She was definitely making a list of pros and cons to determine if she should sleep with Ilya Prakenskii, because listing them was the only sane thing to do.

She sat down with a cup of tea, her pen between her fingers, drumming on the tabletop and trying to remember all the cons she'd thought of the day before. There had been a *lot* of them, but that thing he'd done with her palm had tipped the scales right back in the pro direction. In fact, the cons seemed to be permanently wiped from her mind.

Sarah. Before making up her mind one way or the other about Ilya, Joley should discuss the situation with Sarah. After all, she was the oldest and she really gave good advice—even when no one wanted to hear it.

Joley reached for her cell phone, then hesitated. She had time to do a little exploring and she definitely needed exercise. Maybe calling Sarah right now wasn't such a good idea. Everything was so crazy and she really was mixed up; nothing would make sense. There was no way she'd do more than babble and stammer, and she needed to be coherent and thinking when she talked to her sisters about Ilya. Now was not the right time. Besides, they'd talk too long, and then she wouldn't have time to go exploring before she had to do the sound check . . .

Her cell phone rang and she flipped it open. Joley held the phone away from her ear as Sarah's voice blasted her. "Joley Elizabeth Drake, just what are you up to?"

Joley strove for complete innocence. "I have no idea what you're talking about, I just woke up, and at this precise moment I'm drinking a cup of tea and making out an important list."

"I'm not buying that. You were going to call me and then you decided not to and I could feel the backlash of guilt. What's going on and what do you have to feel guilty over?"

Joley rolled her eyes, thankful her eldest sister couldn't see her. Sarah knew all kinds of things before they happened. She always knew before someone called. "Well, I did want your advice on something, but I just woke up and wasn't certain what time it was, so I didn't want to chance calling and waking everyone up if it was early." She drummed her fingers on the table, looking for a way to distract her sister. "How's Damon doing?"

Joley had grown very fond of Sarah's fiancé. He was a good man, quiet but brilliant, and he obviously adored Sarah, and the minute anyone mentioned him, Sarah was distracted.

"He's wonderful. Libby has spent some time trying to help his hip and leg, but the injury is old enough that she's not getting the results she'd like. But Damon says there isn't as much pain. He's in San Francisco today, working on some project I'd rather not know about."

"I'm so glad Libby's able to help him a little. He's a good man, Sarah."

"Yes, he is. And speaking of men, I'm sensing this problem you have involves one," Sarah said, returning like a dog with a bone to the point of her call.

Joley winced a little at the note of suspicion in her sister's voice. On the blank paper in front of her she wrote out *Pros* and *Cons* with a line separating them. Under cons she wrote, *Gets me in trouble with my sister—received lecture.* Because it was coming—and Sarah's lectures were never pleasant, because she knew exactly what to say to make a person feel guilty.

"Joley?" Sarah prompted. "Tell me what's going on."

"Well . . ." Joley tried to hedge, but that wasn't too smart with Sarah. "It's just that I've been considering having a relationship and I'm trying to be practical." She was fairly certain she heard a snort, and then Sarah was coughing. "Did you choke on something?"

"Sorry. You're being practical—over a man?"

"Hey! I don't think that comment was strictly necessary." Joley was indignant.

There was a small silence. "Really? Who is he?"

Joley pressed the point of the pencil so hard into the paper it broke. Of course Sarah would ask. "Ilya Prakenskii."

There was a silence. Joley felt the gathering explosion and rushed into an explanation. "I don't think he's any of the things everyone says he is. I really don't. He's just too—nice." Even she winced when she said the word. Nice wasn't a description one could use for Ilya.

"He's dangerous, Joley. *Dangerous* is not *nice*. You stay away from him."

Her palm itched and she rubbed it over her thigh. "He has all the same gifts that our family has, Sarah—but the gifts are a little different. When my magic touches his, or our auras get close, they merge and flow together. I can feel the difference in the way he summons and uses energy."

"I noticed that when he was holding Hannah to him," Sarah agreed. "And Hannah spent a lot of time connected to him, and she tried examining the way he gathered and cast energy, but he's cut off. His aura was too dark, hiding everything from her."

"Well, it's definitely different. I know you've been studying the books our ancestors have on the ancient ways, and I wondered if you ever came across anything in our history about marks." Joley drummed out a nervous rhythm with the pencil on the table. "Maybe something to do with binding two people together, or claiming, or I don't know, anything, any mention at all."

"Are you talking about your hand? Describe the mark."

There was comfort in her sister's matter-of-fact, practical voice. That was Sarah, getting to the heart of the matter and gathering information.

"That's the problem, Sarah. There is no visible mark. I can't describe something to you I can't see. There are times when my palm itches and other times I think I see a faint color, like a bluish-purple, but it's never strong enough to be certain and it fades quickly." With a little sigh, she took her pencil sharpener out of the drawer beneath the table and began shaving a new point on the pencil. She had the feeling she'd be doing it a lot.

"When you do see the color, is it linear? Vertical? Horizontal, or all over the place?"

"It's in the exact center of my palm and it appears almost to be two circles intertwined, but that could be my imagination. Most of the time there's nothing there at all." She examined her palm. It looked smooth and unblemished.

"*Joley.*" Sarah bit her name out between her teeth. "Why didn't you ever tell us about this?" She sighed when Joley didn't answer. "I want you to describe to me how you got it again. *Exactly.* Every detail you can remember."

Joley resisted the urge to hang up. The mark was private. Very intimate. And she felt almost as if she was betraying Ilya by describing the events to her sister—although they'd all been there when it happened. "We were at the Caspar Inn dancing. Prakenskii was there and he made me mad. Nikitin had forced me to sing and then he wanted to meet with me. I said no and Prakenskii turned his back to me and was walking away. I pushed energy at his back. It was just a little shove and maybe I shouldn't have done it, but he'd been lecturing me and disapproving of me all evening. I was sick of him. I was only trying to make him stumble, but the energy came back on me. I heard crackling and popping, like electricity, and I could see sparks all around my hand. My palm burned, for just a moment, really burned, deep inside. I remember I sort of yelped and held my hand."

Sarah sighed heavily again. "The girls shielded you from him, but he didn't even turn around."

"That's right. My hand hurt so badly, and we decided to leave. I was angry enough for a confrontation, and Abbey was worried, everyone was, because he seemed to be so powerful. As I walked past him to leave, he reached out and took my hand. His thumb slid over my palm just once, and he let go, but as his skin touched mine and continued a brushing movement, it was as if he wiped away all the pain." Even as she described the gesture to her sister, Joley felt that amazing touch all over again, the single brush of skin to skin that sent flames racing through her body, marking her inside and out.

"When did you first notice the discoloration?" Sarah's question drew Joley back from the memories.

"In the beginning, my hand just kept itching like wounds do when they're healing. Eventually that stopped—now the itching only comes back when he's near, or when I am thinking about him, or when he's talking telepathically to me. And recently I discovered that there's some connection between the mark he put on me and the two of us. It connects us . . ." She searched for the right word. Just thinking about what Ilya did with that mark and his mouth left her damp and needy all over again. "It connects us in a physical way. I suspect it enables him to speak telepathically to me over greater distances."

There was no way she was going to admit to Sarah that the

connection was sexual, that Ilya had given her an orgasm simply by manipulating that spot on her hand.

Sarah made a little noise that alarmed Joley.

"What? Have you read about this?" She carefully drew two circles intertwined right above the words *Pros* and *Cons*.

"I've read references, pretty vague ones. There are a few entries in some of the diaries about a male line with similar gifts. Once in a while one of our ancestors crossed one of theirs."

Joley rubbed her palm along her thigh, then realized that rather than trying to brush the mark off as she used to do, she was now brushing her palm slowly back and forth in a caressing motion. She snatched her hand back. "That doesn't sound particularly bad."

"Well, at one of the points when the male line clashed with our line, it was because a woman had come to the Drake women and claimed someone had marked her with a magical symbol, two circles intertwined. She claimed it bound her to this man and she suspected he was a witch or a sorcerer. She seemed frightened. Of course they took her in."

"I don't like the tone of your voice. This doesn't have a good ending, does it?" Joley asked. She pressed her hand tighter against her body, suddenly afraid. It was one thing to contemplate having an affair by her own choice, but it was something altogether different to think she didn't have free will in the matter.

"Well, even their combined powers and skills couldn't break the bond between the man and the woman. No one knew what happened—just that she got up one night and left the house. He was waiting for her. She went off with him and they never heard of her again."

Joley took a deep breath. "So there is some documentation about another family having similar powers to ours, only male."

"Yes, although I can't find anything in our time, or even Mom's. I can call Mom and ask her if she's read or heard anything more. She always studied the history of our family, and I don't have near the knowledge she has."

Joley swept her hand through her hair, twirled strands around her finger and bit down on her lip, trying to decide. "Ask her, Sarah, but . . ." She trailed off, not wanting to alarm her sister any more. Just the fact that she would consult her mother would elevate Sarah's warning radar.

"You're in way over your head, aren't you, Joley?" Sarah asked.

Joley rubbed her hand along her thigh again. "I don't know. But whatever mark you read about is on my palm, and I'm fairly certain it has somehow, chemically or magically or both, tied me to Ilya Prakenskii." On the paper in front of her, she drew a double circle on the pro side, started to draw a line through it and then left it.

"And you're contemplating a relationship with him?"

Joley had known Sarah wouldn't let her off that easy. She sighed, knowing that if she wanted help she would have to confess, tell the absolute truth and hope her sisters would think of a way to save her.

"I'd have to say it's too late for contemplation. I'm obsessed. I wouldn't admit that to anyone but one of my sisters, but he's all I think about day or night. It's more than obsession. I swear, Sarah, it's like he's become the blood in my veins." She gave a small, derisive laugh and drew her fingertip over the circles on the paper. "How cheesy is that? He's the air in my lungs. I breathe him in and out with every breath I take." And she was cold and lonely without him, without the heat of his body, the heat of his gaze, his voice in her head driving her crazy. "It's like we're merging together. You know me. I may have bad taste in men, but I've never been obsessive and I've never needed a man. Ever. But I need him."

"If Prakenskii is bothering you, Damon and I can fly out today if we have to and get you through the rest of the tour."

"No, it isn't like that. It's more me than him."

"I can't imagine that. You don't exactly chase men, Joley. They chase you."

"I threw myself at him the other night and he turned me down," Joley confessed. "And he spent last night with me and didn't do much but get me to sleep."

Again there was a small silence. Joley counted to ten while her words sank in. She imagined Sarah with a little frown on her face.

"You don't sleep with anyone in the room. You never did even as a child."

"I know. But I did last night. He said he couldn't stand me

not sleeping, and he was going to guard me so I could just relax and sleep all night—and I did."

"And he didn't touch you?"

"He kissed me."

"And?"

"Rockets. Holy cow, Sarah, he's like the greatest kisser of all time."

"That's not good."

"Actually I told him I was putting that in the con section of my list, but he said I couldn't." She couldn't help the bubble of laughter in her voice. She touched her lips, tingling at the memory.

"I'm going to talk to Mom immediately." Sarah sounded more than a little alarmed. "Don't do anything stupid, Joley. If Prakenskii really comes from this other lineage, you could be in real trouble. In the diary, our ancestors wrote that the woman who came to them was terrified of the man who marked her. She was very religious and thought maybe he had made a pact with the devil. The house should have protected her along with all the protections the Drakes could muster for her, yet for some reason, she left the house in the middle of the night and went to him. That doesn't make sense when she was safe."

Joley could have told her why. If the man had been like Prakenskii, he had seduced her with his voice. He had pursued her day and night, until she was in such a state of arousal, she couldn't fight him anymore. "I'm going to be careful. Find out everything you can and call me. I hear a lot of commotion outside. They'll be setting up soon and calling me in for a sound check and I'd like to get in a run at least."

"I love you, Joley. If you need me to help you fight him, I'll come. All of us will."

"I'm good for now. Love you right back. Kiss Damon for me." Joley hit the end call button and sat for a moment, pressing the cell phone to her chin. She had no idea what she was going to do. On the con side of her list she wrote, *Scares the hell out of me.*

She broke the lead in the pencil twice as she wrote out *The hand thing.* She wrote it half on the pro side and half on the con side. Frowning, she was about to add the kiss right in the middle between the two columns as well. And while she was thinking about it, she was pretty sure talking telepathically to her day and night, in an attempt to seduce her, had to go smack in the middle also. She hadn't exactly consulted Sarah over that little piece of information. The pencil snapped in half. Joley took it as a sign she needed to go running.

It was bright outside. She hadn't pulled back the privacy sliders in the bus, and the light from the sun nearly blinded her. Whipping out her sunglasses, she pushed them onto her nose and stepped into the parking lot. Steve would have a fit that she went running without him to guard her, but he had to be tired from driving all night and she didn't want to disturb him.

She looked carefully around her, her breath catching in her throat. Red Rocks was beautiful. The bus was parked in the lot behind the amphitheater, and she looked up at the surrounding natural walls of towering rock that always took her breath. It was as if nature had created an amphitheater with perfect acoustic sound just for the sheer love of hearing music and then had provided the most beautiful backdrop it could offer. For someone like Joley who was all about sound and nature, it was almost perfection on earth. She loved the natural rock formations, the layers and layers of sandstone that had been there millions of years, slowly rising until they were the majestic towers of red rock creating the walls of the theater.

Joley took a deep breath and let it out. Coming to Red Rocks always revitalized her. The sandstone formations, the prehistoric footprints of time rising above her like a cathedral, were inspiring on every level. It had been difficult to talk everyone into a back-to-back concert, but she was grateful she had. She walked toward the stage, where she could hear a commotion as the crew began to set up.

She noticed a couple of Nikitin's guards with dogs searching the rows of the amphitheater. He must have decided to attend, and his security was doing a sweep right along with hers. Loud voices coming from behind several crates attracted her attention. A few of the crew looked uneasy when they saw her, glancing hastily away or acknowledging her with a slight nod of the head. Curious, she moved closer to the commotion.

Jerry and Brian had evidently caught up with Dean, and the discussion didn't appear to be going very well. Dean looked angry, and he was gesturing obscenely at Brian. Joley had to fight her natural inclination to go join the fray. It hadn't been fair to force Jerry and Brian to confront Dean. She was the one who had forbidden underage groupies at the parties. It was her rule and ultimately her decision to fire Dean if he had broken it. She was putting her manager and Brian, her best friend, in the position of looking like the bad guys. She really had become a diva, although, in the music business, everyone knew it was always the star's decision that carried the weight.

She had taken three steps when a woman emerged from the rocks to her left. Joley recognized Tish Voight, Logan's estranged wife. Joy swept through Joley, and she realized just how much she had missed her. Tish had been a mother hen to all of them, but especially to Joley, as she was younger than the band members.

"Joley!" Tish's face lit up and she ran across the parking lot toward her.

"Tish!" Joley, who rarely touched anyone, threw her arms around Tish and hugged her close. "I've missed you. When did you get in? Are you staying?"

Tish hugged her back hard. "Actually I just arrived, my car's down in the lot. You look great, Joley. The band has done so well. I'm really proud of all of you."

"We've never been the same without you. How have you been? Tell me everything."

Joley couldn't believe how good Tish looked. She'd matured in the last few years. Medium height, she had long dark hair, which she still pulled back in a ponytail, but it looked shiny and healthy, as did her skin. She had a woman's body with lots of curves. That was Tish—no makeup, no glamour, but all beautiful. There wasn't a devious bone in her body.

"I've been working; teaching again. Love the kids, you know I do. So it's all been good."

"But you miss us, right? Miss the road and the craziness?" Joley asked hopefully.

"I miss you and the boys, not so much the craziness." Her eyes looked sad, although she was smiling. "Logan called and said it was an emergency and he desperately needed me, so I came." She shrugged. "I didn't want to come, Joley. I can't afford the risk."

"I know. I'm so sorry, Tish, all of us were. You and Logan . . ."

"Don't. I don't want to go there. Logan and I were childhood sweethearts. I guess that's very cliché nowadays. He outgrew me. I'm small town and I like it that way. He's uptown and he likes it that way."

"Neither of you filed for divorce," Joley pointed out. She couldn't tell Tish that she felt her sorrow at the loss of her marriage, and that she knew, after touching her, that Tish still loved Logan. Joley hadn't meant to invade her privacy.

Tish shrugged. "I'm not looking for another relationship, and it seemed too big of a hassle. I figured if he ever wanted to divorce me, he'd just do it. He has the lawyers and I don't care about his money. He knows that. I've made my own living without him."

"But he sends you money, doesn't he?"

"He insisted on a joint account, and apparently he puts money in it every month. He told me once everything he had was in both our names, but I never checked and I've never accessed the bank account."

That was total Tish. Independent and fiercely proud. Joley understood her. "So are you going to stay and help with the baby?"

"I don't know. Logan wants me to, but you know me, I'll get attached to her and then won't be able to let go when the time comes."

"No one would make a better mother, Tish. You were born to be a mother."

"I can't have children—at least I can't give birth to them. I had cancer as a child. The radiation and chemotherapy saved my life, but not anything else." She glanced toward the band's bus. "I always wondered if that . . ."

"Tish! No! Logan was crazy about you. Drugs and alcohol and groupies throwing themselves at the boys ruined everything. You know that. It was too much, too fast, and we couldn't handle it. None of us—except you."

Tish had always stood for them, but as their popularity grew, the band needed someone who knew the business and could handle all the details of a huge venue, and Jerry had come into their lives. With Jerry had come overnight success and all that came with it.

"I didn't handle it all that well either," Tish protested. "Seeing all those girls willing to do anything with Logan—

with the others—they were like brothers to me, it was over-whelming. Maybe I shouldn't have stayed away so long, but I thought our marriage could handle it." She shook her head. "Now look at us. I'm alone and he's got a child."

"Logan has sole custody of the baby, Tish. Lucy gave up all rights to her and she doesn't want her at all. Neither does Lucy's mother. They wanted money. When Lucy found out Logan was married and he had dropped her, she went berserk. She has mental problems and I think she's all the mother can handle. If you're still married to Logan, I don't know the legal ramifications, but I think you should be able to adopt the baby easily. Maybe this is your chance. Talk to Logan about it."

Tish sighed. "That's one more tie to him."

"Is that really such a bad thing?"

Angry voices rose, and Joley looked past Tish to the three men arguing. She had never seen Brian actually lose his tem-per, but he shoved Dean, his posture very aggressive. Jerry stepped in between the two men, pushing Dean away from Brian. She was still too far away to hear what they were say-ing, but body language suggested it was a fairly violent argu-ment. She could see several members of the crew watching the three men while pretending to work.

"Do you know what that's about?" Tish asked.

Joley sighed and filled her in. "I guess I should have been the one to speak with Dean, instead of making Jerry and Brian do it."

"No, you shouldn't," Tish said. "Jerry's your manager and he deals with the crew. You aren't responsible for anything these people do. If Dean took advantage of a minor, Jerry will fire him. And if he knows where she is, they'll get it out of him. You can't be involved in things like that. You're the star, Joley, the band is secondary. If you got involved in a con-frontation with a crew member, someone's going to videotape it and it will end up on television, the Internet and especially the tabloids. Let Jerry do his job."

"I don't want it to come to blows. Brian almost never loses his temper. I can't imagine what would make him get so an-gry." ·

"You can't?" Tish shook her head. "The band looks at you as a younger sister. They're very protective and very loyal. My guess is Dean said something very ugly about you and got

Brian's back up. None of them are going to let anyone say anything bad about you."

Joley felt a tug at her heartstrings. She felt as if the band were family—brothers she loved—but their camaraderie with one another was very different than with her and she always felt the odd man out. "Since you've been gone, I haven't felt as much a part of things as I used to," she admitted, frowning as she watched the argument get a little more heated.

The disturbance had attracted the attention of not only the crew, but also the Russians. They paused in their work and observed the altercation. Joley's palm began to itch. She rubbed it against her thigh, and her heart began to pound. Ilya was nearby—very close. She spotted him making his way to the two Russians and her stomach did a little somersault. He moved with fluid grace, like a large jungle cat, all rippling muscle and power, yet conserving energy with every step.

"Whoa! Mama mia, who is that?" Tish asked. "He's hotter than Hades."

Joley considered feigning indifference, but this was Tish. "Ilya Prakenskii, Nikitin's bodyguard."

"He can guard my body anytime," Tish said appreciatively. "Have you . . ."

"No. But ask me if I want to."

"You'd have to be dead not to want to. I think I'm having an orgasm looking at him."

Joley pressed her palm tighter against her thigh. The center throbbed and burned, and deep inside, in her most feminine core, the same throbbing and burning began. It was going to start all over again, that terrible need, the emptiness that nothing—no one—could fill but Ilya. If she was going to suffer, it was only fair that he should. She wished she could make him feel the same relentless, merciless craving.

Lifting her palm, she studied the center. Already the discoloration was appearing. Faint marks, two circles intertwined. Joley lifted her gaze to Ilya, watching his every move as he approached the two Russian guards. She took a deep breath and ran her finger over the center of her palm, imagining touching him intimately, holding his body close to hers and claiming it for her own.

Ilya's body jerked. He looked up, his gaze locking with hers across the distance. Time seemed to stand still, and for one moment there were only the two of them locked together in the natural wonder of the amphitheater.

I'm sorry. She hadn't believed she could really give him such a jolt of physical awareness.

Be very careful playing with fire you don't understand.

She moistened her lips and turned away from him. It was his magic—not hers—and she didn't understand it. But she knew how dangerous it could be.

"Is something going on between you two?" Tish asked.

"Not yet," Joley answered honestly. "I'm still considering the price tag."

"For a man like that? It's going to be hefty."

Joley laughed. "I missed you, Tish. You're so right, about a lot of things, but especially about this."

"But I bet he'd be worth it."

Joley had the feeling she was going to find out. If she didn't find something huge to put on the con side of the list fast, she would allow him to seduce her, and then she'd be in way over her head. Tish wasn't like Joley's sisters. She looked at the man and saw "hot" all over him. She didn't see the neon warning lights flashing, *danger, danger*. If Joley hung out with Tish, she could easily talk herself into an affair with Ilya, because she desperately wanted him.

"Have you seen Logan yet?" Joley asked, needing to switch the subject. She couldn't think too much about Ilya, especially with him close by. She couldn't afford for him to be reading her thoughts.

The teasing smile faded from Tish's face. "We spoke on the phone, and I said I'd meet him here, but I haven't seen him yet. I drove all night to get here, and now I'm thinking of jumping back in the car and calling him from the safety of two or three hours away."

Joley looked past her. Logan had just stepped out of the bus, and his radar had found Tish immediately. He was staring at her with naked longing. "I think it's too late to run, Tish. He's coming this way."

Tish didn't turn around. Instead, she closed her eyes briefly, as if gathering strength. Joley pressed her hand for courage. "I hope you stay, Tish. You're family to all of us and we've never been the same without you." She kept her voice low. "But I understand if you can't stay."

Tish's fingers clung to hers for a moment, and Joley felt her tremble. Instantly she felt protective and stood her ground, letting Tish hold on to her for courage.

Logan stopped a few steps short of them. "You came, Tish." His voice was low and gravelly, choked even.

Joley was nearly overwhelmed with the mixture of emotions pouring out of Logan. He was close to a breakdown, she realized. The pregnancy had been a nightmare, with Lucy threatening to kill herself every few days and the paparazzi dogging his every footstep. He stood directly behind Tish, his usually good looks worn and tired.

Joley watched the struggle on Tish's face as she turned to face her husband. "I came," she agreed. Her fingers tightened around Joley's.

"Thank you for coming, Tish. Believe me, I know what I'm asking." Logan raked both hands through his hair and then rubbed the shadow along his jaw. "I have the baby here. She's been crying most of the night, kept us all awake. I don't know what's wrong." He glanced over to where Jerry and Brian were now shouting at Dean. "Everyone's temper is a little frayed. They all took turns holding her to try to get her to sleep, but we can't keep that up."

"The baby's in the bus?" Tish asked, obviously melting at the sheer desperation in Logan's voice. "Show me."

Joley took a couple of steps toward Jerry and Brian, but Tish hung on to her like a pit bull. "It looks like it's getting out of hand over there."

"Don't think you'll make it any better," Logan cautioned. "Dean was talking crap about you this morning and Brian overheard him. He was seething when he came into the bus. He's hard to rile, but when he gets going, you've got to look out. Come see the baby."

Joley frowned, torn between hope that she could end the argument that looked like it was coming to blows and fear that she would possibly make it even worse. Dean glanced up, and his venomous gaze met hers across the distance. He spat on the ground and gestured obscenely at her. Even from where she was, Joley could feel the malevolence pouring from him to her. She shivered as waves of hatred and anger washed over her. And something else. She turned her head quickly to see Ilya straighten, his gaze on Dean, hard and cold and glittering with promise. His aura was black and swirled around the edges with blood red. She drew in her breath sharply.

Brian spun Dean around and smashed his fist into his face. Dean staggered back and then flung himself on Brian. Around them the crew sprang into action, surrounding the two men and dragging them apart.

Logan pressed Tish and Joley forward toward the band's bus. "You don't need to be out here. Somewhere, you know someone with a camera is lurking. Let Jerry and Brian toss the bum out on his ass."

"I feel responsible," Joley said.

"He's right, Joley," Tish agreed. "You can't be involved in that. Brian shouldn't have been either. Either the man knows something or he doesn't. If he does, he should just give them the information, and if not, he shouldn't be so resentful that they asked him. It's a perfectly legit question when some kid is missing." She tugged at Joley. "Let's go see the baby."

Joley glanced back toward Ilya, but he was walking away, heading toward the front of the amphitheater, his back toward her.

7

LOGAN stepped out of the bus and put the baby into Tish's arms, standing there with a look of utter, naked, helpless love on his face, for the entire world to see. "I named her Melissa Lacey, the one we picked out together back when we were in high school. We've all been calling her Lissa. Isn't she beautiful?"

Tish looked as if she would cry. She stared down at the little upturned face, the little waving hands with soft, perfect fingers, then pushed the baby into Joley's arms and stepped inside the bus.

Logan caught Joley's shoulders for support, leaning heavily on her, looking down at his child. "She doesn't want her, Joley. She can't forgive me for the things I did."

Joley patted his hand, looking up at him. "I love you, Logan, but you're dense. She's crazy about you and desperately wants to believe she can be a family with you and the baby, but she's afraid. Take the baby and go to her, and for God's sake, eat your pride. Tish is the best in the world. They don't come better. If she accepts you back and takes Lissa as her daughter, she'll never look back. You'll never have anything thrown in your face. You don't deserve her, but if you really want her, I don't think it's going to be all that difficult to convince her. You've got Lissa, and who could resist her?" She smiled at the baby, bent her head and kissed the little forehead. "She's so beautiful."

"If Tish doesn't come back to me, Joley, I don't know what I'm going to do. And now she'll think I only wanted her for the baby. I got here about five in the morning, and we've been passing Lissa back and forth since then. No one's complained, but I can't ask them to help me with her, and I sure can't haul her around the country without help. I don't trust anyone but Tish."

"Tish went into the bus, not back toward her car. Rent an RV or something larger for the three of you for the rest of the tour. We can make them comfortable. If we have to, I can bunk with the boys and the three of you can use my bus. We're family. We'll get through this together." She handed him the baby. "Go tell her you love her and that you're an idiot."

"Thanks, Joley." Logan pressed a kiss to the top of her head.

"I'm going running." She always went jogging to clear her head. Physical exercise was a form of meditation to her.

"Where's Steve?" Logan asked.

"He drove the bus last night. He's asleep, but no one's around yet and I should be fine. Nikitin's security is already here and I noticed a few uniforms showing up."

Logan cradled his daughter close and nodded, although he still looked worried. "Be careful, Joley, and don't go very far."

She glanced at her watch and then over to where Jerry and Brian had argued with Dean. Apparently the fight had broken up and everyone had found something to do. Dean was stalking across the parking lot toward the crew's bus, and Brian was nowhere in sight. She'd have to ask them later what Dean had said about the young girl. "I've got about an hour before this place starts filling up. Jerry told me they'd call me for the sound check around two. That sound about right with you?"

Logan nodded and went up the small steps to the bus. "That's when everything should be ready."

Joley waved, mouthed *good luck* and took off jogging away from the stage area toward the trail leading up into the rocks. Logan was a lucky man. In spite of everything he had done, all the mistakes he'd made, Tish loved him. Even the fiasco with Lucy had turned into something wonderful. Little Lissa would be well loved by Tish and Logan.

In the beginning the band had their lives together, everything had been good. They'd been best friends and had people surrounding them who really loved them. As they'd climbed to success, everything had changed. All of them had been sucked into a life of excess, and they'd all forgotten what really mattered. As the years went by, they'd learned the hard way, and all were trying to find their way back. She hoped Logan and Tish could do it through the baby.

And Denny. She had no idea if Lisa had stuck around to forgive him. Joley hoped so. Love wasn't always forgiving, but at least he'd found it, even if he'd been stupid enough to throw it away.

Her sisters had been lucky. Sarah had found Damon. He was an odd man, brilliant and gruff, but he had embraced Sarah's family and they all had fallen in love with him. Sweet Kate had found Matt Granite, former Army Ranger and now a contractor. He was just what Kate needed. And Abbey was truly in love with her Russian, Aleksandr Volstov.

Love seemed to happen fast to everyone but her. She obsessed over Ilya Prakenskii, but she wasn't in love with him. Just because he took her breath away and set her heart pounding—that was purely physical. Chemistry. They had it in abundance, but she wanted the kind of love her sisters had. Libby and Tyson. Libby was a natural healer, Tyson a renowned researcher for pharmaceuticals, and he looked after Libby, treating her like a precious treasure. And of course there were Jonas and Hannah. Jonas adored Hannah. It was in every look he gave her, every touch of the hand. Joley wanted that. Not just hot sex—and it would be hot with Ilya—but it wouldn't be love.

And maybe no one could love her, not unconditionally, the kind of love her sisters had found, the kind that Tish felt for Logan. She feared it was her. She didn't know how to love, to give herself to someone, to put herself into someone else's keeping and take him into hers. She didn't trust anyone with her heart—or the darker places in her soul.

She picked up her pace, listening to the rhythm of her shoes hitting the trail. She wanted to enjoy being a loner, satisfied with trekking the world and singing wherever she went, in stadiums filled with crowds, but she couldn't live just for those moments. She wanted to share her life with someone else, laugh with him, stay up until all hours of the night talking with him, or just sit quietly side by side and feel at peace.

The morning sun had risen, and the beams of lights shining on the red rock set the hillside ablaze with color. The towers of sandstone that rose up toward the sky were incredible, and she tried to find solace in nature. The trail climbed into the heart of the rock, and she felt surrounded, protected even. Trees and bushes sprang up as life found the sun and stretched toward it. It should have been impossible for her not to be happy, but with every step she took, her heart seemed to grow heavier, until it sat in her chest like a stone and dread filled her.

She didn't want to go back. She didn't want to face Jerry and Brian, or even Tish and Logan with their happy smiles. By now, Lisa might have resolved things with Denny. Joley would have to be happy for everyone. She pressed a hand to her churning stomach. The feeling of dread deepened and she felt sick. A dark shadow slid over her, played over the rocks and trail as a vulture circled lazily. Joley glanced up to see the bird gliding with languid intent in a large circle over the area.

She could see the morning sun glistening off the feathers, the dark underbelly and the fringe as the bird passed overhead. This time the shadow stretched and magnified, casting a bizarre image on the red rock. With the sun shining through, the rock looked like deep blood flowing through the vulture's blackened shadow. With the feathering wing tips and the beak and talons, Joley looked at a specter of death.

She stumbled to a halt and studied the ominous shadow. The bad feeling in the pit of her stomach grew stronger. Something was wrong. Very wrong. Her eyes scanned the area around her, and for the first time she became completely aware that she was alone, unprotected by her usual security.

Nerves tightening, she turned and began jogging back toward the parking lot, this time careful to stay to the center of the trail where she could see anything coming at her from either side. Trees, rocks and brush lined the winding path. An attacker could hide in any number of places. Movement caught her eye, leaves swaying against the slight wind as she ran past a sprawling rock formation. Again the bird circled above her, casting its shadow wide.

Joley kept running, hearing the rhythm of life change around her. The sound of the soles of her shoes echoed the beat of her pounding heart. She heard the wind whistling and leaves rustling. The sharp eyes of the bird seemed filled with evil malice, and the shadow spread wider against the red rock, reaching out to surround her.

She spun around in a circle, unable to shake the feeling of eyes watching her, of evil stalking her. It was a blessing and a curse to feel things, and right now she felt like a hunted rabbit. She took off running again, watching the trail, staying loose and ready, knowing the feeling could be caused by anything from one of her stalkers to a photographer watching with a long-range lens.

"Stupid, stupid, stupid," she hissed under her breath as she rounded a turn. The trail narrowed here, and brush encroached close to the walkway, allowing anyone to conceal himself and jump out at an unwary runner. She picked up her pace, but she was heading downhill and it was dangerous to run too fast.

She was fairly certain the series of switchback bends marked about the halfway point to the bottom of the trail. Rounding the second curve with a smooth, perfect rhythm, she felt she'd managed to hit a good stride, when she ran right into a solid body. She crashed hard, her face pressed tight against a broad chest. Arms swept around her, swinging her off her feet as she lost balance. Joley screamed and brought her thumbs down hard in a stabbing motion for the person's exposed throat, but he had already dropped his chin and covered the spot.

She knew him the moment she inhaled—the moment she got past fear and felt his familiar body, the iron strength in his arms. He was covered in a fine sheen of sweat. He'd been out running, too. Ilya set her on the ground, steadying her, but keeping her close to him.

"Are you okay?"

She licked her lips, taking in his tousled hair, the raw arousal in his eyes, his heavily muscled chest and arms stretching his thin black tee. His narrow waist and hips, the thick bulge in the front of his jeans . . . Her mouth went dry, and a thousand butterflies took flight in her stomach. Her body went damp in instant arousal.

His melody sang to her of heat and fire and passion. She felt the notes, heard them racing through her bloodstream, singing in her ears. Beckoning. Seducing. Whispering to her with such erotic promise she could barely think with wanting him.

"You ran into me," she accused indignantly, trying to hide the excitement seeing him always brought. The tension was still in her from the edgy, ominous signs the shadow of the bird had brought, but it was being taken over by a completely different tension. She caught at his arms to keep contact more than to keep upright, although her knees seemed a little weak. Her palm was itching like mad, burning even, to match the burning emptiness begging to be filled between her legs.

"Actually you ran into me. I heard you coming at the last moment and caught you." He looked around as if expecting to see someone. "Is your bodyguard having a hard time keeping up with you?"

She made a face at him. "You know very well he isn't with me, and I don't appreciate your sarcasm at all." She might be frowning, but as always, when he was near, her body reacted—or maybe it was her soul, because her mouth went dry, her heart beat too fast, and she could hear a strange roaring in her ears. All she wanted to do was slip her hands beneath the thin material stretching over the hard muscles of his chest and lift her face up to his to taste his hot, sinfully seductive mouth again.

His melody shifted, introducing dominant notes, needy and urgent and full of demand. The song pulsed with the same heat and smoldering fire, but this time leapt with the force of an erupting volcano, a demand she couldn't ignore, one that ignited flames in her belly until she craved his kiss beyond all imagination.

It was more than want. She *needed* to kiss him. Needed to feel his mouth on hers, his hands running over her body. She needed to be skin to skin. She licked her lips again, imagining what he might do if she knelt right there and unzipped his tight jeans. Would that famous control of his simply disappear? She desperately wanted his control to slip so she could see that he was as shaken by his reaction to her as she was by hers to him.

Dark lust flickered and burned in the depths of his eyes. He simply lifted her, taking her right off the trail into the shelter of the rocks. He didn't say a word, but trapped her body between his and the towering shelf of sandstone, his mouth coming down on hers. Hot. Hard. Ravaging. *Perfect*. Absolute perfection. Heat burst through her. Music hummed in her veins. Her heart drummed a tune that echoed the throbbing in her deepest core. Joley had no thought other than that she was well and truly lost.

She wrapped her arms around his neck, and his mouth still fastened to hers, he lifted her, half sitting her on a narrow shelf. Joley locked her legs around him, aligning her body with his so that she could feel the hot, hard thickness of him pressing against her. Her nipples tightened, breasts aching and swollen as she melted into him. Her hips moved in a slow, erotic swirl, rubbing her body against his heavy erection. God help her, he felt like home to her.

She gave herself up to him. Offered herself even knowing he would destroy her. There was something more than physical magic, more than pure chemistry; her soul, as stupid and as corny as it sounded, touched his. Her brain that always ran at high speed and prevented her from sleep, that horrible turmoil always raging inside of her—all of it stilled when she was near Ilya.

The moment her mouth touched his, he was inside of her, in her mind, wrapping himself in her thoughts, touching each erotic image and enhancing it with his own. She was stunned by the heat rushing through her, the flames dancing over her skin and in her belly, the tingling in her thighs and the naked longing in her feminine core.

His hand slid under her shirt, cupping the underside of her breast, sending a wave of liquid fire rushing between her legs. The silken wall of small muscles tightened in anticipation, and her song harmonized completely with his until she couldn't tell one from the other.

It was Ilya who pulled away, not putting space between their bodies, but lifting his head inches from hers and running his hands down her arms until he found her hands. His fingers tangled with hers, and he rested his forehead against hers, struggling to get his breathing under control.

"You aren't helping me at all."

"I know." Her voice came out a husky whisper, maybe even an invitation, but she couldn't help it. "I'm sorry." But she doubted if that was true.

"You aren't ready and I'm trying to be noble. Nobility isn't my strong suit, Joley, so you've got to help me out. Otherwise, we'll spend hours in bed and you'll roll over hating me and hating yourself. You have to know I'm the one. You have to accept me as your other half."

"You've been seducing me for months," she reminded him,

trying to absolve herself of the guilt. "With your voice. You know I'm susceptible to sound and you use that against me." It was a pathetic accusation and she knew it. She wasn't helpless, she hadn't even tried to stop him. He'd mesmerized her so completely she hadn't even turned to her sisters for help, not seriously. She wanted him—lusted after him—was consumed by her obsession with him. She grasped at that. "Obsession is not love."

His blue eyes were dark with arousal. "I don't give a damn what it is, Joley. I don't care what you call it. Love, lust, obsession, need, whatever. We belong. That's all that matters. We fit. You're mine and I'm yours, and there doesn't need to be an endless discussion on the subject. We are. Once you accept that, we'll be fine."

"I don't tease men, Ilya, that's not what I'm trying to do."

"I know that."

"Why is it like this between us? We're so obviously wrong for each other."

He pressed a kiss to her forehead. "We're so obviously right, even our songs merge."

That startled her. "You do see melodies."

"And colors. Yours are all over mine."

She shook her head. "No, if that were true, I wouldn't be so afraid. Your colors cover mine until I don't know where one of us starts and the other leaves off."

He kissed her again, long and hard and heartstoppingly slow. "We have to get somewhere safe, Joley. If we stay here alone, this isn't going to turn out the way either of us wants. I'll race you down the mountain."

"No way. I don't like losing, and it doesn't take a genius to see that you're in good shape. We'll go, but casually, no hurry, no competing." She circled his neck with her arms and pulled his head back to hers, kissing him one last time, savoring the taste of him.

Ilya didn't take over. He let her direct the kiss, explore his mouth, caress the nape of his neck with her fingertips. When she pulled away, they looked at each other.

Joley smiled. "You taste good."

"We have to get out of here," he reiterated, tugging at her hand to urge her back onto the trail.

Her smile widened. He definitely was as affected by her

kiss as she was his. She didn't say anything else as they took off running, side by side. Ilya allowed her to set the pace, keeping up easily. She was very aware of him beside her, the smooth way his muscles rippled beneath his shirt, the way the wind ruffled his thick hair, the swing of his arms and his steady breath. Their melodies merged, just as their auras always seemed to when they were close. Joley actually slowed her pace in order to prolong her time with him.

Ilya seemed content to jog beside her quietly. He made no attempt to talk and she was grateful. He was right. She wasn't ready to commit herself to a relationship with him, she had too many doubts about what and who he was, yet she was the one always flinging herself at him, and that was as humiliating as it was disturbing.

They were nearly walking as they rounded the last bend, which opened to a long straight stretch to the beginning of the trail below them. People milled around, and yellow tape surrounded the rocks about halfway down near the bottom and off to the left side.

Joley slowed her pace and caught at Ilya's arm. "Something's wrong; that's a medical examiner's van."

"It doesn't look good." He caught her hand when she would have headed down toward the commotion. "Don't. Let me check it out first."

"It could be one of the band members or my crew. We're practically the only ones here." Her mouth was dry. Something terrible had happened here. She felt violent energy swirling through the rocks. Auras were dark and subdued. The medical examiner's van was parked to one side along with several sheriff cars.

Ilya walked with her toward the officers and security people milling outside the tape. She gripped his arm tightly as a man dressed in a gray suit approached them.

"Miss Drake? Joley Drake?"

"Yes. Tell me what happened." She couldn't stop the anxiety in her voice.

"One of your crew has been killed—murdered. My name is James Branscomb, I'm a detective. I'd like to ask you a few questions."

She wished she could say the murder came as a complete surprise, but with the sick dread weighing so heavily on her, she had expected trouble. She glanced at Ilya. As usual, his expression was unreadable, the calm mask in place, but he had to have known, had to have felt the deep, violent disturbance permeating the amphitheater, just as she had.

"Who? Who was killed?" Unknowingly she stepped closer to Ilya.

He pulled her beneath his shoulder. "I'm Ilya Prakenskii—bodyguard. We've been running up the trail and have no idea what's going on. If you could fill us in, we'd be grateful." He glanced around, his eyes sharp. "You've got several paparazzi here, Detective. Perhaps we should get Miss Drake into her bus and away from the photographers." His voice made the suggestion a command.

The detective's eyes narrowed, but he nodded. "We'll talk inside the bus then."

Ilya slid his arm around Joley's waist, keeping her beneath the protection of his shoulder, his body shielding hers, sheltering her face from long-range lenses as he started her moving past the yellow tape.

"I want to know who it is," Joley insisted.

"A man by the name of Dean Walters." The detective watched her with shrewd eyes.

Joley's breath caught in her lungs. "Dean? I just saw him. Before my run. He was angry with me."

"You spoke to him?"

Ilya kept Joley moving. She seemed stunned. Ilya wanted to be able to watch the cop, to feel his emotions as he questioned Joley, but until he got her in a safe place, he couldn't do that. He didn't want to take a chance on prying eyes, or worse, a photographer, recording Joley's emotions and making money off her distress. And he didn't trust the cop, or anyone for that matter, not to take advantage of the fact that Joley was a high-profile celebrity. He yanked open the door to the bus and almost pushed Joley inside before she could answer. He kept his body between hers and the detective's.

Joley flung herself into a chair and covered her face for a moment. When she looked up, the detective was seated across from her and Ilya was pulling water bottles from the refrigerator. He handed one to her, offered one to the detective, who declined, and took one himself.

"I'm sorry, what did you ask me?" Joley said. "I can't seem

to take this in. Did someone identify the body? When did this happen? I just saw him, before I took off for my run. He was in the parking lot, heading over to his bus. Are you absolutely certain it's Dean?"

"Yes. I'm sorry," Branscomb said. "Several members of your band came forward and positively identified him. You said he was angry with you."

Joley nodded and rubbed at the relentless pounding in her temples. "I have a rule about minors partying with any band or crew member. It's actually written into the contract they sign with us when we go on the road. After the show in New York, I went out to a party to deliver a message to one of the band members, and I saw a group of girls who looked too young to be there. Dean was with one of them. He had his arm around her, and when I called out to him, they took off running."

"How old was this girl?"

Joley sighed. "Thirteen, I later found out. I was going to talk to him about it, but in all honesty, with the traveling and everything else going on, I didn't have a chance and even forgot about it until Chicago. A woman came up to me after the concert and said her daughter had been missing since my show in New York. She handed me a photograph, and I swear, it's the same girl." She looked around the bus. "It's here somewhere."

Ilya retrieved the photograph from the stand by the bed and handed it to the detective. He didn't want to draw attention, so he did what he did best, faded into the shadows and masked his presence with a small, influential push to keep the detective from really noticing him.

"I called the police in New York, and the girl was still missing, so I asked my manager, Jerry St. Ives, and one of the band members, Brian Rigger, to find Dean and ask him about the girl when we reached Red Rocks this morning, before the crew set up. I told Jerry, if Dean had violated our agreement and invited this girl to the party, he was to be fired."

"So they both talked to him this morning."

Joley nodded. "I got ready for my run and stepped off the bus. Tish, the wife of my sax player, had just arrived and I haven't seen her for some time, so I went over to say hello. I saw Brian, Jerry and Dean talking together. They were standing over by the stage. I couldn't hear what was said, but Dean was angry and he kept looking over at me. Eventually he flipped me off and walked to the parking lot. I went for my run, and the last I saw of Dean, he was alone, over by the crew bus."

Ilya stepped out of the shadows. "I observed them as well. He was angry and he stalked off toward his bus. I didn't hear what was said, but he was evidently quite upset at Miss Drake."

"Did your manager fire him?"

Joley leaned her head against the back of the couch. Her headache was getting worse. "I don't know. I haven't had a chance to talk to Jerry about it. I wanted to get in a run before the sound check, and this morning was my only opportunity."

"Did you see the argument becoming heated?"

Joley took a deep breath and let it out. "It got loud, yes. But if you think either Jerry or Brian could have harmed Dean, you're wrong. They just aren't like that." She frowned at the detective, leaning forward so that he would look her directly in the eye. "I've known Brian forever and he doesn't have a mean bone in his body. And Jerry has too much authority over everyone to have to resort to murder. You didn't say what happened. Could it have been an accident?"

"He was shot between the eyes. No, ma'am, I don't think we could call it an accident. Do you know if Rigger or St. Ives own a gun?"

"No. God, no. I'm telling you, they would never do something like that—kill Dean, I mean. Brian is incredibly gentle and Jerry just plain wouldn't bother."

"And you never talked to Walters?"

Joley shook her head. "No. And when I saw he was so angry, I didn't want to." She pressed her fingers to her temples again. "I really have a headache. I've never had one this bad."

Ilya studied her pale face. The headache was worsening. It was essential to keep a low profile, but he couldn't stand by and watch Joley suffer needlessly, not when he could help her. With a small sigh, he moved from the shadows, sat down beside her and turned her face toward his. He rested the pads of his fingers on either side of her head. "You're pale, Joley. Do you get migraines?"

"Not as a rule," she admitted. "But occasionally. This one is bad." And getting worse by the moment. It made her feel vulnerable in front of the detective. Already, her stomach was churning and little white dots flashed in front of her eyes.

"Just close your eyes. This won't take more than a moment."

Ilya sighed to himself. Even with the ability to fade the detective's memories, Branscomb would remember this. Joley was too famous, too beautiful and sexy not to make an impact. A bodyguard ridding her of her headache was something too intimate not to be noted. And Ilya couldn't touch her without being intimate. His hands were that little bit too gentle. His touch more of a caress than anything else. This was the reason a man like Ilya Prakenskii didn't get involved emotionally, because in the end, it was dangerous to both of them.

Inwardly he cursed, but he maintained his expressionless mask. He couldn't hide the body language warning the other man off, or the gentleness of his own touch, but his face gave nothing away as he placed his fingers at her temples and pushed healing energy from his soul to hers. Healing was intimate—giving Joley a part of himself, taking a part from her.

Better, laskovaya moya?

Joley nodded. "Thank you, it's much better."

Ilya glanced at the detective. Shrewd eyes. Cop's eyes. Ilya recognized that look.

"You two went running," Branscomb said, his voice almost casual.

"Running keeps me in shape," Ilya said, "and allows us a small measure of time alone together." He picked up Joley's hand and ran his thumb over the back of it.

"You have an accent. Are you Russian?"

"Yes."

Beside him, Joley stirred. "I need to talk with Brian and Jerry. Where are they?"

The detective closed his notebook. "Mr. Rigger and Mr. St. Ives both agreed to come down to the station and give their statements. Mr. St. Ives insisted on bringing an attorney, but stated they would both cooperate fully."

"This sounds terrible, but we either have to do the show tonight or cancel on all these people, and we have to pull out tonight to make it to Dallas on time for that concert."

"Our forensic people will be working as fast as they can.

I've got officers taking statements from everyone. Obviously if we can allow you to go ahead with the performance, it would be better for everyone, so we'll do our best."

"Thank you," Joley said, "although to be honest, it seems horrible to put on a show after someone is murdered."

The detective rose, taking the photograph of the missing girl with him. "Do you know if Mr. Walters was in any way involved with the mob—specifically the Russian mob?" He asked the question of Joley, but he studied Ilya with his cop's eyes.

"No, but I didn't know him very well. He's been working with us on and off for two years, but we never had much contact. He had a couple of close friends in the crew. I couldn't tell you who they are, although I might recognize them if I saw them." And she was going to look, because there'd been a crew member with Dean that night in New York. She hadn't seen his face, but she'd seen his aura—and fragments of his melody. "Why do you ask about the Russian mob?"

"There were things done to him that are fairly signature mob things, warning others to play ball or else."

Joley glanced at Ilya, took a deep breath and exhaled. "In New York, the party was held by a man named Sergei Nikitin. He surrounds himself with armed guards, and I believe most of them are Russian."

"Do you know Mr. Nikitin?" Branscomb asked Ilya.

"Of course. I work for him often in my capacity as a bodyguard. He's a businessman with powerful enemies."

"Do his enemies include the Russian mob?"

"You would have to ask him that," Ilya said.

Branscomb took a few steps down the corridor. "Thank you for your time, Miss Drake. As for your performance tonight, hopefully we'll have an answer for you within the next hour."

"We'll need to do sound checks," Joley said.

"There's no reason not to. You won't be in the crime scene area. He was killed where we found him. I do want to speak to every one of your crew."

"I'll tell them to cooperate fully with you."

"I would appreciate that." Branscomb turned back, his hand on the door. "Miss Drake. Is there a reason Dean Walters might want to harm you?"

Joley's heart jerked. She remembered the malevolent look he'd shot her as he walked toward the crew bus. There had been genuine, naked hatred on his face. "Harm me?" she echoed, fear tugging at her.

"It looked as if he were heading up the running path after you. Several people mentioned he watched you take off running and that you were alone. They were worried about your lack of security." His gaze flicked to Ilya. "And he had a knife."

Branscomb had known all along they hadn't left together. Ilya had to give him points for that. Of course suspicion would fall on him. He was Russian. He was a bodyguard and very strong. He knew that Dean's death had been a hit, and Nikitin had probably ordered it; he just didn't know why. He had known the body was there. He'd felt the dark, violent energy and gone to investigate, worried for Joley. Fortunately he'd approached the area from above, and he'd seen the body and the mess that had been made of it. Walters had died of a bullet to the head, but they'd stomped every bone in his body first.

Ilya remained silent, waiting for Joley to give him up. He prepared himself for Joley's betrayal. He shouldn't look at it that way. She would think she had to tell the exact truth, and maybe there wasn't anything else for her to do. But the thought of being handcuffed and taken in, and his past brought up to further cast doubt on him in the midst of his investigation, was doubly dangerous.

Joley flicked a glance from Ilya to the detective. It was very obvious where he was going with his questioning. She put a hand on Ilya's arm, her mouth suddenly dry, heart pounding. There was a strange roaring in her ears. Ilya couldn't have killed Dean Walters. He couldn't have. She would have known the moment she touched him. Yes, he was violent, and yes, he had killed, but under what circumstances she didn't know, and right now it didn't matter because he hadn't killed Walters. She trusted her instincts, and her instincts said, not even for her had he done this.

"It's difficult to have a relationship with someone with the paparazzi following everywhere you go and photographing your every move. The things they print—all the lies and innuendos—it ruins any chance at a real bond. We try to be careful so we have the opportunity to build a foundation before it's all over the media and we're both hounded into the ground."

Her voice was soft, persuasive, held a note of pure truth the detective couldn't fail to respond to. Ilya didn't even know if she was aware of the compulsion buried in it. His hand slid against hers, fingers tangling with and then enveloping hers. He brought her knuckles up to his mouth. *Thank you.*

He knew she was protecting him, implying, without saying it, that he had joined her immediately. No one had ever done that for him, stood in front of him, not at their own risk—and she was risking a lot. If Branscomb discovered she was shielding Ilya by deliberately misleading the detective, there was no doubt he'd haul her into his office and make life very uncomfortable for her.

Ilya was fairly certain that strange sensation in his chest was his heart melting. She yanked emotion out of him when all feeling had been buried so deep he'd thought—he'd hoped—it was lost for all time. He loved her in that moment, yet at the same time, a part of him was terrified that she could do that to him, and that part was dangerous and cunning and hated her, because anyone who could make him that vulnerable held power over him—endless power—and he had vowed that would never happen again in his lifetime.

She turned her head and looked at him, her eyes soft and loving, twisting him up inside because she wasn't even aware of it yet. He could rule her sexually, he knew that, and he knew he could bind her to him, and that he'd always be bound to her, but this was more—way, way more than he had bargained for. Joley was more than just his—she was so deep inside of him she was a part of him—and just as she had protected him, he would protect her with his last breath.

Ilya read the cop as intelligent, and he was already cutting Joley a break. "Nikitin sent several of his security force here to sweep the area for bombs. He's had many death threats, as has Miss Drake. And I spotted at least four photographers busily filming the argument as well as the band members from the rocks. If you can find them, they might have caught something on camera that would help."

It was a risk—although a small one. Ilya had a way of blending into the background, making it difficult for people and lenses to spot him. As he was nearly always aware of the photographers, he found it easy enough to hide his presence from them. Branscomb deserved a little help, and in any case, he had probably already thought of it.

Branscomb nodded. "I'll be in touch. If you think of anything more, call my number. I left my card on the table."

8

THE door closed behind the detective. Joley stood very still in the ensuing silence, her gaze locked on Ilya's face, her body trembling. He crossed the distance between them and put his arms around her, pulling her close. She burst into tears.

Ilya pressed her face against his chest, his fingers sliding into her hair to massage her scalp, murmuring softly to her. He didn't know where the words came from, most of it made no sense, just soothing noises, but her distress was so genuine. He hadn't known he could actually feel gentle, or tender; he'd thought those things had long ago been beaten out of him, but she brought out a softer response and he was grateful.

"You feel too much for others, Joley," he said, pressing his lips into the soft disarray of her hair. "This was not a good man."

"He has family. And we don't know that he wasn't good."

"If he had anything to do with the Russian mob, believe me, *laskovaya moya*, he wasn't good. And contrary to popular belief, members of the mob don't kill indiscriminately. If he drew their attention, he was in bed with them." He nuzzled the top of her head, his chin sliding through the soft strands of hair. He loved holding her, and that was terrifying. She made him soft inside, different. This woman could turn him inside out with one look. And dark eyes drowning in tears were enough to turn stone into molten gold.

She sighed and turned her head so her cheek rested against him. "Do you think he was using our band, traveling from one city to another in order to run drugs or something?"

He brushed tears from her cheeks with his fingertips. "Or something."

She pulled away just enough to look up at him. "You knew he was dead, didn't you, when you came up the mountain? Did you see who did it? Do you know why?"

"If I saw who had done it, I would have told the detective and I would have called for help immediately. Do you think I had anything to do with that man's death?"

"No. No, of course not." She wrapped one hand around the nape of his neck and rested against his solid strength. "But the detective was suspicious, I could tell."

"It was dangerous handing him Nikitin," Ilya pointed out. "Nikitin isn't kind to his enemies, and you've skated for a while on the edge of slighting him by refusing his invitations to his parties."

"Branscomb was going to get that connection anyway," Joley said and reluctantly pulled away from him. "There was someone with Dean at the party. I saw him with three other men and the group of girls. One of the three was another member of my crew. I recognized that I'd seen him working on the equipment, but I never saw his face. The others I'd never seen before, and I assumed they were other guests. I was hoping Dean might know the names of the other girls so the police could question them."

"You're not thinking of finding the other man who was with Dean." Ilya made it a statement. "Joley, you always rush into things without thinking. You're not a cop, you're a superstar, with cameras on you every second. You can't conduct a secret investigation into a murder or a child's disappearance."

"Well I can't just do nothing! Dean was in my crew. He worked for me. And the girl went to a party thinking she was going to party with the band. *My* band. Sarah and Elle would investigate. They'd never let it go until they found out the truth."

"Well you aren't your sisters. Stay out of it and let the professionals handle it." Even as he said it, her eyes flashed fire and her mouth set in a firm line. Her chin lifted a little and he cursed under his breath. Joley was a powder keg, and telling her what to do was the same as lighting a match.

"Like you? You said you were going to talk to Dean, that you were looking into that girl's disappearance."

He had the urge to shake her. "You're not a defiant child, rebelling against a parent. I'm telling you this is dangerous and to stay the hell out of it. What good is it going to do if you get yourself—or Brian or Jerry—killed?"

Joley paled visibly. "Why would anyone want to kill Jerry or Brian?"

"They asked Walters questions, didn't they? Has it occurred to you that whoever killed him might not have wanted him to answer questions? He knew something and they didn't want it out, so he's dead. This friend of his, still on your crew, is either part of what Dean was into or entirely innocent. If you question him, you could draw attention to him and the killer might think he knows something, or worse for you, if he's in on it, they might target both of you for execution." He stepped closer to her again, catching her arm and pulling her against his body. "You stay away from all of them. Don't ask questions and let the cops take care of it."

Her large eyes darkened, glittering with anger, and he felt lust hit with a hard punch to the gut. His belly burned and his blood pooled hot and demanding in his groin. He bent his head, one hand anchoring in her hair, and he took her mouth, effectively stopping the protest he knew was coming. Heat spread through his body, rockets went off in his head, and colors burst behind his eyes. He pulled her closer, locking her tight against him, so that he could feel every lush curve of her soft, feminine body.

She tasted just like the honey he remembered so vividly from the beehives outside of the school where he'd spent so many years being trained. He'd stolen that, too, just as he stole his kiss from Joley. And like he'd accepted the stings he'd received as a child, he would accept whatever punishment Joley meted out, because in the end, the pleasure spreading through him at her taste, the feel of her soft skin and silky hair, the fire in her rising up to meet the fire in him made any and all retribution worthwhile.

It wasn't just sparks she gave off, it was a conflagration, and the rush was instant and consumed him. The flames devoured him so quickly he didn't have a chance for control and discipline, the two things that had been drilled—beaten— stomped into him. No woman should be able to shake his control and take over his body, but the moment he touched Joley's soft skin, felt the whisper of her warm breath against him, the touch of her lips, and tasted her, wild and addicting, he was lost.

His hands spanned her throat, tilting her head back so he could take her kiss, devour her the way he needed. Music burst through him, perfect notes he rarely heard. Fire and ice, wind and calm, sky and earth, water and rock all fused together. Joley seemed as wild and turbulent as the sea, yet beneath her fiery passion, at the very core of her, she was as forceful and strong and as constant as the deepest ocean currents. Ilya seemed as calm as a windless sea, yet beneath the surface smoldered a volcano of such explosive magnitude, his power could easily sweep everything from his path. Together they completed each other, his melody and hers merging into a single, perfect harmony.

It took him a moment to realize the odd rhythmic note was pounding on the door, not his heart or hers out of sync. The problem with them was that everything was exactly in sync. He forced himself to pull back, to breathe through the urgent demands of his body. He had to close his eyes to keep from responding to the naked need in her eyes.

"Help me here."

"You started it."

"Someone's at the door." He put her from him, noting that his hands were shaking. His famous control slipped dangerously around her. He could drown in her eyes if he wasn't careful, and he definitely got lost in the taste and texture of her.

Joley nodded, her fingers touching her lips. "I can still feel you—on my mouth—inside me. How do you do that?"

"I wish I was inside you. I ache like a son of a bitch. This has got to stop."

Her smile flashed, just the way he'd known it would. Joley could light up the world. She certainly could chase away the shadows in his.

"If you keep pushing me away, Ilya, we'll never get it to stop."

"Joley!" Brian's voice insisted. "Open up."

Instantly her face changed. "It's Brian. They're back from the police station."

The anxiety in her voice was real enough to slice into Ilya

like the razor edge of a knife. He wanted that anxiety for himself—not another man—not even her lead guitarist.

Joley yanked open the door and actually hauled Brian into the room and, ignoring her own long-standing rule, hugged him tight. "I was worried about you. Are you all right? They didn't hurt you, did they?"

Ilya leaned against the wall and observed the expressions chasing across her face. She looked like a fierce angel. What did she think? That the cops had used a rubber hose on Brian? The idea was absurd that they would touch him, not as famous as he was. And had she forgotten he'd had a lawyer with him?

Damn it. He couldn't stay here smoldering and drawing even more attention to himself. With some effort he managed to look and walk normally as he slipped past them. To his annoyance, Joley didn't do more than wave as he shut the door.

Brian watched Ilya go, a slight frown on his face as he turned back to Joley. "I'm fine. It was uncomfortable, but we got through it."

"I'm so sorry I asked you to talk to Dean in the first place. I should have done it."

"It didn't help that we had an argument right before someone murdered him, but I've never owned a gun in my life and don't even know how to fire one." Brian shrugged. "I just told the truth. I told them you'd asked me to speak to him about the missing girl and inviting teens to parties and hoped they believed me."

"The cops told Jerry we can do the show tonight," Brian added with some relief. "They let us both go. I got here as fast as I could to do the sound check and Jerry's ordered the crew to break everything down fast after the show so we can get on the road as soon as possible." Brian ran both hands through his hair. "Man, I freaked when the FBI agent showed up."

"FBI?" Joley echoed. "What's that about?"

"Branscomb said they were a small town and the local FBI was giving them a hand." Brian sighed. "I never want to do that again. They asked me the same questions over and over, and I began to think I was saying something wrong."

"What exactly did happen between you and Dean?" Joley asked. "Tish didn't want me going over there just in case someone was taking video. I should have though."

"You would have made it worse. He was furious and told

us we didn't have any right to tell him who he could or couldn't see. He didn't remember her name, but he said, and I'm quoting here, 'She wanted it.' "

Joley groaned. "Damn that man. He had to have known she was a child. Give her alcohol and she'd say anything he wanted to hear."

"Well, if you were looking for remorse, he didn't have any, and he could have cared less that the girl was missing. Jerry's pretty hard, but Dean's cavalier attitude that the girl was still missing got to him. Jerry fired him and Dean said all kinds of things about you, which pissed me off." Brian showed her his knuckles, looking a bit sheepish. "I haven't hit anyone since eighth grade. I had to tell the cop I hit him, and believe me, that doesn't sound so good when the guy ends up dead."

"Did they ask you about the Russian mob?"

He nodded. "After our conversation about Nikitin I was worried. And a few of his men have been hanging around here checking things out."

"I was running with Ilya Prakenskii," Joley said. "He gets upset when I don't take a bodyguard with me." She was careful to watch him closely just in case he'd observed Ilya leaving after her.

"That's good, at least we know he didn't do it." Brian frowned at her. "Your face changes when you talk about him. Do you two have something going on?"

"I don't want to talk about him."

Brian scowled at her. "Oh, you *so* have something going on with the bodyguard. Isn't that against the personal protector code or something?"

Joley knew she looked guilty. "He's not my bodyguard and we're not in a relationship. We're just sort of dancing around the idea."

"Look, Joley," he said, rubbing the bridge of his nose and peering at her. "I'll admit he's got some kind of mesmerizing cobra-before-the-strike appeal, but you can't be serious. And before you go all crazy on me, you remember you told me to say something the next time I saw you going off the deep end for a loser." He held up his hand. "And don't say he's not a loser. Maybe he's not a pill-popping, woman-beating asshole, but he's the kind of man who would strangle you with his bare hands if you weren't faithful to him."

Outrage swept through her. "I have *never* cheated on any-one. *Never.*"

"There you go, losing your mind. I knew you would. I meant to point out what kind of man he is, not what kind of woman you are."

Joley threw her arms up into the air, signaling she'd had enough of the conversation. "Let's go," she said. "We have to talk to everyone and settle them down for the show. Everyone has to be freaked."

"Logan was afraid Tish might leave, but she's not like that. She's steady as a rock," Brian said, stepping aside so Joley could exit the bus first.

Lights immediately blinded her as cameras went off all around them. Hands caught at her, tearing at her clothes. She was jerked off the stairs and she nearly fell, catching herself at the last moment. A hard hand shoved her in the back, pro-pelling her forward and down. She fell hard, Brian's shout mingling with the questions coming from all around her. She caught a glimpse of the Reverend's bodyguard disappearing to the back of the swarm, malicious satisfaction on his face.

Flashes went off as she pushed herself off the ground. One cameraman crouched beside her as if to help her up. "Are you and Brian a couple? Are you seeing each other?" He thrust a recorder closer to her.

"Joley!" Brian called to her, clearly trying to get through the mass surrounding her.

More flashes went off. "You're all such gentlemen," she murmured under her breath, wishing she had Hannah's pow-ers. She'd turn them all into toads—well, maybe Hannah couldn't exactly turn them into big, ugly, wart-covered toads, but she might be able to pull off the warts. She rarely went anywhere anymore, not even with her sisters, unless she was in her hometown, where the people protected her. This was her life, every second recorded and photographed until there seemed nothing left for her.

Large hands caught at her and yanked her to her feet, set-ting her up against a hard body. Ilya dragged her beneath his shoulder, his long arm covering her head, and caught at Brian with his other arm, pulling him in his wake as he began to walk them through the pushing and shoving photographers. His eyes were twin glittering diamond chips, hard and burning with fire. He kept moving even when photographers got in his way, wading through them as if they weren't there. He never responded to their questions or taunts, just took Joley and Brian through the mass toward the stage.

Security swarmed around them in the form of police officers, men who worked as security in off-duty hours. They began shepherding the reluctant paparazzi out of the area while Joley's crew formed a line across the entrance to the stage, blocking the cameramen off so Ilya could get the two of them to safety.

"Are you hurt?" Ilya asked, moving faster as the cops took control. He kept his voice low. "Tell me if you're injured."

Joley realized she was shaking. "I'm just angry. I tore my jeans and skinned my knees and hands. RJ's bodyguard shoved me down. I'll bet he got them in."

"What about you, Brian?" Ilya asked. "Are you hurt?"

"Just my pride. I saw Joley go down and couldn't get to her. It's like that anywhere she goes. It's bad, but not like that for the rest of us. She can't get a cup of coffee or go out without them mobbing her. I should have been able to protect her."

"That rotten coward set me up," Joley bit out between her teeth. "I'm *so* going to get him back." She was struggling not to cry, not wanting to admit how terrifying that couple of minutes had been, lying vulnerable and exposed on the ground surrounded by a mob.

The crew opened their line and allowed the three of them onto the stage. As they made it to safety Ilya let go of Brian and turned to fully face Joley, his hands on her arms. "You leave RJ's people to me. This is getting out of hand and you need to be safe, Joley. If RJ is trying to harm you and his people are using the paparazzi to do it, you can't give him any openings."

His eyes swept over her, taking in the torn jeans and the smears of dirt on her clothing. She was trembling. His hands fit around her waist, and he lifted her to the platform where Denny's drums were assembled.

"He's right, Joley," Brian said. "That was plain scary. Anyone could have stuck a knife in you and no one would have known until it was too late. There were too many of them. You went down so fast, and their instincts weren't to help; they all wanted pictures of you on the ground. I'll bet the headlines are going to say you were drunk or doing drugs."

Joley wanted to smash something. That was part of the problem with her life—there were aspects that were so out of control—and she had lost her sense of humor over it. She had money, lots of it, more than she could ever need in her lifetime. She had put it to good use, of course; she had Libby for a sister, and Libby made certain they were all very aware of every environmental issue as well as humanitarian one. But money didn't get her freedom; in fact, just the opposite. The higher she'd risen in fame, the narrower her world had become, the fewer people she could trust.

She loved singing and she loved performing, but she hadn't been able to strike enough of a balance with the paparazzi to get them to give her some space, and she was drowning. For the second time in her career, she was considering quitting—giving it all up. She had no idea what she'd do, but the life was making her physically ill. She couldn't sleep at all anymore, and even her intense exercise was no longer helping.

Ilya's hands were warm on her knees, and she knew he was healing the small scrapes. His energy was strong. She felt his heat, and for one moment white light burst through his darkened aura. She glimpsed a multitude of colors, and then the shadows drew across him like a veil, closing his real character off to her, although she felt she was beginning to see the real Ilya through all the little glimpses.

"Thanks." Her voice was too intimate, and she saw Brian glance at her sharply. She cleared her throat and tried again. "Thanks for getting us out of there, Ilya, I—we really appreciate it. We've got to get moving on the sound check. We've only got a couple of hours before the performance tonight. Where's Jerry?"

"Right here." Jerry came up behind her. "Are you all right?"

She nodded. "Did security clear them all out of here?"

"For now." Jerry stuck out his hand to Ilya. "Thanks for helping out. I'd like to talk to you later if you can spare a couple of minutes." He waved his hand around to encompass the scene. "I'm busy right now, but can we get together after this?"

Ilya nodded.

Joley slid off the platform, brushing at the dirt on her clothes. "Jerry, call everyone in. We need to talk about what happened . . ." Beside her, Ilya stirred, not physically—he didn't move a muscle—but she felt the impact of his reprimand mentally. She sighed. "To settle everyone down before the performance."

As if I have to explain myself to you. I don't need your approval for anything. But she had explained, and that made her angry at herself. She was getting used to his domineering ways, which meant he was wearing down her defenses.

She sent Ilya a snippy look and turned back to the business at hand. "These people have paid money to see us, and we need to be able to deliver a good show if we're going on tonight."

Ungrateful little wretch.

He simply reached for her hand and slid his thumb across her palm. Her body nearly convulsed with pleasure. Shivers slid down her spine; her womb spasmed and her nipples tightened. He sent her the impression of a wicked smirk even though his expression remained absolutely impassive. And then he walked away.

Joley lost her train of thought. She simply stood there with her mouth open and her heart pounding and her body throbbing with urgent need. Damn him. He always seemed to get in the last word. She rubbed her itching palm against her thigh. Maybe not. She lifted her hand to her mouth, rounded her lips to press them tight against her palm, took a long slow lick right over the center and followed it with a sensuous scraping of her teeth along the skin.

Ilya stumbled. His perfectly graceful, fluid walk faltered and he nearly tripped over his own feet. He glanced over his shoulder at her, and she flashed her sweetest smile. Suddenly feeling very good about things, she turned her attention to the assembling crew and band members, leaving Ilya to think about how she could even things out.

The little minx. Ilya walked a short distance away and draped his large body in a casual pose against the wall, crossing his arms and trying to ease the aching discomfort in the front of his jeans. He'd handed her a hell of a weapon to use against him. He was sporting the biggest hard-on he'd ever had, and he'd had a few. Back in school they'd used very talented women to train him. The idea was to stay in control, and when he didn't, the consequences had been immediate, painful and dire.

In one stroke of her tongue, Joley had wiped out years of brutal training. He'd felt her lips suddenly close over him, her tongue stroke down the hard length of him, teeth just barely scraping, and he'd nearly burst out of his jeans. The woman learned fast, and she was just mean enough to use her knowledge. Keeping the upper hand with her wasn't going to be as easy as he'd thought. He willed the blood in his veins to cool to a slow, simmering boil while he stood there watching with hawk eyes the crowd around her.

He could handle sex. Any kind of sex with any woman, and he would stay in complete control; his years of training had seen to that. But he was finding out—much to his horror—that emotion—real emotion—changed everything and made sex something far beyond what he'd ever been shown or taught. There was no controlling his desire or his body when his heart was involved. Damn her, she'd turned his life upside down, turned the very foundations of his life from hard rock to sand. His need for Joley had turned the pleasurable act of sex into something altogether different. Now he knew why people used the phrase "falling in love." The drop was long and scary.

Joley was all too aware of Ilya. He made every nerve ending in her body come alive. Her soul sang to his. It was corny, but true. And his answered. She didn't know what that meant exactly, only that she was hyperaware of him and the fact that his aura was drowning in lust—and *she'd* done that with one stroke of her tongue on the center of her palm. That palm that had plagued her for months. He had seemed stunned by her touch, even if it was through their weird connection. She turned that piece of information over in her mind, even as she addressed her crew. She wasn't exactly as powerless in her odd relationship with Ilya as she had always believed.

Everyone was subdued, some openly distraught and afraid. All had been questioned by the police, and a few were ambivalent about going on with the show. No one seemed terribly upset about Dean's death. He'd kept to himself for the most part, and the crew seemed to want to distance themselves from him. Maybe it was the nature of the murder—the suspicion that it had been a mob hit, and no one wanted any part of that.

She looked them over carefully, noting auras and melodies, unconsciously searching for the one that she'd glimpsed in

New York with Dean. She spotted him toward the back of the pack, a swirling of brownish-green mud coated with speckles of dark gray and streaks of murky pink. The aura puzzled her, as every color was muddy and dirty. She glanced from him to Ilya, her unease difficult to hide.

"Let's give these people a concert. Whatever happened with Dean, the police will handle it. Thank you all for cooperating. The detective was able to clear us to perform, so let's get it done. I believe we have a sound check to conduct."

The crew broke out into assents, nodding heads and talking all at once. She pulled Brian aside and nodded toward the man who was hastily ducking behind heavier equipment, clearly staying out of her way.

"Who is that?"

Brian shrugged. "John or Jake or Joe, something with a 'J.' I don't know, why?"

She glanced around. Several of the crew, a few of the security people, as well as Nikitin's guards were still observing her. For all she knew, the long-range zoom lenses of the photographers were watching—and she could feel Ilya's gaze boring into her back.

"No reason. I just thought maybe I should get to know the people traveling with us a little bit. We used to know everyone, and I think some of our crew have the wrong idea about me." She pushed a hand through her hair, realized she was trembling, and put her fist behind her back. Ilya's warning had affected her more than she liked. She didn't want anyone thinking Brian knew anything he shouldn't. "Never mind. I just don't like people thinking I'm a diva."

Once more her gaze was pulled over toward the man with the muddy aura. She tried not to look, but she couldn't help it. And he was staring back at her with a mixture of fear and anger. He knew she recognized him. He straightened slowly, maintaining eye contact, obviously trying to intimidate her. Suddenly his gaze shifted from her to the three Russian security guards off to his left, and then to Ilya, who had come up behind her.

Ilya took her arm and pulled her slightly away from Brian. "Explain all this to me. What are you doing?" *Keep looking at me.*

She wasn't cut out for intrigue. Her eyes kept shifting toward the crew member she knew had hung out with Dean. Everyone had professed to the detective that Dean was a loner and rarely talked to any of them. That had taken on a sinister aspect when she realized everyone was afraid to be associated with him. She kept her eyes locked with Ilya's. He was so good at it, looking as casual as a coiled rattler, which was the way he always looked.

"Well, each venue where we perform has different acoustics." She tried to keep her voice even, but it trembled.

She cleared her throat. Brian had walked off and was talking to one of the sound crew, and the man with the muddy aura walked over to him. Everything in her shifted. From scared she went into protective mode. She even took a step in their direction, but Ilya shackled her wrist, preventing her from moving.

"Keep talking. I'd like to understand."

He kept his smile easy, although it never reached his eyes. Joley knew he was buffering her. She took a deep breath and tried to play along, even as she kept an eye on Brian. "When I say different, I mean very different. You can hear a perfect pitch, so you're aware of sound quality. We have to make up for the differences at each venue. The PA is tuned before each concert to get the system ready for a performance. Our sound engineer is very particular about his equipment, and he makes certain everything checks out before the band goes up. He always checks each instrument alone and then blended together. That gives us a rough idea how it's all going to sound for the show."

Ilya watched out of the corner of his eye as the man who had been friends with Dean inched closer, all the while talking animatedly to Brian. Ilya had been investigating the band and crew for some time, and he knew the man's name was John Dylan. Dylan had been working on and off for the band for the last two years. He'd traveled to Europe twice with them and had a good reputation as a crew member. He showed up for work, worked hard and didn't party so hard he was hungover the next morning. Most of Ilya's inquiries had resulted in positive things. Dylan was somewhat of a loner, but well liked, hung out mainly with Dean and mostly smoked pot rather than did harder drugs.

Nothing about Dylan had singled him out as someone who

would have a mob affiliation, but he was clearly trying to overhear what Joley was saying, and the look he'd shot her earlier had alarmed Ilya. Fear could make people do things they ordinarily wouldn't consider. And the Russian mob ruled with fear.

The sound engineer called out to the band. "Let's get the instruments. Yours, Brian. Let's hear sound."

The band was already loosely assembled. Joley started over to them, Ilya keeping close pace, his body between hers and Dylan's at all times. He glanced out over the amphitheater. "The audience would change everything," he observed. "Don't they absorb some frequencies, and the sound would echo on the walls and ceilings of most buildings. In this case, the rocks."

She nodded. "That's why I have a genius for a sound engineer. The first two songs during the actual performance generally give him an immediate idea of what's going to happen, and he compensates for it. Are you staying for the check? You might find it interesting. Sometimes we get a few people who sneak in to listen so they can get an idea of what we're doing in the show. When I want to introduce new material into the show, or Brian or Rick has something they've worked on, we rehearse it several times during sound check before adding it in."

She picked up the microphone and turned toward her sound engineer. He lifted a hand and Denny counted off with a drumbeat. The band instantly swung into a familiar song, one that had been a number one hit for weeks on end and was always in demand. Ilya listened, but his gaze was moving over the crew members, yet always keeping Nikitin's security guards in his vision as well. He wanted to know if they even went close to Dylan. The crew member appeared to be concentrating on his job, crouched down back behind the sound engineer. The last notes of the song died away.

"Everyone okay with levels? Okay with guitar, Brian?"

Brian nodded. "Good here. Joley, let's try the new number."

She lifted the microphone to her mouth and smiled at Ilya. His heart nearly stopped beating. She was hazardous to herself as well as to everyone around him. Any woman who could make him forget he was surrounded by danger, by cameras, by the damned Russian mob, was truly dangerous. "I hope you like this one. I wrote it."

She glanced at Denny, who immediately went into action, his drumsticks twirling and then pounding down in a dynamic burst of powerful rhythm. The guitar came in, the music aggressive, and then Joley's voice broke over them, passionate and intense and drowning in a sultry melody of notes. When she stopped, there was a small silence.

"Is everyone okay with everything? Are we good?" Joley turned to survey the band.

Ilya let out his breath. They were used to her, but her voice still got to all of them—he could tell by the short pause.

"A little more bass," the sound engineer finally said. "Can you give me a little more, Rick?"

Denny picked up a glass and swallowed the contents. "I'm having a little trouble hearing."

Each instrument performed a long solo until it received a thumbs-up from the sound engineer. He then nodded to Joley. She swung into the next number, one, Ilya noted, that they sang often. They moved back and forth between the well-known numbers they were familiar with and the newer numbers, to ensure that everything was perfect for their audience.

The natural acoustics of the place were incredible. He watched Joley perform. Her love of music showed in the way she poured herself into every song. Joy was on her face, in her eyes, in the color of her aura. She had a loving relationship, more like siblings, with the band, and an easy, familiar relationship with her sound crew. The others she might not know so well, but those traveling with her obviously cared about her in the same way she cared for them.

"That's it," she said, coming up to him. "We run through our song list once and hopefully nothing goes wrong tonight. What did you think?"

He thought she was the most beautiful, vibrant woman alive, but he merely nodded his head and escorted her back to the bus.

9

JOLEY glanced around the small all-night diner where the buses had stopped. Her band and the crew were traveling together to Dallas in a caravan, and they'd all been hungry. They'd broken down the stage in record time and gotten on the road, still anxious over Dean's death in spite of the fact that the show had been good—not great—but good. Joley hoped they performed better in Dallas.

She walked to the largest round booth, where Denny was sitting, and put a hand on his shoulder. "How'd it go with Lisa?" There was compassion in her voice.

The other band members went silent, waiting, willing things to have gone well for Denny. He had lines on his face that hadn't been there before.

Denny shrugged. "We talked and I think it was good. At least she didn't just walk away from me like I deserved. But she has a son and she said she needed some time to think about us. She doesn't want him getting attached to me and then me walking out on them."

Joley rubbed his arm through his sleeve. "That's fair. She doesn't want to risk her son, and that's admirable. You just have to show her that you mean it, Denny. That you're capable of being faithful and committing to her and your relationship."

"She flew back home after the Red Rocks concert. I didn't want her hanging around just in case it wasn't safe," Denny added.

Joley slid into the booth. "Surely whatever Dean was up to didn't have anything to do with us."

"Whatever it was, I'm hoping it's a long way from us," Rick said. "I heard every single bone in his body was broken. Can I just say ouch?"

"He was an ass, but he didn't deserve that," Jerry said.

Logan wedged himself into the booth, scooting close to Joley. "Do you think his murder had anything to do with the disappearance of that girl? The cops were asking questions about the Russian mob. Maybe Nikitin is involved with them . . ."

"Shut up, Logan," Brian admonished him. "Nikitin isn't involved in the mob."

"You ought to know," Logan said. "You hang out with him all the time." He plopped a stack of tabloids and magazines in front of Joley. "Take a look at these, my little sister."

Joley glanced around the diner. Few people were there at three in the morning, but several of the workers had cell phones with cameras and recorders. They were busy texting their friends. The band would be lucky if the place didn't fill up immediately in spite of the hour. She sighed. It didn't seem to matter where they went, they couldn't ever have a quiet meal.

She glanced at the stack of papers Logan put in front of her. "What are we up to now?"

The rest of the band pushed into the booth, making her grateful Denny'd chosen the largest round one. Everyone peered at the dramatic headlines.

"We're married, Joley. A secret wedding with our secret baby." He pulled one out of the stack and placed it on top. "You had the baby and we've been hiding it."

She laughed. "You have to be kidding me. Your 'love' child was splashed all over the papers a week ago. Let me see that."

"Joley, you rock, girl," Rick said, ripping open a cracker from the little basket on the table. "How could you stay so slim and be pregnant? You hid it well."

"Didn't I?" She spread the paper on the table so they could all see.

The photographs had been taken of the two of them standing with the baby in front of the band's bus. Joley was holding the baby and Logan was standing behind her, hands on her shoulders, looking down at his child. The next picture showed him kissing the top of Joley's head. The third photograph showed Joley placing the baby in his arms, and in the fourth he was climbing into the bus to "hide" their child.

She scanned the article. "Wow. I supposedly had this baby while on tour. How cool is that? All that working out kept me from showing, although apparently once or twice they thought they saw a baby bump." She looked down at her flat stomach. "I need to do more sit-ups."

Brian rolled his eyes. "You've already got a six-pack there, Joley. Pretty soon the tabloids are going to say you swing both ways."

"I think they did that a year or so ago," Logan pointed out.

Joley looked around. "Where's Tish? Has she seen this one?"

Long ago, Tish had told them all to either ignore the tabloids totally or assume every word in them was a lie and just enjoy the ridiculous absurdity of it. Looking back, Joley realized how truly sage her advice had been. Living in the spotlight, with no letup, was an exercise in endurance. It made them all immensely popular, but in the end, they had all begun to crack. They'd come to feel like hunted animals, stalked every moment of every day. Tish had also told them they had to find ways to live out of the spotlight when they weren't touring, which had been one of the things that saved them all. Her advice was one of many things Joley missed about her.

"She just changed the baby, but she's coming."

"Well, make room for her. I don't want to be the only chick at the table."

Logan pulled another paper from the stack and smoothed it out in front of them all. "Yes, Tish has seen the tabloids, and this one is her particular favorite."

The band members crowded closer, hovering over each other's shoulders to peer down at the magazine.

"Wow, Joley," Denny said. "Check it out. You've always wanted a ready-made family, and now you have one without ruining your figure."

Brian whistled. "I had no idea that was so important to you, but hey, it's right here in the headlines. You want children but don't want a matronly body."

"Well I am just so vain." Joley blew on her fingernails.

Rick pointed to another headline. "This says child protective services are investigating you for drug and alcohol consumption, and that you left the baby in a restroom and we had to turn the buses around to go back for her. Wow, Joley, that's kind of sick."

Leo tugged at strands of her hair. "You were in the restroom doing one of the band members and Logan is devastated."

"I'm sorry, Logan, but seriously, you're two-timing me with Tish, so I feel you sort of deserve it. And which band member am I doing this time?" Joley asked, leaning her chin into her hand and batting her eyes at him.

"The handsome one," Rick said. "Me."

"Ooh baby," Joley cooed and blew a kiss at him.

Laughter bubbled up as the waitress came over. She appeared starry-eyed and breathless. "Do you think I could get an autograph? And maybe a picture with you?" she asked.

"How 'bout this, sweetheart?" Brian said. "We'll all sign autographs for you and your crew and take pictures if the place doesn't suddenly fill up with friends, family and reporters. We'd just like a quiet meal."

She nodded her head several times, held up a finger and ran over to the counter to whisper to the other waitress and the cook, before coming back to take their orders. The other waitress struggled with getting orders from the crew.

Joley looked around. Even with no other customers, they took up most of the room. Granted, it was a small diner, but how different this all was from how it had been in the beginning, when the band had no one but Tish traveling with them. Now there were so many . . . Her gaze collided with ice-blue eyes. Her breath caught in her throat. Ilya Prakenskii stood just to the side of the booth where he could hear everything that was said. And she hadn't been aware of him. Her palm hadn't even itched—until now.

"What are you doing here?" Joley asked, trying not to stare. She didn't know whether to feel belligerent or exhilarated.

"I asked him to come," Jerry said. "I felt maybe we should beef security up a little around everyone until the end of the tour."

"But he has a job," Brian protested. "And you should have consulted me."

Joley ducked her head, not looking at any of them, least of

all Ilya. It was scary having him around so much, because the more she saw him, the less resistance she seemed to have.

"He's on temporary loan," Jerry said. He beckoned Ilya to sit down.

Ilya shook his head. "I'm fine right here."

Tish, holding the baby, squeezed in and flashed Ilya a tentative smile. "I feel for you, trying to guard Joley. She's not the most cooperative."

"Hey now!" Joley objected. "I'm the epitome of cooperation."

A groan went up around the booth.

"He's not the kind of bodyguard who needs cooperation," Jerry said, casting Joley a hard look.

She sat up straight. "What does that mean?"

"It means his job is to keep you safe. I'm getting gray hair reading your hate mail lately. And after Dean was murdered, I don't want to sit up nights wondering if some nut is going to kill you right in front of all of us, so I've hired him to keep you alive and told him to use whatever means it takes."

"Umm, Jerry," Joley said, beginning to smolder with fury. She carefully avoided Ilya's slashing blue gaze. "You work for me. You're supposed to clear this kind of thing with me. And it isn't cleared."

"I had a long talk with Jonas and your sister Sarah. They both agreed we need to cover you better, especially if the Russian mob is in any way involved."

"He's Russian," Brian snapped. "Nikitin probably fired him and he's been hanging around making you think we need him, Jerry. Seriously, are you crazy?"

At once Joley felt protective toward Ilya, a complete contradiction. Sometimes she felt her emotions around him were like a Ping-Pong ball, just jumping all over the place. "Rein it in, Brian. Sheesh. The man is standing right there listening to every word you say."

"I'm backing you up," Brian pointed out.

"You're being mean about it. Nikitin didn't fire him, he wouldn't." Probably for more reasons than she wanted to know, but she was certain she was right.

"Nikitin loaned him to us to keep Joley safe."

"You know, I don't know why all of you think I'm the only one in danger. Every one of us is hanging out there."

"Maybe because you live your life in the tabloids," Ilya interjected, his voice low and controlled.

"That's not fair," Brian objected. "It's not like we ask for the paparazzi to follow us everywhere we go and make up lies."

"It's still a choice. And this," Ilya leaned over Joley's shoulder and snapped the paper with his finger, "this is dangerous. There are people who believe this crap. They want to believe it and they fixate on it."

Joley glared at him, crumpled the tabloid and threw it at him. "You don't have to approve of my lifestyle. I don't want or need your approval."

Brian shoved at his glass of water, spilling it on the table. "He can't be her bodyguard, Jerry. Personal protectors can't think clearly when they're in a relationship with the protectee, and he's screwing her."

Tish gasped audibly. The band members looked at one another. Ilya simply caught the front of Brian's shirt in his fist and hauled him over the back of the booth, bringing him up on his toes. Joley covered her face with her hands, imagining all the cells phones out, both recording and taking photos.

"You owe Joley an apology." Ilya's voice was whisper-low, but it cut like a knife. "You're supposed to be her friend and you're deliberately hurting her and trying to publicly humiliate her."

Rick stood, too. "Brian, that was way over the line."

"Whoa, dude," Logan added, "if he doesn't kick your ass for that, I'm going to have to do it and I haven't kicked ass in ten years."

Tish put her arm around Joley and glared at Brian as Ilya shoved him back to solid ground. Brian rocked back on his heels, straightened his shirt and looked at the band, who were all gaping at him in horror.

"That's not cool," Leo weighed in.

"What the hell's gotten into you, bro?" Denny asked. "You've been acting weird for a couple of weeks now. You pissed at Joley for something?"

Brian glared at Ilya, obviously considered trying to punch him and then changed his mind, and climbed over the booth to sit back down. "Sorry, Joley. And I'm apologizing because it was a lousy thing to say, not because muscle man got physical."

Joley didn't look at him. Other than her sisters, Tish, and Jonas, she counted Brian and the others as her best friends—more even—family. Brian had been a little off for a while now. She considered that he might be jealous of Ilya, but truthfully, Brian didn't think of her in that way. He offered, but he wasn't really attracted to her.

Tish shifted, drawing her attention. The baby was sound asleep cradled against her in a sling. Joley was grateful for the distraction. "My sister's pregnant."

Logan snorted and ruffled her hair. "You have like a hundred sisters. Which one?"

"Hannah. I'm so excited for her. Jonas is walking on air, but I'll bet he's turned all bossy on her."

Logan laughed. "From everything you've said about him, I'm betting he was already that way." He leaned in to kiss the baby's cheek, his mouth very close to Tish. "I'm never letting Lissa date. Men are pigs." He rested his head on Tish's shoulder. She didn't look at him, but she didn't move away. "Even the good ones can act like pigs sometimes."

Brian gave an overly loud sigh. "I suppose you're referring to me. Okay, fine. I deserve it."

Everyone laughed, including Joley, although she had to force it. She wanted to forgive Brian, but part of her was still hurt, and she had never been very good at forgiveness, even with her closest friends.

The food was surprisingly good, or maybe they were all just very hungry. Joley tried not to be so aware of Ilya. He had such a powerful energy, yet he seemed to be able to blend into the background, which made no sense until she detected the subtle flow of power in the room. He used his gifts to aid him in disappearing in plain sight, which was probably how he'd kept her palm from giving away his presence earlier.

Conversation flowed around her, and Joley managed to laugh at the appropriate places, but she didn't feel like it. Outside her family and Jonas, Brian had been her closest friend. She had always been extra careful never to intrude on his thoughts. She enjoyed his company and looked forward to their conversations. He came from a very wealthy family and had attended private school, although he'd always remained best friends with the band members, from the time they were young boys first playing sports together. He dressed a little neater and had incredible manners and definitely was more sensitive toward others. He was probably everyone's favorite. And he'd always been the most diplomatic—until now.

"Hey, Joley," Jerry said, "you falling asleep on us?"

"The scintillating conversation is so profound, how could I ever fall asleep?" Joley let her head droop onto the table and pretended to snore.

Ilya's gaze narrowed when Rick threw a biscuit at her and then leaned over to brush the hair from her face, his fingers staying on the silken strands of her hair. The touch held enough affection that Ilya's belly knotted up. He had observed the waitresses and cooks taking numerous pictures of the band and Joley eating. A couple of them had tried to take videos, and he was fairly certain that before dawn the videos would be playing on the Internet.

Joley looked up suddenly and her gaze collided with his. She sent him a small, sad smile that nearly tore out his heart. It was a jolt to feel such deep emotion just from one little exchange. He knew she was upset. Why didn't her friends know? How could they all sit there, joking and laughing when she wanted to cry? He had the urge to simply pick her up, cradle her close and take her out of there.

Jerry glanced at his watch. "Let's give these folks a couple of pictures and get on the road. We have a schedule."

Ilya moved into a better position to protect Joley as the band began to pose for photographs with the waitresses and kitchen staff. She was gracious and talked to each one of them, shaking hands when they were offered, even though he could see by her expression that she was being overwhelmed with emotion and information about each person.

More people entered the diner, and Ilya was aware of cars pulling into the parking lot. He waded through the group and took Joley's elbow, smiling politely, but distantly, making certain to look as intimidating as possible.

"Miss Drake, if you don't leave now, you won't make your next concert on time," he reminded her, already moving her away from the growing crowd.

She went with him, staying close to his body but giving him enough room to maneuver should he have to. Twice she brushed against him, and she had to have felt the harness beneath his jacket as they walked out the door into the parking lot.

Her cell phone rang and she paused to flip it open.

"Bitch." The voice was distorted but loud enough for Ilya to hear.

She looked up at him a little helplessly, her face pale, her gaze colliding with his. He leaned down to listen. She didn't try to pull away from him or stop him. The voice on the other end was filled with menacing hatred, even through the obvious device the person was using to distort their voice. It was impossible to tell if it was a man or a woman. The voice sounded computer-generated.

"You think your sister was fucked up? Back the hell off, or you're going to be cut into so many little pieces no one will ever be able to identify you."

The call ended as abruptly as it had begun. Even as Ilya listened, his eyes slashed around the parking lot, noting where each member of the crew or band was, and whether or not they were using a cell phone. He put the phone in his pocket. "I'll have Jerry get you another."

"They mentioned my sister. Why did they do that? Why would they say anything about what happened to Hannah? That was the mob, Ilya. Ever since Abbey met Aleksandr, we've had nothing but problems with them." As soon as the words were spoken aloud, she clapped her hand over her mouth, her expression horrified. Tears swam in her eyes. "I didn't mean that. I don't know why I thought it, let alone said it. I didn't mean it."

Say nothing, laskovaya moya, *until we are out of the open.*

"Joley!" Brian called. "You want me to ride with you?"

Joley nearly choked. She was suddenly very frightened. The Russian mob had wreaked havoc on her family, nearly killing Hannah. Twice now, they'd had encounters with them, and with Nikitin following her every move, she felt trapped. Brian had been acting so strange, she didn't trust anyone at all. Sea Haven, her hometown, was the only safe place, yet if the mob was after her, she didn't dare head home and endanger her family again.

Wave to Brian. Tell him you're fine. He's feeling guilty for the way he acted and the things he said.

Ordinarily Joley would have objected to the order and tone, but this time she let Ilya take over, waving halfheartedly at Brian and blowing him a kiss as Ilya moved her toward her bus. She could hear laughter and chatter as the band and crew boarded their buses. Ilya kept his body between her and everyone else as they neared her bus.

Coming at you. Keep your head down.

It was all the warning she had. Flashes went off as the paparazzi swarmed around her. Ilya didn't slow down, wading through them without speaking, his face set in grim lines, his arm over her head. She heard her name called countless times. Once she felt the impact as someone bumped into Ilya hard and his weight shifted slightly into her, but with his large muscle mass he was nearly as immovable as a rock.

She moved with him naturally, as if they were dancing, her steps perfectly in tune to his. They could have rehearsed their walk to the bus. Ilya made it all matter-of-fact, without urgency, as if they were simply strolling through a crowd, instead of being mobbed.

She felt safe. Joley took a breath and absorbed that knowledge. In the midst of the threat, the murder, and the crush of paparazzi, Ilya made her feel completely safe. He didn't push or shove or threaten anyone. They stood in front of him and he looked through them, and then walked through them. Something about the set of his shoulders, the expressionless look on his tough features and the cold look in his eyes made even the most hardened veterans of the tabloid press move out of his way.

Ilya yanked open the door to her bus and thrust her in and to the side. "Stay there while I do a quick search."

The door between her driver and the home section of the bus was already closed, which meant Steve was in a hurry to leave. The feeding frenzy of the paparazzi only made him cranky, so it didn't surprise her when the bus roared to life. Ilya moved swiftly through it, checking every conceivable hiding place, including ones she hadn't even thought of. When she would have spoken, he shook his head and walked through a second time with a small device in his hand.

"We're clear," he said and stepped out of her way.

Joley flung herself on the couch. "Thanks. They must have gotten wind of us stopping. Someone at the diner had to have called. They'll get their fifteen minutes of fame, telling lies about us. Or making something out of our conversations."

"Who has your cell number?"

She shrugged. "I have to change it all the time. Usually Jerry and the band and my family. A few friends. I always let Tish have my number, and I think I gave it to Lisa. I meant to change it recently because Logan gave it to that whack job groupie's mother."

"That doesn't mean anything to me."

She sighed. "Logan had this brief fling with a groupie named Lucy Brady. She was absolutely nuts, and I mean certifiable. She caused so many scenes in public. He slept with her a few times, and then dropped her when he realized how crazy she was. She went after him with a broken bottle, which by the way is her favorite weapon. It happened more than once. She turned up pregnant and threatened to kill herself. We tried to tell Logan to just stay away from her, but he felt responsible. She was in and out of institutions the whole time she was pregnant, and in the end, Logan went through an attorney and Lucy gave up the baby. She didn't want it, but she did carry it, although once she was going to cut it out of her stomach, again with a broken bottle. That was really ugly."

"And she has your number?"

She rolled her eyes. "You don't have to sound like that. Her mother had the number, not Lucy. I never had anything to do with Lucy. She was very fixated on Logan, until he told her he was married." She leaned her head back against the cushions. "Our lives sound like a high school soap opera. Sheesh."

"What makes you want to live like this?" Ilya asked. "You have everything you could possibly want. And a family who loves and cares about you. What makes you want—or need— all of this?"

Joley inhaled sharply. The contempt in his voice stung. "You don't know me, Ilya. You only think you do. I may get lost sometimes, and it can be a struggle to stay centered, but I know who I am. I love music. This is my life because it makes sense. And every now and then a letter gets through to me, or someone comes up to me after a show and tells me my songs matter to them. What about you, Ilya? You're so good at handing out judgment. Do you love what you do? Are you sure what you do is the right choice for you?"

"I didn't have a choice. I do what I have to do to survive."
He took the chair across from her and stretched out his legs.
"Your voice changed my life."

The admission was so unexpected, it stunned her into silence for a moment. She searched his expression. As always, he gave nothing away. There was little softness about Ilya. He was hard and capable and could be counted on if he was on your side. She didn't know how she knew that about him, but the feeling in her was strong.

"How did my voice change your life?"

Ilya could see the genuine surprise on her face. Joley was so transparent, every thought that crossed her mind was telegraphed on her mobile features. He had no softer, happier memories. Grim, dark experiences, hard physical and mental labor and unrelenting pain had shaped who and what he had become—until Joley. She had unexpectedly given him back his humanity. Somewhere inside all of that calm discipline and control, she had tapped into long forgotten emotion. She had made the sun shine and taught him laughter. Maybe it was rusty in sound, and came rarely, but he now knew what true happiness felt like.

He cleared his throat, knowing he was going to give a piece of himself away. "I was in a very bad place, an ugly place, when I first heard your voice. You sounded like an angel, and I didn't believe in them. I didn't know joy in life until the first time I listened to a song by you. I knew duty and survival, but not joy or what it meant to really live. You gave that to me. I guess if you give that same thing to others, it's well worth the sacrifices you make, although to be honest, I don't like the danger it puts you in. I suppose that's selfish of me."

Joley's eyes softened, were almost luminous. For a moment he imagined he saw love in them. He'd never seen, or maybe recognized, love or thought much about it until he had crossed paths with the Drake family. They had a great capacity for loving—especially Joley. She was a wild thing, impetuous and compulsive, but she knew how to love fiercely, passionately and protectively. He hadn't known he wanted that for himself until he'd first laid eyes on her.

"I wish I could be as good a person as you make me out to be," Joley said. "I have a temper that I spend half my life having to rein in. I'm not at all like my sisters, Ilya. They really

are good people. I just can't seem to be forgiving and I have a
tendency to fly off the handle when people do stupid things."
She looked away from him, ducking her head as if something
about her character shamed her.

His gut tightened in reaction. "Why are you so afraid of
who you are, Joley? There's nothing wrong with you."

Lights flashed as cars went by and the sounds of traffic
filled the silence in the bus. She twisted her fingers together
and shrugged her shoulders.

"Maybe. Maybe not. You never really know what's inside
of people."

"That's not true of us. We see through different eyes and
hear sounds no one else hears. We touch other people's minds
and thoughts all too easily. You recognize evil when you see it.
So do I. Most people think evil is just a word. We know it ex-
ists and that it does terrible, vicious things and spreads as it
goes. We see one another, and I don't see anything in you that
you should ever be ashamed of."

"Maybe you don't see all of me. I know I don't see all of
you. I can't pierce the shadows of your aura. I've caught
glimpses, but you hide yourself very well—even from me, and
I've touched your mind a thousand times."

"But you know I'm not evil."

She bit her bottom lip and shivered a little. Ilya immediately rose and dragged the comforter from the bed to wrap her
in.

"No, you're not evil," she admitted, almost reluctantly.
"But I don't know what you are. You're not the sweet boy next
door, that's for sure."

"You don't want the sweet boy next door. If you did, you'd
be with Rick."

"Rick?" Her gaze jumped to his. "Why Rick? Brian's my
best friend."

"You're not attracted to Brian and he isn't attracted to you.
But you have some chemistry with Rick." His blue eyes
burned hot. "I don't like it, but it's there."

"You're nuts. He's like a brother. All the band members
are. I've never had sex with any of them, nor would I. It would
be gross."

He shrugged. "I believe you, but that doesn't negate the

fact that you find Rick attractive. In any case," he added before she could protest, "he can't meet your needs."

"My needs?" She stumbled over the last word. Her chin went up a little, and there was defiance in her tone as well as her expression. "And you think you know what I need?"

He leaned toward her. "I know exactly what you need. Why do you think you fight me so hard?"

Joley scowled at him. "You have an archaic view of relationships, Ilya. You think the man should dominate the woman, and that's so last century."

"How do you know what I think? You've never bothered to ask me."

That shut her up. She sat back and studied his face. "Well then, what do you think makes a good relationship?"

"Two people who complete one another. They should each complement the strengths and weaknesses of the other person. And they should meet one another's needs, spiritually, sexually and intellectually. I can do all those things for you. I can also protect the life you want to have. If you keep going as you're doing, you'll burn out in another couple of years. You're already starting to do that. I can provide the buffer you need between you and everyone else in order to allow you to continue with your career."

Okay, that sounded like heaven, too good to be true, but Joley knew life wasn't like that, so perfect and uncomplicated. "Why do you have to say all the right things, Ilya? You and I both know it wouldn't be that easy."

"It would if you let it, Joley." His voice turned tender. "You're exhausted and upset. Lie down and I'll get you to sleep."

"I never sleep."

"Unless I'm with you." He held out his hand to her. "You slept just fine the last time I was here. That's another item for the pro side of that list you were making."

Joley took his hand and let him tug her to her feet. "You got me in trouble with Sarah. That earned a lot of negative points you'll have to make up."

He settled her on the bed and brushed a kiss across her temple. "Fortunately I have a lot of other skills to make those points up fast."

Joley looked alarmed—and intrigued. "Really? Well save them for another time. I'm wiped out."

"I know, *lyubimaya moya*, go to sleep and I'll watch over you." He stretched out beside her. "And this should go on the pro side of your list as well," he muttered under his breath.

Joley curled close to him and, smiling, closed her eyes.

10

LYING beside any attractive woman for three hours could give a man a raging hard-on, but watching Joley sleep, with her lush, curvaceous body and her soft skin, had created a monster.

In those hours she barely moved, her face young and relaxed, the fingers of her hand curled against her palm as if protecting Ilya's mark. Dawn crept in through the blinds, spilling light across her face. She looked like an angel, with her silky hair in disarray on the pillow and her long lashes curving in two thick crescents on her cheeks. And then she moved restlessly, turning toward him, whispering his name, and he lost all pretense of control.

There was nothing saintly about him, and there never would be. There was no way he could lie beside her and not need to touch her soft skin or taste her wild, honeyed flavor. He had known, when the doors of the bus had closed, that he was going to seduce her. She wanted him. The truth was in her eyes when she looked at him, in the feminine fragrance of her body and the seductive sound of her voice. She was fighting her attraction because she didn't trust him, she didn't fully believe he wasn't the bad man he was reputed to be—but she wanted him with every cell in her body, in just the same way he wanted her.

His reaction to her, the first time he'd actually laid eyes on her, had been so physical, so sharp and strong, the ache in his body becoming a permanent part of him in her presence. He'd tried to convince himself he could have her and not be emotionally touched by her. She'd dashed that ridiculous hope completely.

Joley was a strong woman with strong moral convictions. The chemistry between them flared bright and hot, but he was a man in the shadows—and he had to remain there. It would take finesse to overcome Joley's convictions, and there would be repercussions, but damn, he'd waited as long as he could wait.

He needed to touch her silken skin, stroke his hands over her lush, curvy body, sink into the fiery heat of her and bury himself deep and hard, over and over, until she could never think of another man—look at another man—feel the least chemistry with another man, as she did with Rick Henderson, her bass player. She might not acknowledge that she did, but he felt a spark each time the two were together, and that was unacceptable to him. Her emotional dependence on Brian felt like a threat as well. Ilya wasn't into sharing any part of Joley.

He was through being the gentleman and protector; he was going to stake his claim in no uncertain terms, because if he didn't—he would go quietly insane. His body was already so sensitive he couldn't stand the painful press of fabric against his skin for even one more moment. With one hand he tore his shirt over his head, then he went around to every window and slid the privacy screens in place, signaling to everyone that Joley was sleeping and to leave her alone should they stop. He took the precaution of locking the door to the outside as well as the one to the driver's compartment because he wasn't going to allow any interruptions. He left one dim light on because he had to see her face, watch her emotion as he took possession of her.

He shed his jeans, grateful for the cool air on his hot body. His erection was fierce, thick and painful, a reminder of the months of long, sleepless nights when he'd lain in a cold bed and thought of her, his hand on his shaft and emptiness surrounding him. Nothing sated his need for her, no matter how many times he relieved himself or how many cold showers he took. One thought of her, the sound of her voice, her music, a glimpse of her brought the painful lust roaring back stronger than ever.

Joley. Just Joley. She was the sexiest woman he'd ever encountered, and he'd met many trained in the art of driving men wild. Joley needed no such training. She was naturally sensual with her curvy body, her husky voice and the fluid, feminine grace with which she moved. He bent his head to hers, unable to resist that full, beautiful mouth. He'd had a lot of fantasies about her mouth, warm and velvet soft and so perfect it could stop a man's heart.

He wasn't feeling gentle at all, he was feeling animalistic and in desperate need of taking her. He could hear his music now, not at all soft and bluesy, but wild and dominant like a heavy metal band. The pounding pulse of the music matched the way he needed to drive deep into her body. The heavy bass throbbed in his groin, and the drum beat through his veins demanding satisfaction. He caught both wrists as she came awake, stretching her arms above her head and pinning them to the mattress.

"Kiss me, Joley. Don't think. Just kiss me."

Beneath him, she froze, her lashes lifting. She looked dazed and drowsy, a little fearful, but she wanted him. He could see instant desire flare in her eyes.

Joley's breath stilled. For a moment she couldn't think or breathe. Butterflies whirled and danced in her stomach, fluttering their wings until every muscle bunched and tightened in anticipation. Immediately her body responded to his, this one man who would be her downfall if she let him. Desire pulsed hot and wet between her legs. Her entire body vibrated, almost as if humming to his song.

She was aware instantly that he was naked, and her gaze, of its own accord, shifted to his thick, heavily muscled chest, the bulging muscles in his arms. He was lying on his stomach beside her, and his butt was tight and firm and totally sculpted the way she'd always imagined. Her heart kicked in, and her blood heated, drowning her in desire.

She heard his song, blending with hers, the wild, intoxicating timbre, roughened with lust. There were more instruments beneath that hammering beat, the soft and tender notes of a flute, a violin moaning, almost pleading—*save me— save me*—and the saxophone introducing a haunting lonely note, but all that was nearly drowned out by the relentless pounding command of the drums and the crash of cymbals making adamant demands. His song merged with hers, blending and then overtaking hers, the wild strains a fiery, passionate declaration of ownership that swept away her resistance. The combination was heady and enticing, a powerful aphrodisiac she couldn't resist.

Arousal teased her breasts, danced over her thighs, slid into her stomach to wreak chaos. She stared up at the face only inches from hers. Strong-boned, straight nose, firm mouth, eyes as deep blue as the sea itself, eyes that were too old for his years, held too much knowledge and too much pain—or nothing at all. She inhaled sharply. Right now those blue eyes glittered with arousal—with lust—with the need for her—for the heat and fire she could provide.

"Kiss me, Joley." His voice was nearly a growl.

She recognized the command. He wouldn't close that scant inch between them; he was insisting she give herself to him.

"I'm afraid."

"I know." His hands framed her face, his body shifting even more to blanket hers. "Kiss me now."

"If I do this, there's no going back for me. You're asking me to give myself to you, and I won't ever be the same."

One hand, warm and rough, slid down her throat, over the swell of her breast, moved with infinite slowness over her thin shirt to find the hem. Fingers bunched the material and his fist caressed her stomach, still holding her shirt. "Kiss me."

Molten liquid pooled low and wicked. Inner muscles rippled and heated. His voice was implacable. Imperative. Commanding. The sound sent a shiver down her spine, teased her nipples into hard pebbles. She took a ragged breath. She was so susceptible to him.

"Ilya." His name came out a raspy whisper. A plea to save her from herself.

His head lowered, his silky hair brushing over her skin like caressing fingers. His lips brushed over her neck just below her ear, tongue licking wickedly, teeth scraping, sending her nerve endings into shock. He lifted his head again, his gaze, hot and hungry, colliding with her desperate one. "Kiss me, Joley. Stop running and kiss me."

Heat radiated from his body. His need for her surrounded her, enclosed her in raw sexual hunger. His song crashed around her, demanding her compliance, terrifying her even as it seduced her. Her womb contracted. Her obsession for him stole her breath. She knew what he was asking—no—demanding. He wanted surrender—complete surrender.

She touched his lips, tracing the firm, warm curves. "Do you know what you're asking of me? Do you really know who I am?" She was really asking if she was safe, but she could see by his expression he wouldn't let her get away with that. He insisted on blind trust.

"Damn it, Joley. Fucking kiss me now."

His voice was rough, agonized, almost a growl, but so sensual Joley felt a spasm in her deepest core. She cried out, a gasping plea, tormented with hunger for him. It seemed as if she'd needed him for so long she couldn't think of anything else but having him buried inside her. His hand slid down the slope of her belly, sending each muscle curling into a tight ball of desire. In desperation she closed that small distance, her mouth finding his, arms circling his neck, fists bunched in his hair, holding on as if to a life preserver.

Their tongues twined and danced, hot licks, desperate frenzied kisses, devouring one another, feeding on each other's passion. He kissed her as though his very life, his very survival depended on it. He kissed her as if he could never get enough of her or the taste of her.

He shifted again, throwing the cover from the bed onto the floor, his mouth never leaving hers, caging her with his body. She felt his heavy erection, thick and hard, pressed tight against her thigh, and another needy moan escaped.

Her head fell back as his mouth moved across her chin and down her throat, teeth taking small nips as if he wanted to take a bite out of her, his tongue easing each sting. His lips went to the neckline of her thin tee, and he frowned, lifting his head for a minute to look down at the cloth covering her heaving breasts. He simply caught at it with one hand and jerked hard, ripping the material from her body and tossing it aside. Her whole body clenched, her temperature shooting up at his display of impatience.

"Mine," he growled and lowered his head to feast on the swollen, aching mounds.

The harsh sound of his voice sent a ripple of fire shooting through her veins, nearly sending her over the edge, her body pulsing with desire, the muscles of her silken sheath clenching hard. His mouth was fiery hot, closing over her nipple, suckling strongly. Joley shivered as sensations poured through her.

She was terrified he had read her mind and would take her down a seductive path from which she could never return, yet she couldn't stop, couldn't find the will to resist his dark seduction. His body was hard and hot, spreading fire through her, sending electrical currents sizzling through her veins. His mouth was rough, sensuous; his lips pulled at her breast, sending lightning to her thighs and melting her inner flesh. His hands were even rougher than his mouth, teasing and pulling at her nipples, cupping the full mounds possessively. His teeth scraped and taunted, his tongue stroking each nipple with quick hot flicks that drove the breath from her body.

His hands slid down her body, shaping her ribs, her waist, sliding beneath the waistband of her thin cotton pants to strip them from her, leaving her exposed to his hot, hungry gaze. He stared down at her body, the flushed breasts, the tucked-in waist and flared hips, her thighs slightly parted to give him a glimpse of the treasure waiting, already damp with need.

He bent his head to her stomach, finding her sexy little navel, blazing a trail of fiery little bites all the way to the intriguing curls at the junction of her legs.

Joley's head tossed on the pillow and she cried out again, a soft whimper as she tried to make sense of the fire building relentlessly. She'd never experienced such a clawing need in her body, so much pleasure that it bordered on pain. She needed a moment, needed to slow down and get control.

Ilya refused to give her the time. He took her over, driving her out of her comfort zone, pushing her beyond anything she'd ever imagined—even in her darkest erotic fantasies. Her skin was hypersensitive, her inner body pulsing with a tormented need.

His hands swept her thighs open for him, one leg sliding between hers, his arms pinning her hips beneath him, locking her in place as he lifted his head. His blue gaze held stark, raw hunger, ravenous lust and absolute command. "Mine." His tone was raspy and harsh, a wild, arrogant Cossack claiming ownership.

She tried to catch his hair, to stop him. She needed to breathe. To control herself, control the lust crawling through her body and taking over her mind. Ilya ignored the fist jerking his hair and her thrashing body. His mouth ruthlessly covered the hot, sweet core of her, tongue plunging deep, finding her most sensitive spot and flicking hard, over and over. She tried to scream as an orgasm ripped through her, but no sound emerged. She nearly came off the bed in spite of his arms restraining her. His mouth only continued the assault, burning her from the inside out between the suckling and the hot flicks of his tongue.

The more she fought, the firmer he locked her in place, his arms enormously strong, his mouth consuming her, the sensation shattering, rocking her with its intensity. She couldn't catch her breath; her nerve endings were so tight and sensitive she thought she might die. The music was pounding through her veins, thundering in her ears, in her hammering heart, but most of all in her feminine channel, beating too hard and fast, but the crescendo would not come. The inferno built and built. She shook her head back and forth on the pillow, fingernails digging into his back as she tried to either pull him closer or push him away.

He was relentless, taking his pleasure, insisting on her going with him as high as he wanted to take her. He plunged his tongue deep, took the slick, wet offering and reveled in his ability to send her into the next level of sensual sensation. Blood pounded through the muscles of her sheath, tightening, contracting, until she nearly sobbed as his mouth drove her ever higher, and she could feel her body straining for another release. His music vibrated through her, danced against her clit, flinging her hard into another orgasm.

He rose above her like the warrior he was, his eyes fierce and filled with an insatiable lust. He jerked her thighs apart, his hands rough and insistent. She saw him then, savagely aroused, thick and hard and far too intimidating. He pushed the head of his erection against her tight sheath and stilled, holding her gaze with his.

"You're mine. Say it, Joley. Only mine. I want to hear you say it."

He moved, a short thrust that had her biting off a scream as he pushed in a little deeper, stretching her. The burning need increased until she wanted to sob, terrified she'd never be free of it. She had known all along he was the one who would know, who would see beneath her skin, down to her very core, and once he uncovered her need for this—this taking her beyond anything she'd ever known—she'd be lost—and she was. She'd never be free of him. She was his, body and soul, locked together now by something beyond her, and it was terrifying.

She shook her head, tears swimming in her eyes.

Ilya caught her hands, laced his fingers through hers and bent over her, pressing her hands to the mattress, rocking with another short thrust of his hips, stretching her again as he sunk deeper. "Look at me, Joley. Right now. Look at me."

She couldn't look away. She was trapped in his heat. In his lust. His needs. She was trapped by his absolute will and his expertise. He played her body like a maestro, his sensuality beyond her ability to resist. She blinked at the tears stinging her eyes, and he leaned forward and took them with a slow caress of his tongue. Instantly her womb spasmed, convulsed, sending streaks of fire racing through her, her muscles clamping tightly around him.

"Say you belong to me, Joley." He repeated each word in a rough, harsh voice, his hands holding hers tightly. "Say you're mine."

"Damn you," she hissed. "You want everything."

He bent forward again, rocking his hips, forcing another inch, stretching her relentlessly, burning with her. "Everything you are is mine."

"Then you're mine," she said in desperation. "Then you belong to me."

"With everything I am," he agreed and slammed his body home.

He took her breath away, his body driving through her tight inner muscles, spreading fire as she arched into him, her body still fighting for more, or trying to pull away from him as she writhed under him, impaled now and gasping for breath.

"Damn, Joley, you're so tight." His voice was a harsh gasp above her head.

Around them, the music crashed and throbbed and sent electrical currents sizzling through her veins. In some secret place in her mind, she had wanted this, a man who knew exactly what he wanted and took it, a man who dared to push her further than she'd ever been, but reality was different than imagination, and she was terrified she'd never be able to pull herself back together and be Joley. Just Joley.

Ilya easily controlled her body with his own, throwing back his head and losing himself in the heat and fire. He had been born for this moment, trained for this moment, learning from a young age to wield sex like a weapon, to dominate completely without losing himself, to exhibit absolute, utter mastery over a woman. He could ride a partner for hours, have a woman begging and pleading to tell him anything he wanted to know, but nothing in his experience had prepared him for mixing expertise with his own needs, desires and emotions, and the woman who owned him body and soul. He was lost in the absolute carnal pleasure of their bodies.

He set a harsh, demanding tempo, rocking her with streaks of fire. Her silken sheath was tight, strangling him, pulsing and throbbing, squeezing him as he pistoned again and again, hard thrusts that buried him to the hilt. Each time her muscles clamped down and sensations tore through his body, the pleasure burst through him, far more than he'd ever experienced. His strokes became harder, deeper, more rhythmic as she went wild beneath him. Her head tossed on the pillow, her hips arching into him, muscles tightening as the pressure built and built with no relief. She fought the torturous erotic pleasure, sobbing his name.

His hands clamped down on her thighs, holding them apart, shifting her so that she felt the caress of steel stroking over her sensitive knot of nerves already on fire. The more she fought, the higher he took her, biting back a growl, his teeth bared as he drove himself into her, claiming her, riding her, taking her with him into another sensual dimension.

"Stay with me, Joley," he rasped. "Stop fighting it."

"I can't," she gasped.

"You will," he decreed.

Joley couldn't stop the shudders wracking her body, or the involuntary raking at his back with her nails. She was on fire as he rode between her thighs. He felt like velvet-encased steel, driving through tight, stretched muscle already inflamed and in need of release, but the erotic torture didn't end, didn't stop, and she couldn't stand it. The fierce thrusting of his hips, the thick cock driving deep into her, stretching and burning, sending streaks of lightning flashing through her entire body, the tension inside coiling tighter and tighter as she gasped and writhed beneath him was too much. Fear skated through the haze of lust and need, heightening the sensations even more. The sounds of his fierce possession and her pleas added to the crashing music, rising to a crescendo as the firestorm swept over them, engulfing them completely.

Her breath ceased, music thundered in her ears, the room darkened around her, and colors danced behind her eyes as her body tightened unmercifully around his thick erection. And then it came. Wave after wave, multiple orgasms streaking through her womb, blazing through her stomach and breasts, burning her from the inside out, endless, vicious, without mercy, the sensation so intense she wasn't certain if it was pleasure or pain.

The fierce milking of his shaft by her fiery, slick sheath was too much for Ilya. The sensation started in his toes, ran up the column of his thighs, tightened in his balls and burned in his belly. He lost all control for this first time in his life, pouring himself into her, jet after jet of hot semen, as her body gripped him with erotic pleasure. He collapsed over her, breathing roughly, her body pulsing around his.

Joley lay under him, limp, her breathing ragged. His body shuddered from the explosive release. Never in his life had it ever been like that. Her slick, wet heat, burning around his shaft, the tight grasp of her body on his, the torturous brutal release was more pleasure than he'd ever known.

Joley had made him come alive, turning a trained bodily function, an expertise, into a secret paradise of sensation. Before her, sex, like everything else about him, had been a weapon to use, a tool for survival, but she had given him an immeasurable gift. She had surrendered herself to him, entrusted her body, her mind, all that she was to him and in doing so had staked her own claim on him.

"I don't think I'm alive anymore," Joley whispered. "I think you killed me."

She looked dazed, almost uncomprehending. He nuzzled her neck, kissed the pulse beating rapidly behind her ear and rolled over, closing his eyes as he slid from the warmth of her body. "Your body is incredible."

Joley could hear her heart thundering in her ears. She hadn't known sex could be like that, and it was truly terrifying. On one hand to think it might happen again, and on the other to think it might never happen again. She didn't know which was worse. She turned her head to look at him. "You're so far out of my league I can't even play."

He dropped his hand to her bare stomach, fingers splayed wide. "You did more than play, *laskovaya moya*, you drained me. I have never had that happen." The pads of his fingers began slow, circular caresses along her belly, just above the damp curls.

His touch sent ripples through her body, tightening her muscles and creating delicious aftershocks.

"Since neither of us were very responsible, I'll go first. I don't have any diseases and I'd appreciate it if you confess if you have any." She held her breath.

He smiled up at the ceiling, his fingers sliding into the curls, continuing the small, light movements. "I have no disease, Joley."

"And I'm on the pill so you don't have to worry about pregnancy," she said, "but you should have asked."

His eyebrow shot up. "And you think the pill will protect you?"

"From pregnancy, but not from an STD." She was a little alarmed by the smirk in his voice, as if he knew something she didn't.

"I told you I have no diseases, but I did put my mark on you." He took her hand and brought her palm to his lips.

Again she felt his kiss at her very core. The fingers of his other hand continued to weave through her damp curls until they slid into her slick heat, tracing more small circles. He enjoyed the shudders of pleasure and the arching of her restless hips, the way she responded to every touch. Her breathing changed; her breasts heaved and her body tightened on his fingers. She lost all coherent thought.

"Ilya." She caught his wrist. "I'm done. Totally done."

He turned toward her, his blue eyes drifting possessively over her face. "No, you're done when I say you're done. I'm done when you say. That's the way it works, *radost' moya*. And I say you're not done."

"I don't understand."

He bent his head to her breast, his tongue flicking the nipple, teeth tugging, and then his mouth settled to suckle. She gasped, and turned more into him as the flashes of fire went from nipple to sheath. Her arm cradled his head, as she held him to her.

"I'm exhausted. I want more, but I'm so tired."

His fingers plunged deeper, stroking and caressing and circling her clit. This time her orgasm was gentle and washed over her like the receding waves of the seas. He flicked her nipple with his tongue and lifted his head to find her mouth with his. His kiss was infinitely tender.

"You have trust issues, Joley. Serious ones. You gave your body into my keeping, but you don't trust me to know that you're tired and you need to come down slowly. You were flying high and it frightened you."

She kissed him again. He was right, her body was already calmer, the sensations like gentle waves calming turbulent seas. "I'm still scared."

"I don't mind you being afraid, especially if you tell me, but you know I can read you—what you want, what you like, what you need. Trust me to provide you with those things."

"You're talking about sexually." She lay back against her pillow, too tired to prop herself up even to look at his handsome face.

"Emotionally first, Joley. Then, yes, physically, sexually. But this isn't about sex. You still want it to be, but it's not. If you could never have sex with me again, I would still want to be with you. I would still need to be with you. I won't lie and say I don't have a very healthy sex drive. Make no mistake, I'll take from you the things I want and need, but your pleasure, your needs always—*always*—come first, even if you don't know what they are."

She made a face at the ceiling. "You talk and I don't know what you mean."

"You know exactly what I mean. I don't do anything by halves and neither do you. You committed yourself to me and you saw inside of me enough to know what kind of man I am."

Joley inhaled sharply, her breath catching in her lungs. She did know—and yet she didn't. She had been drawn to him, mesmerized and seduced by him, by his aura and his song. By his magic—his strength. Oh, God, his strength was what she craved more than anything in the world. That absolute confidence, that aggression that pushed her out of her comfort zone, that took her places she had only dreamt of—places she craved but feared. He would take her over and she would fight him every inch of the way. He was going to make her life hell—or heaven.

She moistened her lips. "Do you think you're going to rule me? Because if you think so, your fantasy is way beyond reality."

He caught her face between his hands, forcing her toward him. Her startled gaze jumped to his. "Don't start a fight with me, Joley. Not now. We've only got a few hours left together." He leaned down and brushed kisses across her eyelids, the tip of her nose, back and forth across her mouth.

Alarmed, Joley pushed at the wall of his chest. He was stealing her heart. He'd taken her body and her soul, she wasn't handing him her heart to destroy as well. He had given her the most fantastic sexual experience of her life, and she knew she would need him again and again. Nothing would ever compare to what she had with him, but it wasn't lovemaking. She hadn't felt that he was loving her. Possessing her—claiming her—yes. Owning her even, but not loving her, and she could be addicted, she could let him rule her in bed, but she refused, absolutely refused, to hand her heart to a man who might be involved in terrible things.

"Yes," he said softly, kissing her again.

Small, caressing kisses that left her feeling helpless against the onslaught of tenderness. "I won't let you."

He knew what she was afraid of. She could feel him in her mind, touching her inside where there was no way to stop him. He had marked her everywhere, all over her skin, and now he was leaving his mark on the inside.

"It's already too late," he whispered, trailing kisses along her cheekbone to the corner of her mouth.

She was melting inside. Butterfly wings all over again. She wasn't just getting wet and needy, she craved his touch, his voice, the scent of him, but most of all she wanted him to feel that same frightening vulnerability that for her just seemed to grow worse around him.

His hands stroked her skin, memorizing every inch of her, and all the while he whispered to her of faraway places, of being a boy in a cold, hard land, of belonging to her and only her. She could hear the strains of his song wrapping her up in

haunting notes, holding her close while she drifted—
drifted—on a tide of sex and sin and the fragile beginnings of
love.

She went to sleep to the soft murmur of his voice, and
woke to the sensual enticement of it only an hour later. He was
already hard and moving inside her, his kiss taking her breath
while his hands shaped her breasts.

In the tour buses, the trip from Red Rocks to Dallas took a
little over fourteen hours. Ilya woke her over and over, until
Joley thought she would have to crawl to make it to the shower
to relieve the aches in her sore body. He carried her and took
her hard and fast up against the wall. Once they rolled off the
bed, and he just took her there on the floor. They tried to eat,
and he put her on the small table and ate her instead, until she
was sobbing for release, and then he sank into her, first with
her lying on the table and then bending her over it.

When the bus finally pulled into their space and stopped,
and Steve had called to tell her he was going to bed, Joley sat
on the floor, her legs drawn up, head back against her mattress, clutching a blanket around her naked body. Ilya sat beside her, holding a bottle of water so she could sip it.

"Are you all right?"

Joley looked at him, his body fit, the long, thick length of
him semi-hard against the strong column of his thigh. "You're
a freakin' sex machine, Ilya. Nobody can do that. Nobody.
You're either downing Viagra by the bottle or you're a cy-
borg."

He shrugged his shoulders, slipped an arm under her legs
and lifted her back onto the bed, placing her close to the wall
so he could wrap his body around hers. "I was trained to stay
hard no matter what, to ride a woman for hours if need be, to
pleasure her and never let it affect me. But in the end, *angel
moya*, all that training is for nothing with you. No matter how
many times I have you, how many ways I take you, it is never
enough for me. I should be sated, unmoved by what we share,
and yet I'm addicted to you and cannot get enough of you."

She was exhausted beyond anything she'd ever known
but . . . "Ilya." She frowned, sliding her arms around his neck.
"What do you mean, trained? Sexually trained? How? How
can someone train you? And where?"

He was silent, and she sensed—knew—he was uncomfortable and wished he could take the revelation back. She held her breath waiting. For the first time she felt he was as vulnerable and naked as she was.

"I was trained in a lot of things, Joley."

"They hurt you, didn't they?" She guessed.

She had seen scars on his body, felt them under her fingertips; she'd caught glimpses of a young man huddled in a corner with blood running down his back and legs. Now she knew for certain it was Ilya. The glimpses of violence, the black aura—there was so much she didn't know, but she was beginning to get small pieces that fit together, forming a very ugly picture.

"Don't. We're not going there, Joley."

Her hands framed his face and she kissed him gently, her stomach fluttering, her heart reaching for his. Ilya caught her by her shoulders and yanked her back down to the mattress. "I said no. Don't you pity me."

Fury flashed through her. He had spent hours—*hours*—keeping her vulnerable and forcing her to confront her own failings and needs, her own fears, but he refused to share any part of himself with her. She was so angry her body trembled. She dropped her hands immediately, fingers curling into two tight fists.

As she stared up at his handsome face, his ice-cold eyes, the anger drained away. Her breath hitched in her throat, the lump there nearly choking her. Her chest hurt, was too tight, a piercing pain tearing through her heart. He had rejected her again. She could tell herself forever that it had been just sex for her, but she knew better. She had thought he was everything, but he had pushed her away and refused to give anything of himself to her. All his talk was just that—talk. Survival counted now, more than anything she had to survive.

What if he had done what he'd been trained to do? Maybe Nikitin had ordered him to screw her. Well, he'd done a good job. He could go to the tabloids and say he'd screwed a celebrity. She had never felt so betrayed, so ashamed or so stupid. The pain was physical.

She did the only thing possible, she pulled herself back from the brink of that terrible precipice she'd almost gone over. She had to walk away now. This instant. Withdraw and hold a part of herself to her, protected and sheltered, in order to stay alive. He'd taken everything else from her, and she doubted she'd ever get it back, but she wasn't going to give him her life.

She would cry. She would be lonely. She would feel empty forever, but she could survive if she pulled away.

"Joley."

Ilya sensed her withdrawal. Of course he would. He knew her inside and out. He couldn't help but realize she was moving away from him. She did her best to cover.

"No. You're right. I'm sorry. I shouldn't have pried." She turned onto her side. "I've only got a couple of hours to sleep and then I'll be working. When you leave, please don't wake me up."

"Joley, you're angry with me."

"No, I'm just very tired." And she wasn't angry. She was empty. Not even sorrow could fill her emptiness. She would say whatever he needed to hear so he would go and she would be safe. She flashed a fake smile at him and closed her eyes, waiting for him to leave her.

11

"JOLEY. Wake up. Wake up, honey."

Joley groaned and squeezed her eyes closed tighter. "Go away."

There were whispers. She heard them from a distance and tried to turn her head to see who was disturbing her. Her body felt heavy and cumbersome and her eyelids barely opened. Tish and Brian huddled together over the bed. Jerry stood at her table with the shreds of two white packets in his hands.

Joley?

Ilya's voice shredded her heart. That perfect pitch. No one had such a perfect, heartbreaking tone. She closed her eyes and pulled the covers over her head. She couldn't hear him or see him. She needed to stay asleep where he couldn't get to her to destroy her further.

"Joley, what the hell did you take?" Jerry pushed Brian and Tish aside and crouched by the bed, shaking her. "What did you take?" He dipped a finger into the envelope and tasted it, scowled and handed it to Brian.

"She doesn't do drugs," Brian said, repeating the same action and tasting the powder.

"She took something," Jerry snapped. "Joley, what the fuck have you done? I swear you'd better tell me or I'm calling a fucking ambulance right now. Get her up. Walk her up and down the bus. Get some water on her face. What did you take?"

Joley frowned at them, forcing her lashes to lift. "Go away. I'm sleeping."

"You're getting up," Jerry decreed. "I don't expect this kind of drama from you, Joley. Denny maybe, but not you. What the hell did you take?"

Her mouth felt like cotton. "I can't take drugs. You know that. They don't work on my body. They just make me sick." She rolled over and stared at the ceiling, keeping the comforter wrapped tightly around her body.

Tish took the packet from Brian and sat on the edge of the bed. "What is this, honey?"

"Hannah made it up for me. I'm only supposed to use one envelope, but I couldn't sleep so I took two—and it worked." She glared up at Jerry. "Until you decided to barge in."

"What's in it?" Jerry demanded, relief making his voice gruff.

"I don't know. She grows all that stuff. She's like super-gardener, and all her powders and creams work." Joley put her hand over her eyes. "Did you have to raise all the screens?"

"Only two," Brian said. "I'm getting you something to eat. I'll be right back."

"Get her moving, Tish," Jerry said and awkwardly patted Joley's head.

Tish waited until the men had left and shut the door. "You're covered in bruises, Joley, you have marks all over your body. What happened? Do you need a doctor?"

Marks all over her? Ilya's marks. Inside and out. She could feel him touching her, whispering to her, his breath warm against her skin, his hands like magic. She pulled the comforter closer to hold the marks tight against her skin. The absolute compassion and caring in Tish's voice was her undoing. Tears burned in her eyes and clogged her throat. She shook her head. "I'm all right. Nothing bad happened. I was just stupid, the way I'm always stupid."

"You're never stupid, Joley. You might be attracted to the wrong men, but you're careful. You know to keep a distance."

"Does it look like I kept my distance this time, Tish?" Joley raised her head and looked straight at the other woman, letting her see the heartache, the betrayal, the pain that wasn't going to end just because she was smart enough to walk away. She had committed herself to Ilya. She had given herself to him—all that she was, everything—and he'd stolen her heart even when she tried to protect herself. "I'm such an idiot. I know my own weaknesses. I do, Tish. I laugh at them and guard against them. I've never allowed myself to fall in love. *Never.*"

Until now. With the wrong man. Everything about him appealed to her, even his aloofness. "I intended to be the goddess who finally melted his heart of stone. What a crock." She covered her face with her hands. "I can't believe I did this."

"Come here, baby," Tish said.

Joley laid her head in Tish's lap and let her stroke her hair soothingly. She wasn't going to cry. She deserved this for her own stupidity. Men like Ilya Prakenskii didn't really fall in love and live happily ever after, and neither did women like Joley. "I want to be normal."

Tish bent and kissed the top of her head. "You're Joley and that's enough. If he doesn't love you, he's crazy. We all love you. Every single one of us. We know you'd go to hell and back for us. Why do you think Brian's braving the paparazzi right now, getting you something to eat? With the murder, it's even crazier than normal. They've said all kinds of cruel things about him both in the tabloids and in the newspapers, implying he's guilty."

"Oh, no." Joley sat up with a small frown. "Why would they think he'd have a reason to kill Dean?"

Tish sighed. "The heaviest speculation is that you were secretly having an affair with Dean and Brian got jealous. They had words over you and Brian killed him."

Joley swore under her breath. "Can't they just once give us a break? Why do they have to do that?"

"I told you when you got into this business, baby, they feed off scandal and rumors. When there's nothing there, they have to make it up, and when there is, they make it a thousand times worse." Tish pointed to the shower. "Go. He'll be back soon and you're going to want to be on your feet. You'll need cover-up for your neck."

Joley wrapped herself more tightly in the comforter and slid off the bed. Tears were useless, even though she couldn't stop them in the shower.

Joley.

There he was again, a stirring in her mind. A whispered caress. It didn't mean anything. This was a man admittedly trained in the art of seduction—and he had seduced her. He'd used her own dark desires against her. She had to stay focused on reality and not on what she wanted or needed from him.

I'm in a hurry. I'm late getting ready for the sound check and everyone is waiting.

There. Steady. Matter-of-fact. She took a deep breath, let it out and stepped out of the shower to rub a towel over her body. She was sore everywhere, and so sensitized that touching her breasts sent streaks of fire shooting down her thighs.

She stared at herself in the mirror. Her eyes were dark, almost black, filled with pain. She'd let someone do that to her. She had known all along she felt things too deeply. She became attached. She didn't want a lover who could walk away from her, because she could never do that—love someone completely and survive intact if he left her.

Joley, before you go on tonight, we need to talk.

I'm sorry. I doubt there's time. I'm running late and Tish is here. Brian's just come with some food. Later. Much later. As in never. She was going to have to ask Jerry to find a way to get rid of him without tipping him off. Jerry was good at covering for her.

Tish handed her clothes through the door and Joley put them on. Tish knew her so well. She pressed her fingertips to her eyes. Tish knew about pain and loss. She loved Logan and he'd betrayed her. Joley detested the selfish part of her that had pushed Logan to ask Tish to come for the baby. She understood now how hard it had been for Tish. She hadn't wanted to see Logan, to speak to him, to take even his money from him. She wanted nothing to do with him, and now Joley understood.

She was careful with makeup. She rarely wore much other than during a performance, but she needed the added confidence as well as something to mask the dark circles under her eyes.

"Hey," Brian knocked on the bathroom door. "The food I risked my life bringing to you is getting cold. And Tish made you a cup of tea, that special blend Hannah always sends you."

Joley smiled. It was nice to have friends who cared. People who knew you so well. She stepped out and hugged Brian. After his initial shock, he hugged her back. For the first time, she was drowning so much in her own misery, she couldn't catch more than worry and guilt flowing from him.

"Thanks for braving the crazies to get me food, Brian." She managed to look normal as she walked to the table and sat down. She didn't even burst into tears.

"Dallas is wild, Joley. Jerry and I have been tried and convicted in most of the tabloids, and the general speculation is that I'm getting off because I'm a celebrity. It's pretty vicious stuff so don't bother reading it. The newspapers are the same. I was hiding in the bus until Jerry said there was something wrong with you."

Tish nodded. "Security's tight and they've got ropes up, but there's already a mob outside. We've got security going through the usual gifts and things left for you." She glanced at Brian uneasily as she placed the tea in front of the plate of food on the table. "We've gotten a couple more disturbing letters, Joley. Jerry had Prakenskii look at them, and he also faxed copies to Jonas. He said that was standard now, to copy Jonas on everything."

Joley nodded. "Jonas is more than a brother-in-law, he's also like a brother. I've known him my entire life and he's bossy when it comes to safety. All the men in my family are."

Brian sat down and leaned his chin onto his hand, watching her eat. "That's good."

"I suppose," Joley agreed.

Tish touched her hair with a gentle hand. "I've got to check on the baby. You don't have much time for the sound check, Joley. You've only got about two hours before the performance, and you're going to have to get ready. The band did the check, but they need you."

"I know. I'm sorry. I was just so tired. It was dumb to double up on that stuff. Next time, believe me, I'll know better. I'm sorry I scared everyone." Joley caught at Tish's dress. "Are you okay with taking care of the baby, Tish? I should have told Logan it wasn't a good idea. I knew he wanted you back with him, and I did, too. It was wrong of me—of all of us. We were thinking about ourselves, not you."

"I'm taking one day at a time. I won't let Logan push me into anything before I'm ready, but I missed everyone—and him. Especially him. He's treating me like a queen right now."

"He should, Tish. He doesn't deserve you, none of us do."

Tish's eyes went soft, her smile gentle. "I love all of you.

And little Lissa is the sweetest, most beautiful baby in the world."

Brian sighed as she went out. "Lissa is the one who will get Tish back for Logan. We're all crazy about that kid already. She has too many 'uncles' who are going to spoil her rotten." He leaned his elbows on the table and shoved his hands through his hair in agitation. "I have to say it, Joley. I'm sorry. I really shouldn't have talked to you that way the other night. You're my best friend. I just lost it there."

She took a sip of tea and nudged the other cup Tish had made closer to him. "Why did you? What's going on with you? And don't say it's jealousy, because you don't think of me that way. I know we joke all the time, but I've never felt your interest, not once."

"I love you, Joley."

"I know that, but not like that. So what got you so upset?"

"It's that man. Prakenskii. He just irks me. And then Jerry decides to hire him without really giving any of us a choice. What the hell is that about?"

Joley's stomach knotted. She put her fork down. "Why do you dislike him so much?" And why hadn't he told her before she made such a fool out of herself?

"It's the way Nikitin is with him." The words burst from Brian as if he'd been holding them in forever. "I think he's involved with him somehow."

Joley frowned and rubbed her temples. "I have no idea what you mean by involved. Prakenskii works for Nikitin as a bodyguard. Everyone knows that."

Brian shook his head. "It's more than that. Seriously, Joley, something's going on with those two. And suddenly Nikitin loans him to us. Did Nikitin send him on purpose? Does he want something? I think those are legitimate questions we have to ask."

"You've sure changed your mind." Joley pushed away from the table, taking her tea with her. She needed the soothing chamomile. "You defended Nikitin before." Although he'd never liked Prakenskii, she recalled.

"After you talked to me, I thought a lot about the time I'd spent with him, the things I saw and heard, and although I didn't want to admit it, I think there's a possibility that you're right about Sergei."

Her eyebrows shot up at the familiar way Brian said the Russian's name. "You've spent more time with Nikitin than I realized. I'm sorry if you thought he was a friend, Brian. I should have told you my concerns about him earlier. I just thought you all went to his parties for the benefits."

Brian jumped up, knocking hard into the table, sending the plate skittering across it. He righted it, avoiding her eyes. "Yeah. I spent time with him. And I don't trust Prakenskii. Nikitin is weird about him. Really weird."

She wanted to hear but she didn't. The mention of Prakenskii sent pain crashing through her. Pain. Guilt. Shame. She hated feeling stupid. "In what way?"

"At first I thought they had a thing—you know—a sexual thing."

Joley spewed tea across the room, choked and coughed, gasping for air. When she managed to breathe, she scowled at him. "Why in the world would you think Ilya Prakenskii and Nikitin are lovers?"

"You are very naïve, Joley, in a lot of ways. Prakenskii is a dominant, in every sense of the word, and very sexual. He could mesmerize someone, male or female, and keep them tied to him. Nikitin seems under his control, afraid of him, but influenced by him. He obviously won't fire him, you said so yourself. But he doesn't trust him. I saw that with my own eyes. And Nikitin is gay."

"How would you know that?"

There was a small silence that lengthened and grew. Joley slowly put down her teacup and stared at the man she'd known for years. A man she thought of as her best friend. He met her gaze steadily, but she could see the expectance of rejection in his eyes. "You? Brian, why didn't you ever tell me? How could I not know? Do all the guys know?"

He shook his head but remained silent.

Joley looked around for a chair, and when nothing was close by she leaned against the wall. "Why didn't you say something to me?"

"I couldn't."

She swallowed hard. "You didn't trust me. You knew I loved you, but you still didn't trust me, Brian. I don't understand. Did you think it would make a difference in how I feel about you?"

"Right now, I'm just Brian, one of the band, a member of the family, and we all get along and love each other and it's all good. Everyone respects me and comes to me for advice for everything from dating to what to do when they have a problem. In an argument, they all listen to me. What do you think will happen when it comes out I'm gay? I'll be the gay guy who might cry if someone yells at him. Everything will change. My friends will treat me differently, and you can bet the paparazzi will have a field day talking about all of us traveling in the bus together, taking showers, sleeping. They'll speculate on the others, and pretty soon it won't be jokes when we read the tabloids, it will be Brian has to have his own bus because they won't be able to laugh about sleeping with a gay man. They can laugh when the paparazzi claim you're banging all of us, but it won't be so funny if it's them with me."

He was right. She could see how it would happen. "How could you hide this so long and no one know?" She rarely touched him, but she should have had some warning. She'd thought it was just that she felt a lack of sexual attraction toward her.

"Because the band and the music meant more to me than banging someone. I just dated a few girls and made certain we were photographed a lot, and eventually broke up with them. I went to the parties and looked like I fit in. Staying sober helped. I could think clearly and set the stage when I needed to. Our names were linked all the time and I made certain it stayed that way."

"But now? Why are you telling me now?"

"Because Nikitin knows about me, he knows I'm gay. I fell in love with him. He was like a dream come true for me. We'd talk for hours and laugh together. We'd go up to his room and have a cognac and end up in bed. Not at first. At first we just talked, but I couldn't stay away from him, even though I knew I was risking my career. But his risk seemed just as great. He's always with beautiful women. I asked if he was bisexual and he said no, but like me, he needed to keep his image straight. He said it was better for his business. He was perfect. He understood I traveled often; he did, too. He could follow the band on the pretense of loving the music and give extravagant parties and we could be together and no one would be the wiser."

It took a few minutes to digest what he was telling her. Everything she'd ever thought or believed about Nikitin was wrong. Everyone thought Nikitin was obsessed with her, but all along it had been with Brian. He'd followed the band because he'd been Brian's lover.

"How long has this been going on?"

Brian rubbed his forehead in distress. "A long time. Over a year."

"His security has to know."

"You mean Prakenskii. Yeah. I'm pretty certain he knows. Sergei wouldn't discuss him with me. I was so jealous, Joley. So jealous and so stupid. Prakenskii is a very dangerous man. To you. To me. Maybe even to Sergei."

Joley went to the window and stared out. People were milling everywhere, but she felt alone and empty and sad. Terribly sad. Ilya had known about Brian before she had, and Brian was her best friend. Why hadn't Ilya said anything to her? Loyalty toward his boss? Did he have other motives?

And Brian. She sighed. Brian was a good person, and he didn't deserve heartache any more than she did. "I'm afraid for you, Brian. Sergei Nikitin heads up the Russian mob. He isn't just a little part of it, he's the top dog. If he believes you're a threat to him, he'll have you killed."

Brian stood behind her, staring out the window as well. "I broke it off with him, made certain he knew I had as much to lose, and he said he wasn't willing to let it go. He said he would never harm me, but the rest of the band wasn't going to be so lucky." He covered his face with his hands and slid down to the floor. "That kid. Dean. I think his men killed him because of me—as a warning to me. And then he sent Prakenskii here as a warning that you were next. I don't know what to do, Joley. I couldn't bear it if he had you killed, too."

Joley slid to the floor beside him, slinging her arm around him, uncaring that his sorrow and fear only compounded her own. "You know we're going to have to go to the police."

"That won't stop him, Joley. You should have seen him when I talked to him. And God help me, I still love him. I had no idea he was a monster. He was as lonely as I was and I think he really cared. I hope that he did. But he flew into a rage when I told him we had to end it."

"Is he here in Dallas?"

"Yes. And he wants me to go to his party tonight after the performance. He said we have to talk, to clear things up. If I don't go, I don't know what he'll do. Logan's got the baby traveling with him and Tish. Denny we can keep from the party, but Rick and Leo will go for sure. He could do anything to them."

"We're getting ahead of ourselves." She pressed a hand to her churning stomach.

Was it possible that they all had it wrong? Brian insisted that Nikitin feared Prakenskii. Could Nikitin be the front man and Prakenskii be the real boss? Everyone deferred to him—everyone. She'd watched it a million times. The moment he spoke. The moment he moved. Every one of Nikitin's men stopped what they were doing to pay attention. Could he be the real head of the Russian mob? All the violence she'd seen in his memories, all the darkness clouding his aura, even his dominating personality pointed to it. Did he control others through his sexual expertise? The thought sickened her. She rubbed her face against her knees.

"Let's not panic, Brian. No one else knows about this, right?"

He nodded.

"Well, let's do the show. Say you'll go to the party. We can have something go wrong at the performance. I can fall and hurt myself. We've got a couple of hours to think of something to buy us a little more time."

"We have to leave Dallas tonight for some reason."

She nodded. "We'll come up with an excuse and make it seem real. We're performers. Jonas is in law enforcement. I'll talk to him and a couple of my sisters about Nikitin. I'll do my best to cover what he's got on you."

He shook his head. "It's over for me. Once the fact that I'm gay is out, I've got to leave the band."

"No, you don't." She had to get away from him. His misery overwhelmed him. "And you can forget the suicide crap, it's not an option." Because she could feel him considering that as well. "Come on, Brian, we're in this together. We're smart. We'll figure it out." She stood up and brushed herself off. "My family's tangled with the mob before, and we always come out on top. You tell the sound crew I'll be there in a few minutes. I'm calling Jonas."

It had taken a lot of courage for Brian to come to her and tell her the truth. He had served himself up on a platter to her, and she was going to stand by him, by their long-standing friendship and the love she had for him. She loved him all the more for trusting her with his secret. Joley hugged him again hard.

Brian brushed a kiss against her temple. "I'm sorry I brought this to us."

She couldn't let him leave weighed down with so much guilt. "Brian." She caught his sleeve. "Don't do anything stupid. You didn't think Nikitin was anything but a businessman. I suspected Ilya was more than he appeared, so if we're really in trouble here, I'm far more to blame than you."

She had never understood why Denny couldn't just walk away from the groupies and the drugs. She was appalled at Logan for betraying Tish. He'd been so strong, night after night, but in the end, in spite of loving Tish, he'd succumbed to temptation. She hadn't understood how a person could be so weak that they would make the choice to do something they knew was so wrong—until now.

"You didn't do anything wrong, Brian. Of all of us, you're the only one who tried to do the right thing. None of this is your fault. And certainly Dean's death isn't. That's on whoever killed him, and we don't know that it was Nikitin."

"Thank you for that, Joley," Brian said.

He went out the door, leaving her standing alone in the silence. In emptiness. Because that was her life. Empty. Having spent hours of happiness with Ilya, the sheer loneliness was that much harder to take. Maybe that had been Logan's downfall. When Tish stopped traveling so much with them, he couldn't take being alone. Maybe that was the reason Denny couldn't resist the groupies and Rick and Leo partied so much. She could understand how Brian, after so many years of emptiness, had turned to someone he thought it was safe to love.

She flipped open her phone and called Jonas. When it came to her family, she knew they were rock-solid, could always be counted on, but he was going to go berserk on her. She told him the entire story. All of it. Including her downfall with Ilya. She skated over Brian, but she knew he got the gist of it, and one thing about Jonas was his absolute silence when she spoke to him in confidence—which she'd been smart enough to insist on before the conversation even got started.

She had to hold the phone away from her ear until he got done swearing and telling her to get her ass home now. Tonight. On a plane. She stood for what seemed like forever before his rant stopped and she could speak again.

"Jonas, I cannot cancel the rest of my tour. We're sold out at every single venue. In any case, if we did cancel, that would certainly tip off Nikitin that Brian told us everything."

"I don't give a damn. You get home to the house that eats people and I know you'll be safe. Bring the band if you need to, but get where we can protect you."

"It's not like I'm going to be poking around asking questions. I'm not stupid." She made a face. "Okay. I take that back, I'm stupid where men are concerned, but not about safety."

"Nothing can happen to you, Joley. I'll fly to Dallas with Aleksandr and Jackson and we'll help provide protection. Aleksandr knows a great deal about the mob, and once Jackson puts the crosshairs on someone, they're dead."

She sucked in her breath. "You can't do that. I mean it, Jonas. First of all, I absolutely am not risking my family. You promised you'd be reasonable. Don't fly off the handle. If you all come down here, my sisters will come."

"Over my dead body."

"You know they will. Come on. Think with me. If you come to Dallas right now, my sisters will follow, and that would have the same effect as if I canceled the tour. Nikitin would know Brian gave him up and he'd have him killed. Tell me I'm wrong."

There was more swearing on the other end. Jonas finally sighed. "Listen to me, Joley. Really, for once in your life, listen to me. Hannah, your sisters, your parents, and me, Joley, we wouldn't survive it if anything happened to you. You're like the sunshine in this family. Nothing would ever be the same. I'll gather as much information as possible here. Aleksandr will be able to tell us more about Prakenskii, but you stay the hell away from him. My gut says he's some kind of cop, but I've been wrong before. He's sided with our family numerous times, and between you and me, I know he's the one who took out the mobster threatening Hannah. He did it to make certain the feds didn't keep him alive where he could direct reprisals from a cell."

"That hit benefited Nikitin, though, didn't it? I heard you talking to Jackson about it." Joley began pacing up and down the narrow corridor of the bus.

"You shouldn't have been listening." There was an edge now to Jonas's voice, something that happened a lot with Joley.

"Sorry, I find your whispered conversations so intriguing."

"That's not funny, Joley."

Her fingers tightened around the phone. "If I don't laugh, I'm going to cry. I'm counting on you to figure something out. I'm doing the concert tonight, and I'm going to have Jerry announce that we have to leave right after so no one will have a chance to go to that party."

She could feel Ilya's presence now. He was close—very close—and her heart began to beat faster in anticipation of seeing him.

"You just remember there's already been one murder, Joley. If it's about Brian, Nikitin won't hesitate to teach him another lesson."

"I'm scared enough, thank you very much. I've got to do the sound check. My poor sound crew is probably having fits. I've got to go, Jonas, but I'm counting on you to save us."

"That's my specialty, honey. And I'll find out everything I can on Prakenskii, but if he's undercover, I don't want to blow it for him or raise any red flags. Stay away from him."

She closed her eyes for a moment, wishing she had, wishing it wasn't already too late. "Please don't tell Hannah how stupid I've been."

"No one thinks you're stupid, Joley. Please be careful. I'll call back with information and a plan."

"I knew you would. Thanks, Jonas."

Joley slipped the phone into her pocket and went to the door of her bus. Taking a deep breath, she opened it, knowing Ilya would be waiting to escort her to the sound check. She was right, and the sight of him took her breath away. He was so handsome, so mesmerizing, his deep blue eyes hypnotic. She inhaled his scent, and went dizzy with wanting him, weak with need. She forced a small smile and glanced at her watch.

"Sorry. I'm so late. We're going to have to hurry." Deliberately, before Ilya could respond, she looked beyond him to spot Logan stepping out of the other bus. She waved and beckoned him over, trying to hide her relief.

"Joley, stop it," Ilya hissed. "What's this going to prove?" She flicked him a quick look from under her lashes and then shrugged her shoulders. "I don't know what you're talking about other than I'm hours late with my sound check and my crew's had to wait on me."

She kept walking toward Logan as fast as she could, and, thankfully, Logan hurried toward her. Before Ilya could say anything else, Logan was there. Deliberately she stepped to the other side of him, putting him between Ilya and her. She should have known it wouldn't work. Ilya simply dropped a pace back smoothly, looking as stone-cold and as professional as ever.

"Baby all right?" she asked quickly.

"Lissa's great. I think everyone holds her too much. We get her down, and one of the guys will come in and pick her up right out of her little carry crib. Tish deals with it, but I think it makes it hard to keep to a schedule."

"And you and Tish? How's that coming?" Joley prompted. She was so aware of Ilya. So aware of the rise and fall of his chest, his every breath, even his heartbeat. Her palm itched and tingled no matter how much she rubbed it against her thigh seeking relief.

"Not bad. I'm going to have to do a lot more groveling."

She flashed him a look. "And I hope you know you deserve to grovel. She shouldn't take you back."

"I know that. But I'm not stupid enough to ever lose her again. I love Tish, Joley. It was a dumb mistake. I was drunk and she wasn't there and I was lonely, and if I could take it back, believe me, a million times I've thought of that moment, that one moment when I walked out of that room with that woman. I can't remember what she looks like. I don't even remember her name. I only remember Tish standing there with that look on her face, so happy to see me, and then seeing— knowing—and her smile fading. The light just died out of her eyes. Believe me, Joley, I know exactly what I lost. If I get it back, I'm not going to ever lose it again."

She put her hand on his sleeve. "Then I wish with all my heart that she takes you back." They were only steps away from the door, and she wanted to run. She could barely breathe through the pain in her heart. It felt like a knife through her chest. She swore under her breath, counting the steps to safety.

Without warning, Ilya moved fast, a huge graceful tiger inserting his body with fluid grace between her and someone she couldn't see. He actually shoved her to the side and away from him. A woman screamed.

"*Bastard!* You bastard, Logan. I'm going to kill you. I'm going to destroy you." Lucy Brady, the woman who had given birth to Lissa, lunged at Logan, swinging her fist. In her fingers, she clutched a broken bottle.

Ilya restrained her, taking her to the ground. "Keep moving," he ordered. "Both of you. Get inside."

Logan hesitated. Joley grabbed his hand and yanked him with her, running now, into the building and toward the safety of her crew. Glancing back, she saw more security guards converging on the snarling, spitting woman on the ground, and Ilya calm and cool holding her, uncaring of her threats.

12

JOLEY flashed across the stage like quicksilver, looking so sexy Ilya found it hard to tear his gaze from her. She was all glitter and flash, sultry and dazzling, burning so hot, flying so high, he knew she would crash after the performance. He had done that. Driven her to the breaking point. To everyone else she looked strong and confident; to him she looked vulnerable and fragile. She wanted the world to think she was just fine— she wanted *him* to believe it, but he knew her too well.

He had crushed her with his careless handling. For the first time in his life his training had utterly failed him. Joley was everything he had ever dreamt of—more. She had given him back humanity, taught him to feel, to believe in hope. He had been careless for the first time in his life, stealing time for himself, forgetting that his life depended on secrecy. And he had been indiscreet, giving her a truth and then pulling back when she accepted it.

He swore and forced himself to look away from her, to study the audience in the first several rows and then slowly back farther. Her voice played over his skin, a mix of sultry heat and promise that kept his body hard when his chest felt weighed down with sorrow.

He had absolutely no experience when it came to relationships. None. His instinct, when he realized she was withdrawing, had been to pull her close to him, to force the issue, but he couldn't give her what she needed, and she would have fought him with her last breath. It would have turned into a physical confrontation, and there would have been no winner. So he'd backed off, and now he had no idea what to do to regain her trust.

He detested this feeling of inadequacy, of indecision. He was a man confident in his abilities, sure of his responses, quick to make judgment calls, and in the most important area of his life, he felt paralyzed by his lack of knowledge.

His gaze strayed back to Joley. The stage was every body-guard's worst nightmare. The venue was a bowl with the stage in the center, surrounded by thousands of screaming fans. They had people scanning the crowd, but to find trouble was like looking for a needle in a haystack. And there was going to be trouble. The electric energy of the crowd nearly drowned out the small threads of malevolence he could feel, but he was ultrasensitive to danger and it was there, somewhere in that vast sea of faces.

"Check the south side," he said into his radio.

He didn't like the shows in the huge venues. Joley used a rig shaped like a platform bridge that swung her out over the audience. It put her right in the midst of them, up high; she gyrated and sang on a narrow metal path in the air. And when she performed, she was giving it her all. Lights flashed, the sky rained sparkles, and fire rose from the stage. Joley ran and leapt for the platform as it began to swing out over the audience.

"South side. South side," Ilya hissed. His gut was in hard knots now. "Get the camera on her. Make certain there's nothing wrong with that platform." He had inspected it himself. With his belly churning and that heaviness of dread weighing down his chest, he knew the small threads of dangerous energy were gathering fast.

There were a million tricks one learned as a personal protector, but he realized most of them went out the window when the person you were guarding was your soul. He had to keep forcing his gaze from straying toward her. His heart beat too fast, and he tasted fear in his mouth. If someone wanted her dead, it would be so easy. A gun—hell, in this crowd, whoever shot her could probably tuck the gun into his shirt and walk away.

He took a deep breath and pushed it all away, falling back on years of cool distance. He forced himself back under rigid control, knowing that if he allowed emotion to rule him, he would lose this battle. He let his senses flair out, uncaring that he would be gathering information it would take his mind months to get rid of.

The stadium was on its feet as the band swung into one of the favorites. Joley looked like mouthwatering candy as she moved over the bridge. The crowd responded with wild screams and waves, reaching up toward her, thunder filling the bowl as the people stomped feet and clapped hands to the pounding beat.

As the platform swung to the south, Ilya shut everything out of his mind but the people under her; he was watching intently for something beyond his vision, something that would register in his mind, in his senses, long before his brain would recognize what his eyes were seeing. People dancing. Women on men's shoulders, arms lifted. His heart jerked and he began moving fast.

"Just under the bridge. Focus directly under the bridge."

He raced across the stage, leapt for the stairs going up the bridge. Even as he ran, his training didn't fail him. He blurred his image to keep cameras from focusing on him. Below him he could see the man on the shoulders of another man taking his hands away from the steel. Both men ducked, hands over their heads.

Joley. Toward me!

She didn't question or hesitate. As if they had choreographed a dance together, she turned and raced toward him, still singing, still holding the microphone. The charge went off just after she passed the device. Sparks raced to the ceiling, but no more than the dazzling display of light and sound racing around the bowl. The sound of grinding metal was loud as the beam split, one side, jagged and sharp, popping up, catching Joley's arm as she flashed by. The other side dropped down toward the crowd, held only by threads.

"In the crowd. Two men. One is wearing a striped shirt, the other has on a leather jacket, a long one. Get them. I'll be there as soon as possible to question them." He spoke low into the radio, keeping in the shadows as he moved into a better position to help Joley.

She went still, keeping control of the situation like the pro she was. "Swing it slowly over the stage, guys, we don't want anyone hurt." Her voice was absolute calm, and it stopped the crowd beneath her from panicking. She sent them a quick sassy grin. "These little things happen at all shows. That's going to get a lot of play on the Internet. Oops, watch Joley fall off the platform. Maybe I'll get really lucky and become famous!"

The audience went wild cheering. As always, she carried them with her personality and her voice. No one seemed to realize that there was still danger.

He was standing behind her now, his hand on her, as the bridge moved back into position. He felt the shifting under his feet as it wanted to shred and buckle, and he tightened his hands at her waist in case he had to throw her clear. Joley kept talking, seemingly unaware that her arm was dripping blood. He got a good look at the cut as the lights played over them.

It's bad, Joley. Your arm's ripped open.

Tell me something I don't know. Can you do anything to get me through this?

He didn't hesitate. As the platform went level with the stage, he lifted her to firm ground, turning for a moment, his body blocking hers from sight, both hands wrapping around her forearm. She gasped and went pale. Blood dripped steadily. Warmth spread from him to her, and she took a breath and stepped back.

Thanks. I can work with this.

He didn't turn around but kept walking, jumping off the stage as the audience erupted into a round of applause.

"Aren't my guys great?" Joley asked, then turned and sent a mock scowl toward her band. "Hey! I didn't see any of you rushing to be my hero."

Denny held up a glass. "Sorry, love, we were taking a break. Did something happen?" He burst into a drum solo that had the crowd laughing and back on their feet.

The crew discreetly moved the platform back away from the audience as far as possible once it was lowered to the stage, while Joley took the towel Brian handed her and casually wrapped it around her arm.

"Joley." His voice was broken.

"Thanks, babe," she said and stood on her toes to brush a kiss against his cheek where she could whisper reassurances. "I'm fine. We need to keep going here, Brian. Help me, okay?"

He nodded and backed away from her, but his face was stiff with guilt and fear. Joley straightened her shoulders, ignored the pain in her arm and moved to the front of the stage, peering down at the rows in front of her. Spotting a young girl of about ten who looked frightened, she leaned toward her, flashing her famous smile. "Were you scared just then?"

The girl nodded.

"So was I, but not nearly as scared as the time I decided to crawl out my window to go to a girlfriend's house. I was just about your age and she was having a sleepover. My parents said I couldn't go because I'd done something that day at school to get in trouble." She'd put a live mouse in the teacher's drawer because the teacher had yelled at her for writing notes, but she for sure wasn't confessing that. "Well I got stuck half in and half out of that window and I heard my dad coming down the hall. I have to tell you—now *that* was a truly scary moment."

The little girl laughed and visibly relaxed. Joley turned back to the band.

"The father has punished you for your sins." The voice blared over a handheld microphone, loud and commanding.

Ilya, who had been striding up to the office, paused, holding his breath. Joley could turn the crowd ugly with one tone of her voice. She slowly turned back, shading her eyes with her hand, and a small smile broke out. With Joley, that was like watching the sun break free.

"RJ. I see you're back again. You just can't seem to stay away."

"I follow where sin and debauchery take me so I might be an instrument of good. Had you been following the path of righteousness, no evil would have befallen you."

The crowd booed and stomped their feet. Joley held up her hand for silence. Ilya held his breath. She held them in her palm, didn't the Reverend see that? Hear it? She was magic on a stage. She probably didn't even realize how much of her gift she utilized onstage as she performed, but her voice was a powerful weapon and it definitely could incite an ugly riot. He knew the power of sound, he'd used it more than once to hypnotize, incite, or to seduce. Survival was everything, and any and all weapons were exploited.

"No, sir, that was a good old-fashioned accident. They happen all time. These people have worked all week, and they're here to have a good time and enjoy themselves, that's all. So you sit down and let's get on with the fun."

The Reverend sat—and that more than anything showed the power Joley wielded with her voice.

As the band swung into a number, Ilya made his way into the office where security held two men. They were much younger than he'd first thought, and both looked scared. He made them even more terrified by leaning up against the desk, folding his arms and staring at them in silence. One of the security guards handed him the two IDs, showing one was eighteen and the other twenty.

Ilya nodded his head toward the door and the guards left, leaving him alone with the two kids. In silence he pulled on thin leather gloves as he deliberately glanced around the room as if looking for cameras, making certain that the two young men looked as well.

The younger of the two, Raymond Silver, was the one who had planted the charge. He cleared his throat and shifted anxiously when Ilya's cold gaze settled on him. The boy kept sending frightened looks to his friend. The silence stretched and lengthened.

"Look, man," Raymond finally burst out with. "I was just telling those dudes. That wasn't supposed to happen. It was only supposed to rock the platform and unbalance her, not break like that. A guy paid us a hundred apiece to put the device there. He even gave us the tickets for those seats and showed us on a drawing where to place it. He was filming it for the Internet. You know, where they play all the videos."

The other boy, Tony Morano, grinned. "I'll bet it turns out cool."

Ilya reached out, his hand a blur of motion, slapping the kid hard enough to rock him back on his heels. The blow was fast, vicious and shocking, the sound loud in the small confines of the room. Tony staggered and fell against the desk.

"I guess you didn't notice that Miss Drake was injured." Ilya kept his voice low and calm, completely at odds with the blow.

"You can't hit me," Tony yelled, wiping the blood from his mouth. "I could sue you. This is police brutality, man."

Ilya caught him by the throat, again the movement so fast the boy never saw it coming. Ilya yanked him off his feet and slammed him against the door, a foot off the ground, simply holding him there by his throat, while the kid's heels drummed against the wood.

Again he used a calm, mild, unhurried voice. "I guess you didn't hear me, Mr. Morano. I said Miss Drake was injured. A proper response would have been to say you're sorry and that you hope it isn't a bad injury." Ilya ignored the gasping for breath, the ragged, desperate choking and gagging as the boy turned color. Ilya shifted slightly so he could look at Raymond. "Don't you agree that would have been a better response, Mr. Silver?"

Raymond nodded desperately over and over, backing around the desk to put it between them.

Ilya allowed Tony to drop to the ground, releasing him abruptly and not at all gently. Tony fell to the floor, holding his throat, coughing and sputtering.

"Let's try again, Mr. Morano." The voice never changed. It remained casual and matter-of-fact, almost friendly. "I am not the police. I don't arrest people and I have no intention of turning you over to the police. They can find you all by themselves if there's anything left to find when I'm done here. I do, however, do other things besides arrest people. You don't want me to have to do those things to you. There are no cameras in this room, no recorders, and those men outside are my men. They'll walk away and disappear, just like I can make you disappear. So, with that in mind, let's try again. Miss Drake was injured by your little stunt."

Tony tried to get his feet under him twice, but fell back coughing.

"I have a good job. Extermination. At first I wasn't so certain it was a good thing, but after a while I realized there were people that just were never going to get it, you know? They were never going to understand the rules of living in a society." Ilya shrugged. "You know what I mean, Mr. Silver?" He never took his gaze from Tony's face.

Raymond nodded vigorously again.

Ilya sighed and took a step toward Tony.

Tony froze. "I'm sorry she was injured," he managed to blurt out, although the words were strangled and rusty sounding. "I hope it wasn't too bad."

"That wasn't so difficult, was it?" Ilya asked.

Tony shook his head.

"I want a description of the man who paid you money to injure Miss Drake." He held up his hand for silence. "Not out loud. I want separate descriptions written down. Details are important to me." He reached down and with casual strength hauled Tony to his feet, caught a chair with the toe of his shoe, spun it around and slammed the kid down into it. "Get started.

"Keep in mind while you're writing, I know where you both live. I know your names. My men will recover the device and trace the origins. Should you have any involvement other than sheer stupidity, I'll come back and do my job. Are we clear?"

Raymond kept nodding. Tony mumbled an affirmative reply. Both bent to the task the moment Ilya put pen and paper in front of them. The younger boy was an artist with a good memory for every facet of his subject. While Tony wrote down a description, Raymond drew the man who had paid them, and he drew him with close attention to detail. Ilya immediately recognized the emerging face. He waited until the boy finished.

"Both of you look at me. Look directly at me because I don't want you later to say you misunderstood me."

He had already been distorting his image and feeding their imaginations another one, but with Raymond an artist, he needed to implant memories. "I want you to draw me just as you see me, every detail so you won't forget my brown eyes, and long hair, and small dark beard. You won't forget that I'm very tall and lean. I want you to remember the sound of my voice. The pattern of my speech. Everything about me."

The two boys set to work, and Ilya watched the drawing come to life of a security guard who looked anything but like him. He shoved the first sketch, of one of Joley's crew members, John Dylan, into the inside pocket of his jacket and walked out, nodding to his two men, who immediately disappeared into the crowd.

Ilya made his way back inside the bowl, noting that Joley still had her arm wrapped in a towel as she sang a love ballad. She hadn't slowed down at all, giving her audience everything inside of her, sending her beautiful voice to every seat in the stadium with as much energy as she'd had when the show started.

Jerry came up to stand beside him. "Isn't she amazing?"

"She's in pain. Lots of pain."

Jerry nodded. "I've got a medic standing by. We'll take her straight to her bus and let him work on her there, away from cameras. There's a huge crowd of the bastards waiting for her. Ordinarily I'd be happy for the publicity, but she's running on nerves. I'm putting them all on a private plane and flying them out of here tonight. No one knows yet, not even them."

"That's probably for the best. You might give Nikitin a heads-up. He was planning a huge party for them. He won't tip the press."

"Good idea. Why don't you give him a call and let him know. Tell him what's happened and that we can't take any chances with the band. The show's almost over. I want to hustle her out of here fast, Ilya, so make certain we've got a clear path."

Ilya nodded and made the call to Nikitin. The Russian had elected not to come to the night's performance, which was highly unusual, but he'd been acting strange for the last few days. He asked if all the band members were okay, and Ilya gave him the information that Joley had been injured. He wanted the flight time, to meet them at the airport and see for himself that everyone was okay. He ordered Ilya to go with them and make certain nothing more happened to them.

It was a strange conversation, and very unlike Nikitin, who would usually be upset over the cancellation of a group he'd honored with a party. Ilya turned the conversation over and over in his mind as he made his way to the stage.

Lights flashed, the music rose to a crescendo, and the band rushed from the stage. Security lined the aisle, allowing them a quick and safe retreat. Ilya fell into step with Joley, who barely glanced at him. It was obvious he wasn't going to be forgiven anytime soon, nor was she going to acknowledge that she was angry with him.

Joley was hurried straight to her bus, where the medic waited for her. The band members crowded inside, leaving Ilya blending into the shadows where she wouldn't notice him. But she noticed. He caught her irritated and somewhat fearful gaze several times.

"You have to hurry," Jerry told the medic. "She's got a plane to catch."

"She needs stitches and probably some blood. She should go to the hospital."

Joley scowled at him. "Just get it done."

Jerry nodded to the medic, who shrugged and unwrapped Joley's arm, ignoring the manager as he addressed the band. "All of you are leaving tonight. I've got a plane waiting at the airport. Prakenskii called Nikitin and let him know we appreciated all the trouble he went to, but we aren't taking chances with Joley or any of the rest of you. We've lost one crew member—and that was no accident—we're not losing anyone else."

"What about Tish and the baby?" Logan said. "I'm not leaving without them."

"There's room. Tell her to get ready to go."

The medic poured something that burned like acid over Joley's arm, and she cried out and jerked away from him. "Ow, you sadist. What was that for?"

"To clean the wound. Hold still. I'm numbing it."

"By sticking a needle into it? Are you crazy?" She looked around. "He's crazy. Get him out of here. I'll just wrap it up."

Jerry leveled a look at her. "You need that arm sewed up. Either here or the hospital."

She made a face at him. "It was good tonight, boys. We held it together, and I think I can safely say, that's one of the worst 'gone wrong' incidents we've had."

Rick caught her head and kissed the top of it. "Yeah, baby, you were on fire. You rocked their world tonight. Even that preacher was probably jacking off just watching you, you little sinner you."

"Thanks, I think," Joley said and flashed Rick her brightest smile. "I love that shirt on you."

Rick dusted off his chest. "Drives the women wild."

Joley laughed and then quickly changed expression, glaring at the medic. "It hurts—it hurts—it hurts—it hurts," she repeated, wincing as the needle went in and out of her skin. "Damn, can't you do something to make me not hurt?" Tears glimmered in her eyes. "Brian, hit me or something. I heard somewhere you can't hurt in more than one place."

Brian swung around, a mixture of anger, guilt and fear on his face. "I told you not to use that platform. Why don't you ever listen to anyone? You could have been killed."

"Stop jerking your arm away from me," the medic said. "You need a tetanus shot as well."

Joley glared at him. "I'm sure I don't. God, you're a freakin' butcher, and now you want to stab me with another needle. Everyone go away. I'm just fine. And for your information, Dr. Frankenstein, I can sew up my own arm. Jerry, make them all leave."

"You're kicking us out?" Brian said, his gaze shifting toward Ilya.

"Yes." She rocked back and forth. The energy high was giving way under the onslaught of nerves and pain. She needed to be alone, to pull herself back together. She was too exhausted to face any of them, let alone Ilya.

Jerry waved toward the door, and the band went out. She saw Brian glance around, and then he flipped open his cell phone. Instinct told her he was calling Nikitin. Fear skittered down her spine. "Jerry. Call Brian back." Jerry didn't turn around. She yanked her arm away from the medic and stood up.

Immediately the room swirled and the walls began to undulate. The floor shifted out from under her. Ilya caught her before she went down.

"I told you she needed blood," the medic complained.

"She'll be fine," Ilya said. "I'll take it from here."

"At least let me give her the tetanus shot."

"Do it then," Ilya suggested. "Before I throw you out on your ear."

"I'm not the one that did this to her," the medic protested.

"No, but you sure don't know much about suturing wounds either," Ilya pointed out. He waited impatiently for the man to administer the shot to Joley's arm, before placing her on the bed. The medic went out, closing the door, leaving the two of them alone.

Joley tried to say something, to stop her worst nightmare from happening, but no sound came out. She hadn't been able to bring herself to come right out and tell Jerry that she had worries about whether or not Ilya was in the Russian mob. And she certainly wasn't going to admit to sleeping with him. The best she could do was push ineffectually at him with her hand.

Ilya pretended not to notice her distress. "Lie back. I'll get you some orange juice. You can drink that while I finish sewing you up."

She made a face at his back, struggling into a semi-sitting position that made her feel less vulnerable. "You're not coming near me with a needle." She meant to sound firm, but her voice was thin and a little hoarse, as if her throat was raw.

He shot her a quelling look. "Don't waste your energy on arguing. You couldn't fight your way out of a paper bag, Joley." He pushed the glass of juice into her hand and pulled her arm closer to him to inspect it. Swearing under his breath, he placed his hands over the wound and sent warmth to speed healing and hopefully numb the area while he worked.

Tears coursed down her cheeks, but Joley didn't complain or try to pull away from him. He was as gentle as he could be.

"John Dylan is the member of your crew who you thought was friends with Dean. Dylan paid two kids to plant the charge to bring down the platform. He told them it was only going to shake the platform and he'd record you falling on your butt for the Internet. They thought it would be 'cool.' Stupid kids."

Joley let out her breath and pressed her free hand to her mouth to keep from weeping. Her arm hurt like hell, and Ilya's touch was so gentle it ripped at her heart. "I didn't do anything to him. I didn't even talk to him."

"He knows you spotted him. He doesn't know how, but he knows you did. He's covering something up and doesn't want you questioning him or telling anyone that he was the one you saw that night with Dean."

"He'll figure I told you. You were with me."

"He'll try to kill me." Ilya was matter-of-fact. "I'm going to give him his opportunity."

She sucked in her breath sharply. "That's stupid. You aren't a stupid man."

He paused for a moment and waited until she looked up at him. "In some areas, I can be very stupid, Joley. I hurt you and I'm sorry for that."

Her stomach protested the turn in the conversation. She didn't want him to be nice. She didn't want him near her at all, because she didn't trust herself. She was weak when it came to Ilya, and just like every other person in the world, where she was weak, she could make a terrible mistake. "Don't worry about it. I'm a big girl."

His eyes glittered dangerously and her pulse leapt. "Joley, whatever happened the other night . . ."

"Stop. I don't want to talk about it. I don't want to think about it. I'm tired, Ilya. And I have to catch a plane tonight. I hurt like hell and I think someone's trying to kill me. If I had any idea why, maybe I could figure it out, but I don't, so I'm screwed. I don't want you talking to me, or being nice to me, or pretending there's anything at all but sex between us, because you made it clear there wasn't. I don't like mixed signals, so don't throw them at me, especially now."

He bent over her, forcing her across the pillow. The deep sea of his eyes went from calm to stormy. "You're running from yourself, and the things you need in a relationship, not from me. I might not say what you want to hear, but there are no mixed signals. I'm fully committed to you. Now. Always."

Her heart slammed hard in her chest, and as hard as she tried, her body went into meltdown from his aggression, his strength, the raw possession and hunger in his eyes. Even with one hand wrapped around her throat, his thumb tipping her face up toward him and his thick chest weighing her down, she realized he was careful of her arm, careful to keep from jarring her. "You want sex, Ilya. You don't want to share who or what you are." Her gaze slid from his. "You know you can rule me in the bedroom, so yeah, it's probably a great turn-on for you."

"Be very careful what you say to me, Joley. I know you're hurt, and you're pushing me away, but sooner or later we're going to be alone together and you're going to have to face everything you've said or done."

Fear skated down her spine. She moistened her lips. "We're not going to be alone."

His eyebrow shot up. "Really? We are now."

He simply closed the scant inches between their lips and took her mouth. Not savagely. Not with the ravenous hunger she felt smoldering beneath the surface, but with such tenderness it nearly wrenched her heart right out of her body. Tears burned behind her eyelids, but she blinked them away. Before she could stop herself, she was kissing him back. She could try to blame it on exhaustion, but truthfully, the moment he touched her—he owned her.

Someone slammed their palm against the outside of her door. "Car's waiting. Let's go."

Ilya didn't hurry lifting his head. He finished kissing her thoroughly. "We'll figure this out, Joley, give it some time."

Pressing her hand against her burning mouth, she nodded and rushed out, Ilya following at a more leisurely pace. She didn't care if it looked to him as if she was running. She slid into the car beside Brian and closed her eyes, leaving them closed for nearly the entire ride to the airport. Around her, she could hear the others laughing and talking. Inside she wept. She hated that she had become the person she despised most. Weak and helpless against her own needs.

She watched Brian as he hurried away from the band at the airport, making his way to Nikitin's car in what had to be a previously arranged meeting. She felt for him, knew what it was like to want someone that was wrong for you. She wouldn't have understood before, but her own failings had given her a tolerance for and understanding of the weaknesses in others.

Brian returned within a few minutes, his steps heavy, his shoulders slumped. He looked as if the weight of the world was on him. Joley glanced around her to see if anyone else was watching. Tish knew. Joley could see it in her eyes when she looked at Brian as he walked back toward them. The others didn't notice, but Tish knew heartbreak, and Joley was becoming all too familiar with it, and there was no missing the pain in Brian's expression. For once, Joley didn't care about feeling another person's pain or emotion, she only cared about shielding her friend. As Brian approached, his steps heavy, she flung her arm around him and walked with him up the stairs to the plane.

"You okay?"

He shook his head. "When I'm with him, I find it so hard to believe that he's what you say he is. Even with the evidence I've seen with my own eyes, all the little things that add up, I don't want to believe it, Joley." He pressed his fingertips to his eyes hard.

"I'm sorry, Brian."

"He said he didn't mean the things he said. He swore he'd never consider hurting you or anyone else I cared about. He was hurt and angry that I didn't give him a chance to tell his side of things. I should have done that. I should have listened to him."

Joley sank into the seat beside him, noting that Logan, who was holding Lissa, and Tish had their heads close together while Rick strapped an infant seat to the chair for Lissa. Leo took a seat with Denny across from him. She knew, without looking, exactly where Ilya was at the back of the plane. She could feel his gaze on her. She was far too aware of him, every detail, so much so that sometimes she swore she knew when he took a breath. She reached over to Brian and rubbed his sleeve in an attempt to comfort him—or herself.

"If he is the head of one of the branches of mafia, or whatever they call it in Russia, he's dangerous. Being with him isn't worth dying over." She leaned her head back against the seat. "You know my family is different. We have other senses, gifts, magic if you will. We don't think of it that way, but we know things about people when we touch them. It's why I'm careful not to touch skin. I can feel emotions, and sometimes see things others would rather keep private." She smiled at him. "You hid yourself very well from me. I see auras and melodies, and yours has always been rather sad, as if you had suffered a great sorrow."

He shrugged his shoulders. "It's hard to be so alone all the time. I love music, Joley, and I love what we do. I looked after everyone and tried to keep us all together, which wasn't always easy, especially after Tish left Logan, but I was still alone. How can you be anything else when no one knows who you really are?"

Joley sighed. "Strangely, my friend, I felt exactly the same way."

"Joley, how could you? You're so beautiful and talented and easy to love. Hell, if I were straight, I'd be all over you."

She laughed. "There's always an excuse with you. But, seriously, I'm not all that great. I have secrets just like everyone else. We'll have to form the club for worst taste in men."

Brian ducked his head. "He could be good, Joley. He swears he had nothing to do with the incident tonight."

"You know better, Brian. Deep down, you know, that's why it hurts so much." She could feel Ilya's gaze on her and knew he was wondering what they were talking about. Sometimes she felt her palm itching, and a slight flutter of warmth in her mind, but she refused to acknowledge him. She might succumb if he touched her, but in the meantime, she was building defenses as fast as she could.

13

ILYA stood in the shadows as he normally did. The park had little lighting, and with the clouds overhead obscuring the moon, and the thick stand of trees, he doubted anyone could see him, but he wasn't taking chances with this meeting. He'd been followed. He'd lost his pursuers the moment he entered the park, but they'd find him again soon, so he had to hurry.

He watched through night glasses as Jonas Harrington came into view. Jonas wasn't alone, and Ilya recognized Aleksandr Volstov just from the way the man moved. They halted at the appointed meeting place, and with one last look around, he went to join them.

"What part of 'come alone' didn't you understand?" he asked Jonas.

Joley's brother-in-law looked him up and down, his expression a mixture of wariness and respect. Jonas was a man who couldn't be bought, had intense loyalties and would charge hell with a bucket of water if need be. Ilya liked and respected him almost as much as he did Aleksandr. He knew Volstov was engaged to another of Joley's sisters. The man had been a policeman in Russia and then later worked for Interpol.

"What the hell are you doing with Joley?" Jonas demanded.

"This meeting is about our mutual problem with Nikitin, not about Joley. That subject is off-limits," Ilya decreed.

Joley had been safely locked up in a hotel room for the last three days, away from him, and he hadn't realized until that moment how much it disturbed him that she wouldn't see him. She hadn't responded the times he'd whispered to her, shamelessly using his voice through their telepathic link, although he'd known she was awake and could hear him.

"My ass, it's off-limits," Jonas snarled. "You're not going to hurt Joley without getting the pounding of your life. I could care less if you scare everyone on three continents, you don't scare me. Stay the hell away from my sister."

Aleksandr put a restraining hand on Jonas's arm, giving Ilya a clue as to why he was there. Jonas was a hothead when it came to the Drake sisters. He'd been protecting them all of his life.

Ilya found Joley both maddening and endearing in her fight to stay away from him. He knew she thought she was running because of his reputation. His refusal to disclose his past had been another excuse. She feared turning her life, her body, her heart over to him. He knew what her needs were, and that embarrassed her, terrified her, because he would make certain they were met and she was fiercely independent. She didn't want to need him. She didn't even want to *want* him. He hoped she craved him, thought of him night and day the way he did her, because right now, that was all he had to entice her with—sex—and his voice.

Ilya shrugged. "I'm going to marry Joley, so you'd better get used to the idea of having me around."

"She know that?" Jonas asked, somewhat mollified.

"Not yet. She has a few issues with me."

"Don't you hurt her."

Ilya's eyebrow shot up, and for a moment his tough features were stamped with sheer arrogance. "I have no intentions of hurting Joley. And we're done with the subject."

More of the tension drained out of Jonas. "I'm not going to ask who you work for, Ilya, but you're in a bad position. Aleksandr's been hearing rumors from a few friends at Interpol that Nikitin is one of the main traffickers of women and children into Brussels and Indochina. If that's true, and his reputation is growing throughout Europe, then you're smack in the middle of a time bomb. Nikitin is spending so much time in the States that he's in danger of losing his stronghold. There'll be a war soon, and with every side thinking you're the enemy, you're going to be the number one target."

Aleksandr agreed. "Nikitin is spending way too much time here; he's been doing business, and he's made a few enemies, cutting into territories. He's got trouble on two fronts."

Ilya nodded. "I was afraid of that. I need information fast. I can't go through my usual channels so I'm asking for help."

Aleksandr snorted in derision at the tone of his old friend. "That must be hard."

Ilya sent him a look. "Nikitin is gay. He doesn't like women or little children, never has, they represent money and power to him, nothing else. He isn't sampling his products, he just sends them down the line fast."

"Are you sure?" Jonas asked. "Because Joley . . ."

"Not Joley. It's never been Joley. She's his cover. We've known that for some time. He recruited at least one of her crew members to help him move young girls, but his main interest is one of the band members—he's in love. I know you have someone undercover, working the other end to find the routes and the girls. I need to know if she's safe and out of the way because this thing is going to blow up in our faces."

Jonas and Aleksandr exchanged a long look. "Who are you talking about? Interpol has someone inside?"

Swift impatience crossed Ilya's face. "I'm coming clean with you at the risk of my life, not only my life, but blowing years of undercover work, not to mention taking down a major human trafficking ring. I'm asking you to do the same. If she was working for Interpol, I wouldn't need you reaching out, now would I? Where is she? Is she out yet?"

"She?" Jonas was beginning to have an idea of just who Ilya was referring to. "Tell me Elle Drake is not in any way involved in this mess. Do you think Elle is working undercover, trying to bring down this network? What have you heard?"

"You tell me. Nikitin is unstable at best, and now he's crazy. Joley tipped her band friend off, and the idiot did the noble thing and broke up with Nikitin. Nikitin knows the heat's come down on his human-trafficking routes. On top of that, Joley spotted some of the young girls with a couple of her crew members. Nikitin had one of the roadies killed, and did it nice and ugly to scare the other one, but if he loses his lover, his route and everything else he considers his because of Joley, he'll try to wipe out her and everyone close to her. If he gets an inkling Elle's anywhere near him, she'll be the first to go, and he'll make certain she suffers a long time before she's killed. I need to get her out if she isn't already gone."

"Honestly, Prakenskii, I have no idea where Elle is or who she's working for." Jonas swore in frustration. "Do you have enough evidence on Nikitin to take him down?"

"I can take down his routes, and most of his people, but he's never tied directly to anything and he always, *always*, has an alibi. He's got another layer above the one I've compromised, and I need them to make sure the trafficking is closed off for good here. Otherwise, I cut off one head and another grows back. It would take years to get that one and I don't have that much time."

"Jackson can get word to her. They've always been able to connect," Jonas said. "I honestly don't know what Elle's doing. I was fairly certain it involved undercover work, because Jackson's been restless and edgy lately and Elle's disappeared again."

"See if he can get word to her to get out for a while. Any excuse. I don't care how close she thinks she is to shutting things down, she has to get clear. I can't control or guess what Nikitin will do, but he has a tendency to resolve issues with violence."

"Joley has to come home where we can protect her," Jonas said.

"Joley can't go home without finishing her tour. As long as Nikitin is following the band, he'll think he has a chance to put things back together with his lover. The moment she pulls out, he's going to know he's blown and it won't matter anymore. I'm not throwing away years of work, Harrington. I can protect Joley from Nikitin. If I have to, I'll kill him, but I've got to get to his first line of people or all this has been for nothing."

Jonas exchanged another long look with Aleksandr. "Joley only has two performances here in southern California and two in northern California before she's finished. Time's running out, Prakenskii."

Ilya nodded. "I'm aware of that."

"You can't have her and keep up with this kind of work, Ilya. She's an all-or-nothing girl. She's never fallen in love before. She's wanted to, but she doesn't give her trust to anyone. If you're that man, you can't walk away from her. It would destroy her."

Joley was afraid of giving too much of herself and not sur-
viving if something went wrong. Jonas didn't have to tell him
that. He already knew it, because he felt the same way. But he
wasn't going to run from his only chance at happiness. Joley
had a family, he didn't. Joley had people who made her laugh
and could share her troubles. He didn't.

"I wouldn't presume to tell you how best to take care of
Hannah."

"The difference is, Joley's my sister. I've loved her since
she was born." Jonas refused to back down.

"You'll just have to trust me then," Ilya said and pulled on
a thin pair of leather gloves. He drew a very small but wicked-
looking knife from a hidden sheath, palming the handle, blade
up against his wrist. "Get out of here. We're about to have
company, and no one can know you were here."

Aleksandr crouched low, pulling his weapon. "You got any
backup here, Ilya?"

Ilya shook his head. "And you can't stay. If anyone spots
you, it could tip them off. It was a risk calling you. And get me
as much information on John Dylan as you can, as fast as you
can. I put it through channels, but they're going to take some
time."

"You got it," Jonas agreed. "But we're not leaving you to
get killed."

"I don't kill so easy," Ilya said, his voice dropping even
lower. "Get out so I don't have to worry about you. With the
two of you gone, any movement means an enemy in the field,
and I don't have to worry about fucking up."

Aleksandr nodded. "He's always worked alone, Jonas,
we'll just be in the way."

Ilya watched the two of them slip away into the darkness.
He took a deep breath and let it out. He'd deliberately lost the
two men trailing him once inside the park so he could have a
few moments to speak with Jonas, but he was prepared for a
confrontation—in fact, he welcomed it.

Joley's distance had left him edgy and surly inside, his
body demanding hers. The more she refused to speak to him,
the more he whispered to her, seducing her day and night with
his voice. It was a powerful tool, the one he could always fall
back on when all else failed. Hunting would let him expend a
little of that excess energy.

The trees weren't wide enough to hide his shoulders, and he preferred not using the heavier brush because there was more chance to make noise. He dropped low and moved with care toward the sound of approaching footsteps. A shadow lengthened and grew across the grass, as the man approached. He wore all black. He had two guns out and ready, holding them sideways. Joley would have laughed and said the man watched too many movies. It made Ilya want to smile to think of her, and somehow just the thought of her made him warm.

He stayed prone waiting for the man to come to him. As the shadow approached, he heard the soft hum of a radio and stiffened. The man was communicating with someone else. Ilya spoke several languages and manipulated sound easily. He could talk with perfect accents and imitate voices exactly after one hearing. His pitch was so perfect that when using audio scanners, it was impossible to tell the difference between his voice and whoever he was copying.

He let the man move past him. Rising up, Ilya covered the man's mouth and shoved a knife deep into his kidney. The guns dropped to the ground, and Ilya retrieved the radio, slipping it into his ear. He heard the buzz of voices. Not one more man after him, but several. They'd sent a team to kill him, and that told him they knew his reputation. This wasn't some idiot crew member of Joley's thinking he could protect himself by grabbing a couple of buddies and trying to off the bodyguard. This was a professional hit.

Nikitin had too many enemies. He was a highly intelligent man, and if Interpol knew a war was shaping up for Nikitin's turf, then so did Nikitin. Unless Ilya's cover was blown, the Russian mob boss would never order a hit on him. And Ilya doubted if anyone could unravel his cover. Aleksandr had known him most of his life, and he hadn't known for certain until they'd crossed paths recently and Ilya had allowed him glimpses into his real life.

Being alone for so many years had become wearing, and after a while, undercover agents really began to believe their own cover stories. He had wanted Aleksandr and Jonas Harrington to figure out who and what he was. If there was one man in the world he trusted, it was Aleksandr, and now that he'd come to know Jonas, he was beginning to believe there might be a second man he could trust. So if his cover wasn't blown, then who wanted him dead—and why?

The attackers had spread out in a loose line. Ilya had taken out one in the center, but there were men on either side of him, working their way across the park. One appeared to be giving the others instructions. The voice was speaking English perfectly. There was no hint of an accent, other than New York. No European, certainly not Russian. The man he'd killed had also been American.

He pushed through the grass on his belly, rolled a few feet and came up on a second man. This one was much larger than the first. Ilya rose up like a monster, using the same method, taking him from behind, covering his mouth and sinking the blade into flesh. His opponent was enormously strong and wrenched forward, trying to tear out of Ilya's grip. He fired his weapon, making it no longer necessary for silence.

Ilya caught the man's head in both hands and wrenched, breaking the would-be assassin's neck. He crouched beside him, retrieving the knife and wiping the blade on his enemy's shirt. Having shoved the knife into his belt, he pulled his gun and proceeded to run in a straight line toward the next man. Two down. He was certain there were six of them. The other four burst into a furious round of hissing out questions and orders while he gained several yards on them.

He was adept at throwing sound and made certain to make noise to his left. A volley of shots rang out. He fired at the flash, heard a grunt followed by a thud. Ilya dropped to the ground when he heard the body fall. Immediately more gunfire broke out. The earpiece nearly burst as the leader shouted at the others to stop firing, warning them they might hit one another.

Two men nearly came together over the top of him; he rolled to fire off a shot as one fired simultaneously. The bullet kissed his arm hard enough to knock him back, taking a chunk of flesh with it. That would leave DNA he didn't want on scene. Cursing, he rolled and came up on his feet. The man who'd shot him was down, the bullet having taken him between the eyes. The second was on him, swinging a gun at Ilya's head.

He ducked, just not quite fast enough. The metal scraped across his cheekbone as Ilya jerked his head out of the way.

He kicked hard, aiming for a kneecap, striking just above his target. The man grunted, staggered, his leg buckling. Ilya caught him hard with a roundhouse kick to the head, driving him to the ground. He followed through with a kick to the trachea, stomping hard. The man's eyes went wide and the gun slipped out of his nerveless hand.

Ilya hastily tore his shirt and wrapped the wound on his arm to prevent throwing more droplets of blood around the crime scene. Four down. He had two to go and he had to kill them. He couldn't leave anyone alive, since he had only spotted the first two after him. He didn't know if anyone had seen Jonas Harrington and Aleksandr Volstov, but if they had, his cover was blown and Joley was a dead woman for certain.

He retrieved the fallen man's gun, the one that had struck his cheek, ripping his skin. He couldn't leave that on scene either. That would have to be dismantled and gotten rid of far away from here. Tucking it into his belt, he began to move again.

The others were more cautious in the sudden silence. One swore, the other told him to shut up. Ilya slipped into the trees close to the playground. He could see childhood toys, a swing, a slide, a merry-go-round. Not that he'd ever played on such things. He'd climbed cargo nets over two stories high and scaled the walls of buildings, but he'd never even sat in a swing. His life had always been like this—hunted or hunter.

He waited, calm, not feeling the pain in his arm or face. The only thing that mattered was sound and movement. The wind was soft, rustling through trees, lifting the leaves to show glimpses of silver when the moon managed to break through the clouds. In the distance he heard traffic. In his ear, with the earpiece, he heard heavy breathing. A twig snapped a few yards to his right. He slowly lowered his body, keeping close to the brush to conceal his outline, turning toward the sound, waiting. Just waiting.

It occurred to him then that he'd spent most of his lifetime waiting in the shadows for someone to make a wrong move. He was done after this assignment, done with undercover work and living a solitary, cold existence. He was through killing people. He wished the killing mattered, that it bothered him, but he had been closed off to emotion for too long to resurrect guilt now. Undercover work, or taking out someone who lived beyond the arm of the law, was simply a job, and he had a code he tried never to deviate from, one that he could live with in a world of violence. He had a couple of triggers and his bosses knew it. The mistreatment of women and of children. He had seen too much as a child and wouldn't tolerate it, so he was often sent on the jobs demanding cleanup rather than arrest. Like the one he was on now.

The branches of a bush swayed against the wind. Another twig snapped. Loud. Too loud. He turned fast, felt the knife slice across his ribs as he slapped it down and away from him. A second attacker had come up behind him. The only reason the strike hadn't hit home was because Ilya was blurring his image a bit and his assailant hadn't seen him until he was right up on him. He'd swung a knife instead of firing his gun.

Ilya kicked the man's gun arm, smashing through bone, moving inside to whirl the attacker in front of him, facing the swaying bush. Bullets spat out and thunked into his human shield. Ilya dragged the deadweight with him until he had relative cover. He dropped the body, dove for the ground and crawled rapidly into thicker brush. The moment he was clear, he tore a strip from his shirt with his teeth and bound his wound.

He waited in silence again. Minutes ticked by. The shots were bound to have attracted someone's attention. He didn't have the luxury of patience. He began to work his way toward the remaining man. He could still hear heavy breathing, this time rasping, as the air burst from lungs overtaxed with anxiety.

The last attacker decided to make a run for it. He began to withdraw, backing through the brush, cracking small branches and crunching dry leaves. Ilya pinpointed his position and rolled toward him fast, coming up firing several shots in rapid succession. The attacker hunched over on the ground. Ilya crawled close, still covering him. A finger on the man's neck found no pulse. Ilya spent a few minutes looking for the knife that had scraped his ribs, retrieving it so he could leave a relatively clean scene behind.

He glanced at his watch and swore. Joley's performance was nearly over. The feeling of doom inside him hadn't lessened.

The danger he'd sensed hadn't just been this hit squad. He had to get back to Joley fast.

ILYA isn't in the arena. Joley could barely focus. She was worried, worried enough that she'd reached out telepathically and tried to connect with him. He hadn't answered. Uneasily she glanced around at the band. Ordinarily, Staples Center in Los Angeles was another of her favorite performance venues, but this time, she felt overwhelmed instead of energized by the thought of performing that night.

She had a bad feeling. Her stomach churned with a terrible dread she couldn't shake.

"Come on, Joley, get dressed. We've got to go on in a few minutes," Logan said, glancing at Tish for help.

Tish sent Logan a quick quelling look and flashed Joley a bright smile. "Logan can watch the baby while I help you."

"Ten minutes, Tish," Jerry reminded her.

Joley realized they were all treating her carefully. She knew they thought her arm, which was swollen and bruised but healing fast, was much worse than it was. Only Tish and Brian knew the truth. She was pining away for the wrong man. He talked to her at night when she couldn't sleep. She wanted to beg and plead with him to come to her, but she'd remained silent. If she expected Brian to stay away from Nikitin and Denny to stay away from drugs and women, and Logan to toe the line with Tish, then she expected the same high standard of herself.

"It's amazing how you've just fallen right back into taking care of all of us," Joley said as she pulled open the door to the large room she'd been given to get ready. She preferred her own bus, it helped calm her down, but she'd come directly from the hotel, so she used the suite the center set aside for their performers.

"I forgot how much I loved to travel with the band," Tish said, shoving a long narrow box to the back of the table so she could set Joley's makeup case there. "Who sent the flowers?"

"Are there flowers?" Joley's heart leapt. Maybe Ilya had sent them. If he had, she'd do the right thing and throw them away. Or maybe that wouldn't be right. She wouldn't want them to go to waste. "Let me see. Is there a card with them?"

Tish dragged the box back to the center of the table and handed the card to Joley while she lifted the lid. Joley bent over her shoulder, ripping open the small card. She glanced at the card, hoping it was from Ilya.

DIE BITCH

The two words were typed in black bold letters across the white linen card. Tish shoved Joley back and dropped the lid. The box spilled out a dozen long-stemmed blackened roses and a grotesque decapitated doll cut into pieces.

"Okay, that's totally sick," Tish said.

Joley looked around the room. "Maybe it wasn't meant for me. I'm pretty sure I'm not a bitch. Well, at least most of the time."

Tish moistened her suddenly dry lips. "This is crazy, Joley. Who would do this?"

"I don't know, but they have really poor taste in flowers." Joley sank down into a chair and looked up at her friend. "I think I'm done with this life. Really, Tish. I can't deal with the crazies or the paparazzi anymore. Did you see the headlines this morning? There's pictures of me on the ground splashed all over the papers and the Internet. One picture looks as if I'm crawling. The headlines say I'm drunk—too drunk to stand or perform. There's a shot of Brian looking worried and a headline saying he wants an intervention to try to save me. They shoved me, Tish, onto the ground and then took the photographs. I wasn't drinking, Brian was worried because he thought I might be hurt. One of them reached down like he was going to help me up, but instead he asked me a question."

"I know it's hard right now," Tish said. "But you're also upset over other things and that's making it worse."

"You mean Ilya." Joley pushed her head into the heel of her hand. "He isn't here. I know something's wrong. I feel it. He isn't here." The last came out forlorn. "I didn't realize how much I depended on his presence."

Tish used a napkin to push the box of dead flowers to the back of the table and replace the lid. "I'll get the security people to turn that over to whoever takes care of it. In the meantime, Joley, you need makeup. You can't go perform like that."

"I don't want to go on tonight." Joley turned around and

put her head back so Tish could apply the makeup. "Maybe we should say I'm sick."

Tish studied her face. "Are you?"

Joley sighed. "I don't think so. I just feel off. Tired. Exhausted."

"You aren't sleeping again."

"No. I could sleep when he was there. Why is that? If I don't trust him, why would I be able to fall asleep with him when I can't with anyone else?"

"Hold still." Tish frowned as she applied eyeliner. "You're on the pill, right?"

Joley nearly fell off the chair. "Where did that come from? Of course I'm on the pill. Lissa must be putting babies in your brain. I'm just tired, and sick of the whack jobs following me everywhere threatening to kill me because they love me so much."

"I don't think whoever sent the flowers feels that way about you. 'Die bitch' doesn't seem very loving to me."

Joley shoved both hands through her hair. She was still back on Tish's unexpected comment implying she might be feeling sick and miserable because she could be pregnant. She was on the pill and she'd just had sex a few days earlier. Tish was nuts. Sheesh. She struggled to bring her mind away from Ilya, sex and babies and keep the focus on whoever had sent her the dead flowers. "I got a weird phone call on my cell the night we left Red Rocks. Jerry gave me a new cell and number. But Ilya kept that number and phone in case they called back. He said sometimes if they hear your voice it's enough to keep them from escalating." Joley leaned forward to apply lipstick. "How much time do I have?"

"You've got to hurry, hon." Tish patted Joley's hair and nodded her head in satisfaction. "Your hair looks great. Very healthy and lots of shine."

"That's nice to know. I don't feel shiny. Where're my clothes?" Joley looked around. "I thought I hung them outside the closet. I don't know where my brain is tonight." Thinking of Ilya. Worried about him. Worried about the pressing dread that wouldn't go away. She hopped up and stalked across the room to the little clothes closet built into the wall.

Joley yanked open the closet door impatiently. Tish gasped. There was nothing left of the outfit Joley had planned to wear onstage. It hung in shreds, long thin tails of glittering material. Her special jeans, covered in a dazzling rainbow of rhinestones, were in worse shape.

She moistened her lips and blinked up at Tish. "They don't much like the clothes I wear either." Tears burned behind her eyelids. "I'm not going to let them make me cry." But she wanted to cry—not for the flowers or the cut-up doll, or even her stage clothes—although it was her favorite outfit—she wanted to cry because Ilya wasn't there and she was terrified for him.

The dread that had been building for the last hour, making her heart race and her palms sweat, was only growing stronger, and it had nothing to do with what was happening to her.

"You're on in five minutes, Joley. What are you going to do?"

"I'll be going casual tonight." Her chin went up and her eyes glittered with anger. "Because—screw them, Tish. No one's going to scare me off performing. If and when I quit, it will be because I want to, not because I let them beat me. Whoever this sick person is, they can just go buy a ticket and watch me, because I'll be giving the performance of my life out there tonight."

"Good for you, honey," Tish said. "Let's do it. Jerry and I will see to this mess, you take care of giving those people who came to see you the show of their lives."

Joley had to run to catch the band. She nearly missed the huddle. Brian raised an eyebrow at her casual garb, but it didn't seem to matter at all to their audience when they took the stage. She joked about her elegant attire and showed off her running shoes as she skipped across the stage, flashing her famous smile. Her voice was in good form, and she delivered every note as if she was having the time of her life. Her joy in her music carried the crowd to a new high, and they went through the roof, yelling, clapping and stomping for more. And she gave them more, finishing up with several of the audience's shouted requests before ending with her latest, very popular single.

Joley waited until after the performance, when they were back in the suite, before she told the band members about the flowers and her clothes. "Sorry about not dressing up."

"It didn't seem to matter," Denny said. "We rocked the house tonight."

"Yeah, we did," she agreed. "We're leaving for Anaheim in the morning, right? We have one more show before we hit northern California and we're almost home, boys."

She would be so happy to get home to Sea Haven and her sisters. In the meantime, she wanted to see Ilya, just to make certain he was all right. She'd looked for him when she'd come offstage, but he wasn't there and event security had escorted them from the stage. With a sigh, Joley walked through the parking lot toward her bus, looking around for her bodyguard. She'd be grateful to get inside where she could collapse and close her eyes and concentrate on trying to reach him through their telepathic connection.

Steve came toward her from the front of the bus. She waved, stopping him. "Hey, Steve. I needed to ask you about something. I got this box, narrow, like for long-stemmed roses, but it had dead flowers in it and a chopped-up doll. They were in the dressing room along with my clothes, which someone had shredded. Did you happen to see anyone, or have anyone ask you to deliver the box to my dressing room this afternoon?"

"What are you accusing me of, Joley?" he snapped. "You think I brought you dead flowers and cut up your clothes?"

His aura bothered her, the colors swirling in muddy grays and darker greens and browns. She talked to Steve all the time, but usually they were separated by tinted glass or the partition in the bus. His aura indicated he was agitated, nervous—upset even.

Joley frowned. "I wasn't accusing you of bringing the box into the room, Steve, I was asking if you'd seen anyone, or if they'd asked you to drop it off. You've been with me for years. Why would I think you'd want to bring me some dead flowers? Sheesh, if you had a beef with me, I'd assume you'd tell me."

Steve shrugged, visibly calming. "I don't know, Joley. I guess everything is making us all a little on edge. Where's your bodyguard tonight? I thought he'd be with you. I wasn't happy when Jerry gave me the word he was hiring him, but I haven't exactly been doing that job for a long time. You never ask me to do anything but drive, and I've gotten in the habit of just taking you or the band anywhere you want to go."

"I'm comfortable with you, Steve," Joley said, "and I sure don't want you to have to fling your body between mine and a bullet. Or a dead flower." She flashed him a small grin. "Besides, if you were always hanging with me, how would you ever drive the boys to the parties?"

"You knew about that?"

"Sure. I thought it was a great idea. Jerry told me a few years back that if I was tucked safe in my room or on the bus, you were willing to make certain the boys wouldn't try to drive drunk—that you'd get them safely back. I thought it was wonderful. If Jerry hurt your feelings by hiring Prakenskii, you should have told me. Besides, it's a temporary thing."

"And he doesn't appear to be here to do his job." There was satisfaction in Steve's voice.

Joley sighed. She was getting used to people—especially men—not liking Ilya. He was too dominant, and made men uneasy. "He was supposed to be here. Maybe Nikitin held him up. He's here in LA." Joley started again for the bus.

"Yeah, I know. I drove Brian to see him this afternoon." Steve remained where he was.

Joley stopped and looked back at him. "Brian? Before the show?"

"Yes, he asked me to take him to the hotel and I did. Shouldn't I have?"

"Oh no, it was okay. I just seem to be out of the loop lately. You know I'm not all that fond of Nikitin's parties. The last one everyone went to was a big mess." She took a step back toward Steve. "In all the times you drove the band to his parties, did you notice underage girls there?"

He sighed. "I tried not to see anything, Joley. I like my job. I just do the driving."

She nodded and turned back to the bus with a little wave. "What time are we pulling out tonight?"

"Jerry said he wanted us on the road by five this morning. You can probably catch some sleep before we get moving. That's what I'm going to try to do."

"Sounds good." Joley waved again and hurried across the lot to her bus.

She stopped abruptly as she neared her home away from home. A photograph was stuck to the door. It was a picture of her standing in the parking lot talking to Tish. Tish and she each had a bullet painted into the center of her throat. She pulled the picture off and stared down at the words pasted from a magazine onto the glossy print.

BACK OFF THE GIRL OR YOU'RE BOTH DEAD.

The girl? The missing girl? She glanced around, her fingers on the door handle. Where was Ilya? Her stomach was dropping out of her body and her heart pounded like it might leap out of her chest. She was getting an awful lot of notes lately. She yanked the door open.

"Joley! Wait. I need to talk to you about those flowers. Hang on a second."

She turned at the sound of Jerry's voice. His familiar face was a relief. She let out her breath and started toward him, wanting someone else to see the threat, not only to her, but to Tish. The flowers were nothing in comparison. She'd taken several steps when thunder crashed in her ears, and it felt as if a freight train slammed into her.

14

THE explosion rocked the ground and sent the bus walls bursting outward in all directions, including up into the sky. The concussion blasted Joley off her feet, picking her up as if she were a paper doll and hurling her forward through the air. She landed hard, her ears ringing, lungs fighting for air, pain streaking through her body while burning debris rained down around her.

Stunned and uncomprehending, Joley raised her arms to try to cover her head as shards of glass pierced her skin. Splintered wood, paper and materials fell all around her. Her vision blurred, eyes burning. She barely realized what happened as she fought for breath. She'd hit the ground so hard it had knocked the wind out of her. Panic rose sharp and fast. She couldn't breathe, she couldn't get air, and fiery embers and sharp glass rained down on her.

Joley! Breathe, damn it, take a breath. Protect yourself.

She felt hands on her, lifting her rib cage, but they weren't Ilya's hands, and she fought, doubling her fist, striking out blindly, kicking to fight her way free. Someone was trying to kill her—that much registered, and she fought wildly.

I can't see. There was panic in her voice, in her mind, filling her when she should have been worried about breathing. *Where are you?* Because he had to come. If he was there, the world would be right again. He would keep her safe. He had to come. She kicked out blindly, swinging her fist, crying when she didn't connect.

"Joley! Stop it."

Hard hands tried to hold her down. Her ears were ringing so loud the voice was distorted. She didn't recognize the touch. It wasn't him. It wasn't Ilya.

I'm coming, lyubimaya moya. *Take a breath. Breathe for me.*

The hands pinned her to the ground, and something rubbed across her face and eyes. She forced air through her lungs. No matter what, Ilya would come for her. If someone was trying to harm her, they'd never get away with it.

"Let me look, Joley. There's blood everywhere. Stop fighting."

This time she recognized the voice of her manager, Jerry. She wiped at her face, blinked rapidly and looked at his blurry face through stinging eyes. Her hands were covered in blood. Shocked, she stared at the mess around her, the dust settling to the ground, her ears still ringing from the explosion.

She was barely aware of her manager crouching beside her, wiping at her face again. "Are you all right, Joley? Answer me. Should I call an ambulance?"

She could barely see, her vision blurry, but she peered around her at the debris that had been her bus. Smoke and dust littered the air, while splintered furniture and her belongings were scattered around her.

"Joley!" Brian rushed to her, followed by Denny. "Are you hurt? Is she hurt, Jerry? There's blood all over her. Get an ambulance. Get one now, Denny!"

She blinked up at him, shock in her eyes. "My God, Brian. This has something to do with that girl's disappearance. It does." She tried to think, but her brain seemed scrambled, thoughts bouncing so fast she couldn't catch them. She caught a glimpse of Steve off to the side, staring as if dazed at the wreckage.

"She's in shock," Jerry said.

She shook her head, although she was certain he was right. She was cold—too cold—and she couldn't stop shaking. Even her teeth chattered. "No, I'm not. And I don't need an ambulance." She wiped her face and stared down in surprise at the blood smearing her hand. "It's a small cut, nothing serious." She hoped it was true.

"You're bleeding from your leg and arm, too, Joley," Brian said.

She hurt, but in so many places she couldn't process it all. Her hands were trembling. The ringing in her ears was so loud it sounded like a swarm of angry bees. She pressed her hands to her ears in an effort to stop it. "It's nothing, small cuts." They didn't feel small. She couldn't quite move, her body refusing to obey her, and that was terrifying. *Where are you?* He had to come; she didn't know what to do.

"The cuts aren't small," Jerry protested. "And you're losing blood all over the place."

"This is crazy, Jerry." Joley peered around her, more dazed than coherent, her body shaking involuntarily. "Brian, look at this, look at my bus." She couldn't get her mind to work. She tried to stand, but her legs wouldn't hold her up.

Brian kept a hand on her shoulder, keeping her still. "Stay there, Joley. The police are swarming the place, security's everywhere, and they'll be sending in a doctor to look at you, so just sit still until someone gets here and clears you."

"This is about that little girl who went missing. That's what the bomb was all about—getting us to back off trying to find out who she was with. Someone put this on my bus." She still had the picture clutched in her hands and she held it up.

"That's crazy. It's only drawing more attention to her disappearance." Brian pressed a cloth to her forehead. Ignoring her wince, he pressed hard. "And why go for you? You have nothing to do with it. Jerry maybe and me, certainly. We're the ones asking questions, not you."

She pushed harder at his arm. "That hurts."

"You're going to need stitches, so just sit there until we get a doctor in here." Brian scratched his head. "Joley, this doesn't make sense. Why bother to warn you to back off and then try to kill you? How stupid is that?"

Joley could barely think with her ears ringing, the throbbing cut at her temple and the way her heart squeezed hard and painful in her chest. She was really afraid now. Someone wanted her dead. She should have gone into the bus, would have if Jerry hadn't called out to her.

Sirens wailed and voices grew louder. Joley stiffened, feeling energy surging toward her aggressively.

Joley! Answer me. Are you all right?

The voice in her head trembled with anxiety, but held a firm, commanding note, pushing at her mind to obey instantly.

Finally, Ilya Prakenskii, and he was close. Her heart leapt, began pounding a welcome. Adrenaline surged. She clenched her teeth against the need to run to him and fling herself into his arms. She hated weakness in herself, and Ilya was a huge weakness. Cameras were everywhere now. If she turned to him, it would be all over the tabloids, but she wanted to—needed to—be held by him.

Joley. There was a tinge of fear this time, and God help her, she found that small note thrilling.

The voice swore, and the surge of energy grew darker. Someone behind her screamed, and she turned to see Ilya mowing people down as if they were cardboard figures, his glittering blue eyes locked on her, his face grim. He looked like an avenging god, breathtaking, power in motion, his masculine body moving with fluid, lethal grace. The paparazzi, the gathering crowd, even his own security people were knocked flat as he came for her.

He took her breath away. The sheer beauty and energy of him, as if he was power personified, as if he understood the very force of nature and somehow was part of it. Men moved out of his way until he flowed past like the wind of death, holding their breath to keep from taking a chance that they might draw his attention.

Joley couldn't stop the way her body rose and her feet began to run. Her vision blurred again, and this time she was afraid she was crying. She'd been fine—*fine*—in control—until she saw him. Now she couldn't get to him fast enough.

His arms closed around her and he dragged her against his chest. He was so strong—a rock, hard and unyielding, when she needed an anchor to cling to. She knew she was safe. Flashes went off around them, and Joley huddled closer to him, keeping her face buried. Sobs shook her body, and no matter how hard she tried she couldn't stop crying. And the press was already there.

I'm getting you out of here. Dover'sya mne.

He didn't ask. Ordinarily that would have made her crazy, but she didn't want to have to think. He just said trust me and had her in his arms, cradling her close to his chest. Her head hurt and her ears were ringing and her world had just gone up in smoke. She circled his neck with her arms and pressed her face there, accepting his protection.

"Brian," Ilya snapped. "I'm taking her somewhere secure."

"She needs to go to the hospital," Brian called in desperation.

Joley stirred as if she might protest, but she could feel Ilya's absolute resolve and she didn't have the energy to argue with him. Ilya was always a force to be reckoned with, and right now she wanted to just curl up and cry, so she allowed him to take her over.

She felt the brush of his mouth on the top of her head, the strength in his arms, the shift of his muscles as he took her through the crowd to a waiting car. The door of the Town Car was open and he slid in, an easy, fluid move, never once jostling her. The door slammed closed.

"Go," Ilya ordered. "Hurry."

"They're going to follow us, Ilya," Joley warned. "The reporters. They won't stop."

"They're giving chase," the driver confirmed, glancing in the rearview mirror.

"I don't want anyone to see me like this," Joley protested, without lifting her head. She could live with the tabloids falsely portraying her as a partying, hard-living rock-and-roll icon, but she couldn't bear for anyone to see her vulnerable.

"Go to the house," Ilya ordered.

Everything in her stilled. Joley pulled away—or rather tried to. Ilya's arms remained around her like steel bands.

"Nikitin's house?"

"No. My house. I do have one or two when needed." He caught her chin in his fingers and lifted her face so he could examine the cut. "You'll need stitches."

For the first time she really looked at him. There was an angry scrape along his cheekbone, a bloody gash at his ribs and a bloodsoaked cloth wrapped around his upper arm. "Oh my God. *Ilya.* Oh my God." She tried to kneel up on the seat to examine him. "You're hurt. You need a doctor worse than I do. What happened? Tell me. And tell the driver to take us to the hospital."

She touched his raw cheekbone with gentle fingers. "I'm not Libby, but I can help. Where else? Your side. Your arm." Blood soaked through the makeshift bandage on his upper arm, and more spread in a widening patch at his side. "Ilya, this doesn't look good."

"Shh, *laskovaya moya*, the driver will get us somewhere safe and we'll take care of everything. You've got a concussion and you're in shock. Lie quietly."

He settled her back in his arms, holding her to him, his heart still stuttering from the close call. Someone was going to die over this. Threats were a nuisance, but trying to kill Joley was a death sentence.

"You look like you've been in a war," she said softly. "Tell me what happened." She brushed at her head several times, smearing more blood, wincing, and repeating the action.

Ilya pulled her closer, wrapping his arms around her to stop the involuntary movement. He nuzzled the top of her head, feeling the tremors inside his body that never showed on the outside. Joley was far more to him than sex. There was no getting around his emotional ties to her. He might not like them, but they were there, and he was man enough to realize he was no longer the same and never would be. His comfortable world of detachment was gone for all time. Joley had managed to creep inside him and twist herself around his heart so tightly, there was no shaking her loose.

"You look like you've been in a war as well, Joley," he murmured. "Let's just get to a safe house and we'll sort it all out."

She needed the sound of his voice desperately. The ringing in her ears was so loud, and fear clawed and raked at her stomach—fear for her—for him.

"You have a home? Here?" She thought of him as a loner, a lone warrior who moved restlessly through the world. No friends. No family. Never in one place long. She couldn't imagine him with a home—or a family. Shifting in his arms, she glanced at the front to try to glimpse the driver, but the tinted window had already slid smoothly into place, preventing her from being able to see, and later identify, his face.

She shifted again, her legs moving restlessly. She reached for the door handle, but Ilya caught her wrist and brought her hand to his chest.

She should have been afraid, but she felt safe—protected even. Her head throbbed terribly, the cuts and scrapes burning, and she was having trouble reining in her scattered thoughts. The urge to get out of the car was strong, as if she had to run, but Ilya lessened the need by his comforting presence.

Her world was upside down. She couldn't begin to sort

through everything—the accidents, the threats, the missing teenager. Her bus had been blown up, and the paparazzi followed her through the streets to catch a photograph of her with blood running down her face. It wasn't like her condition mattered at all to them, just getting a photograph to show the world that she was injured. She moved restlessly again, the urge to run strong.

"Not exactly a home," Ilya said, soothing her with his voice, "but it will do for now and you'll be safe enough there. No reporters are going to get within miles of it."

"They always do, Ilya." She didn't want him to leave her, but she had to be honest. "If you have anything at all to hide—if you don't want to be photographed with me—you should take me to a hotel and just let me out of the car."

His ice-blue eyes flickered, and just for a moment she caught her breath at what she saw there—raw desire, smoky need—and something else. Affection? Love even? That couldn't be, but there was enough concern in his eyes to melt her heart and give her hope when she shouldn't dare to hope.

"Are you trying to look out for me?"

His voice nearly curled her toes. For one moment all the pain was gone and she felt safe and loved and wrapped up in velvet. She sighed and made herself be strong.

"You value your privacy, and . . ." It had to be said. She rarely asked him about his lifestyle, or the things he did, other than when she was censuring him, but a man in his kind of work couldn't afford to be splashed all over the tabloids. "Your life might depend on it. If they photograph you even once with me, the reporters will be relentless. They'll uncover every secret you've ever had. It would be better to drop me off at the hospital and disappear. You got me out of there and I'm grateful to you."

And she was. She would have hated for the tabloids to get pictures of her so vulnerable, but more than that, she didn't want to make Ilya's life any harder or more complicated than she already knew it was. "There's no reason to risk everything, Ilya."

"They won't find us. The driver will create a diversion."

"He can do that?" She glanced at the tinted partition. "I'll have to lure him away to work for me. And I've got to call my sisters and let them know I'm all right and where I'll be."

She was chattering too much, something she did when she was nervous, and right now she was very nervous. Her beloved bus was gone. Dean Walters had been murdered. She had cuts and bruises everywhere, and her head hurt so bad she could barely think. But she knew one thing for certain—she was with the only person in the world who could make her feel that he could keep her absolutely safe.

"Better wait," Ilya said, and took her cell phone out of her hand. "We can't take any chances until we're safe inside the gates without the reporters hounding us."

Joley bit back a protest. What difference did a few minutes make? "My head really hurts, Ilya." Her hand went to the door handle again as the urge to move, to keep moving drove her. It was more than pain in her head; there was a roaring, as if her mind couldn't be still when she needed calm most. The noise made it impossible to think.

"I know, *laskovaya moya*. Another few minutes and I'll take care of it."

He pressed his hand to the cut on her head. That was the one he was most worried about. The ones on her arms and legs were from glass shards or flying metal. They hurt and a couple might need a stitch or two, but the one on her head was larger and she was obviously still dazed. She was attempting to stay focused by chattering, but she kept trying to move, to get out of the car, to brush at her head, and she didn't even realize she was doing it.

His heart ached with love for her. She was courageous, looking out for his safety when she should have been weeping in his arms.

"That hurts," Joley said, trying to pull away.

"I know, *devochka moya*. I need to slow down the bleeding. It will help get the healing started as well. Relax for me and just let me take care of things."

He kept his hand pressed to her forehead, palm over the cut, warmth moving from his center to her head. Colors spun for a moment, many different ones, spinning in an ever tightening circle until white light burst through, taking all the colors and turning them into flashes of heat.

She had forgotten that he possessed all the talents, just as Elle, her youngest sibling, did, and healing was among them. She knew from experience, watching Libby, that a cut as deep as the one she had wouldn't magically disappear, but he certainly helped slow the flow of blood and took away a great deal of the throbbing. Even the ringing in her ears was better.

"I think I was in shock."

Joley tried to sit up, but Ilya tightened his hold. "Stay still. Relax. Breathe. Let me take care of you for a few more minutes, at least until my heart slows down." He nuzzled the top of her head. "You scared me this time."

"I didn't blow up my bus," she pointed out.

"Who did you make angry this time?" he asked.

She found a small smile forming, and the coldness inside receded a little. "You can compare notes with my security people. They think I'm a nightmare."

"They're right. And don't think I won't be talking to them. What the hell were they doing holding a line instead of getting you the hell out of there? One explosion doesn't mean there's not going to be another. And if you were the target, they should have secured your protection before anything else."

There was an edge to him, not his voice, but his melody, his aura—she felt it and shivered. She was astonished that he could hold her the way he was when he had his own injuries.

"Just let it go, Joley," he murmured softly. "Relax and let me take care of you."

But who was going to take care of him? She closed her eyes and inhaled him. He smelled of blood and sweat, but also that strange male musk she found so enticing about him.

"You can't go to sleep on me," Ilya warned. "We're pulling through the gates now. No one knows about this house, not Nikitin, not anyone. I'm going to have my driver contact the police to send a detective out to interview you after I take care of your wounds. Then you can rest."

"He can't see you," she protested. "No police, Ilya. I'll go down to the station after I take care of my head." Her aching head. Even with his healing energy, her brain was shaken.

He carried her from the car, once again disregarding his own wounds, sheltering her against his heart as he crossed open ground to the door. Once inside, he carried her into an enormous tiled bathroom and set her on the sink.

"This is going to hurt, Joley."

"I know. But I can always sew you up next. You did my arm and it's healing fine."

"I have a little experience with wounds."

Joley was certain that was an understatement. She'd seen his body and the various scars covering him. He had three more to add to his collection.

He washed the gash on her forehead carefully with a fiery liquid that had tears running down her face, but she held still for him. She breathed in deeply as the room began to spin and the edges of her vision blurred.

"Talk to me."

Ilya tried to infuse more healing warmth into the wound before he began the tiny stitches necessary to close it. "Tell me what happened, Joley. Then I'll tell you about my evening."

She pressed her hand to his chest, right over his heart. "Promise?"

He bent to brush a kiss on top of her head before resuming the small even stitches. "Hold still, *devochka moya*, I don't want to leave a scar."

"It's not going to scar, not when you're using healing energy," she said, but she gasped and the tears streamed down her cheeks. "First there were the flowers."

He stiffened. "Someone sent you flowers?"

Her hand was still on his chest and it puffed out aggressively. She smiled through her tears at his male reaction. "Yes. Long-stemmed dead flowers along with a decapitated doll. The torso and legs of the doll were chopped in several pieces. It was very ugly."

He paused and looked down at her face. "Where were the flowers?"

"In the dressing room at the arena. And I'd hung my clothes on a little hook on the closet door, but when I looked around I didn't see them right away."

He sighed. "But you didn't leave the room and get security."

"Are you going to let me tell you? Sheesh, Ilya. I couldn't remember for certain if I'd put the clothes in the closet. I thought maybe I'd just thought about hanging them on the hook." She tried to hold still, but her forehead burned so bad she squirmed. "Someone had shredded the outfit into thin tiny scraps of material. My favorite outfit." Her voice rose to a wail.

Ilya immediately stopped and let her breathe through the pain. "Almost finished with this one. You're doing fine."

"You weren't there." She spoke accusingly even though it didn't make sense to. She'd told herself she'd been relieved when she finally crept out of the hotel like the coward she was and he hadn't been there to guard her. She'd ached to see him, yet at the same time, she was terrified she'd just throw pride away and let him rule her from dusk until dawn without love, without caring. Only for the incredible sex he admitted he'd been trained for.

"I know, *lubov moya.* I'm sorry. You have no idea how sorry. I had an important meeting and should have been back in time." He bent to kiss her again, this time on the corner of her frowning mouth. "A couple more stitches should do it."

She held still, sucking in her breath and counting to herself until he grunted in satisfaction and covered the area with another antiseptic. "I'm giving you a shot, Joley. You need antibiotics. I have them in my field kit."

"I hate needles."

"I know. And you're being very brave." He gave her the shot quickly and then sponged the blood and tears from her face. "You'll have to take off your clothes." He turned from her to run water in the bathtub. "I need to go over the rest of you and stitch up anything too deep or use a butterfly bandage. I'll get you a robe to wear so at least you'll be clean."

"I'll take a shower."

Ilya frowned. "I can't let you do that, Joley. You obviously have a concussion. I wouldn't want you falling down. I'll get you clean."

She frowned up at him. "I'm not going to let you give me a bath. I'm not a baby."

"Right now you're my baby, so don't argue with me." There was the merest hint of steel in his voice. His hands went to her shirt.

She caught his wrists. "Ilya."

"It's all right, Joley. You're not well. Let me take care of you. Tell me what happened after you found your clothes shredded. What did you do?"

She lifted her chin, trying to ignore the way he was so careful to keep from hurting her as he cut off her shirt. It was stained with blood, and she'd never be able to wear it again, but it made her cry anyway. Which was silly, but she couldn't stop, especially when he dropped the rags to the floor, leaving her exposed in her lacy bra.

He drew her close to his body, pressing her face into his shoulder. "You're safe with me. You have to remember, Joley," he stroked a caress down her hair, "I'm very partial to your body. I'll be very careful."

"I know you will. It's not that. This is two outfits today destroyed. Two of my favorites." Which was idiotic, she could care less about her clothes. Her tears had nothing to do with ruined clothes and everything to do with danger and death swirling around her and putting everyone she loved in jeopardy. "I don't know how you live like this." She couldn't stop weeping or shaking, no matter how hard she tried.

She felt so vulnerable, standing there nearly naked with tears she couldn't stop and her body trembling. His hands were warm and strong, and he simply unclipped the bra and tossed it after the shirt. His fingers skimmed down the sides of her breasts, sliding to hook her hips. Her body jerked and a sob escaped. Joley pushed her knuckles into her mouth.

He framed her face with his hands. "I'll buy you a couple of outfits. Nicer ones. Ones you'll love. Come on, *lubov moya*, stand up and let's get the jeans off you. You have a nasty cut on your leg as well. You're exhausted. Don't think about what we're doing. Tell me what you did when you found your clothes shredded."

She swallowed hard and tried not to shiver as he hooked her jeans and boy-short panties, dragging them over her thighs and urging her to step out of them. He lifted her into the bathtub.

"I gave the performance of my life. I rocked the house. I wasn't about to let someone scare me off."

Her teeth chattered as Joley sank down into the heated water. Whatever he had put into it stung, letting her know where the cuts on her body were. She crossed her arms over her breasts and swayed. Her head pounded so hard she bit down on her lip to keep from moaning. Ilya crouched down beside her, sponging her off with a soft washcloth, rinsing the blood away so he could see how deep the cuts were.

Most were superficial, he saw with a sigh of relief. She did look a little worse for wear with her arm torn from the earlier accident, although he could see it was healing fast. Her head was by far the worst cut, followed by the gash in her leg. It was long, but shallow, not really needing stitches, he saw, now that he could examine it. A bandage would do the trick, and with the smaller cuts and bruises he just laid his palm on them, summoning healing energy, and decided he'd apply a topical antibiotic cream.

"That's my woman. Now tell me about the bomb." He dried her shivering body off gently with a towel and wrapped her in a robe. He dropped his voice to a hypnotic, mesmerizing tone. "The pain will lessen in a moment."

Joley sank into the chair by the mirror, her legs too wobbly to hold her up. She drew her knees up, resting her feet on the seat of the chair, and watched as he casually pulled his shirt off. He had such a beautiful body. She wished her eyes would focus just a little better. He had a really ugly slice down his ribs, obviously from a knife, but it looked fairly shallow.

"Here, let me see." She beckoned him closer with her finger. She had recognized the compulsion in his voice; he could spell-sing, although not as well as she could. She hadn't thought of that with her brain so jumbled, but she could do no less for him.

Ilya hesitated but stepped closer when she started to get off the chair. "It's nothing, really, Joley. I'll shower and wash the wounds thoroughly in a few minutes."

Joley ignored his statement and touched around the wound lightly with her fingertips. He felt that touch vibrate through his body like an electrical current. As tired as he was, as fearful as he'd been for her, his control wasn't nearly as good as he'd have liked. He didn't want to react physically when she needed comfort and care most, but it seemed he had no control over his body. He felt the blood pooling hot and insistent in his groin.

"Joley, maybe you'd better not . . ."

"Shh," she cautioned and leaned forward to brush a kiss along the ragged edges.

He'd thought the pads of her fingers were sensual, but her soft lips were a thousand times worse. He cursed and caught her wrists. "Tell me about the bomb."

She looked up at him with slightly glazed eyes. He couldn't help himself—he leaned down and kissed her upturned mouth, running his tongue possessively along the seam until she opened for him. He allowed himself the luxury of losing himself in her, just for a moment, to celebrate that she was alive. He'd known fear as a child, but had lost it along the way as an adult—now it was back because for the first time in his life, he had someone to lose.

He lifted his head and brushed her mouth twice more. "Come on. Let's get you into the living room. The detective should be here in a few minutes. I'm going to shower and stay out of sight. I have to fix my arm. Can you handle him alone?"

She nodded, her eyes enormous, pupils still somewhat dilated.

He carried her into a large, sunken living room and laid her on the couch, arranging the pillows around her and covering her with a blanket. "Don't get up when he comes in. Just stay right there. He knows you're waiting for him and he'll let himself in."

"How do you know that?"

"Because it's my job to take care of details. Tell me about the bomb."

She frowned, trying to remember. "There was a photograph pinned to the door of the bus." She looked around a little helplessly. "I had it. I don't think I dropped it."

He'd taken it out of her hands and put it on the bureau beside several of his weapons. "It's safe. Keep going."

"It was a picture of Tish and me, but someone had drawn in bullets on our throats and they cut out letters from a magazine, which I personally find hokey. It said to back off the girl. And then I started to open the door, but Jerry called to me and I turned, and then the bus exploded."

"You did good, Joley. Tell that to the cop. I'll be in the other room. Try not to mention me if you can help it." He was already moving fast. The detective was coming up the walkway. A small strobe light flashed, indicating his presence. Ilya left her there, trusting that he had reinforced the command enough with his voice that, even in her slightly dazed state, she would obey.

The hot shower felt good on his tired body. It was difficult to sew up his arm when chunks of flesh appeared to be missing, but he managed, although the stitches weren't nearly as small and precise as the ones he'd done for Joley. He closed the wound as best he could, gave himself a shot of antibiotics and attended the other scrapes. He was beat by the time he heard the detective leave.

Exhausted, he set the alarms for the perimeter of the house and then the house itself. Flicking off lights, he carried Joley to the bedroom. She was very drowsy. He would have to wake her up every hour to make certain she was all right, but for the time being both of them could rest. He removed the bulky robe and just pulled a blanket over her body, grateful that he was tired and needed to sleep. Hopefully he could get through the night without going crazy lying beside her.

He stretched out, and then turned on his side to curl his body around hers. He thought he could control her movements, at least minimize them, but she was restless and kept batting at the wound on her face. Each time he caught her hands, it jerked the hell out of his arm, sending pain crashing through him. He cursed the fact that drugs didn't work any better on him than they did on her, and finally, to keep her from hurting herself, he used a soft scarf to tie her wrists together and to the headboard.

Joley murmured a protest, but turned into his body for warmth and eventually slept fitfully. She responded each time he woke her and talked to her, but readily went back to sleep when he left her alone. He drifted off, dreaming of her.

15

JOLEY knew she was dreaming again. She'd had so many erotic dreams, her fantasies getting darker, but much more pleasurable each time. As always it was Ilya with her, because only Ilya saw deep inside her and only Ilya mattered to her. She could barely breathe when he was near, her thoughts and body filled with urgent need.

She was naked, cool air on her bare skin as she lay stretched out on the bed. Ilya stood above her, his features carved and sensual. He was stark naked as well, his body rippling with muscle, his heavy erection already thick and hard. She could see his chiseled body, the defined muscles covered with old scars and new, raw wounds. He looked like a wild Cossack, a warrior, the pagan godlike beauty of his face stamped with lust and sin.

Her breath caught in her lungs and lay trapped there, so that she heard her own ragged gasps. She wet her lips and tried to move, her legs stirring restlessly as her body reacted to his presence with a rush of heated liquid. She could feel her thighs tingle and her nipples harden under his heavy-lidded stare. Her arms were a bit uncomfortable held over her head so that her breasts thrust upward toward him. It took a moment for her to realize that a soft scarf wrapped around her wrists held her hands tied to the headboard.

In her dream, the thought of being his captive added to the already smoldering fire in her body. She burned for him, and it was so unfair. He stood above her looking hot and sexy, his hand casually stroking his heavy erection with a near mesmerizing circle, until he was impossibly thick. She couldn't tear her gaze from the sexy sight of him, the pearl of moisture on the broad head. His eyes were filled with lust, his hunger raw and edgy. She loved the look on his face, harshly sensual, his body hot and hard and so ready for her.

She moved her hips, pushing them toward him in invitation because in a dream, she could enjoy the fantasy, glory in the dominating look on his face, the possession in his eyes. He lowered himself to the bed beside her, one hand sliding up her rib cage to cup her breast, his thumb grazing her nipple so that she jumped and the breath left her body in a strangled gasp. His shaft lay thick and heavy against her bare thigh, the heat radiating up from that single spot like a slow wash of molten lava.

"I love the way you look right now, Joley, helpless and so mine," he whispered. "So soft, all gleaming skin, wet for me, needy, your eyes begging me to take you. You're mine, aren't you? Tell me. Say it. I want you to acknowledge just this once who you belong to."

His voice was low, rough, demanding even. The commanding sound added to the thrill. She was so susceptible to sound. His lips whispered across hers. His tongue licked the corner of her mouth, a sensual rasp that nearly threw her into a climax as his fingers tugged at her nipple in a rhythmic melody. Every nerve ending in her body went on alert. She gasped again and arched into him. She was his. She wanted to be his.

"Of course I belong to you." Dreams and fantasies were safe, and she could have everything she wanted without the risk of giving too much of herself. Right here, now, she could show him how much she loved him, how much she truly was his, because he would never know it any other way than in her dreams.

His hand brushed back the hair from the cut on her forehead, and he leaned in to brush right above it with his lips, fingers tender as he touched her. His palm shaped her face, moved down her neck to her shoulder and then slid over her breasts. She shivered beneath his touch, a broken cry escaping when he leaned over her body and took her breast into his mouth. Hot heat raced from breast to belly as he suckled, his tongue flicking and teeth scraping.

Ilya had meant to slide the scarf from her hands, but Joley

lay stretched out before him and it had been so long—too long. The sight of her lush body—flushed with arousal, waiting for him, open to him, a priceless treasure, a gift he could explore slowly—had him torn between wanting to sink his body into hers and pound unmercifully or go slowly, drawing her to new heights so that she pleaded with him for more.

Her skin was like satin, warm and alive and so soft she felt exquisite beneath his stroking palms. Her thigh felt smooth and enticing against his pulsing cock, and her legs moved against him with restless pleading. He inhaled her fragrance, all woman, the scent of her driving him toward the edge of his control.

The full curve of her mouth tempted him again, and he swallowed her soft moan as his lips took hers, tongue stroking deep to tangle with hers. She tasted even better than he remembered, all honey and spice, a flavor supremely Joley. He lifted his head to take in the picture of her lying there, stretched out across the bed, hands bound, breasts thrust toward his mouth, the flat, exquisite belly and tiny curls at the junction of shapely legs. She was an offering sending another shaft of pleasure rocketing through his body.

He dropped one hand to her leg and ran up the smooth skin to her thigh. The pads of his fingers skimmed the cuts with gentle care, infusing a rush of healing warmth even as his hand parted her thighs. Her body welcomed him, already damp and needy with pleading.

He took her mouth again, that beautiful mouth he always fantasized about. So full, so soft, and inside, a velvet heated secret treasure of sensation he could lose himself in easily. His tongue traced her full lower lip, teased her upper one and claimed each corner of her mouth. He nibbled and teased, taking his time, drawing moans from her. All the while he watched as arousal deepened her color and brought her nipples to harder peaks. For him—all for him.

He reveled in the way she gave herself up to the hot need, allowing it to consume her. His hands slipped over her narrow rib cage to her heaving breasts, cupping them, kneading the soft flesh, pushing them together so he could flick first one nipple and then the other with his tongue. She gasped and arched closer to him, crying out when his mouth closed over one hard bud, sucking it in and flicking back and forth with his tongue until she wailed. He bit down and she cried out brokenly.

"That's what I want, *lubov moya*, burn for me."

One hand slid down her flat belly, exploring the muscles bunched so tight there before slipping lower. He plunged two fingers deep into her hot, wet channel while his mouth closed around her other breast.

Her hips came up, riding his hand, liquid heat flowing along the living silk as her muscles tightened around his fingers in a stranglehold. She moaned, and pushed her breast deeper into his mouth, her head tossing back and forth on the pillow. He suckled hard, tongue tormenting her, his fingers all the while plunging into her, first hard and fast, then slow and easy, so that she tried desperately to relieve the tension building and building. He loved every frantic cry, every involuntary movement of her hips as she twisted and writhed to get more.

"On, no, *lubov moya*, not yet," he whispered softly and began licking over her soft skin, all that wonderful expanse of gleaming satin that was his alone. He took little nips, watching her skin flush with need. So soft. So warm. He teased her belly button and scraped his teeth over her mound.

Joley went wild, pleading with him. She heard herself, shocked by the need and lust in her voice, in her cries to take her. She blinked, focusing, and saw his wicked smile, the demon in his eyes, as he lowered his head again. The need in her was destroying her, consuming her completely, the fire too hot, threatening to burn her alive.

She'd never seen anything more sensual than Ilya in that moment. This was no dream man, but a very strong flesh-and-blood man. He parted her thighs, his hands spreading her legs, palms warm and rough as he positioned her exactly the way he wanted her, open to his hungry gaze. For a tension-filled moment, while she breathed raggedly and her body pulsed and ached with terrible need, he stroked her inner thighs, moving his fingers against her wet, heated flesh.

She would have done anything for him in that moment. Her body screamed for his. Tremors ran through her and her breath caught in her throat when he slowly lowered his head and his tongue slid across her soft lips in a long, curling rasp and then stabbed deep. She opened her mouth wide, but no sound emerged. Nerves jumped in her thighs, and she couldn't stop the way her hips arched and thrust upward toward his greedy mouth.

He licked and sucked and feasted, his tongue as wicked and sinful as his fingers, driving her nearly insane with the wealth of sensations pouring into her. His mouth moved over her clit, and the small growling noise, as if he were a prowling tiger, vibrated right through her, pushing her higher. She cried out again and whispered his name brokenly.

Ilya moved up her body, unable to stop himself, holding her thighs apart, positioning himself between her legs, watching the arousal on her face, the deep red on her breasts, his marks of possession coming up on her soft skin. She whimpered as he dragged her legs over his shoulders and leaned into her, the broad head of his cock seeking the warmth of her tight channel. He waited a heartbeat, his eyes on her face. She was so beautiful, so hungry for him, dazed with pleasure.

He surged forward, sinking in to the hilt in one fast, hard stroke. Her slick, hot feminine channel clamped down on him as he threw her into an orgasm. Muscles constricted, hot silk winding tighter and tighter, rippling with life around him, squeezing and milking until she had him gasping with the fiery streaks tearing through his body. She writhed under him, increasing the fiery sensations so that lightning sizzled and hissed through his bloodstream.

He plunged again, a deep, hard stroke causing those tight muscles to drag over the thick length of him. He swore another bolt of lightning streaked through his body, from his toes to his head. Electricity crackled in the air around them, leaping from his skin to hers.

Joley watched the harsh lines in his face deepen with lust as he stretched her impossibly, filling her to the point of madness. His hips began a rhythm that left her breathless, unable to do more than keen in a thin, ragged voice as the tension in her grew and grew. Fiery heat engulfed her, spreading like a storm through her body, but centering deep, where the torturous pleasure bordered on pain. There was no release, only the continuous building of need—more need—more hunger—more of everything.

It was wrong. This was wrong. She lay stretched out, her hands tied, allowing him to command her body, to do whatever he wanted, and she loved the control he had over her, craved the edge of fear and pain that made the music all the sweeter as he built the song between them with his hands and mouth and body.

Joley began to fight, sobs welling up. She was just giving herself to him, surrendering everything she was again. What was wrong with her? She was sinking further and further into that dark place inside of her, and if she kept it up, she'd never be free.

"This is wrong. There's something wrong with me." Because she liked having him take her over and rule her body. She wanted to be screaming out with pleasure; she didn't care if he tied her up or made her crazy—she wanted to be with him any way she could have him. "This isn't right."

It took a moment, with the blood roaring in his ears and pounding in his groin, for him to realize she was really in distress. Ilya froze, still buried deep in her body, thick and hard and feeling the silken walls encasing his shaft. She wanted him. Her body couldn't lie, yet her distress was genuine. The more she struggled, the more her body tightened around his, until he wanted to give himself up to the loss of control and just drive into her over and over until he was a part of her, imprinted forever deep inside of her, until she recognized fully that they belonged together and only he could give her the things she craved.

He forced his body to remain absolutely still. "*Lubov moya*, what is it?" His voice was gentle, as tender as he could manage when he was at the height of his need. "Tell me what's wrong and we'll fix it."

"Look at me—at us. This isn't love. I'm tied to the bed and letting you do anything you want—begging you to take me. I don't want to be like this. I don't. I want love, Ilya, not just sex. This is sex." She wasn't making sense, the words tumbling over one another, her chest heaving as she sobbed, pushing her hard nipples into the heavy muscles of his chest. She'd promised herself—*promised*, but not only was she under him, she was pleading with him for more.

Ilya immediately braced himself over her with one arm and reached above her head to her wrists with the other. "You're not tied up, Joley. Stop struggling, *laskovaya moya*, and let me get this. It's just looped over your wrists. I was tired last night and afraid you'd open those stitches." He slipped the scarf from her wrists and took each to his mouth, pressing kisses there. "See? You're fine. I would never do anything to you that you didn't want."

She forced herself to be honest with him. She owed him that when she could feel his body stretching hers to the limit, when he was pulsing deep inside of her, breathing hard to control himself, when she had not only encouraged him, but *begged* him to take her.

"That's the trouble, Ilya. I do want this. I want anything I can get from you. I'm terrified of losing myself, of losing who I am and what I stand for. I barely know you, and I'm willing to let you do anything to my body. That's not love. It's obsession with sex. I swore I'd never do this, that when I was with someone it would be because he loved me and I loved him. I'm sorry. I'm so sorry. I know this is my fault. I can't pretend it's yours. I wanted you—I still do." How could she possibly deny that, when her body was rippling around his, demanding he continue? "I think I'm going insane."

Ilya framed her face and brushed kisses over her, catching her tears on his tongue. "You aren't insane, Joley. This was meant. My mark is on you. What do you think that means? Do you think it would work on just anyone? You were born for me. Me alone. To love, to cherish, to protect, to bring you pleasure. I was born for you for those same reasons."

She stopped thrashing and fighting beneath him, lying still, tears running down her face, but she was listening to him and there was hope in her dark eyes.

"Great sex is about total surrender, Joley," he whispered and shifted his body just a little, sending a streak of fire scorching the sensitive knot of nerves deep inside of her. He pressed deeper. "It's giving yourself wholly to another person." He kissed the corner of her mouth, a soft brush of his lips that made her heart want to melt. "In order to do that, you have to truly trust your partner, and trust is a priceless gift."

Joley couldn't close her eyes and savor the sensations rushing through her body because it was too important to watch his face—his eyes, those amazing blue eyes as deep and as turbulent as the sea she loved so much. He moved slow and easy, sending flames dancing over her, but leaving her needing more. The slow buildup was nearly worse than the wild, passionate tango he played for her.

His mouth moved against hers. A soft enticement. "Do you know what I believe love is? It's the same. It's total surrender—giving yourself to your partner, putting their needs and desires above your own and trusting them . . ." He nuzzled her throat. "*Trusting* that person, Joley, to do the same for you. Isn't that what we're doing here? Tell me, *lubov moya*, because that's what I thought we were doing—loving one another."

His voice was pure sin, whispering over her body, sliding past every fear, every guard, and wrapping her heart in warmth. She wanted desperately to believe him, but . . .

"Tell me you do not feel love in my touch, Joley," he continued and bent to brush her throat with his mouth. "Tell me this doesn't feel like love to you."

He pulled back, almost leaving her body, and she wanted to sob for his return. When he surged deep in a fast, hard stroke, he took her breath, sent her stomach flipping and the heated muscles in her sheath melting into a pool of need.

"You don't know me, Ilya. How can you love me?"

The small, forlorn note in her voice tore at his heart. "I've been in your mind every night for nearly a year. We've talked for hours, all night sometimes. I know everything I need to know about you to know I love you. And I can learn the rest, because I'm going to have a lifetime for learning."

His mouth settled on her, a long, slow, almost lazy kiss, while his body began a rhythm similar to his stroking tongue. He kissed her thoroughly, with all the tenderness a man as rough as Ilya could manage. When he lifted his head, he braced himself over her.

"Put your arms around me, Joley. Want me as much as I want you."

Her body clenched around his, tightened and gripped, holding him to her as her stomach muscles bunched and her breasts ached. "You know I want you."

He shook his head. "Not sex, Joley. Want *me*. The man. Your man. Want to spend your life with me, want to be my best friend, my lover, my everything. Put your arms around me and give yourself to me."

She stared up into his blue eyes. The pupils were wide and dark with a need that tugged at her beyond anything she'd ever known. What did she know about him? She'd lived around Jonas too long not to recognize the signs of a man with a code.

She'd spent too much time in Ilya's mind, piecing together all the memories and seeing glimpses of colors behind the darkness of his aura. He had to be working undercover, and that kind of a life molded and shaped men into something altogether different.

She searched his eyes for a long time, looking for truth. "How do I know what's real about you and what isn't?"

"I can't answer that, Joley."

She moistened her lips and tried to be strong, when everything in her ached to hold him close, to comfort him. "You have to give me something, Ilya. You're asking me to trust you with more than just me. I love my family. Several are in law enforcement. I would be trusting you with their lives as well. I need more than my body's absolute trust in you."

He was silent a long time, his body still, but locked with hers. "Joley, you've been around Jonas long enough to suspect what I do. I've spent my entire life training for or living undercover."

"If you lived that long undercover as a hit man, as someone who runs in violent circles, how do you know who you are?" The thought was terrifying, because when she looked at his aura and listened to the strands of his song, there was more blood and death, more darkness than light, and it was so blended, so mixed together, she couldn't tell what the truth was and what the lie was.

He sighed and pressed his forehead to hers. "Do I know what's real and what isn't? Not anymore. I live the way I have to in order to survive every minute of every day. Do I do abhorrent things? Yes. Do they bother me? No, not anymore. The lines blurred a long time ago. You are the only thing real in my life—the only thing for absolute certain. *You.* If you don't save me, I'm lost. I've known that from the moment I heard your voice. I didn't realize I was drowning in the blood until your voice came over the radio and everything in me went to pieces."

If you don't save me, I'm lost. She heard the echo of those words in her mind. His voice was low, unemotional, but so soft the sound stroked over her skin and wrapped her heart in velvet. There was a plea—yet it was the stark truth. Ilya wasn't making a bid for sympathy, he lived his life in black and white and shades of gray.

"I can only give you who I am, whatever that is, Joley, but I can promise you'll never regret it. I'll never betray you. I'll always put you and your needs before my own." He kissed the tip of her nose, slid his tongue over the curve of her lower lip. "Even when you don't know what you want, like right this moment." His hands shifted, cupped her breast, thumbs rasping over her nipples until she wanted to cry out to him for more.

Joley slipped her arms around him and arched her body closer. "Then I'm glad my music touched you, Ilya."

He bent his head to the twin peaks, lapping and nuzzling with his hot mouth, teeth tugging and hands claiming. Each strong pull of his mouth sent a wash of liquid fire sizzling over his thickened cock. "I want to hear your screams again, Joley. I need to hear them and feel your body milking me dry." He braced himself over her.

She swallowed hard as he began to move again, long, slow strokes that sent sizzling fire streaking up and down her body. She gasped and clung to him, trying to be careful not to jar his injured arm.

"Your music saved my life, Joley. It changed my world."

"You've changed mine," she admitted. "I've never felt like you make me feel." Beautiful. Wanted. Needed. Sexy. More than sexy. And so hungry for him. She loved his body— the hard, defined muscles, his enormous strength, the things he could do just by looking at her, let alone touching her.

Every time his body thrust into hers, she felt stretched and full. She was burning alive, from the inside out. He began to pump into her hard and fast, building the aching need until she felt almost desperate for release. She reached for it—that perfect explosion of her body—but he pulled back, slipping her legs through his arms so he held her open for him and gave his body better leverage.

"Ilya." She gasped his name in a plea. "What are you doing?" Because she needed him, needed release from the terrible tension he'd built so fast.

"Marry me, Joley."

His face could have been carved out of stone, a vision of carnal lust, but his eyes—his eyes were alive with love— unmistakable love. Her body pulsed around his; she couldn't stop the involuntary writhing under him, desperate for the release only he could provide.

"Marry you?" She echoed the word almost blankly. Shocked. It was the last thing she'd expected.

"Say it. Promise me. I need to know you love me the way I am."

Her body shook, trembled with the aching tension. She could barely think straight. "Are you sure, Ilya? Are you really sure that's what you want, because marriage for me is forever."

He surged into her, another hard and fast stroke that forced a small scream from her sensitized body. He stretched her out on a rack of tormenting pleasure as he changed his pace, pushing through her tight, swollen muscles with excruciating slowness.

"Forever then, because there is no divorce for a woman with that mark on her palm."

She arched her hips, trying to force his penetration. "Yes then. Yes."

He lost what ragged control he had, plunging into her over and over again, his rhythm fast and hard and utterly devastating. He buried the long, full length of himself completely, driving deep with each stroke into her tight, silken channel. She screamed as every muscle in her body tightened, as her very bones seemed to contract, as every cell and nerve focused on one spot. His hips thrust harder, his arms locking her in place. Her muscles convulsed around him, rippling up and outward, sending shock waves of pleasure rocketing through her. Her body clamped down hard on his, taking him with her so that his hoarse cries echoed around hers.

Ilya collapsed over her, laying his head over her shoulder, fighting for air for a few moments, and then he rolled, taking her with him so that she blanketed his body with hers.

Joley lay as limp as a rag doll over the top of him, her head on his chest, listening to the steady beat of his heart. "I'm exhausted."

"How's your head feeling?"

"I forgot about it. It must be better."

"No nagging headache."

She laughed, she couldn't help it. "That's funny." She kissed his chest and throat, nibbled on his chin and then lay back down again, as if that was all the strength she could muster.

"Why's that funny?"

Joley lifted her head again and studied his face. "Poor baby, you really don't know, do you? Supposedly men say women use headaches as an excuse not to have sex. I personally don't know any women who do that, but it's a standard joke."

"I've never had that happen."

She bit him.

"Ouch!"

His hand came down on her buttocks, but it didn't have the desired effect. Joley just wiggled and gave him a sassy grin. "Feed me. I'm starving. I haven't had anything to eat for days. We can call for takeout or something."

"The reason to have a house is to have a kitchen."

She wrinkled her nose and slowly sat up, straddling him. The movement caused a delicious aftershock. She waited for it to subside before sliding off of him. "I thought a house was for privacy and lots of places to make love."

"I see your point. Your idea is better than mine."

"Only if there's no food in the kitchen. I really am starving."

"Go take a shower and I'll whip something up."

She sat on the edge of the bed. "You mean it? You can cook?"

"You'll see."

Joley didn't wait to hear any more. She was really hungry, and a shower would help to revive her. Now that he'd mentioned her head, it was hurting a little, but she'd never admit it, not when he might toss her on the floor, or against the wall, or maybe the kitchen table. It all sounded good to her.

It didn't take long to shower and find every bruise and sore spot on her body from the explosion, but none of it seemed to matter. She was happy. She was with Ilya and he said he loved her. He made her feel loved. He made her feel so beautiful and sexy she didn't mind wrapping herself in a robe and finding her way to the kitchen.

He'd pulled on a pair of jeans. They were only partially buttoned, leaving his body, so defined with muscle, for her to enjoy. She sank into a chair at the table, drew her knees up and watched him as he moved around the kitchen with sure, purposeful movements. This side of him fascinated her.

"Ilya Prakenskii, all domestic."

"One of us has to be," he pointed out, flicking her a small grin.

The flash of his white teeth sent a small, thrilling somersault sliding through her stomach. She loved making him happy. And he was happy. His melody was joyful, bright colors shining occasionally through that dark shield he always wore. She saw it for what it was now, a cover to keep him safe.

"Fine. I'll admit I'm not great in the kitchen. Hannah loves to cook and bake, and she totally rocks at it. I can make tea though."

"Tea?" His eyebrow shot up. "We're going to have sons, Joley, lots of them. I don't think tea is going to be a big hit on the menu."

She rubbed her chin on her knees and eyed him warily. "Now it's sons. Are you obsessed with having children or something? Because this isn't the first time you've brought the subject up. And I don't like the sound of that word 'lots.' "

He stirred the spaghetti sauce. "In the interests of disclosure, I'm just warning you so you can't ever say you weren't prepared."

She put on her fiercest scowl. "I've disclosed to you that I haven't a clue how to take care of a baby. I'm an artist. I sing onstage and travel around the world. I can hold them, but the entire baby thing is just plain scary. Do you have any idea what it takes to be responsible for a child? I made myself read parenting books, and no way am I trying that."

"I haven't a clue what it takes, Joley. I'll be relying solely on you and your experience." He blew on a spoonful of sauce and tasted it.

"What experience, you crazy man? I have no experience."

He added oregano. "Sure you do. You were raised in a family. You have good parents, a pattern to follow, and we'll just go by what they did."

"You make it sound so easy. Do you really want children, Ilya? Is it that important to you?" She sighed. "If it is, give me a few years and I'll give it a try."

He glanced at her over his shoulder, and his smile had turned into a knowing smirk. "A few years? You think we should wait a few years?"

She shrugged. "We haven't even got to the marriage part. We're at the getting to know you part."

He stirred the sauce again, and she could see from his profile that he was still smiling. "We're past the getting to know you part. That was this past year. Now we're at the we'd better get married fast part."

Joley wrinkled her nose. "You aren't making any sense. We don't want to rush into anything. We have plenty of time to work everything out."

"You said you'd marry me."

She nodded, biting down on her lip. She had said it—and she'd meant it—but that had been in the heat of the moment. Now she wanted to be a little more cautious. "I did say I would, but I was thinking of a long engagement while you got to know my family and maybe figured out what kind of work you wanted to do. Because you're not going to be working undercover anymore, right? Not with a wife and family. You have a lot to think about." That sounded very well thought out and intelligent.

"As long as you're touring and making appearances, I'll be working your security."

He flashed one look at her—the kind that sent tremors down her spine and made her all too aware of the dangerous man she'd committed herself to. He didn't really argue. She'd realized that about him. He would try a short discussion and then he did things his way, expecting everyone to fall in line with his orders. Joley didn't mind that in the bedroom, but he wasn't going to just dictate the rest of her life to her.

"Has it ever occurred to you that I might worry about you, Ilya? That I don't want to take chances with your life? Most of the time I need security for normal reasons, just to get through a crowd, but once in a while there's a real threat. The last person I want in jeopardy is you."

He turned and faced her, looking so incredibly sexy he took her breath away.

"I have no experience with anyone wanting to look out for me. Not even as a small boy." He flashed a small grin at her. "This will be interesting, learning how best to react when you talk this way to me."

She held her breath. "How do you feel like reacting?"

"Honestly?" He put pasta onto two plates, added the spaghetti sauce and two pieces of warm bread. He put one dish in front of her and the other on the side of the table facing her. "I want to sweep the counter clean and put you on it and feast on you in thanks."

The low, wicked voice sent a flood of damp heat between her legs. "That's a good reaction." She tried to keep her voice steady as she twirled pasta onto her fork. "I do need a little fuel and then you can do whatever you want."

The blue eyes glittered at her and her heart jumped.

"Why don't you untie that robe for me?" he suggested.

"It wouldn't be very sexy if I dropped spaghetti down the front of me," she pointed out. "And you're making me so nervous I just might."

His white teeth flashed again, and this time he looked like a wolf. "If you dropped spaghetti down the front of you, Joley, I'd be more than happy to use you for a dinner plate."

She laughed, happiness warming her. "Okay, just stop right there and behave yourself. I'm getting this image that just is so wrong."

"Really?" His eyebrow shot up. "I've got a very erotic one. Want to try it?"

16

"WOO hoo, Joley!" Rick said as they entered the suite. "You were on fire tonight. We were all so worried about you after the bus blew up; we thought for certain we'd have to cancel, but no, you just keep rockin', girl!" He picked her up around the waist, lifting her into the air, and swung her around.

Joley caught a glimpse of Ilya's face before she lost sight of him in the mad spinning. A secret grin tugged at her deep inside. He definitely didn't share well with others.

Keep smiling, lubov moya, *you think this is funny having another man touch you?* The edge to his voice held a warning.

It's not another man, it's Rick. She felt sassy, ecstatic! She had given another great performance in spite of every threat. Only two more shows and she would be home.

Precisely. There was a bite in his voice.

Just like that her body stirred to life. She put her hands on Rick's shoulders and stepped back. "Crazy man, but seriously we all rocked. I wasn't the only one out there exposed, we all were, and I'm so glad we made the decision to go on tonight together."

"No one is going to dictate to us whether or not we perform," Denny said.

"Damn straight," Logan agreed.

She couldn't help herself, she glanced at Ilya standing by the door. He didn't look uncomfortable, he never did. Just— hot. Sexy. His eyes shifted around the room, but she knew he saw her. Watched her. The thought was arousing.

Leo ruffled her hair. "Well the lights caught that bandage

just right and highlighted the bruises and we're going to get so much publicity—all good—because you are the ultimate pro, baby. No one can touch you."

Joley laughed. "Well, I'm hoping not. I felt a lot safer with all the heightened security. I noticed everyone has to have a picture on their IDs."

Jerry nodded as he handed her an ice-cold bottle of water. After a grueling two-and-a-half-hour performance under hot lights, she was tired and sweaty and coming down from an adrenaline high. "We made sure you were totally protected, Joley. And it's going to stay that way. You don't go anywhere without a bodyguard, and when you're getting through a crowd, I want security lining that rope to ensure your safety."

"You've been talking to Jonas, haven't you?" she said accusingly, and flung herself onto the couch beside Tish. She leaned over to kiss the baby's hand. "Hello, little angel. You're so perfect. She's so beautiful, Tish."

"Jonas called me," Jerry said hastily. "And you okayed keeping him in the loop."

Joley laughed again. "Jonas out of the loop would be Jonas sitting on top of me. There's no such thing as keeping him out of it. He sort of steamrolls his way wherever he wants to be."

All the while she was rubbing her palm up and down her thigh. He was only a few feet away, the crowd separating them, but they could have been alone the way her body felt. Ilya. Her Ilya. Wickedly she brought her palm to her mouth, breathing warm air on the center. Her lips brushed back and forth, feather-light. There was something very sensual about sex in a roomful of people when no one else had a clue. It was wicked and exciting and very naughty.

She felt him jump in her mind. *Knock it off.* The voice was a growl. A rasp. She found it sexy and too hot to resist.

Her eyes collided with his. The blue had gone to a molten sea, turbulent and wild. She let her gaze drift lower and was more than satisfied at the obvious bulge in the front of his jeans. She grinned and gave a small salute before responding to the teasing from the band.

"Well, boys, since I have no bus, and you're all pulling out tonight for Sacramento, I think I'll just put my feet up here and relax."

slow lick of her palm, but she wasn't all that adroit at holding babies and she was afraid she might disturb Lissa.

"Hey you," Brian said softly, dropping into the vacated seat beside her. "How are you feeling? They escorted you in so late that I didn't really get much of a chance to talk to you about what happened. Let's see your head." He swept back her hair and whistled low under his breath. "Black and blue and swollen. That looks nasty."

"It hurts," Joley confirmed, stealing a quick glance at Ilya before meeting Brian's eyes. "How 'bout you? Are you doing okay?"

"I went to see Sergei," Brian said in a rush. "I had to. If he was the one who ordered that bombing, I had to try to stop him."

Joley shook her head, glanced around and lowered her voice even more. All around them, the band, their women and friends partied, but she and Brian were isolated by secrets. "You shouldn't have gone, Brian, it's too dangerous."

He slipped his finger into the baby's hand and watched her curl tiny, soft fingers around it. "I don't know what to think—what to believe. He swore—looked me right in the eye and swore—he would never harm you because you're my family and he knows that. He said he had loaned Ilya to you now, when he needed him most, to make certain nothing happens to you—that he did that for me. And God help me, Joley, I believe him."

Joley pressed her cheek against the baby's face. She ached inside for Brian. She knew what loneliness was. And she knew heartache. Brian was a good man and he deserved to be happy. He'd sacrificed any relationship to keep their band going, and now, when he'd finally found someone he could love, it was the wrong person. She wished she could find a way to help him. "Brian, you know I love you very much," she whispered softly. "You're an amazing person. I'm sorry about Nikitin. I really am."

"You're wrong about him. You could be wrong. I know he was once involved in the mob. He was born into it, but he's worked hard to become a legitimate businessman."

"I wish I could say I believed that, but it just isn't true."

"How do you know? You're obviously falling for his bodyguard. Did he tell you that?"

Alarm bells went off. She sat up straight and tried not to look frightened. "No, of course not. My family is in law enforcement. I told you that. I had them double-check, but I think you can dig up the facts yourself, Brian. I'm not saying that to hurt you. If I thought for one moment there was a chance this was all a mistake, I'd totally be on your side, but you know better. Deep down, you know better."

"People change, Joley."

"I know they do, Brian." She couldn't stop the flick of her gaze to Ilya.

Do you need me, lubov moya?

She moistened her lips. She didn't want Ilya to draw Brian's attention. *No. Please don't let him even notice you. He's searching for someone to blame and I don't want it to be you. He's still talking to Nikitin, and Nikitin is trying to convince him that he's just a misunderstood businessman. I don't want Brian to think you've given me any information.* She nuzzled the baby again to keep her gaze from straying to her bodyguard.

"I'm just saying maybe Sergei was into some things he shouldn't have been . . ."

"Brian, maybe you're right, you could be right, but until you know, you can't be with him. It's too dangerous on so many levels. Finish the tour. I'll ask my family to help, and we'll quietly investigate him, not to put him in jail or anything, but to make certain it's safe for you."

Brian ran his fingers through his hair several times. "I hate being so alone, Joley. I can't live like this anymore. With Sergei, half the time we just talked, just laughed together. We didn't have to go out, party, any of that, we were just quiet together and that was enough."

She wanted to weep for him. "Come to Sea Haven with me after the tour. There's something about the town, the people, all of it. The sea is wild there and the sunsets are beautiful. I'd love to have you stay with me. The big house is mostly empty because all my sisters are treacherous wenches and they're getting married. Every last one of them with the exception of my baby sister Elle. She's the only one left with a brain."

He reached over and took Lissa out of her arms, cuddling the baby close to his chest. "I've always envied you your family, Joley. Do you know how really lucky you are? We always had money, but I preferred to hang out with Denny, Logan and Rick and the others, anywhere but home. Alcohol was a huge problem. My mom died in her early forties, but it didn't slow Dad down at all."

Which was why he chose not to drink much, only a rare glass of cognac on a special occasion. She knew all the band members had known one another from childhood and were close. She knew Brian considered the band his family. Would it change everything if they knew he was gay? She hoped it wouldn't, but she knew it often did. Brian looked so sad and alone. All around them his friends partied and laughed, happy about the show they'd put on and deservedly so, but they didn't notice he was apart from them.

Ilya kept his eye on Joley even as he noted all the others in the room, their position, what they were doing, who they were talking to and how close they were to Joley. He was in a good position to get to her if need be, and an even better position to use a weapon. His instincts were on alert, but as always, it was impossible to tell if it was because there'd been threats and attempts on Joley, or because a threat was looming.

Whatever she was discussing with Brian upset her. She looked—and felt—as if she wanted to cry. He wanted to pull her into his arms and shelter her, hold her close and comfort her. She had a good heart and was fiercely loyal to her friends. Ilya wished he could tell her Sergei Nikitin was a good man, but he'd ordered more killings, more torture, and run every kind of operation, from human trafficking to laundering money. While it was true he appeared to have genuine feelings for Brian, if Brian became a threat, Nikitin wouldn't hesitate to kill him just like he'd kill anyone else who threatened him. Violence was Sergei's way of life.

Joley rubbed the baby's hand over her cheek, and deep inside Ilya, something hard and cold warmed and melted. He couldn't wait to watch his child grow in her belly, to lie on the bed with her, waiting the nine months for a life they created together to be born. Joley didn't believe she was the type of woman to be a mother, but she would be fiercely protective, yet fill their lives with love and joy and laughter—all the things he'd never had. Their home would be a sanctuary of laughter and love. It would be Joley who would show them all how to live.

People began to drift out, hugging, laughing, and Ilya stayed to one side, invisible as the band and their friends left.

Brian stood and dusted his clothes off, meticulous as always, walking with Joley over to Logan and Tish. Tish took the baby back with obvious relief. Brian clapped Logan on the back and walked out with Denny. Ilya was very aware that Brian knew exactly where he was at all times, while the others didn't pay any attention at all.

In the end, only Tish, Logan and Joley remained. The two women said something to Logan; he hesitated and then left the suite as well. Silence followed. Tish looked at him, and he knew the moment Joley crossed to his side what she was going to say. The knots in his stomach hardened.

"I'm sorry, Ilya, would you mind stepping out of the room, just for a few minutes? I promised Tish we could talk alone."

"I don't like it," Ilya protested, uneasy with the idea of Joley out of his sight.

She smiled at him, that dynamite smile that tugged on every heartstring and made his blood surge hotly. "You can stand right outside the door, in fact stand in front of it with your gun out."

Ilya had a strong desire to throw her over his shoulder like a primitive caveman and carry her to his lair somewhere safe. Glancing over her head, he saw Tish's anxious face. She held the baby close to her, but her shoulders were stiff, her lips pressed together tightly. He nodded, took another glance around the room and stepped into the hall, leaving the door open behind him. He wasn't happy when Joley closed the door.

"I wasn't certain we'd actually get a chance to be alone," Joley said. "Without the bus, I'm kind of stuck without a place of my own."

"Logan wants us to stay together and he wants me to legally adopt the baby with him." The words came out in a rush, tumbling over one another. "I can't do that and then turn around and lose both of them again. I can't, Joley." Tish nuzzled her chin against the baby's head. "I know you all think I'm really strong, but when I walked in on Logan and that woman, I felt shattered, utterly, absolutely shattered. I was so broken I didn't know if there was any way to ever put me back together again. I've loved him since high school. Maybe grammar school. I've never even looked at another man. His betrayal was so devastating, I came close to suicide." Now her voice was a mere whisper and tears swam in her eyes. "I'm ashamed of that, but it was so close, Joley."

"You should have called me," Joley said, fear gripping her. "We all love you, the entire band. It was horrible after you left and has been ever since. I would have helped you through it, so would all the guys."

"I couldn't call you. I couldn't see any of you. My emotions were all over the place. Part of me blamed all of you, because of the alcohol and drugs. My mother was ill and needed me at home, so I had to stop traveling with the band. I thought Logan would stay away from trouble, but . . ."

The baby in her arms stirred a little and Tish shifted her to pat her back and keep her asleep. She glanced around for the diaper bag. "I think I left her diaper bag in the dressing room. I need to check her in case she needs a change."

"I'm not making excuses," Joley said, following her into the large dressing room, "but it's hard on the road, you know that. It's lonely and isolating. Drinking is a way to be numb, and I would have considered it as an option myself more than once if my body chemistry was different. Logan always loved you, Tish. After you left, we thought we'd lose him. He went crazy, life didn't matter much to him. Drugs, drinking . . ."

"Women," Tish supplied bitterly, glancing over her shoulder at Joley as she snagged the bag. "Believe me, I tried not to read the tabloids, but it was compulsive behavior." Lissa squirmed, and Tish handed Joley the changing pad to put on the makeup table.

Joley smoothed the pad and pulled diapers and wipes from inside the bag. "That, too. That's how he got involved with Lucy. He stayed drunk. We finally did an intervention and told him he was out if he didn't pull his life back together. Unfortunately, or fortunately, depending on how you want to view it, Lucy was already pregnant. She'd tried twice to slice Logan up with bottles when she was angry with him, and then as soon as she found out about the baby, she threatened to cut it out of her stomach. We got the lawyers on it and went the legal route. She didn't want the baby, but she has problems with reality."

"I feel sorry for her," Tish said, kissing Lissa and putting her gently on the pad. "I would give anything if Lissa was Logan's and my child, yet Lucy can't enjoy what she has because she's too ill."

"If she stays on her meds she does fairly well," Joley said. "She makes much more rational decisions when she's on them, but she just won't take them."

"If I stay any longer taking care of Lissa, I'll be lost," Tish admitted as she took the little pink outfit off so she could change the diaper. "I can barely think straight around Logan, but I can't lose myself again like that. It was terrifying to be so depressed, so out of control. Maybe that's why I feel so bad for Lucy. I've had a taste of what depression can do to a person and it's horrible."

"Do you honestly believe Logan would make that mistake again?" Joley slipped her finger into Lissa's little hand. "You're so good at this mom thing. Look at you, Tish, changing that diaper like a pro. I'd be freaking out if it was me. She's too small."

Tish sent her a small grin. "It took me a while, but I was better than the guys. They're so cute with her, all of them, big bad boys, all fighting over who gets to hold her. It's so funny." She sighed. "Right now, Logan's saying everything I want to hear, because he wants me to stay with him. We were never divorced, but I don't want him to be with me because he needs me for the baby. Our relationship wasn't strong enough to sustain being away from each other a few weeks."

"Tish . . ."

She shook her head. "I made all the excuses for him already, but military men and women are apart. Pilots. Lots of couples are apart for long periods of time."

"He was weak. It cost him a huge price, Tish. You didn't answer me. Do you honestly think he'll ever make that same mistake again? He nearly destroyed himself after you left. I was there. I saw him."

The lights flickered and dimmed. Joley frowned. "They can't be finished breaking down the set this fast. Surely they're not closing the building." She turned around to peer out the dressing room door into the larger suite. The lights were off, except the mood lighting over the bar. She was aware of Tish wrapping the baby in a blanket and lifting her into her arms.

Something heavy banged against the outside door. Startled, she looked over at it.

Joley. What the hell is going on?

A chair was stuck under the door handle, effectively blocking the door to the suite. The couch had been pushed up against it as well. Joley caught sight of movement, someone ducking back behind the bar.

Ilya. We're in trouble. Someone's in the room with us and they've barricaded the door. I can't see, but I'm willing to bet they've done the same with the other entrance.

Stay calm, Joley. I'm coming.

The fear subsided a bit, as fast as it had risen. The absolute confidence in his voice calmed her. He would come and nothing would stop him.

She caught Tish's hand, preventing her from entering the suite. "Stay back, hon. We've got company and they barricaded the door from the inside."

"The baby, Joley. What about the baby?"

Joley caught Tish's hand. "It's all right. We'll be all right. Ilya and Logan will come for us. We know the dressing room is clear because we've been here all this time and whoever put the chair against the door is out there. So I want you to stay to the back of the room with Lissa. If they come in here, they'll have to get through me to get to you and the baby."

Tish clutched the baby tighter to her. "Will your cell phone work in here?"

She'd called Ilya, and that was her secret weapon. No one could possibly know they could speak telepathically. "Ilya knows, he's coming for us."

"You know who's out there, don't you, Joley?"

Ilya? It's Lucy, the woman you took down in Dallas. If she's off her meds, she can be very violent and she's tried to kill the baby before.

Does she have a gun?

"Tell me, Joley. I know you suspect someone," Tish insisted.

Joley sucked in her breath, weighing whether or not to tell Tish the truth as they moved together deeper into the dressing room. Her fingers tightened around Tish's hand. "It's Lucy, Tish, the baby's biological mother. I'm just guessing, but she's probably responsible for the flowers, doll, phone call and my clothes. My best guess is, in her twisted and demented mind, she believes the tabloid articles and thinks I've stolen Logan and the baby from her."

"She didn't want the baby. She tried to kill the baby before she was even born and again right afterward in the hospital. She's not supposed to come anywhere near the baby." Tish's voice trembled with fear. She pulled her hand away from Joley and hugged Lissa tighter to her.

"Did Logan mention she attacked him in Dallas just before we entered the building for the sound check?"

Tish made a small sound of assent. "He said she'd been arrested. And she violated a restraining order. The judge specifically said she couldn't go near him."

"Well her mother must have bailed her out, because she's back. I caught a glimpse of her right as I noticed the door was barricaded. She's dressed as a crew member and she ducked back behind the bar, but it was her. And in all honesty, I've never found that restraining orders do much good on people like Lucy. She wants me dead."

Tish put a hand on Joley. "Because she thinks you're with Logan and the baby, but as soon as she sees me, she'll know. I was in the bus when those pictures were taken. But she knows I'm his wife. She sent me a few threatening letters telling me to give him up. That was a while back, but they were ugly."

Joley didn't want to point out that Lucy had to have just now seen Tish holding the baby; that would just frighten her more.

There was the sound of glass shattering, the overpowering smell of whiskey and then a slow, deliberate tread that came closer and closer. Tish gasped and clutched Lissa tighter. The baby began to cry.

"Do you have formula for her?" Joley asked. "Go sit down over there where you're out of the sight of the doorway and feed her. We just need to buy a couple of minutes."

Tish nodded and ducked back into the smaller alcove, sinking into the chair there and hastily pulling a bottle from the bag to keep the baby quiet.

The sound of humming became loud. Lucy stood framed in the doorway dressed in trousers and shirt proclaiming she was a crew member. Around her neck hung an ID badge with a picture of a man on it—John Dylan. Joley recognized his photo immediately. Lucy kept humming as she looked around the room.

"Hi, Lucy," Joley said to greet her. "I didn't know you'd come to the concert. It was a great show. Did you enjoy yourself?"

Lucy's lashes fluttered. A cunning, crafty expression

crossed her face. "Don't pretend to be my friend. I know what you did."

Joley deliberately looked as innocent as possible. "I have no idea what you're talking about, Lucy."

Lucy bared her teeth like a wild animal. "I have friends. You think I don't have friends who tell me what's going on? I know you stole Logan from me. He wanted me and you were jealous—so jealous you crawled into his bed. That bitch of a wife of his thinks you're her friend, just like you're pretending to be mine, but I know the truth."

Joley shook her head. Lucy took a couple of steps to Joley's right, and in her hand, beside her thigh, were the jagged remains of a whiskey bottle. Her fingers were wrapped around the neck of the bottle, and she began to tap it against her thigh.

"Lucy, be careful. You're going to cut yourself," Joley cautioned her.

She had to keep her body between Lucy and Tish, and Lucy taking steps forward didn't give Joley much room.

"Do you think I care?" Lucy demanded, brandishing the bottle. "When I'm finished with you, your face will be in shreds."

"Like my clothes, Lucy? You tore up my clothes, didn't you?"

Joley was aware of a muffled sound coming from just beyond the darkened interior of the suite. Ilya had to be making his way in. She just had to keep Lucy focused on her and he'd be there.

Lucy tossed her head. "Strutting around in front of him in your whore clothes. I know all about you, Joley. You pretend to be so innocent, but you can't stand it when you aren't getting all the attention. That's why you didn't want to have Logan's baby. You insisted I carry the baby so you wouldn't have to ruin your figure. You had me impregnated with your child." She stepped even closer as she lowered her voice, biting out each word between her bared teeth. "I knew you'd done it before *he* told me, and I tried to kill the brat, cut her out of me so your bitch seed wouldn't take root."

"Who told you that, Lucy? Because it isn't true. Lissa is your child." She had to convince her just in case Lucy managed to get past her.

"Lissa?" Lucy snarled the name. "I told Logan he couldn't call her that. He'll see what happens when he tries to leave me."

Joley kept her eyes on the middle of Lucy's chest so she could see her entire body—shoulder movement, foot position, the telegraphing of the attack before it came. She stayed on the balls of her feet, slightly to the side to present less of a target. Both arms were loose, one across her body, so she could bring it up fast and block if need be, one up under her chin, so she could use it to strike. She knew Ilya was close, she could sense him moving into the outer room now. He'd gotten through the barricade Lucy had placed against the far door.

Lucy lunged at her, her fist striking out, bottle rushing at Joley's torso in an arc. Every defense was an offense, and Joley timed hers to catch the arm solidly as she swung her own up in a block, knocking the forearm hard to push the broken glass to the outside, delivering a front kick to Lucy's stomach and doubling her over. Joley followed the kick in and slammed her arm down hard on Lucy's back, driving her to the floor. Lucy crumpled, sprawling at the last moment, trying to recover and swinging wildly with the broken bottle to keep Joley away from her.

"You bitch," she screamed. "I'm fucking going to cut out your heart."

A hand dropped on Joley's shoulder. She whirled around swinging, but Ilya caught her, locking her close. "Everything's fine, *lubov moya*. Please go over to Tish and let me handle this."

"She's ill, Ilya, please don't hurt her," Joley said.

"Of course not." Ilya kept his gaze on Lucy, who slowly climbed to her feet.

Lucy didn't even look at Ilya or acknowledge that he was in the room. She could see only Joley. She straightened her shoulders. "Do you think that hurt? That didn't hurt." Deliberately she made a slow cut across her own arm. "You see that?" Blood dripped. "I don't feel pain. I refuse to feel pain. You're the wimp bitch Logan thinks he's going to run away with, but I don't let anyone steal my man."

Joley knew that backing up often brought an attacker forward. She didn't look at Ilya; certain he was ready, she simply took a tentative step back, putting herself in a vulnerable position. It was difficult to move fast when backing up.

Lucy lunged again, this time striking upward toward Joley's throat. Ilya stepped to the side of her arm, blocking her with his body while he took control of her wrist, his grip merciless. Lucy went insane, kicking and screaming, trying to throw herself over backward, but Ilya held her in a grip of steel. She turned and tried to sink her teeth into his shoulder. He shifted his feet, swinging Lucy into an arc and taking her to the floor, facedown.

Joley rushed to Tish, wrapping her arms around her and the baby. "It's safe now. You're safe."

Logan, along with several security guards, burst into the room. Logan's face was ashen. "Tish. Baby, are you all right? Ilya called me and told me. Are you all right?" He dropped to his knees in front of her and pulled her into his arms.

"Are you crying?" Tish touched his face. "We're safe. We're both safe."

"I thought I'd lost you again. I wouldn't have survived this time, Tish. Thank God you're okay." He rained kisses on her upturned face, careful not to smash the baby.

For the first time since they had broken up, Tish kissed him back.

Joley sank back on her heels, trying not to shake, waiting for Ilya to finish helping put Lucy in handcuffs.

Ilya's eyes met hers. She felt tears clog her throat. Her body trembled. He crossed the distance to her and simply took her into his arms, pressing her against his solid strength, one hand stroking a caress down her hair while the other locked her against his chest.

"Hopefully they'll get her the help she needs, Joley. You were wonderful." He brushed kisses over her temple. She'd scared him to death, but at the same time, the determination, the look on her face as she protected Tish and the baby twisted her even deeper into his heart. "It's over now, *lubov moya*. Let's give a statement and get out of here."

Joley nodded and went with him, careful to keep the appropriate space between them so the paparazzi wouldn't suspect he was anything more than her bodyguard. She knew—and accepted—that he was everything . . . and that meant she would do whatever it took to protect him.

17

⌒

JOLEY was very subdued with her family as they gathered together in a hotel room in Sacramento. She sat alone in a high-backed chair, looking young and fragile, her eyes downcast as Jonas ranted at her. Ilya wanted to gather her into his arms and hold her. He also wanted to smash Jonas in the face. Instead he waited for a sign, anything at all from Joley to tell him how she wanted her family handled, but she just looked at the floor. If she didn't give him an indication soon, he was going to have to throw her brother-in-law out the door—and there'd be some satisfaction in that. Jonas was making it clear that he believed he was in charge.

"You know better, Joley. You could have been killed. Tish and the baby could have been killed. What were you thinking?" Jonas demanded.

"Jonas," Sarah cautioned.

"Get over it already," Kate muttered under her breath.

"Would you like some tea, baby?" Hannah asked her sister, glaring at her husband. The suite had a large kitchen, and Hannah had already taken it over.

Jonas glared right back. "I'm trying to keep you alive, Joley. You've been raised around security. You know what it means, and you certainly have had experience with what can happen when someone tries to kill you . . ."

Ilya stirred. "That's enough. It was my fault, not hers. I walked out of the room and it wasn't secure. We handled it. *She* handled it. She kept Lucy from getting to Tish and the baby and she stalled to give me time to break into the room."

Joley flicked him a small look and his stomach tightened. She might *look* fragile and suitably chastised, but Jonas was only annoying her. Her dark eyes smoldered with fire, and that one telling flash lit a blaze in his belly. *You're so damned sexy when you're pissed.*

She nearly choked, but he felt her laughter in his mind, and it connected them back together when he'd been feeling apart from her. The Drake family was large, and they had no trouble talking to one another, giving their opinions and backing each other up. Watching them together had made him feel a little lonely, which was odd. He preferred being alone, but this was Joley's family and he needed to learn to become part of it, because a huge part of her heart lay with them and she would never be truly happy if he wasn't comfortable with them.

"We're just lucky she handled it, aren't we, Ilya?" Jonas demanded. "Because you fucked up and she nearly was killed."

"Don't say 'fuck,' " Hannah said. "You said you'd clean up your language."

Ilya coughed to cover the sudden laughter welling up. A pained expression crossed Jonas's face at his wife's reprimand in the middle of him dressing Ilya down. Family dynamics could be a lot more fun than Ilya had first thought.

"Laugh it up," Jonas hissed at him, but it was clear Hannah had taken the starch out of his attack. He sighed. "Joley, I know you're sitting there rolling your eyes while you're trying to look like you're listening, but you have to take your protection seriously."

"I'm serious," Joley said. "I thought we were safe in the suite."

"Your bodyguard stays with you at all times."

Joley crossed her arms over her breasts and looked mutinous, but before she could say anything, Ilya made his stand. This was her family, the people she loved most in the world, and whether or not they wanted to accept him into their circle—they were going to have to.

"Joley and I are getting married after the tour."

Everyone in the room froze. The silence stretched. Joley kept her chin on her knees, her lashes hiding her expression. Ilya simply didn't care. He'd had enough of Jonas scolding them as if they were small children, and he wanted to make it very clear that Joley was under his protection—and more—that he belonged there as more than the bodyguard. They could deal with him on equal footing.

"Married?" Sarah finally echoed. She moved closer to her fiancé, Damon, as if he could change what Ilya had said.

Damon shifted slightly and took her hand.

The teakettle whistled, and Hannah waved her hand toward the kitchen. "Joley?"

I don't think they believe me, lubov moya. He injected humor and warmth into the caressing tone of his voice, deliberately stroking her with sound.

Joley shrugged. *I think you're right.*

Ilya kept all expression from his face as he teased her. *Maybe I should tell them I ate spaghetti off your stomach last night and licked sauce off your breasts.* He'd done more than that—a lot more than that. *Do you think they'd believe me then?*

No, they'll just think all the tabloid stories are the truth.

"Joley," Hannah repeated. "Are you really thinking of getting married?" There was a little hitch in her voice and her gaze shifted for a moment to Ilya.

Joley nodded. "I'm not into big weddings. I thought we'd just run off, get it done and then sort of tell Mom and Dad after."

"Before," Ilya corrected.

"After," Joley said.

"We will tell them before we are married and give them the opportunity to join us," Ilya said. *I will not be hidden from your parents as if you are ashamed of me.*

Her gaze jumped to his face. "Ilya. Never. How can you think that?" She was so upset she forgot the others hadn't been privy to their exchange. "It has nothing to do with you. I just can't seem to do anything right and I've given up arguing with my father."

Everyone erupted into speech at the same time.

"No!" Sarah said firmly. "Absolutely not."

Libby shook her head. "Joley, you haven't thought this through."

Abbey stepped directly in front of Ilya. "Mr. Prakenskii, do you kill people for a living?"

The room fell silent again, and Joley hissed, a long, angry note escaping between her teeth. "Don't answer. Don't say anything. She's using her gift of truthspeaking on you." She leapt up and pushed between her older sister and Ilya. "How dare

you? Did you ask Damon that question? Or Matt? What about
Jonas? Did you ask him? Or Tyson? You have no right to do that
to him." Furious, she glared at her family. "I'm done here."

She turned on her heel, yanked open the door and walked
out, slamming it behind her.

Ilya faced her sisters and their men. "She wanted you to be
happy for her. She wanted to share something special with
you. I would have given you any information about myself
freely had you asked. It wasn't necessary to embarrass her."
He followed Joley out into the hall.

Joley walked briskly toward the elevators. She was
furious—*furious*—with her family. It was always the same.
Joley, the one they all had to look out for because she couldn't
make a decent decision to save her life. None of them had lost
their minds over Damon or Matt. Or Jonas. What the hell was
that all about? Jonas was bossy and he worked undercover
even when he promised he wouldn't. What kind of a husband
was he for Hannah?

Ilya caught up to her and took her clenched fist into his
hand, stopping her. "They were objecting out of love for you,
Joley." His thumb slid over her bare knuckles in an attempt to
ease the tension out of her.

She was going to cry. She could feel the tears burning behind her eyes, and that made her even angrier. "I didn't question if Hannah was out of her mind when she chose Jonas. I
supported her decision. Maybe I teased her a bit, but I wanted
her happy and it was obvious that Jonas made her happy."

She had always been so careful in her choice of men because she knew she had a weakness for the dangerous ones.
She'd laughed about it, joked about it, never once hid it from
her sisters, and she'd made certain she stayed away from
them. Her family should have trusted that she knew what she
was doing.

"Is it possible that all of you knew Jonas and had accepted
the man he is already?" he asked gently. "I watch you all when
he's raking you over the coals, and you might roll your eyes
and sigh, but you let him have his say because you know he's
afraid for you. And when he's afraid, he's angry."

"Don't defend them. They don't deserve it."

He brought her hand to his mouth and kissed her clenched
fist before pulling her into the refuge of his arms. "You had the

same fears, *laskovaya moya*. It is a legitimate question after all.
I went to a great deal of trouble to create my reputation."

"Jonas and Aleksandr are standing in that room. Aleksandr
is Abbey's fiancé. She could have asked him privately what he
thought, not tried to embarrass you in front of my entire family."

"I don't embarrass so easily, Joley." He nuzzled her neck,
holding her close in an effort to still the tremors running
through her body. "But I love you all the more for wanting to
defend me." A sound alerted him, and he whirled around,
thrusting Joley behind him as a door opened. Hannah came
down the hall toward them.

"Joley, Ilya, come back inside."

Joley looked stubborn. "I'm really angry," she said. "I'd
better not."

Hannah reached them and drew her sister into her arms, although Joley remained stiff. "You're hurt, baby, that's not the
same thing. And you have every right to be upset. I'm happy
for you and so is Jonas. He says Ilya is a good man."

"By agreeing to marry him, *I* said Ilya was a good man. I
know I've always been attracted to the wrong sort of men, so
why would I marry someone I wasn't certain of?"

"You're right, Joley. Everyone is very sorry. Please come
back and we'll have some tea." Hannah smiled up at Ilya. "Joley is very loved and we're all a little overprotective of her."

Ilya nodded his understanding. He felt very protective of
her as well, and sometimes felt her family didn't protect her
enough. Joley thought of herself as tough, but she was very
sensitive and vulnerable. He slipped his arm around her waist.
"Let's go have some tea."

Joley scowled at them, but she'd never been able to resist
Hannah. She followed her sister back to the room. *You're uneasy. We don't have to go in.*

He looked down at her. She surprised him sometimes. *It
isn't your family. I need to go soon. My gut tells me there's a
problem with Nikitin, and I'm rarely wrong. I need to be
there. In any case he texted me a summons, and you don't
say no to Nikitin.*

She stiffened and threw him a quick shake of the head. *No,
you can't go. I've heard about the Russians when they get upset.*

His expression didn't change, but she had the impression

of a brief smile in her mind. It warmed her as nothing else could.

I am Russian, lubov moya.

Joley stepped very close to him, as if shielding him from her waiting family. They were all on their feet watching soberly as she stepped in front of him. His heart reacted with a curious melting. She looked regal to him, regal and beautiful, and in that moment whatever tiny bit of him he'd held in reserve was gone in an instant. He was completely, utterly hers.

"I am going to marry Ilya Prakenskii. I'm in love with him and I want to spend the rest of my life with him. None of you have to agree with my decision, I'm not asking you to, but I expect you to treat him with respect, the same way you treat every other man in this family."

She wasn't asking. She was stating, and staring her sisters down while she did it.

Hannah reacted first. To Ilya's dismay, she put her arms around him and hugged him. "Welcome to the family. Please forgive our former rudeness, we were just very shocked. Joley normally communicates with us, and she failed to tell us she was even contemplating marriage."

Sarah nodded. "She's been rather opposed to it." She still eyed him warily, as if he might have cast a spell on her sister.

Jonas stuck out his hand. "Why so quick? You'd think you were in a hurry. Mom and Dad are going to want to be there."

"I want to be there, too," Hannah said decisively.

"We all do," Libby added. "Joley, you can't run off and get married without your family."

Hannah waved her hand, and a tray floated in with tea in mugs and a platter of fresh-baked cookies.

"It's just better," Joley said. "Once we're married, he'll have to quit his job." She took a cookie and a mug of tea and went over to Abbey, who was huddled on Aleksandr's lap in the corner. "Here, have some tea, it's good for you, and let's declare a truce."

Abbey broke into a smile and took the mug. "Accept my apology."

"Done." Joley flashed Ilya a smile. "He can't work as Nikitin's bodyguard if he's married to me. He'll be splashed all over every tabloid around the world and there goes his career."

"Is that why you think we're getting married immediately?" Ilya asked. He took a mug as the tray floated past him.

Hannah looked up, her gaze sharp and focused. "Your magic is different from ours, close, but different. The mark on Joley's palm, can that be removed?"

"No man would remove his mark from his woman," Ilya said and took a sip of tea. "I can't stay long, so make your questions count if you need to know something."

The slight smile faded from Joley's face. "They don't need to question you."

"Actually," Hannah interrupted, "I have a question. Are you the seventh son of a seventh son?"

Joley whirled around, sending hot tea streaming out in a half circle. Ilya lifted his hand, and the liquid remained in the air, then refilled the mug.

Joley glared at her sister. "Why in the world would you think that?"

"His magic works differently, yes, but not that much different, and he has all the gifts, not just one or two, and his gifts are highly developed. It makes sense."

Joley raised her chin and glared at Ilya. "Well it might make sense, but he's not. You're not, so don't even pretend. It's not funny. Do *not* give them ammunition." She sank gracefully onto the floor and sipped at her tea. "You aren't funny, Hannah, to even think of that." She sent Ilya another warning look. *You aren't, so forget teasing me.*

"I don't understand," Matt, Kate's fiancé said. "What difference does it make?"

"None!" Joley said. "None whatsoever."

Kate cleared her throat and took the plunge. "If Ilya is the seventh son of a seventh son and his line works anything like ours, then he's destined to produce sevens sons with all the gifts."

Joley shuddered. "Well, he's not."

Ilya grinned at her. "The cookies are very good, Hannah. You'll have to give me the recipe."

Jonas nudged Joley with his foot. "You look a little pale there, Joley. Maybe you're protesting a bit too much." He lifted an eyebrow at Ilya. "*Are* you the seventh son of a seventh son? You know, Joley, I've never forgotten that little pro and con list you made for Hannah when I was trying to convince her I should marry her."

"She did that?" Ilya asked. "She's still doing it. She has a list for me."

Joley narrowed her eyes and looked down her nose at both men. "The cons are stacking up fast, Ilya. I wouldn't get too smug. Siding with them and teasing me goes on the con side."

"Being the seventh son of a seventh son might just go there, too," Jonas said.

"Stop saying that!" Joley put down her mug and clapped her hands over her ears. "I'm not listening to any of you until you start to make sense."

She might not be listening, but she was looking around the room at her family. Every sister was staring at Ilya with a shocked, apprehensive expression. There wasn't the humor Jonas seemed to find in the situation, and Joley's stomach began to tie into little knots. Her gaze jumped to Sarah's face. Sarah, who often knew things. Joley's mouth went dry. Sarah simply stared at the floor, impossible to see what she was thinking—and that was a bad omen. Joley looked up at Ilya. *You're not.*

Ilya bent and brushed a kiss on top of her head. *I told you not to rely so much on your birth control.*

If she'd been pale before, she went white now, blinking up at him, her stomach going from hard knots to a roller coaster. She could feel the blood draining from her face down her body until she was dizzy—actually dizzy. She shook her head. "I'm going to throw up. I am. I'm really going to throw up."

Ilya calmly crouched beside her and laid a hand against her abdomen. The rolling immediately ceased. Joley shoved him backward, hoping to knock him on his butt, but he kept his balance.

"You're not funny. I'm not having children, let alone seven of them. Sheesh. Everyone can just quit looking at us that way. Ilya hasn't a clue about his family, he's making it up." She flashed him another smoldering glare. *You'd better be making it up, because the sex wasn't that great—nowhere near, in fact.*

Then I'll have to work on it, won't I?

No amount of great sex will make me sign on for having seven sons. I mean it, Ilya. I wasn't ever going to get married,

I'm certainly not going to produce seven sons. Have you seen a pregnant woman? Swollen ankles. Labor pains. Water retention. Labor pains! No way. Are you out of your freaky little mind?

He took her hand, the one with his mark, and kissed her palm. "We'll be fine. I can't stay, *lubov moya*, I have a job to do. Have a great performance this evening. Joley, you stay with security at all times. Change your dance patterns, stay away from the edge of the stage."

"I can't do that. I can't be thinking about where I am on the stage while I'm working."

"You're going to have to. And the moment you're done, you get back to your hotel room until I'm there to escort you to the next concert."

She made a face at him.

His expression hardened. "Jonas and Aleksandr are going to make certain you do as I've said. Whoever put that bomb on your bus wants you dead."

"They've arrested Lucy. Jerry called me this morning and told me they found parts she'd used in her hotel room when they searched it."

"Lucy Brady is not capable of making a bomb that sophisticated, Joley," Ilya said. "She was set up. Someone used her to get to you."

"Nikitin?" Sarah asked.

Ilya shook his head. "Nikitin has his own reasons for wanting Joley alive right now. I can't see him for this. We've got another player mixed in, but it sure isn't Lucy."

"When she was threatening me with the bottle, she referred to 'he' several times. At first I thought it was Logan, but that didn't make sense now that I really think about it," Joley admitted. "But I have no clue who she might have been referring to. I can ask . . ."

"You don't ask anyone anything at this point," Ilya said. "You go out on the stage, do your job and get back to cover as soon as possible. I want your word."

Joley looked mutinous.

He shrugged. "You can always cancel tonight if you'd rather. It's your choice. Going onstage isn't the best of ideas when someone is trying to kill you."

"You can't stop me."

"The last time I looked, I was a lot bigger and stronger than you."

His voice was absolutely mild, not a hint that he was angry, or even getting close to getting upset, but there was resolve as well, an implacable determination that made it very clear to her that if she didn't agree, he wasn't above using physical force.

Joley took another sip of tea, waiting for the flickering flames to die down a little in her stomach so she could look at him without wanting to throw something. "I really don't like being told what to do, Ilya. I'm an adult, quite capable of making my own decisions."

"Then as an adult, make the adult decision to be safe. Give me your word now, Joley, or I'll be hauling your ass back to my place and you won't be leaving there until I feel it is safe."

She inhaled sharply. "I don't like threats."

"That wasn't a threat. I don't make threats."

Her breath hissed out between her teeth. "I don't like being treated like I'm not quite bright, that I can't get that there are safety issues."

"I don't think that at all. I know you're bright, Joley. It's just that you think more about other people than you do yourself. So give me your word, because I know you'll never break it and I don't want to have to worry about you."

"Fine then. I'll do whatever." She didn't like the little thrill she'd gotten when he said he knew she was bright, or the way his voice had caressed her when he told her she thought of others, because she just capitulated when she should have made it clear she would follow security for herself, not for him.

With my child growing inside of you, it would be good to take extra precautions.

She snatched her hand away from him. "That's not funny. Run, you coward. You can't know who your brothers are or how many you have or even if you're the youngest. I'm not buying into that. Go away and be careful. I'll kick your ass if anything happens to you."

Ilya stood. "Did you get the information I asked for, Jonas?"

Joley grabbed his hand again. "What information?"

Later, Joley, when we have no one around.

She wanted to protest, but his life was dependent on secrecy, so she just nodded and blew him a kiss he didn't deserve as he followed Jonas and Aleksandr into the kitchen.

"John Dylan seems to be turning up quite often," Ilya said. "Lucy Brady had his ID. He claimed she stole it when he took a break and removed it, then left it on the table in the room where they were eating lunch. Most of the crew sleep during a performance because they have to work again breaking down the set and equipment right after. He says he went to bed and didn't notice he didn't have his ID."

"Bullshit," Jonas said. "They know where their ID is at all times, especially during heightened security. The crew protects their band. They're like a family. Why would he even take it off in the break room?"

"He said he broke the chain and was fixing it when someone called him out of the room." Ilya shrugged. "It's plausible, but not probable. But he wasn't anywhere near that bus, not for a moment, which is a little suspicious in itself. He can account for every moment of his time and has witnesses."

Jonas's eyebrow shot up. "Every moment?"

"Yes. He was questioned along with other members of the crew, and he had his entire day mapped out. Everything checked out just like he said, right down to when he used the can."

Jonas and Aleksandr exchanged a long look. "No one can do that, Ilya."

"Exactly. He's in this up to his ears, but he has an accomplice," Ilya said. "Dylan was also with Dean when Joley saw them with the teenagers, and several of the crew told me he spent a lot of time with Dean, but when I questioned him he said he barely knew him."

"Dylan isn't in any way connected to the Russian mob other than maybe if Dean was working with them to feed them an occasional groupie. He's got connections here in the States," Jonas supplied. "He's a nephew of a man named Dominic Dylan. Have you ever heard of him?"

Ilya shook his head. "Should I have?"

Jonas tapped a manila folder. "Here's what we have on him. He's been making a name for himself. He's got a big family, lots of siblings and cousins, and he's spreading his net. He went to jail for tax evasion, but they suspected him of everything from arms dealing to running a human trafficking ring. Are you starting to see a connection here?"

"He wants Nikitin's front line," Ilya said. "He's looking to take over his business."

Aleksandr nodded. He'd worked for the Russian police for years and then Interpol, and still had the connections. "That's what we suspect. The DEA has been keeping an eye on him for a long time. Homeland Security has their hand in as well. We stepped on a few toes getting that information and we called in a few favors owed. Dominic is bad news. He has a large organization, has mobilized a lot of gangs, mostly from being inside, and his particular plague has spread like wildfire."

"Do you think he had Dean killed?" Ilya asked.

"If the kid was working for Nikitin, bringing him the girls, then yes, I have to say, that's a good bet," Jonas said. "He made it look like a Russian hit to throw suspicion on Nikitin—or you. My guess is, John Dylan took professional pride in showing his uncle he knew how to do a solid hit." Jonas glanced at the door and lowered his voice even more. "Is it possible the bus was meant to take you out? Had anyone seen you with Joley? Could someone have connected you and put you there?"

"Brian knew. Her driver, probably. It's possible Brian voiced his concerns to the other band members. Certainly Tish knew, and if she did, Logan probably did." That hadn't been discreet of him. He could have gotten her killed.

He had known from beginning that getting involved with her would be dangerous to both of them. He shook his head at his own stupidity. He'd been thinking with other parts of his anatomy rather than his brain. "Yeah. Others knew." He hated to admit it, hated making such an amateur mistake. In his entire career he'd never made such a selfish, risky error. He couldn't blame it on Joley and the spell she cast over him. The ultimate responsibility was his.

Aleksandr tapped the folder. "This man, Dominic Dylan, is a huge arms dealer, Ilya. He's been photographed with Kolochek and the German, Heinzman. They only talk to the top men in the business. Word on the street says Dylan wants a bigger piece of the pie. Human trafficking brings in tremendous revenue, as you well know. Anyone who has done their homework knows they have to get rid of you to get to Nikitin.

Without him, that branch goes down here in the United States and creates a vacancy."

"And Dylan wants to fill the vacancy."

Jonas nodded. "That's what we think. So the hit could have been on you, and Joley could have been a by-product. Whoever put the bomb there really didn't give a damn who they killed as long as they took you out. It makes more sense. They create a problem for your girlfriend by using Lucy, feeding her anything that would make her believe Joley was her enemy."

"Great distraction," Ilya said. "And it was. I was very focused on Joley and asked Nikitin for a few days off to help her out."

"They may still come after her to keep you off balance. We'll have our own people all over her tonight, Ilya."

"I've got to put Nikitin somewhere safe. I've spent three years on this investigation and I'm not blowing it. No way does Dominic Dylan take over the human trafficking market. I'm shutting it down for good on this end. What about Elle? Is she out?"

"As far as we can tell, she's not investigating Nikitin. If your paths have crossed, she may be working to nail Dylan, but she didn't respond to Jackson's calls," Jonas admitted, referring to his deputy. "He's pretty pissed. He doesn't get like that often, but when he does, it isn't something anyone wants to witness. We don't know exactly who she's working for. Have you asked Joley? Elle's the loner of the family, keeps everything close to her. If anyone really knows what she's up to, it would be Joley."

Ilya sighed. "Even to me, I doubt if she'd betray her sister's confidence. And if she does know, she keeps it buried deep. As much as I'm in Joley's mind, I've never seen a reference to anything Elle's doing." He glanced at his watch. "I've got to go. I've got a bad feeling that Nikitin is in trouble tonight. You keep close to Joley. If you think, even for a moment, that she's in danger, just get her out, don't wait for her permission."

Jonas shrugged. "You don't have to worry on that score. I'm used to her being upset with me. She gets over things fast."

"That's good to know, because when she finds out I'm not teasing her about the seventh son of a seventh son, I have a feeling she'll be really angry."

Jonas drew in his breath. "That's not right, Prakenskii, you can't do that to her. Are you sure?"

"I don't know much about my family, but I do know I'm the seventh-born son. I don't know if the Drake sisters have exactly the same fate we do, but essentially the seventh carries all the gifts and his partner is destined. In my bloodline, all partners are destined, but they don't seem to have the birth control problems the seventh runs into."

As he spoke, Ilya walked back into the main sitting room. He reached out his hand to Joley. She let him pull her to her feet. He caught a glimpse of her surprised expression as he tipped her face up to his and took possession of her mouth. There was no hesitation on her part; she kissed him back, melting into him, giving herself to him the way she always did.

You're coming back to me. Don't say good-bye.

I'm not saying good-bye. He tried to be reassuring, but he was saying good-bye. In his business, there were no guarantees, and he had a bad feeling about the night. *I'm saying, no matter what, I love you with every breath in my body.* His hand slipped over her hip to press between their bodies, to feel her flat stomach where his child would grow. He wanted that. Wanted everything from her in the same way he had given everything of himself, body and soul, to her.

I love you, too. Joley clung to him, holding him tight. *Ilya, if there's a chance something can happen to you, don't go. Stay here. I won't perform. I'll stay with you.*

The enormity of what she was offering made him soft inside when he needed to be steel. With great reluctance, he lifted his mouth from hers. "Please stay safe, Joley."

"You too, Ilya."

She didn't cry. And she didn't try to stop him. He was proud of her for that. He lifted a hand to her family and slipped out the door, looking back at her face once before he went out. He wanted to memorize every detail. Feel her bone structure on his fingertips. He wanted to know that if he died this night, her face would be his last memory.

18

NIKITIN had always preferred to rent houses, even if he was only staying one night. He liked upscale neighborhoods, and he'd move in and make himself at home for however long he could stay. Ilya had noticed a difference in him the past year. He'd gone from surly and mean to a much more mellow and happy man. That didn't matter, however, when it came down to his job. Nikitin carried hundreds of deaths on his shoulders and had no compunction about ordering the torture and killing of entire families if anyone stood in the way of building his empire.

Ilya drove through the neighborhood slowly. As usual, he'd chosen a car that would fit in. He drove past the house Nikitin was renting, not too slow, not too fast, careful not to draw attention. There were three men standing just inside the gate, bending over a fourth man. At first glance the three men looked like Nikitin's guards, but they weren't men he recognized, and the one on the ground was Eddie, a solid man Nikitin often used for intimidation at his front entrance.

Ilya parked his car down the street and moved into the shadows as he made his way back to the house. The three intruders were inside the gate, which meant he had to go over the wall without being seen. He walked beside it, running a gloved hand along the brick until he found a small indentation he could work with. He jumped, caught the indentation with the toe of his shoe and went over the wall, landing in a crouch on the other side. He waited, orienting himself to the layout.

A low, mocking laugh was followed by a grunt as the taller

of the men dragged Eddie up by his hair and shoved him against the wall. "You're gonna die," he said harshly, and kicked Eddie in the stomach. "But we're gonna have us some fun first."

The other two men laughed.

"You should have stayed in Russia," one with a barbed-wire tattoo across his arm added.

The third pulled a club from under his coat. "Guess you picked the wrong boss."

Ilya broke into a sprint as they closed in on Eddie, forming a loose semicircle. Eddie spat on the ground in front of them defiantly, his eyes bright with rage.

Ilya came in fast and silent, grabbing the bat as it swung toward Eddie's head. He kept turning as he yanked it from the man's hand, swinging at the taller man's hand as he pulled a gun. The club struck him hard enough to break bones and the gun went flying. The tall man swore as he stumbled back.

The man with the tattoo punched at Ilya's open ribs, brass knuckles glinting in the light spilling from the porch. Ilya blocked the shot with his forearm, continued his forward spin going inside and slammed his elbow with full force against the man's sternum. He dropped like a stone, clutching his chest and gasping.

Cursing, the first man, who'd pulled the club, drew a knife and lunged. Ilya stepped into the attack, slamming a brutal fist into the exposed wrist with a short, chopped blow. The knife fell to the ground. Ilya brought up his knee hard into the man's crotch and then turned, shooting the same leg out to slam his foot into the ankle, shattering bone and knocking the man to the ground.

"Hell, Ilya, you didn't give me a chance to help out." Eddie picked up the gun the taller one had dropped. He walked to where the man was still rolling on the ground moaning. He put the gun to his attacker's head and pulled the trigger.

"How many?" Ilya asked.

"I didn't get a chance to count, but it looked like a fuckin' army to me," Eddie answered and shot the second and third man. "They went around to the back, but they're wiping everyone out where they find them."

Ilya ignored the statement, already moving across the lawn to the house. He put his hand on the doorknob and turned slowly. The door was unlocked, which meant the assassination team was already inside. He listened in an effort to get a sense of where everyone was and what was happening. There was a brief murmur of voices. Footsteps. The gun Eddie had picked up had a silencer, so the team was probably similarly equipped. They didn't want a visit from the local police. Neither did he. He bent to pull a knife from his boot, indicated the need for silence from Eddie, and slipped inside.

The living room was empty. The television set remained on, playing the local news channel. Beside the couch, on the small end table, a cut crystal glass sat half-filled. A second glass was on the coffee table, beside several magazines. Nikitin hadn't been alone when the intruders broke in. The secret silent alarm Ilya always set up for Nikitin would have gone off, giving the Russian time to make it to the safe room they always meticulously set up when they occupied a house, whether it was for one night or ten.

With his gloved hand, Ilya lifted the glass and took a small sniff. Cognac. The good stuff. He shook his head as he replaced the glass. Nikitin only drank cognac with one person. Brian Rigger, lead guitarist for Joley's band. She would be so upset if Brian didn't make it out alive. Damn his stupidity. He'd been warned to stay away. There was a part of Ilya that understood. Brian, and Nikitin for that matter, had been every bit as lonely as Ilya had been, and he hadn't been able to stay away from Joley, even though it put both of them in jeopardy. But having Brian there was an unexpected complication.

He did his best to protect Brian, hastily wiping prints from both glasses and any surface he could find that it seemed likely Brian had touched. It was the best he could do when time was short and the enemy was too close.

Ilya began a cautious tread down the hall. Overhead, he could hear footsteps as the assassination squad searched the rooms above him. Eddie caught his sleeve and indicated up the stairs. Ilya shook his head. No one else was ever privy to Ilya's plan to extract Nikitin should there be trouble. If there was a traitor, there would be no chance that he would know where Nikitin would be.

In the first bedroom, a man lay faceup, blood soaking into the carpet from his slit throat, eyes open and staring at the ceiling. Ilya cleared the room, found no target and went to the next one. It was the pool room. Four of Nikitin's soldiers lay dead. One was draped over the pool table with a gun in his hand and the back of his head gone. A second was at the sliding glass door, as if he'd run, a gun inches from his hand where he'd fallen. The third man had been shot first, dead center and never saw it coming. He was slumped just inside the door, a glass of wine soaking the carpet along with his blood. Overturned furniture showed that the fourth man had managed to put up a struggle. He'd been shot several times and lay a few feet to the side of the pool table.

They'd been surprised, which meant either they hadn't noticed the strobe going off—which was difficult for Ilya to believe—or someone inside was a traitor—and that was more likely. "You have any idea how many soldiers we had here tonight, Eddie?"

Hopefully Nikitin had noticed his personal alarm and done exactly as Ilya had instructed—gone without speaking to anyone and hidden. That had probably saved his life. Had the traitor known where he was, certainly he would have given the information to the hit team.

"Hell, Ilya." Eddie wiped his mouth with his sleeve, shaking a little after seeing his friends dead. "Pavel Demidov was here, too, along with Ivan and Klaus."

Continuing down the hall, Ilya peered quickly into the kitchen. Ivan and Klaus lay on the floor in pools of blood, with two men standing over them. One was a stranger and the other was Pavel Demidov, Nikitin's trusted bodyguard. Ilya was certain he was privy to the workings of the human trafficking ring, the one Nikitin had been careful to keep Ilya away from. This assignment was the one time that Ilya's reputation for protecting women and children had hindered him. Nikitin often sent him on errands, or just out of the room so he could talk to this man—Pavel Demidov. He had found his traitor.

The man with Pavel started to turn, and Ilya threw the knife, spinning as he did so and yanking the gun from Eddie's hands to fire three rounds into Pavel's left eye. Both men dropped, and Pavel's gun hit the tile with a clamor. Ilya waited a heartbeat, listening, and then handed the gun back to Eddie. "Make certain they're dead, but don't make a sound. And collect their weapons. We may need them. Get my knife, wipe it on his shirt and give it back to me."

He wasn't about to leave his weapon on scene, or risk leaving evidence if he could help it. He'd always been a ghost at a kill sight; he couldn't afford to let this one be any different.

Eddie nodded and hastily bent over the bodies while Ilya made his way to the den. The door stood wide open as if in invitation. The room had obviously been checked and dismissed. A small gas fire lit it and threw flickering light over the deep wood panels. He moved around the desk toward the small closet. The door stood open there as well, several coats hanging. The closet was very narrow, barely allowing the hangers to fit between the back wall and the front.

Ilya stepped inside and knocked in the prearranged pattern. The back wall was a false steel panel Ilya had designed to fit most standard hall closets. The one in this house by the front door had been too large, but the den unexpectedly had a smaller room which served their purposes perfectly. Staying behind that thin steel panel with its wooden front required endless patience, nerves of iron and the ability to stand for long periods of time.

Ilya didn't hurry, although Eddie hissed a warning at him. He didn't want to make a sound as he stealthily pulled the false back away to reveal Nikitin and Brian flattened against the wall. Both men were soaked with sweat, and Nikitin held a gun, rock steady in his fist.

"Let's go," Ilya said softly. "Stay close to the wall. Make no noise."

Nikitin indicated to Brian to follow Ilya to the door of the den. Brian was trembling almost uncontrollably, but he did as Ilya said, sliding one shoulder along the wall, maintaining contact and staying as close to the bodyguard as possible.

At the door, Eddie handed Ilya the knife and dropped back to guard the rear. Ilya slid the knife into his boot and pulled his gun. There was no silencer on the barrel, so once he fired, he'd bring everyone down on them, and they were severely outnumbered. He hoped they'd make it out clean, but he needed the firepower just in case.

He made his way back toward the kitchen. They'd have to go out the back to avoid the stairs, but no self-respecting assassination team would leave the back open as a means of retreat. They would be walking into their enemies' hands.

He heard Brian gasp when he saw the carnage on the kitchen floor. Glancing back with a hand signal for silence, Ilya glimpsed Brian shoving his hand against his mouth, his stomach obviously rebelling. Nikitin put his hand on Brian's back. "Don't look. Just follow Ilya out. You'll be all right," he said encouragingly, his voice a whisper. "Prakenskii is the best."

Ilya glanced at Brian's white face. Beads of perspiration stood out on his forehead, but he kept moving, trying not to look at the blood and gore on the floor.

Brian swallowed hard and nodded. He reached up and, for one moment, clasped Nikitin's hand. Ilya looked away, feeling he'd caught a sad, intimate moment that was too private for witnesses.

He heard movement and held up his hand, signaling the others to stop. He continued forward, to the back door. Behind him, Brian crouched down against the counter, Nikitin blocked his body with his own, and Eddie placed himself in front of his boss. No one moved, no one breathed.

Ilya listened for movement again, trying to get a sense of how many he was up against and where they were. Again he held his hand up to emphasize that no one move. He had to risk drawing fire in order to get positions. They couldn't wait; the rest of the team that had been searching upstairs in the house would be coming in behind them. They'd be caught in a squeeze trap, with no way out.

The door was a no-win. Once he was through it, every gun would be on him. They expected the door to be used. Ilya went from a crouch to a sprint, leaping and going through the window feet first, gun firing in the direction of the voices he'd heard. He landed and rolled, watching for the flashes of return fire even as he scrambled for cover.

He knew the exact layout of the backyard. It was essential in his business to be familiar with any potential battlefield in or outside a house. It was three feet to the relative cover of brush and an additional two feet to the large boulders placed artistically around the waterfall that flowed down a small stream into a large pool.

Four flashes and a long howl told him he was facing at least five. He felt it then—that stillness in him—the trained warrior taking over. No emotion, only the killing machine that had been developed at such an early age. His vision changed— widened—then tunneled as he saw in targets. Systematically he took them out. Dylan was losing soldiers tonight.

He shot one after another, using kill shots, no mercy, kill or be killed. There could be no mistakes, no mess-ups, not when so many innocent lives were at stake. He wasn't trading one human trafficking ring for another. If he could shut the ring down before they managed to get started, he would do it.

He fired fast—one, two, three, four, five. The fifth shot took out the man who had been wounded. Ilya cleared the area in less than forty seconds and was back to the kitchen, yanking open the door and signaling the others into the night.

"They're coming right behind us," Eddie warned as they ran for the nearest car. "I heard them running down the stairs."

Ilya slid his hand along the visor, dropped the keys into Eddie's hand, grabbed him by the collar and thrust him into the car behind the wheel. He spun around and fired several shots at the door to keep what was left of the assassination squad back.

"You're driving, and do exactly what I say when I say it. Brian, backseat with Sergei. Stay down at all times, and I mean down. They'll be coming after us." He slammed the door behind Nikitin and dove into the front passenger seat. "Go. Get moving."

Eddie shoved the gear into reverse and stomped his foot on the gas pedal. Tires screamed, and they swerved, straightened, and crashed into the gate. The gate crumpled and burst open, so that they emerged backward onto the street, hit the curb, jumped the sidewalk and then Eddie got control and managed to put the car in gear to go forward. Bullets rained on them, hitting the windshield, the doors and the sides of the car.

Ilya leaned over and stomped his foot over Eddie's. The car fishtailed down the street with Eddie cursing every inch of the way. Ilya didn't let up at the corner, forcing Eddie to run the stop sign and shoot them in a wider turn into oncoming traffic before he straightened them out again.

Ilya glanced over his shoulder. "Everybody all right?"

Nikitin nodded. He kept one hand on Brian's back, holding him down. "Who are these fuckers?" the Russian boss demanded, his face tight with anger.

"None of Tarasov's family could have orchestrated this

move against you. A couple of the cousins were left alive, but they don't have the balls to try to take you out." Ilya didn't want to give up the information on Dylan before he was certain he got the names and locations of Nikitin's network of human traffickers.

Ilya tossed his phone to Nikitin then steadied his gun with his other arm, waiting. It wasn't easy to shoot out of a moving car the way they portrayed on television. "Pavel Demidov was a traitor. Whatever he knew of your operation, the competition knows. They'll try to kill everyone. You're going to have to call your people and tell them to get undercover fast. He'll have exposed them all. I need time to find out who's behind this."

Nikitin glanced behind them at the two cars moving through traffic at high speed. "Just get me out of this, Ilya, and I'll . . ." He abruptly switched to Russian to finish his sentence, saying, "I'll kill every one of them and their families. Find out." He kept his hand on Brian's back, his body shielding the guitarist, who had been pushed to the floor.

He was furious. Ilya could hear it in his voice. Nikitin was many things, but he wasn't a coward. He would never tolerate an attempt on his life without brutal, bloody retaliation. There would be a bloodbath the likes of which few had ever seen the moment Nikitin knew who was trying to kill him. And from the way Nikitin was covering Brian, it would be worse for whoever was trying to kill them, their bad luck to catch Brian in the cross fire. Nikitin's feelings for the man had to be real, and that made him all the more dangerous, because if it was true—Brian was probably the only person in the world Nikitin had genuine feelings for.

Ilya needed Nikitin to make those calls. He needed numbers—and names if possible. Pavel Demidov had always been Nikitin's right-hand man in the human trafficking operation. Ilya didn't dare even glance at the Nikitin boss. He needed to appear concerned only with keeping Nikitin alive, but inside, everything stilled. It was now or never that he would get the information they had waited so long for.

Nikitin flipped open the phone, and while Eddie took the car screaming around another corner, weaving in and out of traffic, the Russian made his calls, warning his associates one by one to lie low, put everything on hold, until they could find and remove the threat to their network.

"Coming up on our left," Ilya warned Nikitin calmly. "Eddie, don't evade. Sergei, stay low. Just keep up the speed, but hold the car steady until I say otherwise, then you're going to pull hard to the left."

Eddie nodded his understanding.

Ilya watched the big Cadillac barreling down on them, the calm, centered place inside of him seeing every target, every detail of the night itself and the traffic around them. A small pickup truck swerved, suddenly aware of the drama taking place on the highway, recovered and hit the brakes to allow the Cadillac to move into position. Gun hand braced, Ilya centered on the driver, ignoring the guns flashing, and very deliberately squeezed the trigger.

"Now, Eddie, clip it hard."

Eddie swerved into the larger vehicle, bounced off, recovered and kept going. The driver of the Cadillac slumped over the wheel, the deadweight of his foot on the gas. With their car sideswiping the Caddie, the larger vehicle spun out of control, slamming into the guardrail, breaking through it at high speed.

"They're gone," Nikitin said, looking back, satisfaction in his voice.

"Get down." Ilya hissed the order between his teeth. "Eddie, take the exit and head down toward the river."

"My concert's in an hour," Brian said. "Sergei, I have to be onstage in an hour. Everyone's going to be freaking out."

There was silence. Ilya glanced back at Nikitin and saw the stunned look on his face. He was used to violence, Brian wasn't, and in that moment, Sergei realized how shocked Brian really was. "It will be all right," he promised.

"Why are they doing this?" Brian asked. "I don't understand why they're doing this, Sergei."

Nikitin rubbed his back, all the while looking out the window, watching the other car fishtail down the exit ramp after them. "I don't know, but we'll find out. Just stay down where you'll be safe. I don't want anyone to see you."

Ilya didn't point out that Pavel Demidov had known Brian was in the house, and since he had, then chances were good Dominic Dylan had been told at the very least that Brian was a good friend, or worst-case scenario, that he was Nikitin's lover. Nikitin had always been discreet about Brian. Ilya had guessed at the relationship for a number of reasons. Nikitin had been different since he'd met Brian, definitely mellower and much happier. His aura had changed, and around Brian, sexual colors had grown stronger.

"Okay, Eddie, start slowing down. Stay ahead enough to keep them from getting a good shot, but make sure they follow us."

The road ran along the fast-moving river. It had rained often and hard, and the river was swollen, threatening to breach the banks. In some places the road had a bit of water across it where the current splashed up over the sides.

"They're on us, Ilya," Eddie confirmed, glancing in the rearview mirror. "Not tight, but they're coming, about a curve or so back."

"We want a clear stretch without any witnesses or bystanders that can get hurt," Ilya said. "We should be coming up on a turn that will take us under the bridge. They'll lose sight of us. Slow down, let me out, and keep going."

"No, no, that's not a good idea," Nikitin objected. "We shouldn't separate."

"I'll take out the other car without a risk to you or Brian. Eddie can take you up the road to the exit back to the freeway. You should be able to see from up there. If I take out the car, come back and pick me up; if not, get clear." He tapped Eddie on the shoulder. "Here. Pull over right here."

Eddie shot a quick questioning glance over his shoulder at Nikitin, but he was already stomping on the brakes. Ilya bailed out of the car almost before it stopped moving. It was ironic that he was saving the life of the man he knew he would eventually have to kill. Nikitin had no compunction about killing his enemies, and there would be no quitting undercover work until he was dead. At the same time, Ilya wasn't going to allow Dylan to take over the trafficking network. He knew eventually someone would step in and fill the void once he'd taken down Nikitin, but he hoped to slow things down for a long while.

He shoved a clip into his gun, checked his other and waited. He found a spot on higher ground where he had a clear view of the driver's side of the vehicle. He'd have to take him out first. That was imperative. With the driver dead, the car would be a hazard. The others would have to bail or ride it out and try to survive a crash into the river.

Above the roar of the water, he could hear the powerful engine as the car rounded the bend and accelerated. The driver held it steady in his lane, making the target easier than anticipated. Their attention was on the road, trying to find Nikitin's car. Windows were rolled down, arms and heads hanging out. Ilya concentrated on one target. He steadied his arm and took the shot, drilling the driver through his left eye.

The windshield fragmented, and the car slewed back and forth; then, as someone tried to grab the wheel, it abruptly turned, spun and slid into the rapid current of the river. The car tipped forward, drawn into the powerful current. Water poured into the windows. Ilya heard a shout. Someone fired a wild shot. The car began to be dragged downstream, still sinking.

Ilya made his way down the slippery slope and walked along the embankment. A head popped up, and without hesitation he took the shot. If any of these men lived, and they knew about Brian, the guitarist was dead. He kept his eyes on the body. It was torn loose from the car and carried away, the water rolling over and over the limp form.

A second man emerged, coming up out of the water like a geyser, spewing bullets, aiming wildly, spraying the shore even as he fought to stay afloat. Dirt flew into the air all around Ilya's feet, splattering his jeans as the bullets came close.

Ilya shot the man twice, a quick one-two as the river swept the bobbing head away. The bodyguard was certain he'd killed the shooter, but he raced along the bank to make sure. The body turned facedown, tumbled and churned, a red stain spreading, and then it was pulled under.

Ilya waited, watching the surface of the water. No one could hold his breath that long, but if it had been Ilya, he would have gone out through an open window and swum downstream, letting the current carry him before sticking his head up and chancing it getting blown off. He began to jog along the riverbank heading downstream, reloading as he went and watching both sides of the bank as well as rocks the fourth man might be able to cling to.

Movement caught his attention. At once he dropped to the ground. Bullets spat around him, one actually going through the sleeve of his jacket. He felt the kiss, the heat, and then he rolled, stretching out in a two-handed grip to steady his shot as he fired back. The gun bucked in his hand, feeling familiar, part of him, his aim natural. Where he looked he shot, and the bullet traveled true, striking his target.

He watched the man fall back into the river. He knew his opponent was dead; he knew exactly where the bullet had hit. He turned and began to jog toward the freeway exit. Within minutes, he saw the car driving in reverse back toward him.

Nikitin grinned at him as he slid into the car. "Well done."

"Get us out of here, Eddie," Ilya said. "We have to clean this mess up. You rented that house, Sergei, and your prints are everywhere. I did my best to get rid of Brian's, but I had no way of knowing everything he touched."

"He'd only been there a few minutes when the strobe went off." Nikitin took his hand off Brian and allowed him to sit up. "If you wiped the glass and the couch, we should be good."

Brian pressed an unsteady hand to his mouth. "No one knew I was going there. I had the taxi let me off several blocks away."

"Good, that's good, Brian," Ilya said, praising him to steady him.

"Why is this happening?" he asked again.

Ilya didn't want to take any chances with Nikitin's patience—or the fact that Brian had witnessed a battle between two warring factions of the underworld. "Sergei must have mentioned to you that he was born into a family in Russia that controlled certain aspects of business. They don't want him getting out. He's been legitimate for some time, but a few powerful people fear his knowledge." It was Nikitin's standard story, and it was what Brian wanted to believe. Believing it now might save his life.

Out of the corner of his eye, Ilya saw Nikitin visibly relax.

"I've tried to tell you," Nikitin said. "I know it looks bad, but there's little I can do about the family I was born into."

"We have to go to the police. These people tried to kill you, Sergei. What if there are more of them?"

Nikitin handed Ilya's phone back to him. "Don't worry. This isn't the first time. We don't want the police involved, because these are the kinds of people who buy off the police."

Ilya tucked his cell phone safely into the inside pocket of his jacket. He deliberately glanced at his watch. "Can you perform tonight, Brian? If you can't, say so. Everything has to be exactly as if you never were a part of this. Not only you, but everyone around you would be in danger, and especially Sergei. Can you handle performing?"

Brian swallowed hard. "Will you be there?" he asked Nikitin.

Ilya flinched at the raw emotion in Brian's voice. He didn't want Eddie to have a clue about Brian's relationship with Nikitin. It was too late. Far, far too late. Nikitin flicked a single glance at Eddie, and it was enough to let Ilya know Eddie was a dead man. In spite of his loyalty, in spite of the fact that he'd helped save both Brian and Nikitin, the Russian boss wouldn't take any chances with his relationship being made public.

Brian had no way of knowing what kind of a man Sergei Nikitin really was and what he was capable of doing. Murder was second nature to Nikitin. He'd grown up making hits when other boys were playing ball. He'd learned torture before he ever went on his first date. As with Ilya, there had been no childhood, and violence had become his way of life.

"I have to make certain Sergei is safe, Brian," Ilya said. "Until we know who is trying to kill him, we can't take chances with his life."

Brian nodded. "That's right. You're right. Maybe you should get out of town, Sergei. Leave tonight. We have one more gig to play in San Francisco and then we're finished with the tour."

"Where do we go?" Eddie asked.

"We have to switch cars. This is full of bullet holes. Then we take Brian to the Arco Arena if he thinks he can put on a show."

"Yes, yes, if it will help," Brian agreed. "Of course."

"You have to act as though nothing happened. You have to be normal, Brian," Ilya reiterated and pulled a cell phone from inside his jacket. His hand slid over the other one, the one with the special chip that had sent every number Nikitin called to Ilya's bosses. They'd be moving on the information, matching numbers with names in order to set up raids.

The two phones were identical, just in case Nikitin wanted the phone destroyed. Ilya would have cooperated fully. He wanted the original phone for evidence, but if not, they still had the numbers.

He spoke briefly into the phone then turned to Eddie. "Take this next exit, Eddie. A car will be waiting at the McDonald's parking lot. We'll ditch this one in the parking garage just next to it." He glanced back at Brian. "You don't have any blood on your clothes, do you? Or your shoes?"

Brian shuddered, but inspected his clothing. "No. I'm fine."

"Good. You're doing great."

Nikitin nodded. "I'm sorry this happened. It comes with the territory. At least you know I was telling you the truth."

Brian took a deep breath as Eddie pulled into the parking garage and found a dark corner on the second level. "You don't lead a boring life, Sergei." He made an attempt to smile.

Ilya pulled open the door. "Don't touch anything. Eddie and I will wipe the car down. Stand over there, where I can see you, but no one can approach you."

Ilya worked vigorously, wiping the steering wheel, seats and door handles in the front seat, while Eddie wiped down the back and floor.

"Let's go. Brian, walk normally, we're just looking for a Big Mac," Ilya instructed. "You're recognizable, so hunch a little and keep your head down so no one sees your face. You're doing fine," he added as he herded the men through the parking garage and out onto the street.

Darkness had fallen. If they were going to get Brian to his performance, they would have to hurry. Ilya wanted him gone. He didn't want to give Nikitin an opportunity to regret protecting Brian, or to figure out that Brian was an intelligent man who would sooner or later realize Nikitin was no legitimate businessman.

Ilya glanced down at the guitarist as they walked, noting his aura, and everything in him went still. Brian *did* know the truth. The shakiness, the trembling, his fear, had nothing to do with the attempt on their lives, and everything to do with his knowledge of what and who Sergei Nikitin really was. Brian's melody was sobbing, wailing, every note drawn out in utter and real despair.

He rested his hand briefly on Brian's shoulder, the merest of touches, but sending healing warmth and encouragement to him, a small salute that the man was holding up under the worst circumstances. Brian kept his head down, stumbled a little, recovered and kept walking.

The car was waiting right where Ilya had instructed. Nikitin didn't ask who had put it there, but if he had, Ilya had a ready answer. He covered every detail—that was how he stayed alive.

The Arco Arena was already filled with cars and a crush of people. They drove around the top where the buses were parked, and Brian slid from the car.

"You can do this, Brian," Ilya said, keeping his gaze steady.

Brian nodded. "Don't worry. I won't let you down."

"I know you won't," Nikitin said.

Brian lifted his hand and turned and walked away.

Some of the tension that had coiled in Ilya's stomach drained away. "Let's go, Eddie. Take us to the safe house."

"Do you have any idea who those fuckers were?" Nikitin asked.

"Not Tarasov," Ilya said. "Someone here in the U.S. How much did Demidov know about your operation?"

"Everything. He knew everything. He's been with me for years."

"So how did they get to him? Money wouldn't have done it. What did they use to turn him against you?"

"I don't know," Nikitin said, "but I'm going to find out."

19

"WHAT the hell were you doing out there, Brian?" Rick demanded, throwing a towel on the low-slung couch. They were in the suite at the Arco Arena, surrounded by some of the crew, a few friends and girlfriends. "You played worse than an amateur. Joley covered for you time after time. You were lagging. You forgot which song you were playing. Shit. It was crap tonight."

Brian swung around, his expression going from upset to furious instantly. "You know what, Rick?" Brian shouted back. "Fuck you and your opinion. I don't see you playing the kind of music I play. You're all safe back there on your bass, playing off my lead."

Rick took several aggressive steps forward. "Lead? Is that what you think you were doing tonight? You couldn't pick up the beat. You were all over the place tonight. It was my bass that saved your ass more times than I can count."

"Then you can fucking take over." Brian picked up his guitar, swung it over his head and smashed it repeatedly against the floor.

There was a shocked silence. Brian was the mellow one, the diplomatic one. The band counted on him for stability.

The baby started to cry, and Logan put his arm around Tish and pushed her toward the door. He held it open. "Everyone out. You too, Jerry. Just the band stays."

The members of the crew, Rick's girlfriend, and Jerry went out. Logan shut the door firmly, stood in front of it and crossed his arms.

Joley took what was left of the guitar from Brian's hand.

He jerked away from her and paced across the room. He was trembling. His melody and aura was so sorrowful she felt weighed down, drained. A hopeless, shattering despair ate at her, and she knew it was coming from him.

Brian flung up both hands. "I'm out. How 'bout that, Rick? I'm gone. You fucking play the guitar if you're so damned good at it."

Rick puffed out his chest. "You think I can't? Hell, I could play better than that any day of the week."

"Stop!" Joley stepped between them. "Everyone has bad nights. All of us have had them. Flu, hangovers, losing a girlfriend—all of us have had accidents and lost our mikes, pulled wires. Come on. This is crazy. Everyone's on edge here. We've been on tour for months. We're tired and need a break."

"We're all tired, we all need a break. But we're not fucking throwing a tantrum," Rick snapped.

"That's exactly what you're doing," Logan said. "Shut up, Rick. Can't you see something's wrong? What the hell's going on, Brian?"

"Nothing. Nothing at all." Brian couldn't control the rush of adrenaline, the buildup of aggressive energy. He was looking for a target, pacing back and forth, his fists doubled up.

Joley had a bad taste in her mouth. She knew. It had to be Nikitin. Brian wouldn't look at her, wouldn't meet her eyes. He'd gone to see him again, and this time something had happened. He knew the truth about the man he'd grown to love. She felt sick for him.

Denny leaned against the door, watching his friend with worry in his eyes. "Dude. Don't blow us off. We've been your family. You've never been upset like this. I've never seen you angry. Not once in all the years we've been hanging together." He spread his hands out in front of him. "Whatever it takes, man, it's yours. Whatever you need. You've always been there for us, we're not walking away from you now."

"Really? Really, Denny?" Brian's eyes glittered with anger. His face was flushed red, his hands balled into two tight fists. "I'm your friend? Your family? What the hell are you going to say when I tell you I'm fucking gay? Yeah, man, that's right, I'm a fucking fag."

"You say it like that again, Brian," Joley snapped, "and I'll slap your face."

Brian stood in the center of the room, his chest heaving as he fought for air. He looked defiant, ready to fight. His challenging gaze fell on Rick.

Rick glared right back. "Shit, man, that's what this is about? If coming out of the closet was going to make you play like an asshole, why the fuck didn't you wait until after the tour was over."

"I . . ." Brian's mouth opened and then closed; he stared at them in shock. "You . . . *knew* about me . . . about . . . How long?"

"Hell, Bri, of course we knew." Logan shook his head. "We've known each other since grammar school. Did you really think you were that good at keeping a secret?"

"You never said anything," Brian said. He was still breathing hard, trying to assimilate what they were saying. He was stunned, staring around the room in astonishment at his friends.

"What was there to say? You never brought anyone around, not that it would have mattered, and then we figured you were careful because of the paparazzi. If you didn't want it splashed all over the tabloids, neither did we."

Brian looked at each one of the band members. "I can't believe this. All this time you knew and never said anything?"

Denny shrugged. "It wasn't our business. What's the big deal, man?"

Brian shoved both hands through his hair several times. "I thought it would change everything between us if you knew."

"Why the hell should we care what you do, Brian?" Denny asked.

"I don't believe this. Weren't you afraid the tabloids would make up a bunch of stories about us traveling together?"

"They make up shit all the time," Leo said. "What the hell, Brian? You've known us since we were five. Did you really think it would make a difference to us?"

Brian shook his head. "I told my old man after my mother died and he told me he never wanted to see me again. Hasn't anyone ever wondered why I never go home?"

"Your old man's a drunk, Brian," Rick pointed out. "Screw him. You never liked your family anyway. You slept on my couch half the time and on Denny's the other half."

"Well, shit," Brian said and sank down onto the couch. He

stared around him in a kind of dazed confusion. "I *really* don't believe this." He flashed the beginnings of a faint grin. "I ruined my fucking guitar for no damned reason."

Rick toed the wreckage. "Waste of a damned fine Gibson Les Paul." He sat down beside Brian. "Next time you decide to come out of the closet, Bri, smash a cheap guitar instead. This just makes me wanna cry."

Brian managed a faint smile. "You all knew?" He repeated. "You all discussed it? Talked about me?"

Denny snorted. "Hell yeah, we talked about you. We talk about everyone, why should you be any different? But, no, if you think we sat around talking shit, it was never like that. I'd beat the crap out of someone who talked shit about you. Any of us would."

Brain rubbed his hands over his face again and shook his head, obviously dazed by their reaction. "I don't know what to say."

"You can say you need a new guitar before tomorrow night," Joley said with a quick grin. She'd never loved her band members more than at that moment. But she could see the raw pain still swirling around Brian. In spite of what he'd revealed, in spite of everyone's reaction, he wasn't all right. He was struggling to maintain. She had to find a way to distract the attention from him. "The next time you have a secret, try not to go all Jimi Hendrix on your guitar. Of course, if you really wanted to do it right, you could have smashed your guitar onstage. Then we could have gathered up the pieces, autographed them and sold them as souvenirs."

She redirected the conversation, all the while keeping watch on Brian. The anger had drained away, but the dark moody colors still swirled around him and his melody was sad and lonely, as if his heart were breaking.

Talk gathered around them, the band members teasing Brian about breaking his guitar into tiny matchsticks and selling the pieces on eBay. Brian took the teasing in his normal good-natured way, but while his mouth was smiling, there were shadows in his eyes, so she stayed with the band, being there with him, with them, laughing and teasing in a way she hadn't done in years.

Eventually, as the others drifted out and made their way to the hotel, she sat down beside Brian. "Are you all right?"

He shook his head. "It hurts, Joley. I've never hurt like this before. Not even when my father disowned me."

"What happened?"

"Someone tried to kill Sergei tonight. I was with him. If it wasn't for the bodyguard, Prakenskii, we'd all be dead."

Joley inhaled sharply and reached out. Ilya didn't answer her. She closed her fingers over the mark on her palm and pressed her hand to her heart. "Is everyone okay?"

Brian glanced at her sharply. "You mean the bodyguard? He just about killed everything that moved, but he got us out alive. I have to take back everything I said about him. He didn't hesitate to come into that house after us, when we were completely surrounded. I thought we were dead, Joley. I really did." He hung his head, scrubbing his face with his hand, over and over, as if he could wipe away the memory.

Her heart pounded hard. She tried to still it by taking deep breaths. "But everyone's okay?"

"Yeah. After a car chase and a shoot-out."

"And then you came here and performed."

A ghost of a smile touched his mouth. "Not very well, apparently."

Joley answered his smile with a teasing one of her own. "I don't know. After all that, I'd say you did pretty well."

The smile faded from Brian's face, and he looked as if someone had ripped out his heart. "He's a mobster, Joley. Prakenskii tried to cover for him, and I knew he was doing it for my protection." The words stumbled over one another fast, coming out in a rush, as if all the air in his lungs was bursting out with the revelation. "Prakenskii was worried Sergei would hurt me if he guessed I knew the truth."

She bit at her lip, frowning. "How did you find out?"

"You mean aside from all the dead bodies? Bodyguards aren't like that. Prakenskii is a machine, Joley, cool and without emotion; he didn't hesitate to pull the trigger, not one time. There were so many of them, and he killed them all. Sergei and the other guy, Eddie, took it all as if it happened every day—and for normal people that's just not the case. And then, when we were in the car, Sergei told Prakenskii he would kill the people who attacked us and kill their families."

"He said that in front of you?" She tried not to let her alarm show.

"He spoke in Russian. I know he thought I wouldn't understand, but I've been studying Russian for the last year. It was supposed to be a surprise for him . . ." He trailed off, tears swimming in his eyes. "It doesn't matter. Businessmen don't say they're killing not only their enemies, but the families of their enemies. I knew right then."

Joley put her arms around him and held him close. "I'm sorry, Brian. I'm really, really sorry." She didn't like the crazy thoughts swirling around in his head. "Come back to the hotel with me tonight, Brian, and we'll just talk for a while."

"I don't want to intrude."

"Don't be silly, you wouldn't be intruding. Say you'll come. Steve can drive us both back together. And if you don't want to hang with my family, you can call it an early night."

Brian looked around the empty room. "I loved all this. The music—the life—all of you." He spread his hands out in front of him. "Now it seems so empty."

"Because you need someone to share it all with," Joley said. She stood up and tugged at his hand. "You know you shouldn't be alone, Brian. I may not be Nikitin, but I love you, and I'm always here for you. Come on back with me. You can sit in a corner and read a book if you don't want to talk. I'll spoil you with gourmet chocolate," she added, using a clear bribe.

He managed another laugh and toed the wreck of his guitar. "I can't believe I did that."

"Me either. That was your favorite guitar."

Brian put his hand in hers and they walked out of the room. Jonas and Aleksandr shot her an inquiring look as they stood and closed ranks around Brian and Joley.

"Everything okay?" Jonas asked.

Joley nodded. "It's all good."

They walked through the halls until they came to the exit. Security was everywhere, and a few lifted their hands when Joley flashed them a smile. Steve stood beside the car waiting as they came over.

"I'm sorry I held you up," Joley greeted. "We got talking."

Steve shrugged. "It's my job. No big deal."

Jonas opened the door for her. "We'll follow behind you in the other car."

"That's dumb. There's plenty of room and no need to take

two cars. Just tell the other driver you're coming with us," Joley protested. Steve started the car and at once warm air began to fill the interior. Joley hadn't realized she was cold until that moment. "And hurry up because I want to get back and have a hot cup of tea."

Jonas nodded and shut the door. Steve put the car in gear and began to pull away.

"Wait. Wait for my brothers-in-law," Joley said, leaning forward in her seat. "They're coming with us."

A smoky window went up between the front and back seats. At the same time, the locks snicked into place.

"Steve. What the hell are you doing?" Joley demanded as the window continued to rise between them. "We need to wait for Jonas. Steve, damn it. What are you doing?" She knocked on the window. When there was no response, she tried the doors. The lock wouldn't respond. "Great." She slumped back in her seat. "This is just great."

Joley pulled her cell phone out of her pocket and flipped it open to call Jonas. "Shit. No service. He must have a jamming device in the car with us."

Brian's eyebrow shot up, and in spite of the situation he laughed. "A jamming device? You sound like a spy. Are there jamming devices? And if so, how do you know about them?"

Joley flung herself back against the seat. "This is such bull, Brian. My own driver-slash-bodyguard is kidnapping us. And my bodyguard brother put us in the car. And my bodyguard boyfriend is off playing with his friends. Sheesh." She crossed her arms across her chest and kicked the front seat hard, right in the middle of Steve's back. "And when he stops this car, I'm kicking his ass."

Brian laughed again. "You're so crazy, Joley. Most women would be scared at this point. Hell, if I hadn't seen a dozen dead bodies today, I'd be scared, too."

"I'm tired and mad. Really mad. We've been working for months nonstop. I'm one show away from going home. Sea Haven is about four hours from here, Brian. That's it."

"So what are we going to do?"

She scowled and drove the toe of her shoe deep into the middle of the back of the driver's seat a second time just for emphasis. "I have no idea. But these idiots are messing around with the wrong woman. My sisters are not going to be happy

about this." Joley looked around her. "All right. What do we
have back here that can be used as a weapon? We just have to
buy ourselves a little time. Jonas and Aleksandr will be following. Ilya will come, and my sisters are going to be a force
to contend with. Give me a minute and let me see if I can
reach any of them."

But it was Ilya she called first. She closed her eyes, blocked
out everything around her—all sounds, all thoughts—and
concentrated on him. Her palm itched, and she ran her fingertip over the mark, as if she could physically touch him.

Ilya. I'm in trouble.

She felt him moving through her mind, and then there was
warmth. *That's nothing new.* The faint note of humor caressed
her with a soothing touch. *The word just came in to Nikitin
that the kidnappers want to meet. They're using you and Brian,
who apparently is with you, as a bargaining chip to work out a
deal. Nikitin would never have shown up for you. They don't
know it, but they're holding a winning hand with Brian.* There
was that same reassuring warmth. *Don't worry, I'd show up
for you, but as Steve's involved, they probably expect that.*

Joley sent him an impression of haughty disdain. *I wasn't
in the least bit worried.* She sobered with a little sigh. Everything was falling into place now. All the clues had been there;
she just hadn't read them. *I talked to Steve the evening the bus
blew up. He asked where you were. He was coming from the
bus and we talked for a minute, but it was a bizarre conversation. Do you think he's the one who planted the bomb?* The
thought made her angry. She'd known Steve and trusted him.
She *liked* Steve. How had she missed that he would betray
her? Some psychic she was. She hadn't known her best friend
was gay, and she hadn't realized Steve was in the employ of
people trying to kill her.

*Magic isn't science, Joley. You rely too heavily on your
gifts. People are different, and they can be a multitude of
things—not all bad, not all good.*

She didn't want a lecture, she wanted help. Nikitin and
whoever his rival mobster was might have a small army with
tons of firepower, but she had her family—her sisters. And she
had Ilya. The combination was unstoppable.

She reached for her closest connection with absolute faith.
Hannah?

We're here, honey. We feel it. We'll be waiting.

She wasn't afraid. Deep inside she felt centered and calm, definitely in control. Already she could feel the energy building around her as her sisters united. She flashed a reassuring smile at Brian and tapped her fingers against the back of his hand. "We'll be all right. If they mention Nikitin to you, act like you don't know anything."

"You think these are the same people who tried to kill him earlier?"

"I think they have to be. And I think Steve planted the bomb that blew up my bus, so don't think he's going to have any loyalty toward us. Ilya will come for us."

"I've seen him in action. He inspires confidence."

Joley nodded. He did that. She was amazed how safe she felt, how reassured. She'd always had that with her family. Having Ilya only made the feeling more so. Whatever differences they had to work out, trust was no longer one of them, because she knew he was coming for her—nothing would stop him.

The ride was long. North on the freeway for what seemed an hour and then west toward the coast. They drove through a series of twists and turns. They were definitely off the highway and running along a narrow, winding road that led to the foothills. She recognized the area.

Bear Valley. They're taking you on the road to Bear Valley. Hannah's voice was soothing and calm in Joley's mind. *We're not far behind you. Jonas picked us up. We're tracking your energy.*

All people left a specific trail behind, a part of their aura, their song, the same as fingerprints, and Joley knew each sister could find one of the others if she ran across that energy trail.

Ilya? She couldn't help reaching out to him. She wanted to feel the warmth of his touch, the comforting caress of his voice.

We were sent a map to follow. He's distraught, Joley, genuinely distraught.

You know it's a trap. They have cover everywhere. This is heavy brush country, lots of trees, and they'll have the advantage of knowing the terrain. They chose it.

You worry too much. It will be all right.

She wanted the reassurance, and his voice, that amazing voice, provided it. She believed in him, which was almost shocking to her. She believed in her family and never thought anyone could come close to making her feel safe in the way they did, but Ilya had slowly inserted himself into her life until she found herself believing. And now that belief was so strong, she had no doubts he would find a way to rescue her.

Joley stared out the window into the night, watching the lights of cars flashing past. For Joley, marriage was sacrosanct. In her profession, marriage often ended up in a quick and easy divorce. She didn't want that. Her parents had a long and happy marriage, and her ancestors had done the same. One by one her sisters had found men they felt were true partners—best friends, astonishing lovers. Joley had never believed that would happen to her. She had always believed the bond of her sisters would be all that she had, and she'd been determined to make that enough—until Ilya. He was everything. Her heart, her soul, and he certainly commanded her body. She knew what love was, and she had finally made that sacred commitment with every fiber of her being.

The car slowed, and Joley let her senses flair out as much as possible, trying to send impressions of movement or heat or anything that might help Ilya. Her sisters would be somewhere safe, and no one would ever know they'd been there, helping in the battle, but Ilya would be on the front line and she wanted him to have every advantage.

"Look for guards on your side," she hissed to Brian.

Jonas let us out a few miles away from you. We're going to high ground so we can command the wind, Hannah informed Joley.

They were coming up on a cabin. Steve parked the car and they sat for a few minutes. He slowly lowered the glass between them. "Don't do anything stupid, Joley, and you might get out of this alive."

"Maybe I will," she said, "but you won't."

Brian kicked her ankle. "Don't provoke him."

"You haven't seen provocation yet," she answered, tossing her head in defiance, not bothering to lower her voice.

Steve opened the door and reached in to pull Joley out.

She slapped his hand away. "Don't you touch me, you

miserable slug, slimy, worthless, traitorous piece of shit." She put all the contempt she could muster into her voice—the one weapon that none of them had even considered. She let him feel her disgust, allowed her voice to influence, not only him, but everyone within hearing distance to look at Steve the way she did. "You have no honor. If you would turn on me after being my friend for years, you would turn on anyone. No one can trust you."

Steve reddened visibly, her voice leaving him exposed not only to the others, but to himself. He shifted his feet and stepped back.

Joley shot him a look of utter disdain and climbed out on her own, carrying herself as regally as possible. She looked him up and down and stepped past him, going straight to the cabin and the men waiting on the porch. She flashed a cold smile at John Dylan, who half sat on the railing, swinging one leg, arms crossed over his chest.

"If you'd wanted a meeting, John, you might have just said so at the hotel or the arena. It's a little on the chilly side here."

Brian trailed after her, and just as he reached the porch stairs, the man behind him shoved him. Brian stumbled and fell into her. Joley staggered, recovered her balance, turned and in one precise move, snapped out a front kick, catching the guard square in the chest. She wanted the attention centered solely on her, especially now that John Dylan was present. Nobody could guess at Brian's relationship with Nikitin.

Dylan stepped up to her and slapped her hard, rocking her backward. She tasted blood in her mouth, but she refused to flinch. She just stood there, staring him down.

What the hell just happened? The voice was utterly cold, white-hot but arctic-cold, the voice of death.

Joley shivered. There was that underlying fury, the volcano beneath the ice cap. *I kicked one of Dylan's guards, so Dylan slapped me. John Dylan is here and everyone is deferring to him. Looks to me like he's in charge.*

She could feel Ilya making an effort to tamp down his fury. *Stay away from that son of a bitch. I'll be there in another couple of minutes. Aleksandr and Jonas will take out as many guards as possible to give us a clear escape route. Just don't provoke him.*

Brian took her arm, drawing her against him.

"Now that I have your attention," Dylan sneered, "where's your friend, the bodyguard?"

She smirked. "You mean the one you're all so afraid of?" She embedded the suggestion in her voice, as well as amplifying their fears. "What do you want, Dylan?"

"In a few minutes you'll find out." He pulled out a pack of cigarettes, offered Brian one, and when he declined, Dylan pulled one from the pack and lit it. "Sorry you got mixed up in this, Brian, you weren't part of the deal. You just were in the wrong place at the wrong time. You never should have gotten in the car with her."

The wind shifted slightly, coming in from the west. It tasted of salt water, as if blowing off the ocean that was behind several mountains. Joley lifted her face to the cool breeze and inhaled the scent of sea. Around them the branches of the trees rustled, murmuring softly, the leaves flashing silver in the night. She heard the faint sound of feminine voices rising in an age-old chant. Soft. Insistent. Musical. She recognized the surge in power surrounding her like a protective cloak.

"Car coming," Steve announced.

"Shoot the bodyguard the moment he steps out of the car," Dylan ordered. "Grab them."

They're planning to shoot you on sight, Ilya, Joley warned, ignoring the man who grabbed her arms and yanked them behind her back. *Turn around. Get out of here.*

Dylan caught at Brian as the car swept up to the house, using his body as a shield, and dragging him backward toward the door of the cabin. Joley was thrown facedown over the railing, a gun pressed to the back of her neck, a hard hand against her back.

The car rolled slowly toward the cabin. The guards began to shoot, the bullets drilling holes into the vehicle until it looked like a sieve. Joley could see it coming toward the porch at the same steady speed.

Don't move.

It was all the warning she got. The gun suddenly shifted, pointing away from her. She felt the guard jerk. He was flung back and away from her. Blood spattered across her back and arms. The gun clattered to the floor.

Now. Toward the trees.

Joley leapt onto the railing and jumped off of it, sprinting toward the tree line. Around her the wind whirled and screamed, creating a mini-cyclone. Branches broke off from the trees above her head, hurtling toward the porch, knocking men down. Ilya came out to meet her, the gun bucking in his fist, spitting death, laying down a covering fire as he yanked her behind him.

"Go! Get down."

Deliberately, Ilya fired three shots into Steve's throat, sending him over backward.

"Brian. They've got Brian," Joley said as she raced deeper into the trees and shrubbery.

Ilya aimed over Brian's head and squeezed the trigger, but at the last moment, Dylan went through the door.

"No! Hold your fire." Nikitin grabbed Ilya's gun arm. "You might shoot Brian."

"You shouldn't even be here. They want you dead, I told you that. Get to cover," Ilya snapped.

In the distance they heard the crack of a rifle, then another shot. Jonas and Aleksandr were protecting their escape route. The wind tore at the house, whirling around it, loosening boards and rattling the windows. It increased in strength, vicious, finally ripping boards loose so that they flapped. Shingles flew from the roof.

Nikitin pulled out his gun, speared Ilya a fierce look and ran toward the cabin. Ilya swore and ran after him. Twice he shot one of Dylan's soldiers as they reared up in front of Nikitin. The Russian made it to the porch in spite of the wind and kicked at the door. Ilya grabbed his shirt and jerked him to the side as bullets splintered the door from the inside.

Sergei Nikitin was no coward, he never had been. He was used to giving orders and expected his men to obey him. He was going in after Brian, which told Ilya more than anything else that his feelings for the guitar player were absolutely genuine, because Nikitin never took an unnecessary risk.

Ilya took a breath and summoned energy to him, tapping into the Drake sisters' combined strength, gathering the wind so that it pulled back for a moment and then slammed into the door with the force of a battering ram. The door buckled and crashed to the floor, and the wind swept inside.

A volley of shots poured out of the room, the flashes bright in the darkness. Ilya waited for the sudden silence, sent another blast of wind ahead of him and rolled in behind it, going to the left, at an angle from the gunfire. He tried to track Dylan, but the man had already moved. Brian began to struggle violently, kicking and hitting until he broke free and made a dash for the window, obviously intending to dive out of it.

Ilya couldn't get a clear shot at Dylan, who had overturned furniture to provide cover. He saw Dylan's gun sweep up and track Brian. Heart in his throat, he rolled to get a better angle. Nikitin ran at Dylan, firing round after round. Most of the bullets thunked harmlessly into furniture, but the distraction forced Dylan to turn the gun from Brian to Nikitin. The two mobsters exchanged a ferocious storm of bullets until Ilya aimed, squeezed the trigger and shot John Dylan through the heart.

The wind retreated, leaving behind silence. The room smelled of blood, gunpowder and death. Brian turned slowly, his fingers still clutching the windowsill. Nikitin lay on the floor, the gun still in his hand, blood pouring from several wounds.

Brian dropped to the floor and crawled to Nikitin, taking his hand. "Don't." He rocked himself. "Don't go."

Nikitin glanced at Ilya, who shook his head. "Get him out of here." He tried to say more words, but blood choked his throat, poured out of his mouth. He coughed, tried to clear his throat. "Don't let any of this touch him." More blood streamed.

"I'll take care of it," Ilya promised.

Nikitin looked up at Brian, and, as their eyes locked together, he died.

20

THE sea crashed and foamed, spraying over rocks and up into the darkened sky in white bursts, the sound loud, but familiar and comforting. Joley walked along the captain's walk, pacing slowly back and forth, knowing one of her ancestors had traced exactly the same path—waiting, watching, hoping for her man to return home from the perils of the sea. She felt a kinship with that woman from long ago; she knew what it was like to wait and watch and worry. She knew what it was like to love someone else with every breath in her body. She desperately wanted Ilya to escape unscathed from his dangerous job and return to her.

Ilya had been away, tying up the remnants of his operation for three long weeks. The first week, she and the band members had spent with Brian, helping him through the first rush of terrible grief. Now he was staying with Logan and Tish, living quietly and trying to come to terms with what he wanted to do in the future.

Joley had returned to her family home and tried very hard to fit in again, but without Ilya, her world, even the sanctuary of the Drake house, was gone. She concentrated on the ocean, watching the way the endless waves rose and fell. At night the water appeared black and shiny, with sudden bursts of silver as it foamed against the rocks.

She ached, inside and out, worried about Ilya, afraid for him. He'd gone after Sergei Nikitin's human trafficking network, determined to shut it down. With Nikitin gone, his front line would scramble and hide, so Ilya had very little time to catch them before they disappeared into the shadows where they preferred to live. Working undercover for so long had made Ilya a loner, rarely using or even having a backup, or checking in as regularly with his bosses as he should. Jonas had told her what little he could, but Ilya preferred being alone and didn't often give much information. Bottom line—she had no idea where he was or even if he was safe.

Joley sighed and leaned on the railing, the wind blowing her hair from around her face. She inhaled the salt air, tasted the sea spray, felt restless and empty. *Where are you?* She would wait as long as it took for him to come to her. It was two in the morning. She accepted that there would be another night without sleep. She missed Ilya so much that she could barely go into the house anymore. She wanted to stay outside, close to the sea, where the wind could carry her news of her man. *Where are you?*

She pulled her cloak closer around her and continued her lonely vigil. Deep inside, her stomach churned like the wild sea, her brain refused to quiet, wave after wave of anxiety crashing through her mind, conjuring images of every conceivable injury or death that could befall Ilya. What if he never returned to her? So many women before her had stood in this very place waiting for a man who never came home, and they never knew where his ship had gone down. That could happen. He would just disappear and no one would ever know.

Where are you? She pressed a hand to her stomach. She needed peace. She needed Ilya. *Come home to me. Just come home.*

The wind tugged at her hair, teasing her with small fingers of awareness over her skin. She inhaled and caught a faint scent. Everything inside of her went still. Fear held her paralyzed for a moment. Her mind might be playing tricks on her. She turned slowly and walked to the rail, looking down away from the sea and for the first time toward the path leading up to her house. She had refused to allow herself to look—to hope—to believe he would really be there.

In the distance, emerging out of the dark and the few tendrils of fog, she made out a man with wide shoulders and a long stride. Joley would recognize that walk anywhere. In the night he was a dark shadow, moving with stealth and power.

As he approached the gates, she held her breath. The Drake home had power of its own, and the padlock was on those high gates. The house would protect any Drake woman from a threat if need be. Ilya never even broke stride, although he had to have seen that the iron gates were locked. He would know those ancient symbols of protection, yet he walked, head up, his strides covering ground fast.

Joley's heart began to beat too fast—too hard. Her legs went weak so that she clutched at the rail. Tears burned in her eyes and blurred her vision. She felt a lump rising in her throat, choking her. Ilya. *Her* Ilya. At that moment she couldn't speak or move, not even to call out to him, absolute joy bursting through her.

The padlock simply fell from the gates, and they swung open. The creak was loud in the silence of the night as the metal parted in the middle and welcomed him inside. Ilya kept walking up the winding path, through the garden still over-grown with flowers in the dead of winter. Behind him the gates closed, clanking hard, and the padlock leapt from the ground, back to its place to guard the entrance.

Joley dropped her cloak and ran. She waved her hand and the door opened for her. She raced down the hall and took the stairs two at a time. The house was dark and cold, mirroring the way she felt inside. She hadn't been able to bring herself to light a fire or even make a cup of tea, but the darkness didn't hinder her, she knew every step of the way to the front door and she sprinted, her heart bursting.

The door swung open before she even managed to send it a command, and he was there. On her front porch. Real. Solid. *Alive.* Joley leapt on him, so that he had no choice but to catch her in midair. She wrapped her legs around his waist, her arms around his neck, sank her face into the hollow of his shoulder and burst into tears.

He buried his face in her silky hair and just held her on the porch while the wind whipped around them in a joyous frenzy and the waves climbed higher and higher as if dancing in their delight.

Ilya carried Joley inside and kicked the door closed behind him. At once a fire sprang up in the fireplace. Candles on the mantel lit one by one, lending the room an amber glow. The mosaic beneath his feet seemed to come alive, swirling with colors and shooting stars. He swore for a moment that he heard whispers, feminine voices welcoming him home, but when he looked around, they were completely alone.

Ilya let Joley's legs slide back to the floor, but he caught the nape of her neck and turned her face up to his. He had never in his life had a home, but when he walked through the gates, and the door to her house had swung open, and Joley had been there, her face lit up like Christmas morning—he had known. He was home.

Emotion overwhelmed him, robbed him of speech, leaving him without words to tell her how much he loved her. He brought his mouth to hers, slowly, inch by inch, watching her face—her eyes. Watching the way she loved him back. He had dreamt of this moment, feeling the soft silk of her mouth, warm and tasting of that long-ago honey that had been so good. The dream didn't come close to the reality. He sank into her arms, into her kiss, and knew he was truly home. She held nothing back; she simply melted into him, her body soft and pliant, sensual with promise.

Joley couldn't stop her tears, and he tasted them, too, his lips wandering over her face, memorizing the shape and feel of her.

"I was so scared," she whispered, linking her fingers behind his neck. "Please never go away like that again."

"I have no intention of ever leaving you, Joley. I handed in my resignation and walked away."

"What happened? Were you able to take the network down?"

"The bust covered four countries and netted us sixteen major players. I found your missing teen and we brought her home. She was traumatized, but she was alive and HIV-free, luckier than some of the others."

"Thank God!"

Ilya kissed her again, a long, slow savoring of her, pulling her closer, needing to feel her warmth. "How is Brian?"

Joley pulled off his jacket, needing to inspect him for injuries. She almost dropped it on the floor, but something made her go and hang it in the entryway closet beside her coat. The two jackets looked as if they belonged together. "We're all taking turns watching over him, and hopefully he'll come to terms with his loss. It makes it so hard for him because he can't really talk about Nikitin to anyone and have them under-stand why he might have fallen in love with a monster."

She turned her head and stared at him—drank him in. She still could barely believe he was really there.

Ilya swept her into his arms, cradling her close to his chest. "Tell me where the bedroom is." He was already going up the stairs.

She just pointed and nuzzled his neck, much more inter-ested in the scent and texture of him than their destination.

The walls were covered with pictures, and as they passed, the photographs rustled softly and two wall sconces glowed with light.

Joley's bedroom faced the sea. There was a large window, already open, the sheer curtains billowing, like ghostly dresses, with the wind coming off the ocean. Her bed lay beside the window, giving her a huge view of the sea. Ilya put her down beside the large four-poster bed and tugged her shirt over her head. Joley kicked off her sandals as his hands went to the waistband of her jeans. He unzipped them and tugged, taking her panties as well. She held his arm while she stepped out of them. The moment he unhooked her bra, the cold air shaped her nipples into twin hard peaks.

She stood with the moonlight spilling over her soft skin, her dark eyes luminous, her silky hair tousled from the wind.

"You're so beautiful," he said, his breath catching in his lungs. He unbuttoned his shirt with one hand, reaching out with the other to cup her breast, his thumb sliding over her nipple, watching her reaction. "I missed you."

She leaned into him for another kiss. She couldn't get enough, would never get enough. She ached with missing him. His arms slid around her, and he simply lifted her, kissing her the entire time, even as he laid her on the bed. The darkened shadow on his face rubbed erotically against her sensitive skin. When he raised his head, she felt bereft. He sank down beside her and removed his shoes.

Joley couldn't take her gaze from him, afraid that if she did, he might disappear. She wanted to inspect him for in-juries, and the moment he shed his clothes, she came up on her knees and ran her hands over him. Of course there were fresh bruises, scrapes and a couple of raw-looking gashes.

His hand slid over her bare bottom, shaping the naked

cheek lovingly as he brought his mouth down to the hollow of her shoulder. She went still, the breath leaving her lungs in a rush. She slid her arms around his neck and pressed close, still shaken by his absence—by his return—tears burning behind her eyelids even while her body was soft and aching with need.

He lifted her hips. "Put your legs around me, *lubov moya.*"

She was almost afraid to—she wanted to have him deep inside, yet she didn't want anything to interfere with this time, this moment when the love was so overwhelming she could barely breathe.

He whispered to her in Russian, bit gently at her earlobe, her neck, kissed her upturned mouth again. "Lock your ankles, Joley." This time there was that edge of command to his voice, and it brought a rush of damp heat, a small thrill in her stomach.

She raised her legs obediently and sank down on his thick length, impaling her body. He was larger than she remembered, forcing his way through the tight velvet folds, stretching her impossibly. She was slick with liquid heat and the sensation of pleasure washing over her, but love was also there in abundance. She felt surrounded by her deep commitment and emotion for this man, she felt lifted by it, but most of all—complete. She felt his ragged gasp, the heat and raw honesty in his whisper of love.

Ya lublu tebya.

I love you. The three words meant everything. She was a spell-singer, and her world was sound. She knew truth when she heard it. She tightened her arms around him, holding him closer, wanting to share the same skin, wanting to crawl inside the shelter of his body and have them be as close as they could to each other.

"I love you, Ilya, more than anything," she answered, meaning it, knowing he heard sound in the same way she did.

Around them their colors swirled and merged like the notes of their song. It no longer frightened her. Ilya was part of her—the best part—and he felt the same way about her.

His lovemaking started gentle, so incredibly tender she felt tears run down her face. Each stroke was slow and easy as his hands shaped and memorized her body. She felt as if he was worshiping her, the sweet pleasure washing through her in

gentle waves. As his hips maintained that same gentle rocking, the tension began to rise, to build, until she couldn't
think, until she was desperate for him to pick up the pace. She
tried to force it, writhing and moving her own hips, but no
amount of squirming or eventual pleading could change his
tempo.

Heat became an inferno; around them she heard the notes
of their song catch fire as passion sizzled and burned through
her veins. That slow burn grew hotter and brighter, threatening
to consume her. She threw her head back, absorbing the sheer
erotic magic of Ilya.

Tongues of fire began to lick along her breasts, her belly,
deep inside where that relentless stroke of velvet-encased
steel continued to drag over sensitive nerves, until she heard
her own sob and her body clenched and spasmed and began to
coil tighter and tighter. Each stroke was precise, driving deep,
a hard, thick piston that only tightened the stranglehold her
body had him in. When it came, her orgasm rushed, overtook,
consumed them both, throwing them into an explosive series
of waves, roaring through their bodies, taking Ilya with her,
her feminine sheath like hot silk gripping hard, forcing him to
submit and surrender.

She cried out his name, dropped her head onto his shoulder
as she collapsed, kissing his neck, her arms holding him tight.

"If you didn't understand what I just told you, I am in love
with you," Ilya said. He didn't mean just what he'd told her
when he was speaking Russian, he meant what he'd said with
every beat of his heart, every stroke of his body. He remembered her fears of his wanting only sex from her, and he
wanted to lay them to rest forever.

"I understood perfectly."

He felt her lips curve against his neck and knew she was
smiling. He laid her back, careful of her smaller body as he
blanketed her, holding her close to him, unable to break away
yet. He wanted to feel the beat of her heart, hear her soft
breath, feel the silk of her hair and the satin of her skin against
his. She was soft, all woman; she was—everything.

"Listen to that, Ilya," she said softly.

"What am I listening to?" He was listening to her song, almost purring like a contented kitten. He would never hear that
song enough.

"The sea. Earlier, before you were here, the waves were wild and crazy. I could hear the roaring and crashing against the rocks." She pressed a hand to her stomach. "Inside I felt the same way, moody and stormy and all on edge. And then you came home. The sea is at peace." And so was she. Deep inside, everything had become calm and still and at peace.

He looked at her instead of the inky water. Her heart leapt. His eyes, his beautiful eyes, often so like the turbulent sea in the midst of a wild coastal storm, were as serene as the clear skies after a storm passes. She could see his colors; the dark shadow was still there—and it probably would always be second nature to Ilya to hide who he was—but she could see the colors swirling beneath the darkness, light and happy and tranquil. His music was soft and sensuous, a blend of notes that made her heart melt and her world right.

"You make everything in me still and relaxed, Joley. You make my body and heart sing. I swear, when I saw you coming toward me, the rest of the world fell away and I knew I was home. It didn't matter where, just as long as I was with you."

Joley smiled and kissed him again, a long, lingering kiss that stole his breath. "Look at the sea, Ilya. The ocean is so enormous and beautiful. Especially at night, it just sweeps everything bad in your life under those pounding waves and takes it out to somewhere in the middle of all that vast space, leaving life good."

His smile was slow and heart-stopping. She got another kiss, and then he braced himself above her to look out the window at the continually moving water. "It is beautiful, Joley," he agreed. "I had hoped we could buy the property next to Jonas. There's twenty acres for sale, a huge home with enough bedrooms for our sons, but we're not on the ocean. You have to look over the tops of the trees to see it in the distance."

There was a small silence. "You were looking at property? When? How?"

"Jonas sent me a link on the Internet. I had to do something while I was traveling, so I went through my e-mail. It sounded perfect, but now that I can hear the sea, maybe we should be closer." He lowered his body over hers again, bending his head to kiss her. It was difficult resisting her, the shape and texture of her curves when she melted the way she did each time he sank into her.

"I hadn't thought that far ahead," she admitted, running her hands up and down his arms. It was necessary to touch him, to feel every inch of his skin. "But I'd love to live close to Hannah."

"Our children can play together." He rolled over to lie beside her, one hand massaging her stomach.

"There you go with the children again. Get over it already. We're not having children for a long, long time." But she was already a *little* enticed by the prospect of letting him see a real childhood by watching their son grow up in a loving home.

"Really?" He bent his head and kissed her stomach, his dark hair falling across her skin and tickling her. "I don't know that I'd call eight months a long time, but I guess by the end of it, most women think it's a very long time."

Joley couldn't help but immerse her fingers into that wealth of silky hair as he pressed his ear to her stomach and then rubbed another caress over her. "You are so insane. I told you, I'm on birth control."

"Does birth control work for Elle?"

She frowned and, with her fingers curled into his thick hair, yanked to bring his head up. "I am *not* Elle."

He flashed a small grin. "No, but I am—well—the masculine version of her, and I'm feeling life here in your womb. I felt it the first time I ever made love to you."

Joley gaped at him. It wasn't true. A baby? She put her hands on her belly. Could she be pregnant with a baby? *His* baby? That little boy with dark curls who would never hide in a corner trying to make himself small? She imagined Ilya carrying the child on his shoulders, laughing. Ilya needed to laugh; he needed to see a childhood the way it was meant to be. Secretly, she thought she might like the motherhood thing—with *one* child—but there would be no admitting it to him.

"You'd better be wrong. That would be like a fate worse than death. I'm not having seven children. Do you know how many times I'd have to be in labor?"

He nuzzled her stomach. "Not if we did it two at a time."

She sat up, pushing his head away from her. "Did I say I missed you, because if I did, I was sadly mistaken." She pointed across the room. "Go over there and sit down."

He grinned at her, unrepentant. "I think we should have at

least one girl, too. I want to find her trying to get out of windows when she's been naughty at school."

Joley groaned. "Don't wish that on us!" She wrapped her arms around him and pulled him back to her. "Seven sons, for real? You'd better be really good at the daddy role."

"I'll do my best," he promised, nuzzling her neck, "but I intend to be dynamite at the husband role." He kissed her several times, unable to stay away from her soft mouth. "And thank you for the way you lit up the house when I returned, the fire in the fireplace, the candles—it was so beautiful and made me feel unlike anything I've ever felt. It was perfect."

Joley's hands smoothed through his hair lovingly. "I didn't do that," she whispered, knowing the truth. "The house recognized you and welcomed you home."

Turn the page for a special preview of

DARK CURSE
by Christine Feehan

"LARA, let's get out of here," Terry Vale said. "It's getting dark and there's nothing here. Look below us. There're caves crisscrossing the entire mountain. Take your pick."

Lara Calladine didn't bother looking away from where she was scanning the mountainside for the smallest crack that might signal the presence of a cave. She wasn't wrong—not this time. Power surged and crackled the moment she set foot on the upper slopes of the mountain. She took a deep breath and pressed a hand over her pounding heart. This was *it*. This was the place she had spent her life searching for. She would recognize that flow of energy anywhere. She knew every weave, every spell, her body absorbing the gathering power so that veins sizzled and her nerve endings burned with the electrical current building inside of her.

"I've got to go with Terry on this," Gerald French agreed. "This place gives me the creeps. We've been on a lot of mountains, but this one doesn't like us." He gave a nervous laugh. "It's getting dicey up here."

"No one says 'dicey,'" Lara murmured, running her hand along the face of the rock about an inch from the surface, looking for threads of power.

"Whatever," Gerald snapped. "It's getting dark and there's nothing here but mist. The fog is creepy, Lara. We've got to get out of here."

Lara spared the two men an impatient glance and then surveyed the countryside around them. Ice and snow glittered, coating the surrounding mountains with what appeared to be sparkling gems. Far below she could see castles, farms and churches in the distance despite the gathering dusk. Sheep dotted the meadows and she could see the river running, filled to capacity. Birds cried overhead, filling the sky and dive-bombing toward her, only to break off abruptly and circle again. The wind shifted continuously, biting at her face and at every bit of exposed skin, tugging at her long thick braid, moaning and wailing all the while. Occasionally a rock fell down the slope and bounced off the ledge to the hillside below. A trickle of snow and dirt slid near her feet.

Her gaze swept the wild countryside. Gorges and ravines cut through the snowcapped mountains, plants clung to the sides of the rocks and shivered naked along the plateaus. She could see the entrances to several caves and felt the strong pull toward them as if they were tempting her to leave where she was to explore. Water filled the deeper depressions below, forming a dark peat bog and beds of moss, which were a vivid green in stark contrast to the browns surrounding them. But she needed to be here—in this spot, this place. She had studied the geography carefully and knew that deep within the earth, a massive series of ice caves had formed.

The higher she climbed, the smaller everything below her looked and the thicker the white mist surrounding her became. With each step, the ground shifted subtly and the birds overhead shrieked a little louder. Ordinary things, yes, but the subtle sense of uneasiness, the continual voice whispering, warning her to leave before it was too late, told her this was a place of power. Although the wind continued to shriek and blow, the mist remained a thick veil that shrouded the upper slope.

"Come on, Lara," Terry tried again. "It took us forever to get the permits, we can't waste time on the wrong area. You can see nothing's here."

It had taken considerable effort this time to get the permits for her study, but she had managed the usual way—using her gifts to persuade those who disagreed with her that, with the universal global warming, the fate of the ice caves was unknown and needed immediate attention. More than that, microbes—extremophiles—not only survived within the caves, but thrived in extreme conditions. The hope was that the microorganisms that lived and reproduced far from sunlight and traditional nutrients could aid medical science in the fight against cancer or even produce an antibiotic capable of wiping out the newer superbugs emerging.

Her research project was fully funded and, although she was considered young at the age of twenty-seven, she was acknowledged as the leading expert in the field of ice-cave study and preservation. She'd logged more hours exploring, mapping and studying the ice caves around the world than most other researchers twice her age. She'd also discovered more superbugs than any other caver. NASA, one of the leading researchers of the extremophiles, was one of her biggest supporters.

"Didn't it strike you as odd that no one wanted us in this particular region? They were fine giving us permits to look virtually anywhere else," she pointed out. Part of the reason she'd persisted when no caves had been mapped in the area was because the department head had been so strange— strange and rather vague when they went over the map. After studying the area, the natural geographical deduction was that a vast network of ice caves lay beneath the mountain, yet the entire region seemed to have been overlooked.

Terry and Gerald had exhibited exactly the same behavior, as if they didn't notice the odd structure of the mountain, and both men were superb at finding ice caves from the geographical surface. Persuasion had been difficult, but all of that work was for this moment, this cave, this find.

"It's here," she said with absolute confidence.

Her heart continued to pound with excitement, not at the find, but because walking had become such a chore, her body not wanting to continue forward. She breathed away the compulsion to leave and pressed through the safeguards, following the trail of power, judging how close she was to the entrance by how strong her need to run away was.

Voices rose in the wind, swirled in the mists, telling her to go back, to leave while she could. Strangely, she heard the voices in several languages, the warning much stronger and insistent as she made her way along the slope searching for a crack, for anything at all that might signal an entrance to the caves she knew were there. All the while she kept her senses alert to the possibility that monsters might lurk beneath the earth. But she had to enter—to find the place of her nightmares, the place of her childhood. She had to find the two dragons she dreamt of nightly.

"Lara!" This time Terry's voice was sharp with protest. "We have to get out of here."

Barely sparing him a second glance, Lara stood still for a long moment, studying the outcropping that jutted out from smoother rock. Thick snow covered most of it, but there was an oddity about it that kept drawing her gaze back to the rock. She approached cautiously. Several small rocks lay at the foot of the larger boulders, and strangely, not a single snowflake stuck to them. She didn't touch them, but studied them from every angle, carefully observing the way they were arranged in a pattern at the foot of the outcropping.

"Something out of place," she murmured aloud.

Instantly the wind wailed, the sound rising to a shriek as it rushed toward her, blowing debris into the air so that it shot at her like small missiles.

"It's the rocks. See, they should be arranged differently." Lara leaned down and pushed the small pile of rocks into a different pattern.

At once the ground shifted beneath them. The mountain creaked in protest. Bats took to the air, pouring out of some unseen hole a short distance from them, filling the sky until it was nearly black. The dark crack along the outcropping split wider. The mountain shuddered and shook and groaned as if alive, as if it were coming awake.

"We shouldn't be here," Terry nearly sobbed.

Lara took a deep breath and held her palm to the narrow slit in the mountainside, the only entrance to this particular cave. Power blasted out at her, and all around she could feel the safeguards, thick and ominous, protecting the entrance.

"You're right, Terry," she agreed. "We shouldn't." She backed away from the outcropping and gestured toward the trail. "Let's go. And hurry." For the first time she was really aware of the hour, the sun setting, the gathering darkness spreading like a stain across the sky.

She would be coming back early morning—without her two companions. She had no idea what was left in the elaborate ice caverns below, but she wasn't about to expose two of her closest friends to danger. The safeguards in place would confuse them, so they wouldn't remember the location of the cave, but she knew each weave, each spell, and how to reverse it so that the guards wouldn't affect her.

Ice caves as a whole were dangerous at all times. The continual pressure from overlying ice caps often sent great frozen chunks of ice blasting out of the walls, like rockets being fired, capable of killing anything they struck. This ice cave held dangers that far outweighed natural ones, and she didn't want her companions anywhere near it.

The ground shifted again, throwing all of them off balance. Gerald grabbed her to keep her from falling and Terry caught at the outcropping, fingers digging into the widening crack. Beneath their feet, something under the ground moved, raising the surface several inches as the creature raced toward the base of the rocks Lara had realigned.

"What is that?" Gerald shouted, backpedaling. He thrust Lara behind him in an effort to protect her as the dirt and snow spouted into a geyser almost at his feet.

Terry screamed, his voice high-pitched and frightened as he tipped over backward and the unseen creature raced toward him beneath the earth.

"Get up! Move!" Lara called, trying to get around Gerald's solid bulk to throw a holding spell. As he swung around, Gerald's backpack knocked her off her feet and sent her rolling down the steeper slope. Her birthmark, the strangely shaped dragon positioned just over her left ovary, suddenly flared into life, burning through her skin and glowing red hot.

Two dark-green tentacles burst from the snow-covered ground, slick with blood, the color so dark it nearly was black. They emerged on either side of Terry's left ankle. The sound of bubbling mud rose, along with a noxious, putrid stink of rotten eggs and sulfur, so overpowering the three of them gagged. The bulbous ends of the tentacles reared back, revealing coiling snake heads, and then struck with brutal speed. Two curved, venomous fangs clamped through Terry's skin nearly to the bone. Blood dripped into the pristine snow. The small gap in the ground began to widen into a larger hole a few feet from Terry. At once, the tentacles retreated toward the hole, slithering across the surface, dragging Terry by his ankle. His screams of fear turned to pain and terror.

Gerald flung himself forward, gripping Terry under his arms and throwing his weight in the opposite direction. "Hurry, Lara!"

Lara scrambled to the top of the slope. The mist whirled

and thickened around her, making it difficult to see. She spread
her arms as she ran, gathering energy from the darkening sky,
uncaring of her companions, knowing she was Terry's only
chance at survival. She hadn't used the knowledge inside of
her, the wealth of information her aunts had shared with her—
indeed, she hadn't been certain it was real—until that moment.
Power flooded her. Her mind opened. Expanded. Reached into
the well of knowledge and found the exact words she needed.

"It's too strong." Gerald dug his heels into the earth and
held on to Terry with every ounce of strength he possessed.
"Stop wasting your energy and help me, damn it. Come on,
Terry, fight."

Terry abruptly ceased screaming and began to fight in
earnest, kicking with his free leg in an attempt to dislodge the
two snake heads.

The vine threw more tentacles out, the greenish-black
stems writhing hideously, looking for a target. The teeth sank
deeper into Terry's ankle, sawing at flesh and bone in an effort
to keep their prey.

Lara flung herself forward, lifting her face to the sky as she
muttered the words she found in her mind.

*I call forth the power of the sky. Bring down lightning to
my mind's eye. Shaping, shifting, bend to my will. Forging a
scythe to sharpened steel. Hot and bright the fire be, guide my
hand with accuracy.*

Lightning zigzagged across the sky, lighting the edges of
the clouds. The air around them was charged so that the hair
on their bodies and heads stood on end. Lara felt electricity
snapping and sizzling in her fingertips and focused on the
thinner space between the long, thick bodies and the bulbous
heads of the snake-vines.

White light streaked across the short distance and pierced
the necks of the creatures. The smell of rotting flesh burst
from the vine. Both severed bodies dropped limply to the
ground, leaving the teeth, with the heads attached, still sunk
deep into Terry's ankle. The rest of the tentacles reared back
in shock and then burrowed beneath the dirt and snow.

Terry grasped one of the heads to pull it out.

"No!" Lara protested. "Leave it. You don't know if the
teeth are barbed. We have to get out of here right now."

"It burns like acid," Terry complained. His face was pale,

nearly as white as the covering of snow, and beads of sweat dotted his forehead.

Lara shook her head. "We have to get off this mountain now. And you can't take chances until I can look at it."

She took his arm and signaled to Gerald to grab his other one. They steadied Terry between them and began to hurry from the slope to the well-traveled path off to their right.

"What was that?" Gerald hissed, his eyes meeting hers over Terry's head. "Have you ever seen a snake like that before?"

"Was it two-headed?" Terry asked. Anxiety made him hyperventilate. "I didn't get all that good a look at it before it struck. Do you think it's poisonous?"

"It isn't attacking the central nervous system, Terry," Lara said. "At least not yet. We'll get you back down to the village and find a doctor. I know a few things about medicine, I can treat you when we get to the car."

The mountain rumbled ominously, shivering beneath their feet. Lara glanced up at the swirling white mists. Above them, spiderweb cracks appeared in the snow and began to widen.

Gerald swore, renewed his grip on Terry, and started sprinting along the thin, winding trail. "It's going to come down."

Terry gritted his teeth against the pain radiating up from his ankle. "I can't believe this is happening. I feel sick."

Lara kept her eyes on the mountain behind them as they raced, dragging Terry every step of the way. "Faster. Keep moving."

The ground shifted and rolled and small fans of snow slid in artful patterns toward the slope below them. The sight was dazzling, hypnotic even. Gerald shook his head several times and looked at Lara, puzzled, slowing down to gaze at the undulating snow. "Lara? I can't remember what happened. Where are we?"

"We're about to be creamed by an avalanche, Gerald," Lara advised. "Terry's hurt and we've got to run like hell. Now move it!"

She put every ounce of compulsion and command into her voice that she could muster on the run. Fortunately both men obeyed, concentrating on getting down the steep slope as quickly as they could and asking no more questions. The safeguards protecting the cave were not only lethal, but they confused and disoriented any traveler stumbling across them. The warning system was usually enough to make people so uneasy they left the area, but once triggered, the safeguards fought to erase memories or even kill to protect the entrance to the cave.

It was the place she had been looking for. Now she had to survive in order to come back and discover the long-buried secrets of her past. Gerald stumbled and Terry screamed as one of the snake heads slammed against a particularly dense pile of snow and ice, shoving the teeth further into his flesh.

Lara felt the mountain tremble. At first there was silence, and then a distant rumbling. The sound increased in strength and volume until it became a roar. The snow slid, slowly at first, but picking up speed, churning and roiling, rushing toward them. Lara forced back panic and reached into the well of knowledge she knew was deep inside of her. Her aunts had never appeared human to her, but their voices had been, and the immense wealth of information they had collected over centuries had been stored in Lara's memories.

She was Dragonseeker, a great Carpathian heritage. She was human, with courage and strength of the ages. She was mage, able to gather energy and use it for good. All of her ancestors were powerful beings. The blood of three species mingled in her veins, yet she belonged in none of those worlds and walked her chosen path—alone, but always guided by the wisdom of the aunts.

She felt strength pour into her, felt the crackle of electricity as the sky lit up with lightning. Looking over her shoulder once more, she sent a command to the wilds of nature to counteract the protection guard the dark mage had used on the mountain.

I summon thee, water ice, fit to my hand, provide me with shelter as I command.

The snow stopped moving abruptly, sprayed in air, frozen in place, curled over their heads like a giant wave motionless in mid-air.

"Run!" Lara shouted. "Go, Gerald. We've got to get off the mountain."

Night was falling and the avalanche was not the worst they might face. The wind had stilled, but the voices remained, shrieking warnings she dared not ignore. They gripped Terry and half ran, half slid down the steep slope. Above their heads, the heavy mantle of snow formed a wave, cresting over them, motionless like an ominous statue.

Terry left behind streaks of blood as they skidded over the icy surface. They were sweating profusely by the time they made it to the bottom. Breathing heavily, they paused, looking around for their car. It stood out like a sore thumb. In this particular area of Romania, most of the locals used carts with tires pulled by horses. Cars weren't a common sight at all and, as small it as it was, it looked far too modern in a place centuries old.

Gerald dragged Terry through the meadow to where the car was parked beneath some naked branches. Lara turned back toward the mountain, let out her breath and clapped her hands together three times. There was an odd, expectant pause. The wave rolled, snow dropped. The mountain slid, raising a cloud of white into the air.

"Lara," Terry gasped. "You have to get these teeth out of my ankle. My leg burns like hell and, I swear, something's crawling inside of me—inside my leg."

He sprawled on the small backseat, his skin nearly gray. Sweat soaked his clothes and his breathing came in ragged gasps.

Lara knelt in the dirt and examined the hideous heads. She knew what they were—hybrids of the dark mage, bred to do his bidding. She'd seen the beginnings of them in her nightmares. The snakes injected a poisonous brew, including tiny microscopic parasites, into their victim's body. The organisms would eventually take over Terry's body and then his brain, until he was a mere puppet to be used by the dark mage.

"I'm sorry, Terry," she said softly. "The teeth are barbed and have to be removed carefully."

"Then you've seen this before?" Terry gripped her wrist and held her close to him as she crouched beside the open door of the car. He was sprawled across the back seat, rocking in pain. "I don't know why, but the fact that you know what they are makes me feel better."

It didn't make her feel any better. She'd been a child, dragged into a laboratory. The sights and smells had been so hideous she'd tried to forget them. The stench of blood. The screams. The grotesque tiny worms in a putrid ball, wiggling in a frenzy, consuming blood and human flesh.

Lara took a deep breath and let it out. They didn't have much time. She needed to get Terry to a master healer who could handle such things, but she could slow down the deterioration.

Gerald looked around him, then back up at the mountain, now quiet and still. White mists swirled, but the voices were gone. Overhead the clouds grew heavier and darker, but the mountain looked pristine—untouched—certainly not as if anyone had climbed it and been attacked.

"Lara?" He sounded as puzzled as he looked. "I can't remember where we were. I can't remember how these snakes attacked Terry. Don't snakes need warm weather? How did this happen, and what's wrong with me?"

"It doesn't matter right now. What matters is getting these teeth out of Terry's leg and getting him to the inn where someone who knows what they're doing can help him." Someone with healing skills, more than medical skills. If they were in the vicinity where she had been held as a child, then it stood to reason that someone knew how to treat a mage wound.

She closed her eyes to block out the sight of Terry's gray face and Gerald's anxious one. Deep inside, where that wealth of knowledge lay, she found her calm center. She could almost hear the whisper of her aunts' voices, directing her as the information flooded her mind. The curved fangs had a barb at the tip.

Severed head that now does bite, fangs be removed with heat and light. Draw the poison that would remain, holding the harm, stop the pain.

"There might be someone much better at taking these out," Lara said. "We can get you to the inn fast and the couple that owns it might be able to find someone for us who has dealt with this before."

Terry shook his head. "I can't stand it, Lara. If you don't take them out now, I'm going to rip them out. I really can't stand it."

She nodded her understanding and reached beneath her jacket for the knife on her tool belt. "Let's get it done then. Gerald, get in the back seat on the other side and hold Terry's shoulders." More than anything, she didn't want Gerald positioned where some of the tainted blood might spatter on him. The tiny microorganisms were dangerous to everyone.

Gerald obeyed her without question and Lara studied the first snake head. The hybrid was part plant, part living animal, and all frightening. It was meant to take over a person, no matter what the species, and bring them under the dark mage's control. It hadn't been just Carpathians and humans he had tortured, but his own people as well. No one was safe, not even his own family, as Lara could attest to.

She closed her eyes and swallowed hard, slamming the door on memories that were too painful, too frightening to remember when she had such a complex task before her. She had rarely used her healing abilities on anyone else in the last few years. In her childhood, she'd made the mistake several times, traveling with gypsies. She'd knit broken bones. Healed a wound from a blade that would have killed a man. Removed harmful bacteria from children's lungs. At first people would be grateful, but inevitably they would come to fear her.

Never show that you are different. You must blend in wherever you are. Learn the language and the customs. Dress the way they dress. Speak as they speak. Cloak who and what you are and never trust anyone.

She liked Gerald and Terry—very much. They'd worked together for several years, and she'd been careful never to intrude on either of them or to show them that she was different in any way. That had been a difficult lesson she'd learned repeatedly, every time she was kicked out of the family taking care of her.

"Lara."

Terry's pleading voice forced her thoughts to the task at hand. She steadied herself and gave him a reassuring nod. They were used to her being the leader in caving, and it was natural to look to her now. She took another breath and let it out, pushing down the revulsion that was welling up.

The words to the healing chant rose out of that same bank of knowledge, and she repeated them under her breath as she slid the razor-sharp knife beneath Terry's skin and found the barb.

Kunasz, nelkul sivdobbanas, nelkul fesztelen loyly.
Ot elidamet andam szabadon elidadert.
O jela sialem jorem ot ainamet es sone ot elidadet.
O jela sialem pukta kin minden szelemeket belso.
Pajnak o susu hanyet es o nyelv nyalamet sivadaba.
Vii o vermin sone o verid andam.

The ancient Carpathian language came easily; it was one she'd known since childhood. She might be rusty, having never used it other than to murmur to herself before she fell asleep, but the words, spoken in a chant, were always soothing to her.

As she whispered the healing words, she blocked Terry's pain. The tooth was wicked and nasty. It curved into the skin, growing wider, digging deep, and at the end was a small barb, curving in the opposite direction. She had to slit the skin carefully to allow the points on either side to become loose enough to slide out without further damaging Terry's leg.

At first she used her human sight, blocking all other ability to see until she had the barb out. Only then did she allow herself to look with the eyes of a mage. Tiny white worms writhed and burrowed, swarming to the cells to reproduce as quickly as possible. Her stomach lurched. It took tremendous effort to shed her awareness of her own thoughts and physical self and become a blaze of healing white light, which she then poured into Terry's wound to burn the organisms as quickly as she found them.

The wormlike creatures tried to hide from the light, and given the chance, they reproduced quickly. She tried to be thorough, but Terry squirmed and moaned, distracting her, all at once reaching down to the other bite, trying to yank the remaining snake head free.

She found herself abruptly back in her own body, disoriented and panic-stricken. "Terry! Leave it. I'll take it out."

She was too late. He screamed as he yanked at the foul snake head, tearing it loose from his ankle. The barb ripped through his skin and muscle. Blood sprayed the back of the car and shot across the seat, splattering Gerald's chest.

"Don't touch the blood with your hands!" Lara yelled. "Use a cloth. Get your jacket off, Gerald."

She clamped both of her hands over the wound, pressing hard, ignoring the burning pain as the blood coated her skin, burning to the bone. She fought past her own fear and panic to reach for the cool, centered place inside of her, calling healing light, burning white-hot and pure, to counteract the acid of the snake blood. The way her birthmark was burning there had to be vampire blood mixed in the foul brew.

Gerald ripped his jacket open and threw it away as the material smoldered with a grayish smoke. He rubbed at his face and eyes, slapping his palms down his face and chest to rid himself of the sensation of things crawling on him.

Terry grew quiet as Lara sent healing light streaking through his body to the gaping wound in his leg. The bleeding slowed to a trickle and the tiny wormlike creatures retreated from the spreading heat Lara generated. She cauterized the wound, destroying as many of the parasites as she could before bathing her hands and arms in the same hot energy.

"Did you get any blood on you, Gerald?"

He shook his head. "I don't think so, Lara. It felt like it, but I wiped my hands and face and there aren't any smears."

"Once we get Terry to a healer, take a shower as soon as you can. And burn your clothes. Don't just wash them, burn them. Everything."

She backed out of the seat, helping Terry to swing his legs out of the way of the door so she could close it and rush around to the driver's side. Terry's coloring was terrible, but more importantly she didn't like the way he was breathing. Part of it could be shock, the shallow, too-fast breathing of panic, but she feared she hadn't stopped the parasites from assaulting his body. He needed a master healer immediately.

She drove as fast as she could over the narrow, pitted mountain road, sliding through some of the sharper turns and bumping over the muddy holes. Dirty water sprayed into the air as the car fishtailed through mud and snow, throwing up debris in its wake. All around them the peaceful countryside seemed in sharp contrast to the terror of the snake heads that had been embedded in Terry's ankle.

Haystacks and cows surrounded them. Small thatched houses and horse-drawn carts with huge tires gave the impression of stepping back in time to a much more slower-paced and happier time. The castles and abundance of churches lent the area a medieval look, so that one expected knights on horses to come charging over the hills any moment.

Lara had traveled all over the world searching for her past. She remembered little of her journey from the ice cave, and once the gypsies had found her she'd traveled all over Europe. Passed from family to family, she'd never been told where they found her. Coming to the Carpathian mountains had been like coming home. And when she had entered Romania, she *felt* home. This place was still wild, the forests untamed and the land alive beneath her feet.

The car slid around another corner and they were out of the

heavier forest and into the peat bogs. The trail narrowed even more, winding on solid ground while the smell of the bog permeated the air around them. Trees swayed and drooped under the heavy weight of snow. Lights in the distance heralded farms, and for a moment she thought to stop at one of the nearest ones for aid. But Terry had been bitten by a hybrid, a mage-bred snake carrying vampire blood. Healing a mage wound was difficult enough, but a hybrid with vampire blood—that required skills far beyond her knowledge or that of a human doctor.

Their one hope lay with the innkeepers. The couple had been born and raised in the area and had lived their entire lives there. Lara couldn't imagine that they wouldn't have some knowledge of the danger lying beneath the mountain. Over time it became difficult to tamper with the same memories. And there had been something about that inn—something that had drawn Lara to it. A suggestion of power, as if perhaps there was subtle influence at work, pushing tourists and visitors to the area to want to stay at the homey, friendly inn.

Lara had allowed herself to be susceptible to the flow of power because it was the first time since the dragon had shoved her onto the upper cavern ledge that she had encountered the light delicate touch of flowing energy. She had forgotten what it was like to bathe herself in the crackle of electric power, to feel it surrounding her, flowing through every cell until her body hummed with it. The inn and the entire village gave off the amazing feeling, although it was so subtle she had nearly missed it.

"Lara," Gerald called from the back seat. "My skin is starting to burn."

"We're almost there. Go in and take a shower, first thing." She didn't want to think what Terry was suffering. He was very quiet, other than making a soft moaning sound. "Gerald, when we get to the inn, we'll need to talk to the owners and ask right away who the village healer is."

"The owner's name was Slavica and she seemed very nice."

"Hopefully she's very discreet as well. She certainly seems to know everyone."

"Wouldn't it be better to ask for the nearest doctor?" Gerald asked.

Lara tried to sound casual. "Sometimes the local healers

know so much more about plants and animals in the area. Although we've never encountered this particular species before, it's a good bet the villagers have and the local healer probably knows exactly what to do to extract the poi—" She broke off and hastily changed her description. "Venom."

Lara drove the car up the twisting road to the inn on the edge of town. It faced the forest with its long porch and inviting balconies. She parked as close to the stairs as she could get and raced around to help Gerald get Terry out.

Shadows lengthened and grew as the clouds overhead thickened with the threat of snow. The wind howled and the trees swayed and rustled in protest. Lara glanced around her with sharp, wary eyes as she opened the door to the back seat and reached inside for Terry.

"I'll come back for the snake heads to show the innkeeper. Don't touch them," she cautioned.

Terry was nearly deadweight as he hung between them. Gerald had to practically carry him as they stumbled through the snow. The walkway was clear, but they took a shortcut, tramping across the front slope to get to the porch faster.

A tall, dark-haired man opened the door for them and reached to help. Even under the dire circumstances, Lara found him handsome, compelling even.

"Don't get the blood on you," she warned. "It's highly venomous."

The dark-haired man's gaze swept up to her face and froze, locking on her. For one moment there was shocked recognition in his eyes and then it was gone as he got his shoulder under Terry to relieve her of the weight.

Lara whirled around, back toward the car. "Get him inside and ask the innkeeper to find a healer. I'll get the snake heads."

She rushed back down the steps, crossing the distance to the car in a run. As she yanked open the door, her birthmark, the one shaped like a dragon, began to burn hot against her skin.

There was only one thing that brought forth the dragon's warning. Vampire. And he had to be close. She closed the door and looked carefully around her, one hand sliding beneath her thick red cloak to find the knife on her belt.